I AM stepping on the gas, air is pouring into the truck and curses are pouring out, because I feel like I get up on the wrong side of the gutter this morning. So, I'm looking ahead on the road, squinting hard. Then I slam on the brakes.

There is a *thing* blocking the road, instead. *Two* things.

One of these things is a horse. At least, it looks more like a horse than anything else I could see on four drinks. It is a horse covered with a kind of awning, or tent that hangs down over its legs and out on its neck. In fact, I noticed that this horse is wearing a mask over its head with eyeholes, like it belonged to the Ku Klux Klan.

The other *thing* is riding the horse. It is all silver; from head to foot, and I notice that there is a long plume growing out of its head. It looks like a man, and it has a long, sharp pole in one hand and the top off a garbage can in the other.

Now when I look at this party I am certain of only one thing. This is not the Lone Ranger.

—from "A Good Knight's Work"
by Robert Bloch

UNKNOWN

EDITED BY
STANLEY SCHMIDT

BAEN
BOOKS

UNKNOWN

A Baen Books Original

Baen Publishing Enterprises
260 Fifth Avenue
New York, N.Y. 10001

First printing, October 1988

ISBN: 0-671-69785-4

Cover art by Tom Kidd

Printed in the United States of America

Distributed by
SIMON & SCHUSTER
1230 Avenue of the Americas
New York, N.Y. 10020

CONTENTS

ACKNOWLEDGMENTS

"A Good Knight's Work" by Robert Bloch, copyright © 1941 by The Condé Nast Publications, Inc., reprinted by permission of the author.

"The Compleat Werewolf" by Anthony Boucher, copyright © 1942 by The Condé Nast Publications, Inc., reprinted by permission.

"The Angelic Angleworm" by Fredric Brown, copyright © 1942 by Street & Smith Publications, Inc., reprinted by permission of Scott Meredith Literary Agency, Inc.

"Nothing in the Rules" by L. Sprague de Camp, copyright © 1939 by Street & Smith Publications, Inc., renewed copyright © 1967 by L. Sprague de Camp, reprinted by permission of Blassingame-Spectrum Corporation.

"The Coppersmith" by Lester del Rey, copyright © 1939 by Street & Smith Publications, Inc., reprinted by permission of the author and Scott Meredith Literary Agency, Inc.

"Even the Angels" by Malcolm Jameson, copyright © 1941 by The Condé Nast Publications, Inc., reprinted by permission.

"The Devil We Know" by Henry Kuttner, copyright © 1941 by Street & Smith Publications, Inc., renewed copyright © 1969 by Catherine Kuttner, reprinted by permission of Don Congdon Associates, Inc.

"Smoke Ghost" by Fritz Leiber, copyright © 1941 by The Condé Nast Publications, Inc., reprinted by permission of the author.

"A God In a Garden" by Theodore Sturgeon, copyright © 1939 by Street & Smith Publications, Inc., reprinted by permission of Kirby McCauley, Ltd.

INTRODUCTION

Stanley Schmidt

THE UNKNOWN UNIVERSE

In March of 1939 a new magazine appeared, titled simply *Unknown*. On its first page, its editor promised, "Street & Smith present herewith a new magazine, dedicated to a new type of entertainment. *Unknown* is both our title and our only classification; the material we plan to present is to be like none that has ever, anywhere, been presented consistently before. . . . We will deal with the Unknown, but in a manner uniquely and completely different from the stories you have seen in the past.

"One rule only we apply as limitation to an author's imagination: that the resultant story must be pure entertainment."

That editor was John W. Campbell, Jr., already famous for revolutionizing science fiction as editor of *Astounding Science Fiction*. How did he revolutionize it? By demanding equal emphasis on both words: *science* and *fiction*. For *Astounding*, Campbell demanded entertaining, thought-provoking stories about

1

believable people in situations created by new developments in science and technology. He demanded that those fictitious developments be so solidly rooted in what was known about real science that a thoughtful reader could believe that the events of the story could, someday or somewhere, happen in reality.

What was different about *Unknown*? Simply put, *Unknown* was the fantasy companion of *Astounding*. But what is the difference between science fiction and fantasy? Science fiction is based on the known— things like physics, chemistry, astronomy, and biology. Fantasy is based on the unknown—all those things that *may* exist on the fringes of human experience but about which we have little or no real knowledge, like gods and demons, werewolves and leprechauns, genies and witches and magic. When science fiction writes about something that sounds impossible, it tries to rationalize it, to provide a believable way that it really *could* happen. Fantasy doesn't bother. For that reason, many *Astounding* readers, liking their stories solidly logical, didn't like fantasy.

Until *Unknown* came along. *Unknown* was a lot like *Astounding* in that it was dedicated to the proposition that stories ought to be *fun*—and, given the premise, no matter how strange, *logical*. Just because a story rests on a fantastic and unexplained assumption doesn't mean the rest of the story has to be fast and loose. Campbell expected writers to work out the consequences of their assumptions just as logically for *Unknown* as for *Astounding*. Many of the same writers appeared in both magazines—people like Theodore Sturgeon, Lester del Rey, Fredric Brown, Henry Kuttner, and L. Sprague de Camp. The stories had an exuberant, often zany flavor of their own, with plots set in the everyday contemporary world, with just one or two little things out of the ordinary. Things like a mermaid entered in a swimming meet, a werewolf thrust into a search for suitable employment, an accidental visitor to a mine full of gnomes setting out to unionize them, or a linotype machine with a mind of its own.

You'll read some of those, and more, in this book. Not all of them are wacky, of course. *Unknown* had a wide enough scope to encompass the occasional darker piece like Fritz Leiber's modern ghost story reprinted herein, or his sword-and-sorcery tales of Fafhrd and the Grey Mouser.

Unknown fulfilled its editor's promise for four and a half years—but after the October 1943 issue, it fell victim to the wartime paper shortage. It has lain dormant ever since, fondly remembered by those fortunate enough to have known it firsthand, its name mysteriously evocative to those who hear the fuss others make over it but were born too late to know why. Despite its short life, *Unknown* printed far more of its special brand of fantasy than this book could hold—but I hope it will give those readers new to it a good sampling of its flavor.

And for those who do remember the original . . .

A reminder, yes. But might it be more than that? One thing you'll notice in reading these stories is that, while most of them have "contemporary" settings, "contemporary" here means a few years of the World War II period. They're still fun to read, but inevitably reflect the time in which they were written. *Our* contemporary scene, some 45 years later, has changed a lot. Our world is full of potential for brand-new stories in the *Unknown* vein. What if your VCR went beyond recording shows at preselected times to deciding which ones it would let you play back? What would the AIDS scare do to a vampire's lifestyle?

The possibilities are endless—but where is today's magazine to print them? I sneak one into *Analog* (as *Astounding* is now called) from time to time—Timothy Zahn's recent tale of voodoo acupuncture and poli-

tics, for example—but I can't get away with it too
often. *Analog*'s readers, like *Astounding*'s, mostly
want their science fiction undiluted and their fantasy
somewhere else. What many of us would not-so-
secretly like to see, whether we remember *Unknown*
personally or secondhand, is a new *Unknown*, restored to its original vigor and once more exploring
the unknown universe at the fringes of our own real
world.

What are the chances of that happening? Well, I'm
not in a position to make any promises, but I would
certainly enjoy the chance to edit *Unknown* for the
first time in almost half a century. So if you enjoy
this book and would like to see a magazine of new
stories like these, please write and tell me. If I get
enough such letters . . .

Who knows?

THE COMPLEAT WEREWOLF

Anthony Boucher

Author's note: In my criminological researches, I have occasionally come across references to an agent of the Federal Bureau of Investigation who bids fair to become as great a figure of American legend as Paul Bunyan or John Henry. This man is invulnerable to bullets. He strikes such terror into criminals as to drive them to suicide or madness. He sometimes vanishes from human ken entirely, and at other times he is reported to have appeared with equal suddenness stark naked. And perhaps the most curious touch of all, he engages in a never-ceasing quest, of Arthurian intensity, for someone who can perform the Indian rope trick.

Only recently, after intensive probings in Berkeley, where I have certain fortunate connections particularly with the department of German, and a few grudging confidences from my old friend Fergus O'Breen, have I been able to piece together the facts behind this legend.

*Here, then, is the story, with only one important
detail suppressed, and that, I assure you, strictly for
your own good.*

The professor glanced at the note:

>   Don't be silly—Gloria.

Wolfe Wolf crumpled the sheet of paper into a
yellow ball and hurled it out the window into the
sunshine of the bright campus spring. He made several choice and profane remarks in fluent Middle
High German.

Emily looked up from typing the proposed budget
for the departmental library. "I'm afraid I didn't
understand that, Professor Wolf. I'm weak on Middle High."

"Just improvising," said Wolf, and sent a copy of
the *Journal of English and Germanic Philology* to
follow the telegram.

Emily rose from the typewriter. "There's something the matter. Did the committee reject your
monograph on Hager?"

"That monumental contribution to human knowledge? Oh, no. Nothing so important as that."

"But you're so upset—"

"The office wife!" Wolf snorted. "And pretty poly-
androus at that, with the whole department on your
hands. Go 'way."

Emily's dark little face lit up with a flame of righ-
teous anger that removed any trace of plainness.
"Don't talk to me like that, Mr. Wolf. I'm simply
trying to help you. And it isn't the whole department. It's—"

Professor Wolf picked up an inkwell, looked after
the telegram and the "Journal," then set the glass
pot down again. "No. There are better ways of going

to pieces. Sorrows drown easier than they smash—
Get Herbrecht to take my two o'clock, will you?"

"Where are you going?"

"To hell in sectors. So long."

"Wait. Maybe I can help you. Remember when
the dean jumped up for serving drinks to students?
Maybe I can—"

Wolf stood in the doorway and extended one arm
impressively, pointing with that curious index which
was as long as the middle finger. "Madam, academi-
cally, you are indispensable. You are the prop and
stay of the existence of this department. But at the
moment this department can go to hell, where it will
doubtless continue to need your invaluable services."

"But don't you see—" Emily's voice shook. "No.
Of course not. You wouldn't see. You're just a
man—no, not even a man. You're just Professor Wolf.
You're Woof-woof."

Wolf staggered. "I'm what?"

"Woof-woof. That's what everybody calls you because your name's Wolfe Wolf. All your students,
everybody. But you wouldn't notice a thing like that.
Oh, no. Woof-woof, that's what you are."

"This," said Wolfe Wolf, "is the crowning blow.
My heart is breaking, my world is shattered, I've got
to walk a mile from the campus to find a bar; but all
this isn't enough. I've got to be called Woof-woof.
Good-by!"

He turned, and in the doorway caromed into a
vast and yielding bulk, which gave out with a noise
that might have been either a greeting of "Wolf!" or
more probably an inevitable grunt of "Oof!"

Wolf backed into the room and admitted Professor
Fearing, paunch, pince-nez, cane and all. The older
man waddled over to his desk, plumped himself
down, and exhaled a long breath. "My dear boy," he
gasped. "Such impetuosity."

"Sorry, Oscar."

"Ah, youth—" Professor Fearing fumbled about for a handkerchief, found none, and proceeded to polish his pince-nez on his somewhat stringy necktie. "But why such haste to depart? And why is Emily crying?"

"Is she?"

"You see?" said Emily hopelessly, and muttered "Woof-woof" into her damp handkerchief.

"And why do copies of the J.E.G.P. fly about my head as I harmlessly cross the campus? Do we have teleportation on our hands?"

"Sorry," Wolf repeated curtly. "Temper. Couldn't stand that ridiculous argument of Glocks's. Good-by."

"One moment." Professor Fearing fished into one of his unnumbered handkerchiefless pockets and produced a sheet of yellow paper. "I believe this is yours?"

Wolf snatched at it and quickly converted it into confetti.

Fearing chuckled. "How well I remember when Gloria was a student here! I was thinking of it only last night when I saw her in 'Moonbeams and Melody.' How she did upset this whole department! Heavens, my boy, if I'd been a younger man myself—"

"I'm going. You'll see about Herbrecht, Emily?"

Emily sniffled and nodded.

"Come, Wolfe." Fearing's voice had grown more serious. "I didn't mean to plague you. But you mustn't take these things too hard. There are better ways of finding consolation than in losing your temper or getting drunk."

"Who said anything about—"

"Did you need to say it? No, my boy, if you were to— You're not a religious man, are you?"

"Good God, no," said Wolf contradictorily.

"If only you were— If I might make a suggestion, Wolf, why don't you come over to the Temple tonight? We're having very special services. They might take your mind off Glo—off your troubles."

"Thanks, no. I've always meant to visit your Temple—I've heard rumors about it—but not tonight. Some other time."

"Tonight would be especially interesting."

"Why? What's so special about April 30th?"

Fearing shook his gray head. "It is shocking how ignorant a scholar can be outside of his chosen field—But you know the place, Wolfe; I'll hope to see you there tonight."

"Thanks. But my troubles don't need any supernatural solutions. A couple of zombies will do nicely, and I do *not* mean serviceable stiffs. Good-by, Oscar." He was halfway through the door before he added as an afterthought, " 'By, Emily."

"Such rashness," Fearing murmured. "Such impetuosity. Youth is a wonderful thing to enjoy, is it not, Emily?"

Emily said nothing, but plunged into typing the proposed budget as though all the fiends of hell were after her, as indeed many of them were.

The sun was setting, and Wolfe's tragic account of his troubles had laid an egg, too. The bartender had polished every glass in the joint and still the repetitive tale kept pouring forth. He was torn between a boredom new even in his experience and a professional admiration for a customer who could consume zombies indefinitely.

"Did I tell you about the time she flunked the midterm?" Wolf demanded truculently.

"Only three times," said the bartender.

"All right, then; I'll tell you. Y'unnerstand, I don't do things like this. Profeshical ethona, that's what's I've got. But this was different. This wasn't like somebody that doesn't know just because she doesn't know; this was a girl that didn't know because she wasn't the kind of girl that has to know the kind of things a girl has to know if she's the kind of girl that ought to know that kind of things. Y'unnerstand?"

The bartender cast a calculating glance at the plump little man who sat alone at the end of the deserted bar, carefully nursing his gin-and-tonic.

"She made me see that. She made me see lossa things and I can still see the things she made me see the things. It wasn't just like a professor falls for a coed, y'unnerstand? This was different. This was wunnaful. This was like a whole new life like."

The bartender sidled down to the end of the bar. "Brother," he whispered softly.

The little man with the odd beard looked up from his gin-and-tonic. "Yes, colleague?"

"If I listen to that potted professor another five minutes, I'm going to start smashing up the joint. How's about slipping down there and standing in for me, huh?"

The little man looked Wolf over and fixed his gaze especially on the hand that clenched the tall zombie glass. "Gladly, colleague," he nodded.

The bartender sighed a gust of relief.

"She was Youth," Wolf was saying intently to where the bartender had stood. "But it wasn't just that. This was different. She was Life and Excitement and Joy and Ecstasy and Stuff. Yunner—" He broke off and stared at the empty space. "*Uh-mazing!*" he observed. "Right before my very eyes. *Uh-mazing!*"

"You were saying, colleague?" the plump little man prompted from the adjacent stool.

Wolf turned. "So there you are. Did I tell you about the time I went to her house to check her term paper?"

"No. But I have a feeling you will."

"Howja know? Well, this night—"

The little man drank slowly; but his glass was empty by the time Wolf had finished the account of an evening of pointlessly tentative flirtation. Other customers were drifting in, and the bar was now about a third full.

"—and ever since then—" Wolf broke off sharply. "That isn't you," he objected.

"I think it is, colleague."

"But you're a bartender and *you* aren't a bartender."

"No. I'm a magician."

"Oh. That explains it. Now like I was telling you— Hey! Your bald is beard."

"I beg your pardon?"

"Your bald is beard. Just like your head. It's all jussa fringe running around."

"I like it that way."

"And your glass is empty."

"That's all right, too."

"Oh, no, it isn't. It isn't every night you get to drink with a man that proposed to Gloria Garton and got turned down. This is an occasion for celebration." Wolf thumped loudly on the bar and held up his first two fingers.

The little man regarded their equal length. "No," he said softly. "I think I'd better not. I know my capacity. If I have another—well, things might start happening."

"Lettemappen!"

"No. Please, colleague. I'd rather—"

The bartender brought the drinks. "Go on, brother," he whispered. "Keep him quiet. I'll do you a favor sometime."

Reluctantly the little man sipped at his fresh gin-and-tonic.

The professor took a gulp of his *n*th zombie. "My name's Woof-woof," he proclaimed. "Lots of people call me Wolfe Wolf. They think that's funny. But it's really Woof-woof. Wazoors?"

The other paused a moment to decipher that Arabic-sounding word, then said, "Mine's Ozymandias the Great."

"That's a funny name."

"I told you I'm a magician. Only I haven't worked for a long time. Theatrical managers are peculiar, colleague. They don't want a real magician. They won't even let me show 'em my best stuff. Why, I remember one night in Darjeeling—"

"Glad to meet you, Mr. . . . Mr.—"

"You can call me Ozzy. Most people do."

"Glad to meet you, Ozzy. Now about this girl. This Gloria. Yunnerstand, donya?"

"Sure, colleague."

"She thinks being a professor of German is nothing. She wants something glamorous. She says if I was an actor now or a G-man— Yunnerstand?"

Ozymandias the Great nodded.

"Awright, then! So yunnerstand. Find. But whatdayou want to keep talking about it for? Yunnerstand. That's that. To hell with it."

Ozymandias' round and fringed face brightened. "Sure," he said, and added recklessly, "Let's drink to that."

They clinked glasses and drank. Wolf carelessly tossed off a toast in Old Low Frankish, with an unpardonable error in the use of the genitive.

The two men next to them began singing "My Wild Irish Rose," but trailed off disconsolately. "What we need," said the one with the derby, "is a tenor."

"What I need," Wolf muttered, "is a cigarette."

"Sure," said Ozymandias the Great. The bartender was drawing beer directly in front of them. Ozymandias reached across the bar, removed a lighted cigarette from the barkeep's ear, and handed it to his companion.

"Where'd that come from?"

"I don't quite know. All I know is how to get them. I told you I was a magician."

"Oh. I see. Pressajijijation."

"No. Not a prestidigitator; I said a magician. Oh,

blast it! I've done it again. More than one gin-and-tonic and I start showing off."

"I don't believe you," said Wolf flatly. "No such thing as magicians. That's just as silly as Oscar Fearing and his Temple and what's so special about April 30th, anyway?"

The bearded man frowned. "Please colleague. Let's forget it."

"No. I don't believe you. You pressajijijated that cigarette. You didn't magic it." His voice began to rise. "You're a fake."

"Please, brother," the barkeep whispered. "Keep him quiet."

"All right," said Ozymandias wearily. "I'll show you something that can't be prestidigitation." The couple adjoining had begun to sing again. "They need a tenor. All right; listen!"

And the sweetest, most ineffably Irish tenor ever heard joined in on the duet. The singers didn't worry about the source; they simply accepted the new voice gladly and were spurred on to their very best, with the result that the bar knew the finest harmony it had heard since the night the Glee Club was suspended en masse.

Wolf looked impressed, but shook his head. "That's not magic, either. That's ventriloquism."

"As a matter of fact, that was a street singer who was killed in the Easter Rebellion. Fine fellow, too; never heard a better voice unless it was that night in Darjeeling when—"

"Fake!" said Wolfe Wolf loudly and belligerently.

Ozymandias once more contemplated that long index finger. He looked at the professor's dark brows that met in a straight line over his nose. He picked his companion's limpish hand off the bar and scrutinized the palm. The growth of hair was not marked, but it was perceptible.

The magician chortled. "And you sneer at magic!"

"Whasso funny about me sneering at magic?"

Ozymandias lowered his voice. "Because, my fine furry friend, you are a werewolf."

The Irish martyr had begun "Rose of Tralee" and the two mortals were joining in valiantly.

"I'm what?"

"A werewolf."

"But there isn't any such thing. Any fool knows that."

"Fools," said Oxymandias, "know a great deal which the wise do not. There are werewolves. There always have been, and probably always will be." He spoke as calmly and assuredly as though he were mentioning that the earth was round. "And there are three infallible physical signs; the meeting eyebrows, the long index finger, the hairy palms. You have all three. And even your name is an indication. Family names do not come from nowhere. Every Smith has an ancestor somewhere who was a Smith. Every Fisher comes from a family that once fished. And your name is Wolf."

The statement was so quiet, so plausible, that Wolf faltered. "But a werewolf is a man that changes into a wolf. I've never done that. Honest I haven't."

"A mammal," said Ozymandias, "is an animal that bears its young alive and suckles them. A virgin is nonetheless a mammal. Because you have never changed does not make you any the less a werewolf."

"But a werewolf—" Suddenly Wolf's eyes lit up. "A werewolf! But that's even better than a G-Man! Now I can show Gloria!"

"What on earth do you mean, colleague?"

Wolf was climbing down from his stool. The intense excitement of this brilliant new idea seemed to have sobered him. He grabbed the little man by the sleeve. "Come on. We're going to find a nice quiet place. And you're going to prove you're a magician."

"But how?"

"You're going to show me how to change!"

Ozymandias finished his gin-and-tonic, and with it drowned his last regretful hesitation. "Colleague," he announced, "you're on!"

Professor Oscar Fearing, standing behind the curiously carved lectern of the Temple of the Dark Truth, concluded the reading of the prayer with mumbling sonority. "And on this night of all nights, in the name of the black light that glows in the darkness, we give thanks!" He closed the parchment-bound book and faced the small congregation, calling out with fierce intensity, "Who wishes to give his thanks to the Lower Lord?"

A cushioned dowager rose. "I give thanks!" she shrilled excitedly. "My Ming Choy was sick, even unto death. I took of her blood and offered it to the Lower Lord, and he had mercy and restored her to me!"

Behind the altar an electrician checked his switches and spat disgustedly. "Bugs! Every last one of 'em!"

The man who was struggling into a grotesque and horrible costume paused and shrugged. "They pay good money. What's it to us if they're bugs?"

A tall, thin, old man had risen uncertainly to his feet. "I give thanks!" he cried. "I give thanks to the Lower Lord that I have finished my great work. My protective screen against magnetic bombs is a tried and proven success, to the glory of our country and science and the Lord."

"Crackpot," the electrician muttered.

The man in costume peered around the altar. "Crackpot, hell! That's Chiswick from the physics department. Think of a man like that falling for this stuff! And listen to him: He's even telling about the government's plans for installation. You know, I'll bet you one of these fifth columnists could pick up something around here."

There was silence in the Temple when the congregation had finished its Thanksgiving. Professor Fearing leaned over the lectern and spoke quietly and impressively. "As you know, brothers in Darkness, tonight is May Eve, the 30th of April, the night consecrated by the Church to that martyr missionary, St. Walpurgis, and by us to other and deeper purposes. It is on this night, and this night only, that we may directly give our thanks to the Lower Lord himself. Not in wanton orgy and obscenity, as the Middle Ages misconceived his desires, but in praise and in deep, dark joy that issues forth from Blackness."

"Hold your hats, boys," said the man in the costume. "Here I go again."

"*Eka!*" Fearing thundered. "*Dva tri chatur! Pancha! Shas sapta! Ashta nava dasha ekadasha!*" He paused. There was always the danger that at this moment some scholar in this university town might recognize that the invocation, though perfect Sanskrit, consisted solely of the numbers from one to eleven. But no one stirred, and he launched forth in more apposite Latin: "*Per vota nostra ispe nunc surgat nobis dicatus Baal Zebub!*"

"Baal Zebub!" the congregation chorused.

"Cue," said the electrician, and pulled a switch.

The lights flickered and went out. Lightning played across the sanctuary. Suddenly out of the darkness came a sharp bark, a yelp of pain, and a long-drawn howl of triumph.

A blue light now began to glow dimly. In the faint reflection of this, the electrician was amazed to see his costumed friend at his side, nursing his bleeding hand.

"What the—" the electrician whispered.

"Hanged if I know. I got out there on cue, all ready to make my terrifying appearance, and what happens? Great big dog up and nips my hand. Why didn't they tell me they'd switched the script?"

In the glow of the blue light the congregation reverently contemplated the plump little man with the fringe of beard and the splendid gray wolf that stood beside him. "Hail, O Lower Lord!" resounded the chorus, drowning out one spinster's murmur of "But, my *dear*, I *swear* he was *much* handsomer last year."

"Colleagues!" said Ozymandias the Great, and there was utter silence, a dread hush awaiting the momentous words of the Lower Lord. Ozymandias took one step forward, placed his tongue carefully between his lips, uttered the ripest, juiciest raspberry of his career, and vanished, wolf and all.

Wolfe Wolf opened his eyes and shut them again hastily. He had never expected the quiet and sedate Berkeley Inn to install centrifugal rooms. It wasn't fair. He lay in darkness, waiting for the whirling to stop and trying to reconstruct the past night.

He remembered the bar all right, and the zombies. And the bartender. Very sympathetic chap that, up until he suddenly changed into a little man with a fringe of beard. That was where things began getting strange. There was something about a cigarette and an Irish tenor and a werewolf. Fantastic idea, that. Any fool knows—

Wolf sat up suddenly. He *was* the werewolf. He threw back the bedclothes and stared down at his legs. Then he sighed relief. They were long legs. They were hairy enough. They were brown from much tennis. But they were indisputably human.

He got up, resolutely stifling his qualms, and began to pick up the clothing that was scattered nonchalantly about the floor. A crew of gnomes was excavating his skull, but he hoped they might go away if he didn't pay too much attention to them. One thing was certain; he was going to be good from now on. Gloria or no Gloria, heartbreak or no heartbreak, drowning your sorrows wasn't good enough. If you felt like this and could imagine you'd been a werewolf—

But why should he have imagined it in such detail? So many fragmentary memories seemed to come back as he dressed. Going up Strawberry Canyon with the fringed beard, finding a desolate and isolated spot for magic, learning the words—He could even remember the words. The word that changed you and the one that changed you back.

Had he made up those words, too, in his drunken imaginings? And had he made up what he could only barely recall—the wonderful, magical freedom of changing, the single, sharp pang of alteration and then the boundless happiness of being lithe and fleet and free?

He surveyed himself in the mirror. He looked exactly what he was, save for the unwonted wrinkles in his conservative single-breasted gray suit; a quiet academician, a little better built, a little more impulsive, a little more romantic than most, perhaps, but still just that—Professor Wolf.

The rest was nonsense. But there was, that impulsive side of him suggested, only one way of proving the fact. And that was to say The Word.

"All right," said Wolfe Wolf to his reflection. "I'll show you." And he said it.

The pang was sharper and stronger than he'd remembered. Alcohol numbs you to pain. It tore him for a moment with an anguish like the descriptions of childbirth. Then it was gone, and he flexed his limbs in happy amazement. But he was not a lithe, fleet, free beast. He was a helplessly trapped wolf, irrevocably entangled in a conservative, single-breasted gray suit.

He tried to rise and walk, but the long sleeves and legs tripped him over flat on his muzzle. He kicked with his paws, trying to tear his way out, and then stopped. Werewolf or no werewolf, he was likewise still Professor Wolf, and this suit had cost thirty-five dollars. There must be some cheaper way of securing freedom than tearing the suit to shreds.

He used several good, round, Low German expletives. This was a complication that wasn't in any of the werewolf legends he'd ever read. There, people just—boom!—became wolves or—bang!—became men again. When they were men, they wore clothes; when they were wolves, they wore fur. Just like Hyperman becoming Bark Lent again on top of the Empire State Building and finding his street clothes right there. Most misleading. He began to remember now how Ozymandias the Great had made him strip before teaching him the words—

The words! That was it. All he had to do was say the word that changed you back—*Absarka!*—and he'd be a man again, comfortably fitted inside his suit. Then he could strip and start all over again. You see? Reason solves all. "*Absarka!*" he said.

Or thought he said. He went through all the proper mental processes for saying *Absarka!* but all that came out of his muzzle was a sort of clicking whine. And he was still a conservatively dressed and helpless wolf.

This was worse than the clothes problem. If he could be released only by saying *Absarka!* and if, being a wolf, he could say nothing, why, there he was. Indefinitely. He could go find Ozzy and ask—but how could a wolf wrapped up in a gray suit get safely out of a hotel and set out hunting for an unknown address?

He was trapped. He was lost. He was—
"*Absarka!*"

Professor Wolfe Wolf stood up in his grievously rumpled gray suit and beamed on the beard-fringed face of Ozymandias the Great.

"You see, colleague," the little magician explained, "I figured you'd want to try it again as soon as you got up, and I knew darned well you'd have your troubles. Thought I'd come over and straighten things out for you."

Wolf lit a cigarette in silence and handed the pack to Ozymandias. "When you came in just now," he said at last, "what did you see?"

"You as a wolf."

"Then it really— I actually—"

"Sure. You're a full-fledged werewolf, all right."

Wolf sat down on the rumpled bed. "I guess," he ventured slowly, "I've got to believe it. And if I believe that— But it means I've got to believe everything I've always scorned. I've got to believe in gods and devils and hells and—"

"You needn't be so pluralistic. But there is a God." Ozymandias said this as calmly and convincingly as he had stated last night that there were werewolves.

"And if there's a God, then I've got a soul?"

"Sure."

"And if I'm a werewolf— Hey!"

"What's the trouble, colleague?"

"All right, Ozzy. You know everything. Tell me this: Am I damned?"

"For what? Just for being a werewolf? Shucks, no; let me explain. There's two kinds of werewolves. There's the cursed kind that can't help themselves, that just go turning into wolves without any say in the matter; and there's the voluntary kind like you. Now most of the voluntary kind are damned, sure, because they're wicked men who lust for blood and eat innocent people. But they aren't damnably wicked because they're werewolves; they became werewolves because they are damnably wicked. Now you changed yourself just for the fun of it and because it looked like a good way to impress a gal; that's an innocent-enough motive, and being a werewolf doesn't make it any less so. Werewolves don't have to be monsters; it's just that we only hear about the ones that are."

"But how can I be voluntary when you told me I was a werewolf before ever I changed?"

"Not everybody can change. It's like being able to roll your tongue or wiggle your ears. You can, or you can't; and that's that. And, like those abilities, there's probably a genetic factor involved, though nobody's done any serious research on it. You were a werewolf *in posse;* now you're one *in esse.*"

"Then it's all right? I can be a werewolf just for having fun, and it's safe?"

"Absolutely."

Wolf chortled. "Will I show Gloria! Dull and unglamorous, indeed! Anybody can marry an actor or a G-Man; but a werewolf—"

"Your children probably will be, too," said Ozymandias cheerfully.

Wolf shut his eyes dreamily, then opened them with a start. "You know what?"

"What?"

"I haven't got a hangover any more! This is marvelous. This is— Why, this is practical. At last the perfect hangover cure. Shuffle yourself into a wolf and back and— Oh, that reminds me. How do I get back?"

"*Absarka.*"

"I know. But when I'm a wolf I can't say it."

"That," said Ozymandias sadly, "is the curse of being a white magician. You keep having to use the second-best form of spells, because the best would be black. Sure, a black-magic werebeast can turn himself back wherever he wants to. I remember in Darjeeling—"

"But how about me?"

"That's the trouble. You have to have somebody to say *Absarka!* for you. That's why I did last night, or do you remember? After we broke up the party at your friend's Temple— Tell you what. I'm retired now, and I've got enough to live on modestly because I can always magic up a little— Are you going to take up werewolfing seriously?"

"For a while, anyway. Till I get Gloria."

"Then why shouldn't I come and live here in your hotel? Then I'll always be handy to *Absarka* you. After you get the girl, you can teach her."

Wolf extended his hand. "Noble of you. Shake." And then his eye caught his wrist watch. "I've missed two classes this morning. Werewolfing's all very well, but a man's got to work for his living."

"Most men." Ozymandias calmly reached his hand into the air and plucked a coin. He looked at it ruefully; it was a gold moidora. "Hang these spirits; I simply canot explain to them about gold being illegal."

"From Los Angeles," Wolf thought, with the habitual contempt of the northern Californian, as he surveyed the careless sport coat and the bright-yellow shirt of his visitor.

This young man rose politely as the professor entered the office. His green eyes gleamed cordially and his red hair glowed in the spring sunlight. "Professor Wolf?" he asked.

Wolf glanced impatiently at his desk. "Yes."

"O'Breen's the name. I'd like to talk to you a minute."

"My office hours are from three to four Tuesdays and Thursdays. I'm afraid I'm rather busy now."

"This isn't faculty business. And it's important." The young man's attitude was affable and casual, but he managed none the less to convey a sense of urgency that piqued Wolf's curiosity. The all-important letter to Gloria had waited while he took two classes; it could wait another five minutes.

"Very well, Mr. O'Breen."

"And, alone, if you please."

Wolf himself hadn't noticed that Emily was in the room. He now turned to the secretary and said, "All right. If you don't mind, Emily—"

Emily shrugged and went out.

"Now, sir. What is this important and secret business?"

"Just a question or two. To start with, how well do you know Gloria Garton?"

Wolf paused. You could hardly say, "Young man, I am about to re-propose to her in view of my becoming a werewolf." Instead he simply said—the truth if not the whole truth—"She was a pupil of mine a few years ago."

"I said *do*, not *did*. How well do you know her now?"

"And why should I bother to answer such a question?"

The young man handed over a card. Wolf read:

FERGUS O'BREEN

Private Inquiry Agent

Licensed by the State of California

Wolf smiled. "And what does this mean? Divorce evidence? Isn't that the usual field of private inquiry agents?"

"Miss Garton isn't married, as you probably know very well. I'm just asking you if you've been in touch with her much lately?"

"And I'm simply asking why you should want to know?"

O'Breen rose and began to pace around the office. "We don't seem to be getting very far, do we? I'm to take it that you refuse to state the nature of your relations with Gloria Garton?"

"I see no reason why I should do otherwise." Wolf was beginning to be annoyed.

To his surprise, the detective relaxed into a broad grin. "O.K. Let it ride. Tell me about your department: How long have the various faculty members been here?"

"Instructors and all?"

"Just the professors."

"I've been here for seven years. All the others at least a good ten, probably more. If you want exact figures, you can probably get them from the dean, unless, as I hope"—Wolf smiled cordially—"he throws you out flat on your red pate."

O'Breen laughed. "Professor, I think we could get on. One more question, and you can do some pate-tossing yourself. Are you an American citizen?"

"Of course."

"And the rest of the department?"

"All of them. And now would you have the common decency to give me some explanation of this fantastic farrog of questions?"

"No," said O'Breen casually. "Good-by, professor." His alert, green eyes had been roaming about the room, sharply noticing everything. Now, as he left, they rested on Wolf's long index finger, moved up to his heavy meeting eyebrows, and returned to the finger. There was a suspicion of a startled realization in those eyes as he left the office.

But that was nonsense, Wolf told himself. A private detective, no matter how shrewd his eyes, no matter how apparently meaningless his inquiries, would surely be the last man on earth to notice the signs of lycanthropy.

Funny. Werewolf was a word you could accept. You could say, "I am a werewolf," and it was all right. But say "I am a lycanthrope," and your flesh crawled. Odd. Possibly material for a paper on the influence of etymology on connotation for one of the learned periodicals.

But, hell! Wolfe Wolf was no longer primarily a scholar. He was a werewolf now, a white-magic werewolf, a werewolf-for-fun; and fun he was going to have. He lit his pipe, stared at the blank paper on his desk, and tried desperately to draft a letter to Gloria. It should hint at just enough to fascinate her and hold her interest until he could go south when the term ended and reveal to her the whole wonderful new truth. It—

Professor Oscar Fearing grunted his ponderous way into the office. "Good afternoon, Wolf. Hard at it, my boy?"

"Afternoon," Wolf replied distractedly, and continued to stare at the paper.

"Great events coming, eh? Are you looking forward to seeing the glorious Gloria?"

Wolf started. "How— What do you mean?"

Fearing handed him a folded newspaper. "You hadn't heard?"

Wolf read with growing amazement and delight:

GLORIA GARTON TO ARRIVE FRIDAY

Local Girl Returns to Berkeley

As part of the most spectacular talent hunt, since the search for Scarlett O'Hara, Gloria Garton, glamorous Metropolis starlet, will visit Berkeley Friday.

Friday afternoon at the Campus Theater, Berkeley canines will have their chance to compete in the nation-wide quest for a dog to play Tookah the wolf dog in the great metropolis epic, "Fangs of the Forest," and Gloria Garton herself will be present at the auditions.

"I owe so much to Berkeley," Miss Garton said.

"It will mean so much to me to see the campus and the city again." Miss Garton has the starring human role in "Fangs of the Forest."

Miss Garton was a student at the University of California when she received her first chance in films. She is a member of Mask and Dagger, honorary dramatic society, and Rho Rho Rho Sorority.

Wolfe Wolf glowed. This was perfect. No need now to wait till term was over. He could see Gloria now and claim her in all his wolfish vigor. Friday— today was Wednesday—that gave him two nights to practice and perfect the technique of werewolfry. And then—

He noticed the dejected look on the older professor's face, and a small remorse smote him. "How did things go last night, Oscar?" he asked sympathetically. "How was your big Walpurgis night services?"

Fearing regarded him oddly. "You know that now? Yesterday April 30th meant nothing to you."

"I got curious and looked it up. But how did it go?"

"Well enough," Fearing lied feebly. "Do you know, Wolf," he demanded after a moment's silence, "what is the real curse of every man interested in the occult?"

"No. What?"

"That true power is never enough. Enough for yourself, perhaps, but never enough for others. So that no matter what your true abilities, you must forge on beyond them into charlatanry to convince the others. Look at St. Germain. Look at Francis Stuart. Look at Cagliostro. But the worst tragedy is the next stage; when you realize that your powers were greater than you supposed and that the charlatanry was needless. When you realize that you have no notion of the extent of your powers. Then—"

"Then, Oscar?"

"Then, my boy, you are a badly frightened man."

Wolf wanted to say something consoling. He wanted to say, "Look, Oscar. It was just me. Go back to your half-hearted charlatanry and be happy." But he couldn't do that. Only Ozzy could know the truth of that splendid gray wolf. Only Ozzy and Gloria.

The moon was bright on that hidden spot in the canyon. The night was still. And Wolfe Wolf had a severe case of stage fright. Now that it came to the real thing—for this morning's clothes-complicated fiasco hardly counted and last night he could not truly remember—he was afraid to plunge cleanly into wolfdom and anxious to stall and talk as long as possible.

"Do you think," he asked the magician nervously, "that I could teach Gloria to change, too?"

Ozymandias pondered. "Maybe, colleague. It'd depend. She might have the natural ability, and she might not. And, of course, there's no telling what she might change into."

"You mean she wouldn't necessarily be a wolf?"

"Of course not. The people who can change, change into all sorts of things. And every folk knows best the kind that most interests it. We've got an English and Central European tradition; so we know mostly about werewolves. But take Scandinavia, and you'll hear chiefly about werebears, only they call 'em berserkers. And Orientals, now, they're apt to know about weretigers. Trouble is, we've thought so much about were*wolves* that that's all we know the signs for; I wouldn't know how to spot a weretiger just off-hand."

"Then there's no telling what might happen if I taught her The Word?"

"Not the least. Of course, there's some werethings that just aren't much use being. Take like being a wereant. You change and somebody steps on you and that's that. Or like a fella I knew once in Mada-

gascar. Taught him The Word, and know what?
Hanged if he wasn't a werediplodocus. Shattered the
whole house into little pieces when he changed and
almost trampled me under hoof before I could say
Absarka! He decided not to make a career of it. Or
then there was that time in Darjeeling— But, look,
colleague, are you going to stand around here naked
all night?"

"No," said Wolf. "I'm going to change now. You'll
take my clothes back to the hotel?"

"Sure. They'll be there for you. And I've put a
very small spell on the night clerk, just enough for
him not to notice wolves wandering in. Oh, and by
the way—anything missing from your room?"

"Not that I noticed. Why?"

"Because I thought I saw somebody come out of it
this afternoon. Couldn't be sure, but I think he came
from there. Young fella with red hair and Hollywood
clothes."

Wolfe Wolf frowned. That didn't make sense. Point-
less questions from a detective were bad enough, but
searching your hotel room— But what were detec-
tives to a full-fledged werewolf? He grinned, nodded
a friendly good-by to Ozymandias the Great, and
said The Word.

The pain wasn't so sharp as this morning, though
still quite bad enough. But it passed almost at once,
and his whole body filled with a sense of limitless
freedom. He lifted his snout and sniffed deep at the
keen freshness of this night air. A whole new realm
of pleasure opened up for him through this acute
new nose alone. He wagged his tail amicably at Ozzy
and set up off the canyon on a long, easy lope.

For hours loping was enough—simply and purely
enjoying one's wolfness was the finest pleasure one
could ask. Wolf left the canyon and turned up into
the hills, past the Big C and on into noble wildness
that seemed far remote from all campus civilization.

His brave new legs were staunch and tireless, his wind seemingly inexhaustible. Every turning brought fresh and vivid scents of soil and leaves and air, and life was shimmering and beautiful.

But a few hours of this, and Wolf realized that he was lonely. All this grand exhilaration was very well, but if his mate Gloria were loping by his side— And what fun was it to be something as splendid as a wolf if no one admired you! He began to want people, and he turned back to the city.

Berkeley goes to bed early. The streets were deserted. Here and there a light burned in a rooming house where some stolid grind was plodding on his almost-due term paper. Wolf had done that himself. He couldn't laugh in this shape, but his tail twitched with amusement at the thought.

He paused along the tree-lined street. There was a fresh human scent here, though the street seemed empty. Then he heard a soft whimpering, and trotted off toward the noise.

Behind the shrubbery fronting an apartment house sat a disconsolate two-year-old, shivering in his sunsuit and obviously lost for hours on hours. Wolf put a paw on the child's shoulder and shook him gently.

The boy looked around and was not in the least afraid. "He'o," he said, brightening up.

Wolf growled a cordial greeting, and wagged his tail and pawed at the ground to indicate that he'd take the lost infant wherever it wanted to go.

The child stood up and wiped away its tears with a dirty fist which left wide, black smudges. "Tootootootoo!" he said.

Games, thought Wolf. He wants to play choochoo. He took the child by the sleeve and tugged gently.

"Tootootootoo!" the boy repeated firmly. "Die way."

The sound of a railway whistle, to be sure, does

die away; but this seemed a poetic expression for such a toddler, Wolf thought, and then abruptly would have snapped his fingers if he'd had them. The child was saying "2222 Dwight Way," having been carefully brought up to tell its address when lost. Wolf glanced up at the street sign. Bowditch and Hillegas—2222 Dwight would be just a couple of blocks.

Wolf tried to nod his head, but the muscles didn't seem to work that way. Instead he wagged his tail in what he hoped indicated comprehension, and started off leading the child.

The infant beamed and said, "Nice woof-woof."

For an instant Wolf felt like a spy suddenly addressed by his right name, then realized that if some say "bow-wow" others might well say "woof-woof."

He led the child for two blocks without event. It felt good, having an innocent human being put his whole life and trust in your charge like this. There was something about children; he hoped Gloria felt the same. He wondered what would happen if he could teach this confiding infant The Word. It would be swell to have a pup that would—

He paused. His nose twitched and the hair on the back of his neck rose. Ahead of them stood a dog, a huge mongrel, seemingly a mixture of St. Bernard and Husky. But the growl that issued from his throat indicated that carrying brandy kegs or rushing serum was not for him. He was a bandit, an enemy of man and dog. And they had to pass him.

Wolf had no desire to fight. He was as big as this monster and, certainly, with his human brain, much cleverer; but scars from a dog fight would not look well on the human body of Professor Wolf, and there was, moreover, the danger of hurting the toddler in the fracas. It would be wiser to cross the street. But before he could steer the child that way, the mongrel brute had charged at them, yapping and snarling.

Wolf placed himself in front of the boy, poised and ready to leap in defense. The scar problem was secondary to the fact that this baby had trusted him. He was ready to face this cur and teach him a lesson, at whatever cost to his own human body. But halfway to him the huge dog stopped. His growls died away to a piteous whimper. His great flanks trembled in the moonlight. His tail curled craven between his legs. And abruptly he turned and fled.

The child crowed delightedly. "Bad woof-woof go way." He put his little arms around Wolf's neck. "*Nice woof-woof.*" Then he straightened up and said insistently, "Tootootootoo. Die way," and Wolf led on, his strong wolf's heart pounding as it had never pounded at the embrace of a woman.

"Tootootootoo" was a small, frame house set back from the street in a large yard. The lights were still on, and even from the sidewalk Wolf could hear a woman's shrill voice.

"—since five o'clock this afternoon, and you've got to find him, officer. You simply must. We've hunted all over the neighborhood and—"

Wolf stood up against the wall on his hindlegs and rang the doorbell with his front right paw.

"Oh! Maybe that's somebody now. The neighbors said they'd— Come, officer, and let's see— Oh!"

At the same moment Wolf barked politely, the toddler yelled "Mamma!" and his thin and worn-looking young mother let out a scream half delight at finding her child and half terror of this large, gray canine shape that loomed behind him. She snatched up the infant protectively and turned to the large man in uniform. "Officer! Look! That big dreadful thing! It stole my Robby!"

"No," Robby protested firmly. "Nice woof-woof."

The officer laughed. "The lad's probably right, ma'am. It *is* a nice woof-woof. Found your boy wandering around and helped him home. You haven't maybe got a bone for him?"

"Let that big nasty brute into my home? Never! Come on, Robby."

"Want my nice woof-woof."

"I'll woof-woof you, staying out till all hours and giving your father and me the fright of our lives. Just wait till your father sees you, young man; he'll— Oh, good night, officer!" And she shut the door on the yowls of Robby.

The policeman patted Wolf's head. "Never mind about the bone, Rover. She didn't so much as offer me a glass of beer, either. My, you're a husky specimen, aren't you, boy? Look almost like a wolf. Who do you belong to, and what are you doing wandering about alone? Huh?" He turned on his flash and bent over to look at the nonexistent collar.

He straightened up and whistled. "No license. Rover, that's bad. You know what I ought to do? I ought to turn you in. If you weren't a hero that just got cheated out of his bone, I'd— I ought to do it, anyway. Laws are laws, even for heroes. Come on, Rover. We're going for a walk."

Wolf thought quickly. The pound was the last place on earth he wanted to wind up. Even Ozzy would never think of looking for him there. Nobody'd claim him, nobody'd say *Absarka!* and in the end a dose of chloroform— He wrenched loose from the officer's grasp on his hair, and with one prodigious leap cleared the yard, landed on the sidewalk, and started up the street. But the instant he was out of the officer's sight he stopped dead and slipped behind a hedge.

He scented the policeman's approach even before he heard it. The man was running with the lumbering haste of two hundred pounds. But opposite the hedge he, too, stopped. For a moment Wolf wondered if his ruse had failed; but the officer had paused only to scratch his head and mutter, "Say! There's something screwy here. *Who rang that doorbell?* The kid couldn't reach it, and the dog— Oh, well," he concluded. "Nuts," and seemed to find in that monosyllabic summation the solution to all his problems.

As his footsteps and smell died away, Wolf became aware of another scent. He had only just identified it as cat when someone said, "You're were, aren't you?"

Wolf started up, lips drawn back and muscles tense. There was nothing human in sight, but someone had spoken to him. Unthinkingly, he tried to say, "Where are you?" but all that came out was a growl.

"Right behind you. Here in the shadows. You can scent me, can't you?"

"But you're a cat," Wolf thought in his snarls. "And you're talking."

"Of course. But I'm not talking human language. It's just your brain that takes it that way. If you had your human body, you'd just think I was going *meowrr*. But you are were, aren't you?"

"How do you . . . why do you think so?"

"Because you didn't try to jump me, as any normal dog would have. And, besides, unless Confucius taught me all wrong, you're a wolf, not a dog; and we don't have wolves around here unless they're were."

"How do you know all this? Are you—"

"Oh, no. I'm just a cat. But I used to live next door to a werechow named Confucius. He taught me things."

Wolf was amazed. "You mean he was a man who changed to chow and stayed that way? Lived as a pet?"

"Certainly. This was back at the worst of the depression. He said a dog was more apt to be fed and looked after than a man. I thought it was a smart idea."

"But how terrible! Could a man so debase himself as—"

"Men don't debase themselves. They debase each other. That's the way of most weres. Some change to keep from being debased, others to do a little more effective debasing. Which are you?"

"Why, you see, I—"

"*Sh!* Look. This is going to be fun. Holdup."

Wolf peered around the hedge. A well-dressed, middle-aged man was walking along briskly, apparently enjoying a night constitutional. Behind him moved a thin, silent figure. Even as Wolf watched, the figure caught up with him and whispered harshly, "Up with 'em, buddy!"

The quiet pomposity of the stroller melted away. He was ashen and aspen, as the figure slipped a hand around into his breast pocket and removed an impressive wallet.

And what, thought Wolf, was the good of his fine, vigorous body if it merely crouched behind hedges as a spectator? In one fine bound, to the shocked amazement of the were-wise cat, he had crossed the hedge and landed with his forepaws full in the figure's face. It went over backward with him on top and then there was a loud noise, a flash of light, and a frightful sharp smell. For a moment Wolf felt an acute pang in his shoulder, like the jab of a long needle, and then the pain was gone.

But his momentary recoil had been enough to let the figure get to his feet. "Missed you, huh?" it muttered. "Let's see how you like a slug in the belly, you interfering—" and he applied an epithet which would have been purely literal description if Wolf had not been were.

There were three quick shots in succession even as Wolf sprang. For a second he experienced the most acute stomach-ache of his life. Then he landed again.

The figure's head hit the concrete sidewalk and he was still.

Lights were leaping into brightness everywhere. Among all the confused noises, Wolf could hear the shrill complaints of Robby's mother, and among all the compounded smells, he could distinguish scent of the policeman who wanted to impound him. That meant getting out, and quick.

The city meant trouble, Wolf decided as he loped off. He could endure loneliness while he practiced his wolfry, until he had Gloria. Though just as a precaution he must arrange with Ozzy about a plausible-looking collar, and—

The most astounding realization yet suddenly struck him! He had received four bullets, three of them square in the stomach, and he hadn't a wound to show for it! Being a werewolf certainly offered its practical advantages. Think what a criminal could do with such bullet-proofing. Or— But no. He was a werewolf for fun, and that was that.

But even for a werewolf, being shot, though relatively painless, is tiring. A great deal of nervous energy is absorbed in the magical and instantaneous knitting of those wounds. And when Wolfe Wolf reached the peace and calm of the uncivilized hills, he no longer felt like reveling in freedom. Instead he stretched out to his full length, nuzzled his head down between his forepaws, and slept.

"Now the essence of magic," said Heliophagus of Smyrna, "is deceit; and that deceit is of two kinds. By magic, the magician deceives others; but magic deceives the magician himself."

So far the lycanthropic magic of Wolfe Wolf had worked smoothly and pleasantly, but now it was to show him the second trickery that lurks behind every magic trick. And the first step was that he slept.

He woke in confusion. His dreams had been

human—and of Gloria—despite the body in which
he dreamed them, and it took several full minutes
for him to reconstruct just how he happened to be in
that body. For a moment the dream, even that episode in which he and Gloria had been eating blue-
berry waffles on a roller coaster, seemed more sanely
plausible than the reality.

But he readjusted quickly, and glanced up at the
sky. The sun looked as though it had been up at least
an hour, which meant that the time was somewhere
between six and seven. Today was Thursday, which
meant that he was saddled with an eight-o'clock class.
That left plenty of time to change back, shave, dress,
breakfast and resume the normal life of Professor
Wolf, which was, after all, important if he intended
to support a wife.

He tried, as he trotted through the streets, to look
as tame and unwolflike as possible, and apparently
succeeded. No one paid him any mind save children,
who wanted to play, and dogs, who began by snarling and ended by cowering away terrified. His friend
the cat might be curiously tolerant of weres, but not
so dogs.

He trotted up the steps of the Berkeley Inn confidently. The clerk was under a slight spell and would
not notice wolves. There was nothing to do but rouse
Ozzy, be *absarka'd*, and—

"Hey! Where you going? Get out of here! Shoo!"

It was the clerk, a staunch and brawny young man,
who straddled the stairway and vigorously waved
him off.

"No dogs in here! Go on now. Scoot!"

Quite obviously this man was under no spell, and
equally obviously there was no way of getting up that
staircase short of using a wolf's strength to tear the
clerk apart. For a second Wolf hesitated. He had to
get changed back. It would be a pity to use his
powers to injure another human being—if only he

had not slept and arrived before this unmagicked day clerk came on duty—but necessity knows no—

Then the solution hit him. Wolf turned and loped off just as the clerk hurled an ash tray at him. Bullets may be relatively painless, but even a werewolf's rump, he learned promptly, is sensitive to flying glass.

The solution was foolproof. The only trouble was that it meant an hour's wait, and he was hungry. He found himself even displaying a certain shocking interest in the plump occupant of a baby carriage. You do get different appetites with a different body. He could understand how some originally well-intentioned werewolves might in time become monsters. But he was stronger in will, and much smarter. His stomach could hold out until this plan worked.

The janitor had already opened the front door of Wheeler Hall, but the building was deserted. Wolf had no trouble reaching the second floor unnoticed or finding his classroom. He had a little more trouble holding the chalk between his teeth and a slight tendency to gag on the dust: but by balancing his forepaws on the eraser trough, he could manage quite nicely. It took three springs to catch the ring of the chart in his teeth, but once that was pulled down there was nothing to do but crouch under the desk and pray that he would not starve quite to death.

The students of German 31B, as they assembled reluctantly for their eight o'clock, were a little puzzled at being confronted by a chart dealing with the influence of the gold standard on world economy, but they decided simply that the janitor had been forgetful.

The wolf under the desk listened unseen to their gathering murmurs, overheard that cute blonde in the front row make dates with three different men for that same night, and finally decided that enough had assembled to make his chances plausible. He slipped out from under the desk far enough to reach the ring of the chart, tugged at it, and let go.

The chart flew up with a rolling crash. The students broke off their chatter, looked up at the blackboard, and beheld in a huge and shaky scrawl the mysterious letters

ABSARKA

It worked. With enough people, it was an almost mathematical certainty that one of them in his puzzlement—for the race of subtitle readers, though handicapped by the talkies, still exists—would read the mysterious word aloud. It was the much bedated blonde who did it.

"*Absarka*," she said wonderingly.

And there was Professor Wolfe Wolf, beaming cordially at his class.

The only flaw was this: He had forgotten that he was only a werewolf, and not Hyperman. His clothes were still at the Berkeley Inn, and here on the lecture platform he was stark naked.

Two of his best pupils screamed and one fainted. The blonde only giggled appreciatively.

Emily was incredulous but pitying.

Professor Fearing was sympathetic but reserved.

The chairman of the department was cool.

The dean of letters was chilly.

The president of the university was frigid.

Wolfe Wolf was unemployed.

And Heliophagus of Smyrna was right. "The essence of magic is deceit."

"But what can I do?" Wolf moaned into his zombie glass. "I'm stuck. I'm stymied. Gloria arrives in Berkeley tomorrow, and here I am—nothing. Nothing but a futile, worthless werewolf. You can't support a wife on that. You can't raise a family. You can't . . . you can't even propose—I want another. Sure you won't have one?"

Ozymandias the Great shook his round, fringed head. "The last time I took two drinks I started all this. I've got to behave if I want to stop it. But you're an able-bodied, strapping, young man; surely, colleague, you can get work?"

"Where? All I'm trained for is academic work, and this scandal has put the kibosh on that forever. What university is going to hire a man who showed up naked in front of his class without even the excuse of being drunk? And supposing I try something else, I'd have to give references, say something about what I'd been doing with my thirty-odd years. And once these references were checked— Ozzy, I'm a lost man."

"Never despair, colleague. I've learned that magic gets you into some tight squeezes, but there's always a way of getting out. Now take that time in Darjeeling—"

"But what can I do? I'll wind up like Confucius the werechow and live on charity, if you'll find me somebody who wants a pet wolf."

"You know," Ozymandias reflected, "you may have something there, colleague."

"Nuts! That was a gag. I can at least retain my self-respect, even if I go on relief doing it. And I'll bet they don't like naked men on relief, either."

"No. I don't mean just being a pet wolf. But look at it this way: What are your assets? You have only two outstanding abilities. One of them is to teach German, and that is now completely out."

"Check."

"And the other is to change yourself into a wolf. All right, colleague. There must be some commercial possibilities in that. Let's look into them."

"Nonsense."

"Not quite. For every merchandise there's a market. The trick is to find it. And you, colleague, are going to be the first practical commercial werewolf on record."

"I could— They say Ripley's Odditorium pays good money. Supposing I changed six times a day regular for delighted audiences?"

Ozymandias shook his head sorrowfully. "It's no good. People don't want to see real magic. It makes 'em uncomfortable—starts 'em wondering what else might be loose in the world. They've got to feel sure it's all done with mirrors. I know. I had to quit vaudeville because I wasn't smart enough at faking it; all I could do was the real thing."

"I could be a Seeing Eye dog, maybe?"

"They have to be female."

"When I'm changed I can understand animal language. Maybe I could be a dog trainer and— No, that's out. I forgot; they're scared to death of me."

But Ozymandias' pale-blue eyes had lit up at the suggestion. "Colleague, you're warm. Oh, are you warm! Tell me: Why did you say your fabulous Gloria was coming to Berkeley?"

"Publicity for a talent hunt."

"For what?"

"A dog to star in 'Fangs of the Forest.'"

"And what kind of a dog?"

"A—" Wolf's eyes widened and his jaw sagged. "A wolf dog," he said softly.

And the two men looked at each other with a wild surmise—silent, beside a bar in Berkeley.

"It's all the fault of that Disney dog," the trainer complained. "Pluto does anything. Everything. So our poor mutts are expected to do likewise. Listen to that dope! 'The dog should come into the room, give one paw to the baby, indicate that he recognizes the hero in his Eskimo disguise, go over to the table, find the bone, and clap his paws gleefully!' Now who's got a set of signals to cover stuff like that? Pluto!" he snorted.

Gloria Garton said, "Oh." By that one sound she managed to convey that she sympathized deeply, that the trainer was a nice-looking young man whom she'd just as soon see again, and that no dog star was going to steal "Fangs of the Forest" from her. She adjusted her skirt slightly, leaned back, and made the plain wooden chair on the bar theater stage seem more than ever like a throne.

"All right." The man in the violet beret waved away the last unsuccessful applicant and read from a card: "Dog: Wopsy. Owner: Mrs. Channing Galbraith. Trainer: Luther Newby. Bring it in."

An assistant scurried offstage, and there was a sound of whines and whimpers as a door opened.

"What's got into those dogs today?" the man in the violet beret demanded. "They all seem scared to death and beyond."

"I think," said Fergus O'Breen, "that it's that big, gray wolf dog. Somehow, the others just don't like him."

Gloria Garton lowered her bepurpled lids and cast a queenly stare of suspicion on the young detective. There was nothing wrong with his being there. His sister was head of publicity for Metropolis, and he'd handled several confidential cases for the studio, even one for her, that time her chauffeur had decided to try his hand at blackmail. Fergus O'Breen was a Metropolis fixture; but still it bothered her.

The assistant brought in Mrs. Galbraith's Wopsy. The man in the violet beret took one look and screamed. The scream bounced back from every wall of the theater in the ensuing minute of silence. At last he found words. "A wolf dog! Tookah is the greatest role ever written for a wolf dog! And what do they bring us! A terrier yet! So if we wanted a terrier we could cast Asta!"

"But if you'd only let us show you—" Wopsy's tall, young trainer started to protest.

"Get out!" the man in the violet beret shrieked. "Get out before I lose my temper!"

Wopsy and her trainer slunk off.

"In El Paso," the casting director lamented, "they bring me a Mexican hairless. In St. Louis it's a Pekinese yet! And if I do a wolf dog, it sits in a corner and waits for somebody to bring in a sled to pull."

"Maybe," said Fergus, "you should try a real wolf."

"Wolf, *schmolf!*" He picked up the next card. "Dog: Yoggoth. Owner and trainer: Mr. O. Z. Manders. Bring it in."

The whining noise offstage ceased as Yoggoth was brought out to be tested. The man in the violet beret hardly glanced at the fringe-bearded owner and trainer. He had eyes only for that splendid gray wolf. "If you can only act—" he prayed, with the same fervor with which many a man has thought, "If you could only cook—"

He pulled the beret to an even more unlikely angle and snapped, "All right, Mr. Manders. The dog should come into the room, give one paw to the baby, indicate that he recognizes the hero in his Eskimo disguise, go over to the table, find the bone, and clap his paws joyfully. Baby here, here, here, baby here. Got that?"

Mr. Manders looked at his wolf dog and repeated, "Got that?"

Yoggoth wagged his tail.

"Very well, colleague," said Mr. Manders. "Do it." Yoggoth did it.

The violet beret sailed into the flies, on the wings of its owner's triumphal scream of joy. "He did it!" he kept burbling. "He did it!"

"Of course, colleagues," said Mr. Manders calmly.

The trainer who hated Pluto had a face as blank as

a vampire's mirror. Fergus O'Breen was speechless with wonderment. Even Gloria Garton permitted surprise and interest to cross her regal mask.

"You mean he can do anything?" gurgled the man who used to have a violet beret.

"Anything," said Mr. Manders.

"Can he— Let's see, in the dance-hall sequence— can he knock a man down, roll him over, and frisk his back pocket?"

Even before Mr. Manders could say "Of course," Yoggoth had demonstrated, using Fergus O'Breen as a convenient dummy.

"Peace!" the casting director sighed. "Peace— Charley!" he yelled to his assistant. "Send 'em all away. No more try-outs. We've found Tookah! It's wonderful."

The trainer stepped up to Mr. Manders. "It's more than that, sir. It's positively superhuman. I'll swear I couldn't detect the slightest signal, and for such complicated operations, too. Tell me, Mr. Manders, what system do you use?"

Mr. Manders made a Moopleish *kaff-kaff* noise. "Professional secret, you understand, young man. I'm planning on opening a school when I retire, but obviously until then—"

"Of course, sir. I understand. But I've never seen anything like it in all my born days."

"I wonder," Fergus O'Breen observed from the floor, "if your marvel dog can get off of people, too?"

Mr. Manders stifled a grin. "Of course! Yoggoth!"

Fergus picked himself up and dusted from his clothes the grime of the stage, which is the most clinging grime on earth. "I'd swear," he muttered, "that beast of yours enjoyed that."

"No hard feelings, I trust, Mr—"

"O'Breen. None at all. In fact, I'd suggest a little celebration in honor of this great event. I know you can't buy a drink this near the campus, so I brought along a bottle just in case."

"Oh," said Gloria Garton, implying that carousals were ordinarily beneath her, that this, however, was a special occasion, and that possibly there was something to be said for the green-eyed detective, after all.

This was all too easy, Wolfe Wolf-Yoggoth kept thinking. There was a catch to it somewhere. This was certainly the ideal solution to the problem of how to earn money as a werewolf. Bring an understanding of human speech and instructions into a fine animal body, and you are the answer to a director's prayer. It was perfect as long as it lasted; and if "Fangs of the Forest" was a smash hit, there were bound to be other Yoggoth pictures. Look at Rin-tin-tin. But it was too easy—

His ears caught a familiar "Oh" and his attention reported to Gloria. This "Oh" had meant that she really shouldn't have another drink, but since liquor didn't affect her any way and this was a special occasion, she might as well.

She was even more beautiful than he had remembered. Her golden hair was shoulder-length now, and flowed with such rippling perfection that it was all he could do to keep from reaching out a paw to it. Her body had ripened, too; was even more warm and promising than his memories of her. And in his new shape he found her greatest charm in something he had not been able to appreciate fully as a human being, the deep, heady scent of her flesh.

"To 'Fangs of the Forest'!" Fergus O'Breen was toasting. "And may that pretty-boy hero of yours get a worse mauling than I did."

Wolf-Yoggoth grinned to himself. That had been fun. That'd teach the detective to go crawling around hotel rooms.

"And while we're celebrating, colleagues," said Oyzmandias the Great, "why should we neglect our star? Here, Yoggoth." And he held out the bottle.

"He drinks yet!" the casting director exclaimed delightedly.

"Sure. He was weaned on it."

Wolf took a sizable gulp. It felt good. Warm and rich—almost the way Gloria smelled.

"But how about you, Mr. Manders?" the detective insisted for the fifth time. "It's your celebration really. The poor beast won't get the four-figure checks from Metropolis. And you've taken only one drink."

"Never take two, colleague. I know my danger point. Two drinks in me and things start happening."

"More should happen yet than training miracle dogs? Go on, O'Breen. Make him drink. We should see what happens."

Fergus took another long drink himself. "Go on. There's another bottle in the car, and I've gone far enough to be resolved not to leave here sober. And I don't want sober companions, either." His green eyes were already beginning to glow with a new wildness.

"No, thank you, colleague."

Gloria Garton left her throne, walked over to the plump man, and stood close, her soft hand resting on his arm. "Oh," she said, implying that dogs were dogs, but still that the party was inevitably in her honor and his refusal to drink was a personal insult.

Ozymandias the Great looked at Gloria, sighed, shrugged, resigned himself to fate, and drank.

"Have you trained many dogs?" the casting director asked.

"Sorry, colleague. This is my first."

"All the more wonderful! But what's your profession otherwise?"

"Well, you see, I'm a magician."

"Oh," said Gloria Garton, implying delight, and

went so far as to add, "I have a friend who does black magic."

"I'm afraid, ma'am, mine's simply white. That's tricky enough. With the black you're in for some real dangers."

"Hold on!" Fergus interposed. "You mean really a magician? Not just presti . . . sleight of hand!"

"Of course, colleague."

"Good theater," said the casting director. "Never let 'em see the mirrors."

"Uh-huh," Fergus nodded. "But look, Mr. Manders. What can you do, for instance?"

"Well, I can change—"

Yoggoth barked loudly.

"Oh, no," Ozymandias covered hastily, "that's really a little beyond me. But I can—"

"Can you do the Indian rope trick?" Gloria asked languidly. "My friend says that's terribly hard."

"Hard? Why, ma'am, there's nothing to it. I can remember that time in Darjeeling—"

Fergus took another long drink. "I," he announced defiantly, "want to see the Indian rope trick. I have met people who've met people who've met people who've seen it, but that's as close as I ever get. And I don't believe it."

"But, colleague, it's so simple."

"I don't believe it."

Ozymandias the Great drew himself up to his full lack of height. "Colleague, you are about to see it!" Yoggeth tugged warningly at his coat tails. "Leave me alone, Wolf. An aspersion has been cast!"

Fergus returned from the wings dragging a soiled length of rope. "This do?"

"Admirably."

"What goes?" the casting director demanded.

"*Shh!*" said Gloria. "Oh—"

She beamed worshipfully on Ozymandias, whose chest swelled to the point of threatening the security of his buttons. "Ladies and gentlemen!" he announced, in the manner of one prepared to fill a vast amphitheater with his voice. "You are about to behold Ozymandias the Great in—The Indian Rope Trick! Of course," he added conversationally, "I haven't got a small boy to chop into mincemeat, unless perhaps one of you— No? Well, we'll try it without. Not quite so impressive, though. And will you stop yapping, Wolf?"

"I thought his name was Yogi," said Fergus.

"Yoggoth. But since he's part wolf on his mother's side— Now quiet, all of you!"

He had been coiling the rope as he spoke. Now he placed the coil in the center of the stage, where it lurked like a threatening rattler. He stood beside it and deftly, professionally, went through a series of passes and mumblings so rapidly that even the superhumanly sharp eyes and ears of Wolf-Yoggoth could not follow them.

The end of the rope detached itself from the coil, reared in the air, turned for a moment like a head uncertain where to strike, then shot straight up until all the rope was uncoiled. The lower end rested a good inch above the stage.

Gloria gasped. The casting director drank hurriedly. Fergus, for some reason, stared curiously at the wolf.

"And, now, ladies and gentlemen—oh, hang it, I do wish I had a boy to carve—Ozymandias the Great will ascend this rope into that land which only the users of the rope may know. Onward and upward! Be right back," he added reassuringly to Wolf.

His plump hands grasped the rope above his head and gave a little jerk. His knees swung up and clasped about the hempen pillar. And up he went, like a monkey on a stick, up and up and up—

—until suddenly he was gone.

Just gone. That was all there was to it. Gloria was

beyond even saying "Oh." The casting director sat his beautiful flannels down on the filthy floor and gaped. Fergus swore softly and melodiously. And Wolf felt a premonitory prickling in his spine.

The stage door opened, admitting two men in denim pants and work shirts. "Hey!" said the first. "Where do you think you are?"

"We're from Metropolis Pictures," the casting director started to explain, scrambling to his feet.

"I don't care if you're from Washington, we gotta clear this stage. There's movies here tonight. Come on, Joe, help me get 'em out. And that pooch, too."

"You can't, Fred," said Joe reverently, and pointed. His voice sang to an awed whisper. "That's Gloria Garton—"

"So it is. Hi, Miss Garton, wasn't that last one of yours a stinkeroo!"

"Your public, darling," Fergus murmured.

"Come on!" Fred shouted. "Out of here. We gotta clean up. And you, Joe! Strike that rope!"

Before Fergus could move, before Wolf could leap to the rescue, the efficient stage hand had struck the rope and was coiling it up.

Wolf stared up into the flies. There was nothing up there. Nothing at all. Some place beyond the end of that rope was the only man on earth he could trust to say *Absarka!* for him; and the way down was cut off forever.

Wolfe Wolf sprawled on the floor of Gloria Garton's boudoir and watched the vision of volupty change into her most fetching negligee.

The situation was perfect. It was the fulfillment of all his dearest dreams. The only flaw was that he was still in a wolf's body.

Gloria turned, leaned over, and chucked him under the snout. "Wuzzum a cute wolf dog, wuzzum?"

Wolf could not restrain a snarl.

"Doesn't um like Gloria to talk baby talk? Um was a naughty wolf, yes, um was."

It was torture. Here you are in your best beloved's hotel room, all her beauty revealed to your hungry eyes, and she talks baby talk to you! Wolf had been happy at first when Gloria suggested that she might take over the care of her co-star pending the reappearance of his trainer—for none of them was quite willing to admit that "Mr. O. Z. Manders" mighty truly and definitely have vanished—but he was beginning to realize that the situation might bring on more torment than pleasure.

"Wolves are funny," Gloria observed. She was more talkative when alone, with no need to be cryptically fascinating. "I knew a Wolf once, only that was his name. He was a man. And he was a funny one."

Wolf felt his heart beating fast under his gray fur. To hear his own name on Gloria's warm lips— But before she could go on to tell her pet how funny Wolf was, her maid rapped on the door.

"A Mr. O'Breen to see you, madam."

"Tell him to go 'way."

"He says it's important, and he does look, madam, as though he might make trouble."

"Oh, all right." Gloria rose and wrapped her negligee more respectably about her. "Come on, Yog— No, that's a silly name. I'm going to call you Wolfie. That's cute. Come on, Wolfie, and protect me from the big, bad detective."

Fergus O'Breen was pacing the sitting room with a certain vicious deliberateness in his strides. He broke off and stood still as Gloria and the wolf entered.

"So?" he observed tersely. "Reinforcements?"

"Will I need them?" Gloria cooed.

"Look, light of my love life." The glint in the green eyes was cold and deadly. "You've been playing

games, and whatever their nature, there's one thing
they're not. And that's cricket."

Gloria gave him her slow, languid smile. "You're
amusing, Fergus."

"Thanks. I doubt, however, if your activities are."

"You're still a little boy playing cops and robbers.
And what boogyman are you after now?"

"Ha-ha," said Fergus politely. "And you know the
answer to that question better than I do. That's why
I'm here."

Wolf was puzzled. This conversation meant nothing to him. And yet he sensed a tension of danger in
the air as clearly as though he could smell it.

"Go on," Gloria snapped impatiently. "And remember how dearly Metropolis Pictures will thank
you for annoying one of its best box-office attractions."

"Some things, my sweet, are more important than
pictures, though you mightn't think it where you
come from. One of them is a certain federation of
forty-eight units. Another is an abstract concept called
democracy."

"And so?"

"And so I want to ask you one question: Why did
you come to Berkeley?"

"For publicity on 'Fangs,' of course. It was your
sister's idea."

"You've gone temperamental and turned down better ones. Why leap at this?"

"You don't haunt publicity stunts yourself, Fergus.
Why are you here?"

Fergus was pacing again. "And why was your first
act in Berkeley a visit to the office of the German
department?"

"Isn't that natural enough? I used to be a student
here."

"Majoring in dramatics, and you didn't go near the
Little Theater. Why the German department?" He

paused and stood straight in front of her, fixing her with his green gaze.

Gloria assumed the attitude of a captured queen defying the barbarian conqueror. "Very well. If you must know—I went to the German department to see the man I love."

Wolf held his breath, and tried to keep his tail from thrashing.

"Yes," she went on impassionedly, "you strip the last veil from me, and force me to confess to you what he alone should have heard first. This man proposed to me by mail. I foolishly rejected his proposal. But I thought and thought—and at last I knew. When I came to Berkeley I had to see him—"

"And did you?"

"The little mouse of a secretary told me he wasn't there. But I shall see him yet. And when I do—"

Fergus bowed stiffly. "My congratulations to you both, my sweet. And the name of this more than fortunate gentleman?"

"Professor Wolfe Wolf."

"Who is doubtless the individual referred to in this?" He whipped a piece of paper from his sport coat and thrust it at Gloria. She paled and was silent. But Wolfe Wolf did not wait for her reply. He did not care. He knew the solution to his problem now, and he was streaking unobserved for her boudoir.

Gloria Garton entered the boudoir a minute later, a shaken and wretched woman. She unstoppered one of the delicate perfume bottles on her dresser and poured herself a stiff drink of whiskey. Then her eyebrows lifted in surprise as she stared at her mirror. Scrawlingly lettered across the glass in her own deep-crimson lipstick was the mysterious word

A B S A R K A

Frowning, she said it aloud. *"Absarka—"*

From behind a screen stepped Professor Wolfe Wolf, incongruously wrapped in one of Gloria's lushest dressing robes. "Gloria dearest—" he cried.

"Wolf!" she exclaimed. "What on earth are you doing here in my room?"

"I love you. I've always loved you since you couldn't tell a strong from a weak verb. And now that I know that you love me—"

"This is terrible. Please get out of here!"

"Gloria—"

"Get out of here, or I'll sick my dog on you. Wolfie—Here, nice Wolfie!"

"I'm sorry, Gloria. But Wolfie won't answer you."

"Oh, you beast! Have you hurt Wolfie? Have you—"

"I wouldn't touch a hair on his pelt. Because, you see, Gloria, darling, I am Wolfie."

"What on earth do you—" Gloria stared around the room. It was undeniable that there was no trace of the presence of a wolf dog. And here was a man dressed only in one of her robes and no sign of his own clothes. And after that funny little man and the rope—

"You thought I was drab and dull," Wolf went on. "You thought I'd sunk into an academic rut. You'd sooner have an actor or a G-man. But I, Gloria, am something more exciting than you've ever dreamed of. There's not another soul on earth I'd tell this to; but I, Gloria, am a werewolf."

Gloria gasped. "That isn't possible! But it all fits in. What I heard about you on campus, and your friend with the funny beard and how he vanished, and, of course, it explains how you did tricks that any real dog couldn't possibly do—"

"Don't you believe me, darling?"

Gloria rose from the dresser chair and went into his arms. "I believe you, dear. And it's wonderful!

I'll bet there's not another woman in all Hollywood that was ever married to a werewolf!"

"Then you will—"

"But of course, dear. We can work it out beautifully. We'll hire a stooge to be your trainer on the lot. You can work daytimes, and come home at night and I'll say *Absarka!* for you. It'll be perfect."

"Gloria—" Wolf murmured with tender reverence.

"One thing dear. Just a little thing. Would you do Gloria a favor?"

"Anything!"

"Show me how you change. Change for me now. Then I'll *Absarka* you back right away."

Wolf said The Word. He was in such ecstatic bliss that he hardly felt the pang this time. He capered about the room with all the litheness of his fine wolfish legs, and ended up before Gloria, wagging his tail and looking for approval.

Gloria patted his head. "Good boy, Wolfie. And now, darling, you can just stay that way."

Wolf let out a yelp of amazement.

"You heard me, Wolfie. You're staying that way. You didn't happen to believe any of that guff I was feeding the detective, did you? Love you? I should waste my time! But this way you can be very useful to me. With your trainer gone, I can take charge of you and pick up an extra thousand a week or so. I won't mind that. And Professor Wolfe Wolf will have vanished forever, which fits right in with my plans."

Wolf snarled.

"Now, don't try to get nasty, Wolfie darling. Um wouldn't threaten ums darling Gloria, would ums? Remember what I can do for you. I'm the only person who can turn you into a man again. You wouldn't dare teach anyone else that. You wouldn't dare let people know what you really are. An ignorant person would kill you. A smart one would have you locked up as a lunatic."

Wolf still advanced threateningly.

"Oh, no. You can't hurt me. Because all I'd have to do would be to say the word on the mirror. Then you wouldn't be a dangerous wolf any more. You'd just be a man here in my room, and I'd scream. And after what happened on the campus yesterday, how long do you think you'd stay out of the madhouse?"

Wolf backed away and let his tail droop.

"You see, Wolfie darling? Gloria has ums just where she wants ums. And ums is going to be a good boy."

There was a rap on the boudoir door, and Gloria called, "Come in."

"A gentleman to see you, madam," the maid announced. "A Professor Fearing."

Gloria smiled her best cruel and queenly smile. "Come along, Wolfie. This may interest you."

Professor Oscar Fearing, overflowing one of the graceful chairs of the sitting room, beamed benevolently as Gloria and the wolf entered. "Ah, my dear! A new pet. Touching."

"And what a pet, Oscar. Wait till you hear."

Professor Fearing buffed his pince-nez against his sleeve. "And wait, my dear, until you hear all that I have learned. Chiswick has perfected his protective screen against magnetic bombs, and the official trial is set for next week. And Farnsworth has all but completed his researches on a new process for obtaining osmium. Gas warfare may start any day, and the power that can command a plentiful supply of—"

"Fine, Oscar," Gloria broke in. "But we can go over all this later. We've got other worries right now."

"What do you mean, my dear?"

"Have you run into a red-headed young Irishman in a yellow shirt?"

"No, I— Why, yes. I did see such an individual

leaving the office yesterday. I believe he had been to see Wolf."

"He's on to us. He's a detective from Los Angeles, and he's tracking us down. Some place he got hold of a scrap of record that should have been destroyed. He knows I'm in it, and he knows I'm tied up with somebody here in the German department."

Professor Fearing scrutinized his pince-nez, approved of their cleanness and set them on his nose. "Not so much excitement, my dear. No hysteria. Let us approach this calmly. Does he know about the Temple of the Dark Truth?"

"Not yet. Nor about you. He just knows it's somebody in the department."

"Then what could be simpler? You have heard of the strange conduct of Wolfe Wolf?"

"Have I?" Gloria laughed harshly.

"Everyone knows of Wolf's infatuation with you. Throw the blame onto him. It should be easy to clear yourself and make you appear an innocent tool. Direct all attention to him and the organization will be safe. The Temple of the Dark Truth can go its mystic way and extract even more invaluable information from weary scientists who need the emotional release of a false religion."

"That's what I've tried to do. I gave O'Breen a long song and dance about my devotion to Wolf, so obviously phony he'd be bound to think it was a cover-up for something else. And I think he bit. But the situation is trickier than you guess. Do you know where Wolfe Wolf is?"

"No one knows. After the president . . . ah . . . rebuked him, he seems to have vanished."

Gloria laughed again. "He's right here. In this room."

"My dear! Secret panels and such? You take your espionage too seriously. Where?"

"There!"

Professor Fearing gaped. "Are you serious?"

"As serious as you are about the future of Fascism. That is Wolfe Wolf."

Fearing approached the wolf incredulously and extended his hand.

"He might bite," Gloria warned him a second too late.

Fearing stared at his bleeding hand. "That, at least," he observed, "is undeniably true." And he raised his foot to deliver a sharp kick.

"No, Oscar! Don't! Leave him alone. And you'll have to take my word for it—it's way too complicated. But the wolf is Wolfe Wolf, and I've got him completely under control. He's absolutely in our hands. We'll switch suspicion to him, and I'll keep him this way while Fergus and his friends the G-Men go off hotfoot on his trail."

"My dear!" Fearing ejaculated. "You're mad. You're more hopelessly mad than the devout members of the Temple." He took off his pince-nez and stared again at the wolf. "And yet Tuesday night— Tell me one thing: From whom did you get this . . . this wolf dog?"

"From a funny plump little man with a fringy beard."

Fearing gasped. Obviously he remembered the furor in the Temple, and the wolf and the fringe-beard. "Very well, my dear. I believe you. Don't ask me why, but I believe you. And now—"

"Now it's all set, isn't it? We keep him here helpless, and we use him to—"

"The wolf as scapegoat. Yes. Very pretty."

"Oh! One thing—" She was suddenly frightened.

Wolfe Wolf was considering the possibilities of a sudden attack on Fearing. He could probably get out of the room before Gloria could say *Absarka*! But after that? Whom could he trust to restore him? Especially if G-Men were to be set on his trail—

"What is it?" Fearing asked.

"That secretary. That little mouse in the department office. She knows it was you I asked for, not Wolf. Fergus can't have talked to her yet, because he swallowed my story; but he will. He's thorough."

"Hm-m-m. Then, in that case—"

"Yes, Oscar?"

"She must be attended to." Professor Oscar Fearing beamed genially and reached for the phone.

Wolf acted instantly, on inspiration and impulse. His teeth were strong, quite strong enough to jerk the phone cord from the wall. That took only a second, and in the next second he was out of the room and into the hall before Gloria could open her mouth to speak that word that would convert him from a powerful and dangerous wolf to a futile man.

There were shrill screams and a shout or two of "Mad dog!" as he dashed through the lobby, but he paid no heed to them. The main thing was to reach Emily's house before she could be "attended to." Her evidence was essential. That could swing the balance, show Fergus and his G-Men where the true guilt lay. And, besides, he admitted to himself, Emily was a nice kid—

His rate of collision was about one point six six per block, and the curses heaped upon him, if theologically valid, would have been more than enough to damn him forever. But he was making time, and that was all that counted. He dashed through traffic signals, cut into the path of trucks, swerved from under street cars, and once even leaped over a stalled car which obstructed him. Everything was going fine, he was halfway there, when two hundred pounds of human flesh landed on him in a flying tackle.

He looked up through the brilliant lighting effects of smashing his head on the sidewalk and saw his old Nemesis, the policeman who had been cheated of his beer.

"So, Rover!" said that officer. "Got you at last, did I? Now we'll see if you'll wear a proper license tag. Didn't know I used to play football, did you?"

The officer's grip on his hair was painfully tight. A gleeful crowd was gathering and heckling the policeman with fantastic advice.

"Get along, boys," he admonished. "This is a private matter between me and Rover here. Come on," and he tugged even harder.

Wolf left a large tuft of fur and skin in the officer's grasp and felt the blood ooze out of the bare patch on his neck. He heard an oath and a pistol shot simultaneously, and felt the needlelike sting drive through his shoulder. The awestruck crowd thawed before him. Two more bullets hied after him, but he was gone, leaving the most dazed policeman in Berkeley.

"I hit him," the officer kept muttering blankly. "I hit the—"

Wolfe Wolf coursed along Dwight Way. Two more blocks and he'd be at the little bungalow that Emily shared with a teaching assistant in something or other. That telephone gag had stopped Fearing only momentarily; the orders would have been given by now, the henchmen would be on their way. But he was almost there—

"He'o!" a child's light voice called to him. "Nice woof-woof came back!"

Across the street was the modest frame dwelling of Robby and his shrewish mother. The child had been playing on the sidewalk. Now he saw his idol and deliverer and started across the street at a lurching toddle. "Nice woof-woof!" he kept calling. "Wait for Robby!"

Wolf kept on. This was no time for playing games with even the most delightful of cubs. And then he saw the car. It was an ancient jalopy, plastered with wisecracks even older than itself; and the high-school youth driving was obviously showing his girl friend how it could make time on this deserted residential street. The girl was a cute dish, and who could be bothered watching out for children?

Robby was directly in front of the car. Wolf leaped straight as a bullet. His trajectory carried him so close to the car that he could feel the heat of the radiator on his flank. His forepaws struck Robby and thrust him out of danger. They fell to the ground together, just as the car ground over the last of Wolf's caudal vertebrae.

The cute dish screamed. "Homer! Did we hit them?"

Homer said nothing, and the jalopy zoomed on.

Robby's screams were louder. "You hurt me! You hurt me! *Baaaaad* woof-woof!"

His mother appeared on the porch and joined in with her own howls of rage. The cacophony was terrific. Wolf let out one wailing yelp of his own, to make it perfect and to lament his crushed tail, and dashed on. This was no time to clear up misunderstandings.

But the two delays had been enough. Robby and the policeman had proved the perfect unwitting tools of Oscar Fearing. As Wolf approached Emily's little bungalow, he saw a gray sedan drive off. In the rear was a small, slim girl, and she was struggling.

Even a werewolf's lithe speed cannot equal a motor car. After a block of pursuit, Wolf gave up and sat back on his haunches panting. It felt funny, he thought even in that tense moment, not to be able to sweat, to have to open your mouth and stick out your tongue and—

"Trouble?" inquired a solicitous voice.

This time Wolf recognized the cat. "Heavens, yes," he assented wholeheartedly. "More than you ever dreamed of."

"Food shortage?" the cat asked. "But that toddler back there is nice and plump."

"Shut up," Wolf snarled.

"Sorry; I was just judging from what Confucius told me about werewolves. You don't mean to tell me that you're an altruistic were?"

"I guess I am. I know werewolves are supposed to go around slaughtering, but right now I've got to save a life."

"You expect me to believe that?"

"It's the truth."

"Ah," the cat reflected philosophically. "Truth is a dark and deceitful thing."

Wolfe Wolf was on his feet. "Thanks," he barked. "You've done it."

"Done what?"

"See you later." And Wolf was off at top speed for the Temple of the Dark Truth.

That was the best chance. That was Fearing's headquarters. The odds were at least even that when it wasn't being used for services it was the hang-out of his ring, especially since the consulate had been closed in San Francisco. Again the wild running and leaping, the narrow escapes; and where Wolf had not taken these too seriously before, he knew now that he might be immune to bullets, but certainly not to being run over. His tail still stung and ached tormentingly. But he had to get there. He had to clear his own reputation, he kept reminding himself; but what he really thought was, *I have to save Emily*.

A block from the Temple he heard the crackle of gunfire. Pistol shots and, he'd swear, machine guns, too. He couldn't figure what it meant, but he pressed on. Then a bright-yellow roadster passed him and a vivid flash came from its window. Instinctively he ducked. You might be immune to bullets, but you still didn't just stand still for them.

The roadster was gone and he was about to follow

when a glint of bright metal caught his eye. The bullet which had missed him had hit a brick wall and ricocheted back onto the sidewalk. It glittered there in front of him—pure silver.

This, he realized abruptly, meant the end of his immunity. Fearing had believed Gloria's story, and with his smattering of occult lore he had known the successful counter weapon. A bullet, from now on, might mean no more needle sting, but instant death.

And so Wolfe Wolf went straight on.

He approached the Temple cautiously, lurking behind shrubbery. And he was not the only lurker. Before the Temple, crouching in the shelter of a car every window of which was shattered, were Fergus O'Breen and a moonfaced giant. Each held an automatic, and they were taking pot shots at the steeple.

Wolf's keen, lupine hearing could catch their words even above the firing. "Gabe's around back," Moonface was explaining. "But it's no use. Know what the steeple is? It's a revolving machine-gun turret. They've been ready for something like this. Only two men in there, far as we can tell, but that turret covers all the approaches."

"Only two?" Fergus muttered.

"And the girl. They brought a girl here with them. If she's still alive."

Fergus took careful aim at the steeple, fired, and ducked back behind the car as a bullet missed him by millimeters. "Missed him again! By all the kings that ever ruled Tara, Moon, there's got to be a way in there. How about tear gas?"

Moon snorted. "Think you can reach the firing gap in that armored turret at this angle?"

"That girl—" said Fergus.

Wolf waited no longer. As he sprang forward, the gunner noticed him and shifted his fire. It was like a needle shower in which all the spray is solid steel.

Wolf's nerves ached with the pain of reknitting. But at least machine guns apparently didn't fire silver.

The front door was locked, but the force of his drive carried him through and added a throbbing ache in his shoulder to his other discomforts. The lower-floor guard, a pasty-faced individual with a jutting Adam's apple, sprang up, pistol in hand. Behind him, in the midst of the litter of the cult, ceremonial robes, incense burners, curious books, even a Ouija board, lay Emily.

Pasty-face fired. The bullets struck Wolf full in the chest and for an instant he expected death. But this, too, was lead, and he jumped forward. It was not his usual powerful leap. His strength was almost spent by now. He needed to lie on cool earth and let his nerves knit. And this spring was only enough to grapple with his foe, not to throw him.

The man reversed his useless automatic and brought its butt thudding down on the beast's skull. Wolf reeled back, lost his balance, and fell to the floor. For a moment he could not rise. The temptation was so strong just to lie there and—

The girl moved. Her bound hands grasped a corner of the Ouija board. Somehow, she stumbled to her rope-tied feet and raised her arms. Just as Pasty-face rushed for the prostrate wolf, she brought the heavy board down.

Wolf was on his feet now. There was an instant of temptation. His eyes fixed themselves on the jut of that Adam's apple, and his long tongue licked his jowls. Then he heard the machine-gun fire from the turret, and tore himself from Pasty-face's unconscious form.

Ladders are hard on a wolf, almost impossible. But if you use your jaws to grasp the rung above you and pull up, it can be done. He was halfway up the ladder when the gunner heard him. The firing stopped, and Wolf heard a rich German oath in what he automatically recognized as an East Prussian dialect with possible Lithuanian influences. Then he saw the man himself, a broken-nosed blond, staring down the ladder well.

The other man's bullets had been lead. So this must be the one with the silver. But it was too late to turn back now. Wolf bit the next rung and hauled up as the bullet struck his snout and stung through. The blond's eyes widened as he fired again and Wolf climbed another round. After the third shot he withdrew precipitately from the opening.

Shots still sounded from below, but the gunner did not return them. He stood frozen against the wall of the turret watching in horror as the wolf emerged from the well. Wolf halted and tried to get his breath. He was dead with fatigue and stress, but this man must be vanquished.

The blond raised his pistol, sighted carefully, and fired once more. He stood for one terrible instant, gazing at this deathless wolf and knowing from his grandmother's stories what it must be. Then deliberately he clamped his teeth on the muzzle of the automatic and fired again.

Wolf had not yet eaten in his wolf's body, but food must have been transferred from the human stomach to the lupine. There was at least enough for him to be extensively sick.

Getting down the ladder was impossible. He jumped. He had never heard anything about a wolf landing on his feet, but it seemed to work. He dragged his weary and bruised body along to where Emily sat by the still unconscious Pasty-face, his discarded pistol in her hand. She wavered as the wolf approached her, as though uncertain yet as to whether he was friend or foe.

Time was short. With the machine gun dead, Fergus and his companions would be invading the Temple at any minute. Wolf hurriedly nosed about and found the planchette of the Ouija board. He pushed the heart-shaped bit of wood onto the board and began to shove it around with his paw.

Emily watched, intent and puzzled. "A," she said aloud. "B—S—"

Wolf finished the word and edged around so that he stood directly beside one of the ceremonial robes. "Are you trying to say something?" Emily frowned.

Wolf wagged his tail in vehement affirmation and began again.

"A—" Emily repeated. "B—S—A—R—"

He could already hear approaching footsteps.

"—K—A— What on earth does that mean? *Absarka*—"

Ex-Professor Wolfe Wolf hastily wrapped his naked human body in the cloak of Dark Truth. Before either he or Emily knew quite what was happening, he had folded her in his arms, kissed her in a most thorough expression of gratitude, and fainted.

Even Wolf's human nose could tell, when he awakened, that he was in a hospital. His body was still limp and exhausted. The bare patch on his neck, where the policeman had pulled out the hair, still stung, and there was a lump where the butt of the automatic had connected. His tail, or where his tail had been, sent twinges through him if he moved. But the sheets were cool and he was at rest and Emily was safe.

"I don't know how you got in there, Mr. Wolf, or what you did; but I want you to know you've done your country a signal service." It was the moonfaced giant speaking.

Fergus O'Breen was sitting beside the bed, too. "Congratulations, Wolf. And I don't know if the doctor would approve, but here."

Wolfe Wolf drank the whiskey gratefully and looked a question at the huge man.

"This is Moon Lafferty," said Fergus. "F.B.I. man.

He's been helping me track down this ring of spies ever since I first got wind of them."

"You got them—all?" Wolf asked.

"Picked up Fearing and Garton at the hotel," Lafferty rumbled.

"But how—I thought—"

"You thought we were out for you?" Fergus answered. "That was Garton's idea, but I didn't quite tumble. You see, I'd already talked to your secretary. I knew it was Fearing she'd wanted to see. And when I asked around about Fearing, and learned of the Temple and the defense researches of some of its members, the whole picture cleared up."

"Wonderful work, Mr. Wolf," said Lafferty. "Any time we can do anything for you— And how you got into that machine-gun turret— Well, O'Breen, I'll see you later. Got to check up the rest of this round up. Pleasant convalescence to you, Wolf."

Fergus waited until the G-Man had left the room. Then he leaned over the bed and asked confidentially, "How about it, Wolf? Going back to your acting career?"

Wolf gasped. "What acting career?"

"Still going to play Tookah? If Metropolis makes 'Fangs' with Miss Garton in a Federal prison."

Wolf fumbled for words. "What sort of nonsense—"

"Come on, Wolf. It's pretty clear I know that much. Might as well tell me the whole story."

Still dazed, Wolf told it. "But how did you know it?" he concluded.

Fergus grinned. "Look. Dorothy Sayers said some place that in a detective story the supernatural may be introduced only to be dispelled. Sure, that's swell. Only in real life there comes times when it won't be dispelled. And this was one. There was too much. There were your eyebrows and fingers, there were the obviously real magical powers of your friend, there were the tricks which no dog could possibly do without signals, there was the way the other dogs whimpered and cringed— I'm pretty hard-headed, Wolf, but I'm Irish. I'll string along only so far with the materialistic, but too much coincidence is too much."

"Fearing believed it, too," Wolf reflected. "But one thing that worries me—if they used a silver bullet on me once, why were all the rest of them lead? Why was I safe from then on?"

"Well," said Fergus, "I'll tell you. Because it wasn't 'they' who fired the silver bullet. You see, Wolf, up till the last minute I thought you were on 'their' side. I, somehow, didn't associate good will with a werewolf. So I got a mold from a gunsmith and paid a visit to a jeweler and— I'm glad I missed," he added sincerely.

"You're glad!"

"But look. Previous question stands. Are you going back to acting? Because if not, I've got a suggestion."

"Which is?"

"You say you fretted about how to be a practical, commercial werewolf. All right. You're strong and fast. You can terrify people even to committing suicide. You can overhear conversations that no human being could get in on. You're invulnerable to bullets. Can you tell me better qualifications for a G-Man?"

Wolf goggled. "Me? A G-Man?"

"Moon's been telling me how badly they need new men. They've changed the qualifications lately so that your language knowledge'll do instead of the law or accounting they used to require. And, after what you did today, there won't be any trouble about a little academic scandal in your past. Moon's pretty sold on you."

Wolf was speechless. Only three days ago he had been in torment because he was not an actor or a G-Man. Now—

"Think it over," said Fergus.

"I will. Indeed I will. Oh, and one other thing. Has there been any trace of Ozzy?"

"Nary a sigh."

"I like that man. I've got to try to find him and—"

"If he's the magician I think he is, he's staying up there only because he decided he likes it."

"I don't know. Magic's tricky. Heaven knows I've learned that. I'm going to do all I can for that fringe-bearded old colleague."

"Wish you luck. Shall I send in your other guest?"

"Who's that?"

"Your secretary. Here on business, no doubt."

Fergus disappeared discreetly as he admitted Emily. She walked over to the bed and took Wolf's hand. His eyes drank in her quiet, charming simplicity, and his mind wondered what freak of debated adolescence had made him succumb to the blatant glamour of Gloria.

They were silent for a long time. Then at once they both said, "How can I thank you? You saved my life."

Wolf laughed. "Let's not argue. Let's say we saved our life."

"You mean that?" Emily asked gravely.

Wolf pressed her hand. "Aren't you tired of being an office wife?"

In the bazaar of Darjeeling, Chulundra Lingasuta stared at his rope in numb amazement. Young Ali had climbed up only five minutes ago, but now as he descended he was a hundred pounds heavier and wore a curious fringe of beard.

THE COPPERSMITH

Lester del Rey

In the slanting rays of the morning sun, the figure trudging along the path seemed out of place so near the foothills of the Adirondacks. His scant three feet of stocky height was covered by a tattered jerkin of brown leather that fell to his knees, and above was a russet cap with turned-back brim and high, pointed crown. Below, the dusty sandals were tipped up at the toes and tied back to the ankles, and on each a little copper bell tinkled lightly as he walked.

Ellowan Coppersmith moved slowly under the weight of the bag he bore on his shoulders, combing out his beard with a stubby brown hand and humming in time with the jingling bells. It was early still and a whole day lay before him in which to work. After the long sleep, back in the hills where his people lay dormant, work would be good again.

The path came to an end where it joined a well-kept highway, and the elf eased the bag from his shoulder while he studied the signpost. There was

69

little meaning for him in the cryptic marker that bore the cabalistic 30, but the arrow below indicated that Wells lay half a mile beyond. That must be the village he had spied from the path; a very nice little village, Ellowan judged, and not unprosperous. Work should be found in plenty there.

But first, the berries he had picked in the fields would refresh him after the long walk. His kindly brown eyes lighted with pleasure as he pulled them from his bag and sat back against the signpost. Surely even these few so late in the season were an omen of good fortune to come. The elf munched them slowly, savoring their wild sweetness gratefully.

When they were finished, he reached into his bag again and brought forth a handful of thin sticks, which he tossed on the ground and studied carefully. "Six score years in sleep," he muttered. "Eh, well, though the runes forecast the future but poorly, they seldom lie of the past. Six score years it must be."

He tossed the runes back into the bag and turned toward a growing noise that had been creeping up on him from behind. The source of the sound seemed to be a long, low vehicle that came sweeping up the road and flashed by him so rapidly that there was only time to catch a glimpse of the men inside.

"These men!" Ellowan picked up his bag and headed toward the village, shaking his head doubtfully. "Now they have engines inside their carriages, and strange engines at that, from the odor. Even the air of the highway must be polluted with the foul smell of machines. Next it's flying they'll be. Methinks 'twere best to go through the fields to the village."

He pulled out his clay pipe and sucked on it, but the flavor had dried out while he had lain sleeping, and the tobacco in his pouch had molded away. Well, there'd be tobacco in the village, and coppers to buy it with. He was humming again as he neared the town and studied its group of houses, among which the people were just beginning to stir. It would be best to go from house to house rather than disturb them by crying his services from the street. With an expectant smile on his weathered old face, Ellowan rapped lightly and waited for a response.

"Whatta you want?" The woman brushed back her stringy hair with one hand while holding the door firmly with the other, and her eyes were hard as she caught sight of the elf's bag. "We don't want no magazines. You're just wastin' your time!"

From the kitchen came the nauseating odor of scorching eggs, and the door was slammed shut before Ellowan could state his wants. Eh, well, a town without a shrew was a town without a house. A bad start and a good ending, perchance. But no one answered his second knock, and he drew no further response than faces pressed to the window at the third.

A young woman came to the next door, eyeing him curiously, but answering his smile. "Good morning," she said doubtfully, and the elf's hopes rose.

"A good morning to you, mistress. And have you pots to mend, pans or odds that you wish repaired?" It was good to speak the words again. "I'm a wonderful tinker, none better, mistress. Like new they'll be, and the better for the knack that I have and that which I bring in my bag."

"I'm sorry, but I haven't anything; I've just been married a few weeks." She smiled again, hesitantly. "If you're hungry, though . . . well, we don't usually feed men who come to the door, but I guess it'd be all right this time."

"No, mistress, but thank'ee. It's only honest labor I want." Ellowan heaved the bag up again and moved down the steps. The girl turned to go in, glancing back at him with a feeling of guilt that there was no work for the strange little fellow. On impulse, she called after him.

"Wait!" At her cry, he faced her again. "I just thought; Mother might have something for you. She lives down the street—the fifth house on the right. Her name's Mrs. Franklin."

Ellowan's face creased in a twinkling smile. "My thanks again, mistress, and good fortune attend you."

Eh, so, his luck had changed again. Once his skill was known, there'd be no lack of work for him. "A few coppers here and a farthing there, from many a kettle to mend; with solder and flux and skill to combine, there's many a copper to spend."

He was still humming as he rounded the house and found Mrs. Franklin hanging out dish towels on the back porch to dry. She was a somewhat stout woman, with the expression of fatigue that grows habitual in some cases, but her smile was as kindly as her daughter's when she spied the elf.

"Are you the little man my daughter said mended things?" she asked. "Susan phoned me that you'd be here—she took quite a fancy to you. Well, come up here on the porch and I'll bring out what I want fixed. I hope your rates aren't too high?"

"It's very reasonable you'll find them, mistress." He sank down on a three-legged stool he pulled from his bag and brought out a little table, while she went inside for the articles that needed repairs. There were knick-knacks, a skillet, various pans, a copper wash boiler, and odds and ends of all sorts; enough to keep him busy till midday.

She set them down beside him. "Well, that's the lot of them. I've been meaning to throw most of them away, since nobody around here can fix them, but it seems a shame to see things wasted for some little hole. You just call me when you're through."

Ellowan nodded briskly and dug down into his seemingly bottomless bag. Out came his wonderful fluxes that could clean the thickest tarnish away in a twinkling, the polish that even the hardest grease and oldest soot couldn't defy, the bars of solder that became one with the metal, so that the sharpest eye would fail to note the difference; and out came the clever little tools that worked and smoothed the repair into unity with the original. Last of all, he drew forth a tiny anvil and a little charcoal brazier whose coals began to burn as he set it down. There was no fan or bellows, yet the coals in the center glowed fiercely at white heat.

The little elf reached out for the copper boiler, so badly dented that the seam had sprung open all the way down. A few light taps on his anvil straightened it back into smoothness. He spread on his polish, blew on it vigorously, and watched the dirt and dullness disappear, then applied his flux, and drew some of the solder onto it with a hot iron, chuckling as the seams became waterproof again. Surely now, even the long sleep had cost him none of his skill. As he laid it down, there was no sign to show that the boiler had not come freshly from some shop, or new out of the maker's hands.

The skillet was bright and shiny, except for a brown circle on the bottom, and gleamed with a silvery luster. Some magic craftsman must have made it, the elf thought, and it should receive special pains to make sure that the spell holding it so bright was not broken. He rubbed a few drops of polish over it carefully, inspected the loose handle, and applied his purple flux, swabbing off the small excess. Tenderly he ran the hot iron over the solder and began working the metal against the handle.

But something was very wrong. Instead of drawing firmly to the skillet, the solder ran down the side in little drops. Such as remained was loose and refused to stick. With a puzzled frown, Ellowan smelled his materials and tried again; there was nothing wrong with the solder or flux, but they still refused to work.

He muttered softly and reached out for a pan with a pin hole in it.

Mrs. Franklin found him sitting there later, his tools neatly before him, the pots and pans stacked at his side, and the brazier glowing brightly. "All finished?" she asked cheerfully. "I brought you some coffee and a cinnamon bun I just baked; I thought you might like them." She set them down before the elf and glanced at the pile of utensils again. Only the boiler was fixed. "What—" she began sharply, but softened her question somewhat as she saw the bewildered frustration on his face. "I thought you said you could fix them?"

Ellowan nodded glumly. "That I did, mistress, and that I tried to do. But my solder and flux refused all but the honest copper, yonder, and there's never a thing I can make of them. Either these must be wondrous metals indeed, or my art has been bewitched."

"There's nothing very wonderful about aluminum and enamelware—nor stainless steel, either, except the prices they charge." She picked up the wash boiler and inspected his work. "Well, you did do this nicely, and you're not the only one who can't solder aluminum, I guess, so cheer up. And eat your roll before it's cold!"

"Thank'ee, mistress." The savory aroma of the bun had been tantalizing his stomach, but he had been waiting to make certain that he was welcome to it. "It's sorry I am to have troubled you, but it's a long time ago that I tinkered for my living, and this is new to me."

Mrs. Franklin nodded sympathetically; the poor little man must have been living with a son, or maybe working in a side show—he was short enough, and his costume was certainly theatrical. Well, hard times were hard times. "You didn't trouble me much, I guess. Besides, I needed the boiler tomorrow for wash day, so that's a big help, anyway. What do I owe you for it?"

"Tu'pence ha'penny," Ellowan said, taking out for the bun. Her look was uncertain, and he changed it quickly. "Five pence American, that is, mistress."

"Five cents! But it's worth ten times that!"

"It's but an honest price for the labor, mistress." Ellowan was putting the tools and materials back in his bag. "That's all I can take for the small bit I could do."

"Well—" She shrugged. "All right, if that's all you'll take, here it is." The coin she handed him seemed strange, but that was to be expected. He pocketed it with a quick smile and another "thank'ee," and went in search of a store he had noticed before.

The shop was confusing in the wide variety of articles it carried, but Ellowan spied tobacco and cigars on display and walked in. Now that he had eaten the bun, the tobacco was a more pressing need than food.

"Two pennies of tobacco, if it please you," he told the clerk, holding out the little leather pouch he carried.

"You crazy?" The clerk was a boy, much more interested in his oiled hair than in the customers who might come in. "Cheapest thing I can give you is Duke's Mixture, and it'll cost you five cents, cash."

Regretfully Ellowan watched the nickel vanish over the counter; tobacco was indeed a luxury at the price. He picked up the small cloth bag, and the pasteboard folder the boy thrust at him. "What might this be?" he asked, holding up the folder.

"Matches." The boy grinned in fine superiority. "Where you been all your life? Okay, you do this . . . see? Course, if you don't want 'em—"

"Thank'ee." The elf pocketed the book of matches quickly and hurried toward the street, vastly pleased with his purchase. Such a great marvel as the matches alone surely was worth the price. He filled his clay pipe and struck one of them curiously, chuckling in delight as it flamed up. When he dropped the flame regretfully, he noticed that the tobacco, too, was imbued with magic, else surely it could never have been cured to such a mild and satisfying flavor. It scarcely bit his tongue.

But there was no time to be loitering around admiring his new treasures. Without work there could be no food, and supper was still to be taken care of. Those aluminum and enamelware pans were still in his mind, reminding him that coppers might be hard to get. But then, Mrs. Franklin had mentioned stainless steel, and only a mighty wizard could prevent iron from rusting; perhaps her husband was a worker in enchantments, and the rest of the village might be served in honest copper and hammered pewter. He shook his shoulders in forced optimism and marched down the street toward the other houses, noting the prices marked in a store window as he passed. Eh, the woman was right; he'd have to charge more for his services to eat at those rates.

The road was filled with the strange carriages driven by engines, and Ellowan stayed cautiously off the paving. But the stench from their exhausts and the dust they stirred up were still thick in his nostrils. The elf switched the bag from his left shoulder to his right and plodded on grimly, but there was no longer a tune on his lips, and the little bells refused to tinkle as he walked.

The sun had set, and it was already growing darker, bringing the long slow day to a close. His last call would be at the house ahead, already showing lights burning, and it was still some distance off. Ellowan pulled his belt tighter and marched toward it, muttering in slow time to his steps.

"Al-u-mi-num and en-am-el-ware and stain-*less*

STEEL!" A row of green pans, red pots and ivory bowls ran before his eyes, and everywhere there was a glint of silvery skillets and dull white kettles. Even the handles used were no longer honest wood, but smelled faintly resinous.

Not one proper kettle in the whole village had he found. The housewives came out and looked at him, answered his smile, and brought forth their work for him in an oddly hesitant manner, as if they were unused to giving out such jobs at the door. It spoke more of pity than of any desire to have their wares mended.

"No, mistress, only copper. These new metals refuse my solder, and them I cannot mend." Over and again he'd repeated the words until they were as wooden as his knocks had grown; and always, there was no copper. It was almost a kindness when they refused to answer his knock.

He had been glad to quit the village and turn out on the road to the country, even though the houses were farther apart. Surely among the farming people, the older methods would still be in use. But the results were no different. They greeted him kindly and brought out their wares to him with less hesitancy than in the village—but the utensils were enamelware and aluminum and stainless steel!

Ellowan groped for his pipe and sank down on the ground to rest, noting that eight miles still lay between him and Northville. He measured out the tobacco carefully, and hesitated before using one of the new matches. Then, as he lit it, he watched the flame dully and tossed it listlessly aside. Even the tobacco tasted flat now, and the emptiness of his stomach refused to be fooled by the smoke, though it helped to take his mind away from his troubles. Eh, well, there was always that one last house to be seen, where fortune might smile on him long enough to furnish a supper. He shouldered the bag with a grunt and moved on.

A large German shepherd came bounding out at the elf as he turned in the gate to the farmhouse. The dog's bark was gruff and threatening, but Ellowan clucked softly and the animal quieted, walking beside him toward the house, its tail wagging slowly. The farmer watched the performance and grinned.

"Prinz seems to like you," he called out. "Tain't everyone he takes to like that. What can I do for you, lad?" Then, as Ellowan drew nearer, he looked more sharply. "Sorry—my mistake. For a minute there, I thought you was a boy."

"I'm a tinker, sir. A coppersmith, that is." The elf stroked the dog's head and looked up at the farmer wistfully. "Have you copper pots or pans, or odds of any kind, to be mended? I do very good work on copper, sir, and I'll be glad to work for only my supper."

The farmer opened the door and motioned him in. "Come on inside, and we'll see. I don't reckon we have, but the wife knows better." He raised his voice. "Hey, Louisa, where are you? In the kitchen?"

"In here, Henry." The voice came from the kitchen, and Ellowan followed the man back, the dog nuzzling his hand companionably. The woman was washing the last few dishes and putting the supper away as they entered, and the sight of food awoke the hunger that the elf had temporarily suppressed.

"This fellow says he's good at fixin' copper dishes, Louisa," Henry told his wife. "You got anything like that for him?" He bent over her ear and spoke in an undertone, but Ellowan caught the words. "If you got anything copper, he looks like he needs it, Lou. Nice little midget, seems to be, and Prinz took quite a shine to him."

Louisa shook her head slowly. "I had a couple of old copper kettles, only I threw them away when we got the aluminum cooking set. But if you're hungry, there's plenty of food still left. Won't you sit down while I fix it for you?"

Ellowan looked eagerly at the remains of the supper, and his mouth watered hotly, but he managed a smile, and his voice was determined. "Thank'ee kindly, mistress, but I can't. It's one of the rules I must live by not to beg or take what I cannot earn. But I'll be thanking you both for the thought, and wishing you a very good night."

They followed him to the door, and the dog trotted behind him until its master's whistle called it back. Then the elf was alone on the road again, hunting a place to sleep. There was a haystack back off the road that would make a good bed, and he headed for that. Well, hay was hardly nourishing, but chewing on it was better than nothing.

Ellowan was up with the sun again, brushing the dirt off his jerkin. As an experiment, he shook the runes out on the ground and studied them for a few minutes. "Eh, well," he muttered, tossing them back in the bag, "they speak well, but it's little faith I'd have in them for what is to come. It's too easy to shake them the way I'd want them to be. But perchance there'll be a berry or so in the woods yonder."

There were no berries, and the acorns were still green. Ellowan struck the highway again, drawing faint pleasure from the fact that few cars were on the road at that hour. He wondered again why their fumes, though unpleasant, bothered him as little as they did. His brothers, up in the grotto hidden in the Adirondacks, found even the smoke from the factories a deadening poison.

The smell of a good wood fire, or the fumes from alcohol in the glass-blower's lamp were pleasant to them. But with the coming of coal, a slow lethargy had crept over them, driving them back one by one into the hills to sleep. It had been bad enough when coal was burned in the hearths, but that Scotchman, Watts, had found that power could be drawn from steam, and the factories began spewing forth the murky fumes of acrid coal smoke. And the Little Folk had fled hopelessly from the poison, until Ellowan Coppersmith alone was left. In time, even he had joined his brothers up in the hills.

Now he had awakened again, without rhyme or reason, when the stench of the liquid called gasoline was added to that of coal. All along the highway were pumps that supplied it to the endless cars, and the taint of it in the air was omnipresent.

"Eh, well," he thought. "My brothers were ever filled with foolish pranks instead of honest work, while I found my pleasure in labor. Methinks the pranks weakened them against the poison, and the work gives strength; it was only after I hexed the factory owner that the sleep crept into my head, and six score years must surely pay the price of one such trick. Yet, when I first awakened, it's thinking I was that there was some good purpose that drew me forth."

The sight of an orchard near the road caught his attention, and the elf searched carefully along the strip of grass outside the fence in the hope that an apple might have been blown outside. But only inside was there fruit, and to cross the fence would be stealing. He left the orchard reluctantly and started to turn in at the road leading to the farmhouse. Then he paused.

After all, the farms were equipped exactly as the city now, and such faint luck as he'd had yesterday had been in the village. There was little sense in wasting his effort among the scattered houses of the country, in the unlikely chance that he might find copper. In the city, at least, there was little time wasted, and it was only by covering as many places as he could that he might hope to find work. Ellowan shrugged, and turned back on the highway; he'd save his time and energy until he reached Northville.

It was nearly an hour later when he came on the boy, sitting beside the road and fussing over some machine. Ellowan stopped as he saw the scattered parts and the worried frown on the lad's face. Little troubles seemed great to twelve-year-olds.

"Eh, now, lad," he asked, "is it trouble you're having there? And what might be that contrivance of bars and wheels?"

"It's a bicycle; ever'body knows that." From the sound of the boy's voice, tragedy had reared a large and ugly head. "And I've only had it since last Christmas. Now it's broke and I can't fix it."

He held up a piece that had come from the hub of the rear wheel. "See? That's the part that swells up when I brake it. It's all broken, and a new coaster brake costs five dollars."

Ellowan took the pieces and smelled them; his eyes had not been deceived. It was brass. "So?" he asked. "Now that's a shame, indeed. And a very pretty machine it was. But perchance I can fix it."

The boy looked up hopefully as he watched the elf draw out the brazier and tools. Then his face fell. "Naw, mister. I ain't got the money. All I got's a quarter, and I can't get it, 'cause it's in my bank, and mom won't let me open it."

The elf's reviving hopes of breakfast faded away, but he smiled casually. "Eh, so? Well, lad, there are other things than money. Let's see what we'll be making of this."

His eyes picked out the relation of the various parts, and his admiration for the creator of the machine rose. That hub was meant to drive the machine, to roll free, or to brake as the user desired. The broken piece was a split cylinder of brass that was arranged to expand against the inside of the hub when braking. How it could have been damaged was a mystery, but the ability of boys to destroy was no novelty to Ellowan.

Under his hands, the rough edges were smoothed down in a twinkling, and he ran his strongest solder into the break, filling and drawing it together, then scraping and abrading the metal smooth again. The boy's eyes widened.

"Say, mister, you're good! Them fellers in the city can't do it like that, and they've got all kinds of tools, too." He took the repaired piece and began threading the parts back on the spindle. "Gosh, you're little. D'you come out of a circus?"

Ellowan shook his head, smiling faintly. The questions of children had always been candid, and honest replies could be given them. "That I did not, lad, and I'm not a midget, if that's what you'd be thinking. Now didn't your grandmother tell you the old tales of the elves?"

"An elf!" The boy stopped twisting the nuts back on. "Go on! There ain't such things—I don't guess." His voice grew doubtful, though, as he studied the little brown figure. "Say, you do look like the pi'tures I seen, at that, and it sure looked like magic the way you fixed my brake. Can you really do magic?"

"It's never much use I had for magic, lad. I had no time for learning it, when business was better. The honest tricks of my trade were enough for me, with a certain skill that was ever mine. And I wouldn't be mentioning this to your parents, if I were you."

"Don't worry, I won't; they'd say I was nuts." The boy climbed on the saddle, and tested the brake with obvious satisfaction. "You goin' to town? Hop on and put your bag in the basket here. I'm goin' down within a mile of there—if you can ride on the rack."

"It would be a heavy load for you, lad, I'm thinking." Ellowan was none too sure of the security of such a vehicle, but the ride would be most welcome.

"Naw. Hop on. I've carried my brother, and he's heavier'n you. Anyway, that's a Mussimer two-speed brake. Dad got it special for Christmas." He reached over for Ellowan's bag, and was surprised by its lightness. Those who help an elf usually found things easier than they expected. "Anyway, I owe you sumpin' for fixin' it."

Ellowan climbed on the luggage rack at the rear and clutched the boy tightly at first. The rack was hard, but the paving smoothed out the ride, and it was far easier than walking. He relaxed and watched the road go by in a quarter of the time he could have traveled it on foot. If fortune smiled on him, breakfast might be earned sooner than he had hoped.

"Well, here's where I stop," the boy finally told him. "The town's down there about a mile. Thanks for fixin' my bike."

Ellowan dismounted cautiously, and lifted out his bag. "Thank'ee for helping me so far, lad. And I'm thinking the brake will be giving you little trouble hereafter." He watched the boy ride off on a side road, and started toward the town, the serious business of breakfast uppermost in his mind.

Breakfast was still in his mind when midday had passed, but there was no sign that it was nearer his stomach. He came out of an alley and stopped for a few draws on his pipe and a chance to rest his shoulders. He'd have to stop smoking soon; on an empty stomach, too much tobacco is nauseating. Over the smell of the smoke, another odor struck his nose, and he turned around slowly.

It was the clean odor of hot metal in a charcoal fire, and came from a sprawling old building a few yards away. The sign above was faded, but he made out the words: MICHAEL DONAHUE—HORSESHOEING AND AUTO REPAIRS. The sight of a blacksmith shop aroused memories of pleasanter days, and Ellowan drew nearer.

The man inside was in his fifties, but his body spoke of strength and clean living, and the face under the mop of red hair was open and friendly. At the moment, he was sitting on a stool, finishing a sandwich. The odor of the food reached out and stirred the elf's stomach again, and he scuffed his sandals against the ground uneasily. The man looked up.

"Saints presarve us!" Donahue's generous mouth opened to its widest. "Sure, and it's one o' the Little Folk, the loike as my feyther tolt me. Now fwhat— Och, now, but it's hungry ye'd be from the look that ye have, and me eatin' before ye! Here now, me hearty, it's yerself as shud have this bread."

"Thank'ee." Ellowan shook his head with an effort, but it came harder this time. "I'm an honest worker, sir, and it's one of the rules that I can't be taking what I cannot earn. But there's never a piece of copper to be found in all the city for me to mend." He laid his hands on a blackened bench to ease the ache in his legs.

"Now that's a shame." The brogue dropped from Donahue's speech, now that the surprise of seeing the elf was leaving him. "It's a good worker you are, too, if what my father told me was true. He came over from the old country when I was a bit of a baby, and his father told him before that. Wonderful workers, he said you were."

"I am that." It was a simple statement as Ellowan made it; boasting requires a certain energy, even had he felt like it. "Anything of brass or copper I can fix, and it'll be like new when I finish."

"Can you that?" Donahue looked at him with interest. "Eh, maybe you can. I've a notion to try you out. You wait here." He disappeared through the door that divided his smithy from the auto servicing department and came back with a large piece of blackened metal in his hand. The elf smelled it questioningly and found it was brass.

Donahue tapped it lightly. "That's a radiator, m'boy. Water runs through these tubes here and these little fins cool it off. Old Pete Yaegger brought it in and wanted it fixed, but it's too far ruined for my hands. And he can't afford a new one. You fix that now, and I'll be giving you a nice bit of money for the work."

"Fix it I can." Ellowan's hands were trembling as he inspected the corroded metal core, and began drawing out his tools. "I'll be finished within the hour."

Donahue looked doubtfully at the elf, but nodded slowly. "Now maybe you will. But first, you'll eat, and we'll not be arguing about that. A hungry man never did good work, and I'm of the opinion the same applies to yourself. There's still a sandwich and a bit of pie left, if you don't mind washing it down with water."

The elf needed no water to wash down the food. When Donahue looked at him next, the crumbs had been licked from the paper, and Ellowan's deft hands were working his clever little tools through the fins of the radiator, and his face was crinkling up into its usual merry smile. The metal seemed to run and flow through his hands with a will of its own, and he was whistling lightly as he worked.

Ellowan waited intently as Donahue inspected the finished work. Where the blackened metal had been bent and twisted, and filled with holes, it was now shining and new. The smith could find no sign to indicate that it was not all one single piece, now, for the seams were joined invisibly.

"Now that's craftsmanship," Donahue admitted. "I'm thinking we'll do a deal of business from now on, the two of us, and there's money in it, too.

Ellowan, m'boy, with work like that we can buy up old radiators, remake them, and at a nice little profit for ourselves we can sell them again. You'll be searching no further for labor."

The elf's eyes twinkled at the prospect of long lines of radiators needing to be fixed, and a steady supply of work without the need of searching for it. For the first time, he realized that industrialization might have its advantages for the worker.

Donahue dug into a box and came out with a little metal figure of a greyhound, molded on a threaded cap. "Now, while I get something else for you, you might be fixing this," he said. " 'Tis a godsend that you've come to me. . . . Eh, now that I think of it, what brings you here, when I thought it'd be in the old country you worked?"

"That was my home," the elf agreed, twisting the radiator cap in his hands and straightening out the broken threads. "But the people became too poor in the country, and the cities were filled with coal smoke. And then there was word of a new land across the sea, so we left, such of us as remained, and it was here we stayed until the smoke came again, and sent us sleeping into the hills. Eh, it's glad I am now to be awake again."

Donahue nodded. "And it's not sorry I am. I'm a good blacksmith, but there's never enough of that for a man to live now, and mostly I work on the autos. And there, m'boy, you'll be a wonderful help to be sure. The parts I like least are the ignition system and generator, and there's copper in them where your skill will be greater than mine. And the radiators, of course."

Ellowan's hands fumbled on the metal, and he set it down suddenly. "Those radiators, now—they come from a car?"

"That they do." Donahue's back was turned as he drew a horseshoe out of the forge and began ham-

mering it on the anvil. He could not see the twinkle
fade from the elf's eyes and the slowness with which
the small fingers picked up the radiator cap.

Ellowan was thinking of his people, asleep in the
hills, doomed to lie there until the air should be
cleared of the poisonous fumes. And here he was,
working on parts of the machines that helped to
make those fumes. Yet, since there was little enough
else to do, he had no choice but to keep on; cars or
no cars, food was still the prime necessity.

Donahue bent the end of a shoe over to a calk and
hammered it into shape, even with the other one.
"You'll be wanting a place to sleep?" he asked casually. "Well, now, I've a room at the house that used
to be my boy's, and it'll just suit you. The boy's at
college and won't be needing it."

"Thank'ee kindly." Ellowan finished the cap and
put it aside distastefully.

"The boy'll be a great engineer some day," the
smith went on with a glow of pride. "And not have to
follow his father in the trade. And it's a good thing,
I'm thinking. Because some day, when they've used
up all their coal and oil, there'll be no money in the
business at all, even with the help of these newfan-
gled things. My father was a smith, and I'm by way
of being smith and mechanic—but not the boy."

"They'll use up all the coal and oil—entirely?"

"They will that, now. Nobody knows when, but
the day's acoming. And then they'll be using electricity or maybe alcohol for fuel. It's a changing world,
lad, and we old ones can't change to keep with it."

Ellowan picked up the radiator cap and polished it
again. Eh, so. One day they'd use up all the sources
of evil, and the air would be pure again. The more
cars that ran, the sooner that day would come, and
the more he repaired, the more would run.

"Eh, now," he said gayly. "I'll be glad for more of
those radiators to mend. But until then, perchance I

could work a bit of yonder scrap brass into more such ornaments as this one."

Somehow, he was sure, when his people came forth again, there'd be work for all.

A GOD IN A GARDEN

Theodore Sturgeon

Kenneth Courtney, anyone could see, was plenty
sore. No man works so hard and viciously digging his
own lily pond on his own time unless he has a
man-size gripe against someone. In Kenneth's case it
was a wife who allowed herself to be annoyed by
trifles. The fact that in her arguments she presented
a good case made Kenneth all the angrier because it
made him sore at himself too. Suppose he *had* come
in at four a.m.? And suppose he *had* told Marjorie
that he was working late? A lie like that was nothing—
much. The only trouble with lies was that people—
especially wives and bosses—can make such a damn
fool out of a man when they catch him in one. All
right; so it was a poker game, and he had lost a few
bucks.

Marjorie, as usual, got all the details out of him;
but she didn't stop there. She cited instance after
instance when he had done the same thing. Her
kick, it developed, was not so much the poker, but

the fact that he had lied to her about it. Well, and why should a man brag to his wife about losing twenty-four bucks? If only she'd take his simple little explanations without all those fireworks, life would be more worth living. At least he wouldn't have to retreat into the garden and take out his fury on a pick and shovel.

He had reached about this stage in his mental monologue when his shovel rang dully against old Rakna.

Of course, he didn't know then that it was Rakna. He might well have stopped digging altogether if he had known. And then again, he might not. It didn't work out so badly in the end.

At any rate, all he knew was that there was an unyielding mass, and a large one, in his way, and he couldn't finish digging the little lily pool until he moved it. That *would* have to happen now, he thought bitterly. Everything's going wrong today.

He threw down his shovel and stamped up the garden path toward the house. Sore as he was, he still found room in his sulking mind to admire that garden. It began at the house, almost as if it were part of it, and led downwards into a little gully. Kenneth had, by ranking trees and shrubs carefully, built a small lot up to look like something twenty times as big.

The sunken rockery, well out of sight, was the hidden theme of the whole; you stumbled on it, that rock garden; and yet because of the subtle placing of the trees and plants around it, you knew that it had been there all the time. There was a miniature bridge, and a huge pottery teapot—all the fixings. And once you were in the rock garden, you and your eye were led to the shrinelike niche by the lily pool.

For months Kenneth had been searching for an idol ugly enough for that niche; he wanted it there so that it would frighten people. Something nice and hideous, to be a perfect and jarring foil for the quiet and beautiful effect of all that surrounded it. Kenneth determined to leave that niche empty until he found a stone face ugly enough to turn an average stomach—not wrench it, exactly; Kenneth was not altogether fiendish in his humorous moments!—but plumb ugly.

He went into the back kitchen—it served as a tool shed as well—and took down a crowbar. His wife came to the door when she heard him.

"How's it going?" she asked in the dutifully interested tone of a wife whose most recent words to her husband were violent ones.

"Swell," he said, his casualness equally forced.

"See?" she cried in feminine triumph. "You even lie to me about a little thing like that. If everything was swell down there, you wouldn't need a crowbar to dig with. This ground isn't rocky. Why can't you tell the truth just *once*?" Then she fled into her own territory, to be alone with her indignation.

Kenneth shrugged. Fight all morning with your wife, and you're up against things like that. He hesitated. She was probably crying, after that blowup. That's a woman for you. Fire and water all at once. Oh, well. He shrugged again and started back with his crowbar. The tears would wait, he reflected callously. There were more where they came from.

His conscience bothered him a little, though. Maybe she had something there. It did seem as if he couldn't tell her—or anyone—the absolute truth. It was just a conversational habit, that lying; but it did make trouble. But what could a man do? Maybe he'd be a little more careful in future—but, damn it, why did she have to be so picky?

As usual, he took it out in work, picking and prying and heaving. Well, this lump of brownstone or whatever it was, was something worth while working on. Not like digging in the soft earth around it.

He began to forget about Marge and her annoyances in the task on hand.

Slipping the bar well under the brown mass, he heaved strongly and lifted it a few inches at the corner. Kicking a rock under it, he stepped back for a look at the thing, and was confronted by quite the most hideous imaginable face. He stared, shook his head, stared again.

"Well, I'll be . . . here's my idol, right where I need it. Now where the devil did that thing come from?" he asked no one in particular.

Yes, it was an idol, that brown mass in the half-finished lily pool. And what a face! Hideous—and yet, was it? There was a certain tongue-in-cheek quality about it, a grim and likable humor. The planes of that face were craggy and aristocratic, and there was that about the curve of the nostril and the heavily lidded eyes that told Kenneth that he was looking at a realistic conception of a superiority complex. And yet—again; was it? Those heavy eyelids—each, it seemed, had been closed in the middle of a sly wink at some huge and subtle joke. And the deep lines around the mouth were the lines of authority, but also the lines of laughter. It was the face of a very old little boy caught stealing jam, and it was also the face of a being who might have the power to stop the sun.

"Or a clock," thought Kenneth. He shook himself from his apathy—the thing nearly hypnotized by its ugliness—and walked around it, knocking off clods of dirt with his hands.

The face was lying on its side. Yes, he discovered, it was more than a face. A body, about half the size of the head, was curled up behind it. Kenneth shuddered. The body looked like unborn fetus he had seen at the Fair, floating in alcohol. The limbs were shriveled, and the trunk was big-bellied with an atrophied chest, jammed up against the back of that enormous head. The whole thing was, maybe, five feet high and three wide, and weighed a good ton.

Kenneth went back to the house shrugging off an emotional hangover, and called up Joe Mancinelli. Joe had a two-ton hoist at his "Auto Fixery" that would do the trick.

"Joe," he said when he got his connection, "I want you to come right over with your truck and the two-ton lift. And listen. What I've got to lift will knock your eye out. Don't let it scare you."

"Hokay, Kan," said Mancinelli. "I feex. I no scare. You know me, boy!"

Kenneth had his doubts.

"Who are you calling, dear?" Marjorie called.

"Joe Mancinelli. I've got to have help. I ran across a . . . a big rock in the lily pool." There it was again. Now, why did he have to say that?

Marjorie came across the room and put her hands on his shoulders. "That's so much better, sweetheart. It isn't terribly hard to tell the truth, now, is it?"

Her eyes were a little red, and she looked very sweet. He kissed her. "I . . . I'll try, kiddo. You're right, I guess." He turned and went out to the shed, muttering to himself.

"Can you beat that? Tell her a lie and she raises hell. Tell her another and everything's all right. You can't win."

He rigged a set of shear poles so that the chain hoist would have some kind of a purchase, and dragged them down to the rock garden. The sight of the half-buried idol gave him another fascinated shock. He looked at it more closely. It seemed old as time itself and carved—was it carved? Its execution made him think that if nature had carved rock into idols, then this was a natural work. And yet, it was so flawless! What human artist could do such macabre sculpture? Kenneth had seen the *striges* on the carved galleries on Notre Dame cathedral in Paris, and had thought that they were tops in *outré* art. But this— He shrugged and went back to the shed for a wire strap to slip under the thing, meeting Joe halfway to the house. Joe was staggering under the coils of chain over his shoulders.

"Hi, keed! Ware you got heem, thees beeg theeng?"

"Down at the bottom of the garden, Joe. What made you come over here so fast?"

"I like to see thees theeng make scare Joe Mancinelli," wheezed Joe.

"Well, look it over for yourself. It's half buried. I've got shear poles rigged. Be with you in a jiffy."

As he reached the shed, Kenneth smiled at the roar of polylingual profanity which issued from the rock garden. Joe was evidently impressed. Coming to the door with the wire strap in his hand, Kenneth called: "Scared, Joe?"

The answer came back hollowly: "I no scare. I sorry I come. But I no scare!"

Kenneth laughed and started down. He had taken about five steps when he heard a sound like a giant champagne cork, and Joe Mancinelli came hurtling up the path as if he were being chased by one of the devil's altar boys.

"Hey! Whoa there!" Kenneth called, laughing. "What happened? Hey!"

He surged forward and tackled the Italian low. They slid to a stop in a cloud of dust. "Easy, now, boy. Easy."

"The 'oist is down dere. You do you work, calla me, I come back, get heem. I don't *never* touch that theeng."

"All right, all right. But what happened?"

"You don' tell nobody?"

"No, Joe. Course not."

"So I see thees face. Thees not so gooda face. Maybe I scare, maybe no. I tell this face, 'I no lika

you. So. I speet on you. So. *Ptui.'* " Joe turned white
at the recollection, and swallowed hard. "Thees theeng
shake all over like wan piece jally, is make the mouth
like dees"—Joe pursed his lips— "an' . . . *ptow*! Is
speet on me. So. Now, I go."

"You dreamed it," Kenneth said unconvincingly.

"So, I dream. But I tella you, boy, I go now to
church. I take wan bat' in holy water. I light wan
dozen candles. An' I bring you tomorra plenty dynamite for feex that theeng."

Kenneth laughed. "Forget it, Joe," he said. "I'll
take care of old funnyface down there. Without
dynamite."

Joe snorted and went back to his truck, starting it
with a violence that set its gears' teeth on edge.
Kenneth grinned and picked up the wire strap. "I no
scare," he said, and laughed again.

He was not, evidently, the only one who was
amused by the episode. Old funnyface, as Ken had
called the idol, really seemed to have deepened the
humorous lines around his tight-lipped, aristocratic
mouth. A trick of the light, of course. "You know,"
said Kenneth conversationally, "if you *were* alive
you'd be a rather likable dog."

He burrowed under the idol and pushed the end
of the strap as far under as he could reach. He was
flat on his stomach, reaching out and down, with his
shoulder against the mass of the thing, when he felt
it settle slightly. He pulled his arm out and rolled
clear, to see old funnyface settling steadily back into
the hole.

"You old devil!" he said. "You almost had me that
time. Bet you did that on purpose."

The idol's face seemed to have taken on a definite
smirk.

"—is speet on me," Joe had said. Well, he was no
better than Joe. He picked up a clod of earth, held it
poised, and expectorated explosively, following up

by ramming the clod into the sardonic lips of the idol. There was a small but powerful explosion and Kenneth found himself flat on his back six feet away.

Now Kenneth Courtney was no story-book hero. He was just an ordinary driver for an ordinary trucking firm. But in his unbrilliant but satisfying past, he had found that the best thing to do when he had this cold, crawling feeling at the pit of his stomach was to smile at his antagonist. Nine times out of ten, said antagonist was floored by it. So he reared up on his elbow and smiled engagingly at the idol.

The smile faded quickly; one glance at the idol's mouth took care of that. The lower lip was quivering, like an angry child's, or like a railroad bull about to take a poke at a tramp. Suddenly it snapped shut. The jaws bulged and contracted, and little bits of earth fell into the hole around its cheeks.

More than a little shaken, Kenneth got his feet under him and walked over to the idol. "I'd bury you where you are, though guy, but you're in my lily pool. Come up out of there!"

He went furiously to work, rigging the hoist over the idol. In a remarkably short time he had the ends of the strap hooked into the chain-fall, and was heaving merrily. To his surprise, he found that the idol came up easily—there could not have been more than three or four hundred pounds' load on the hoist. He stopped hauling and stood off a bit.

"Why, you son of a gun!" he exclaimed. "So you've decided to co-operate, hey?"

It was true. The idol's emaciated legs and arms straddled the pit, and were lifting the massive head steadily. Even as he watched, the chain-fall began to slacken as the weight came off it. By this time Kenneth was almost beyond surprise at anything.

"O. K., buddy," he cried, and heaved away. Higher and higher rose the idol, until the shear poles creaked and their bases began to sink deeper into the soft earth. Finally it swung clear. Gauging the distance nicely, Kenneth toppled the shear poles and the idol swung face inward into the niche, landing with a rubbery thump. Kenneth grinned.

"Stay that way, old boy," he told the idol. "You're no uglier behind than you are face-outward." He threw the strap over his shoulder, lifted the shear poles at the lashing and dragged them back up to the shed.

When he came back with a spouting garden hose, the idol was facing outward.

"On second thought," said Kenneth conversationally, as he busily sluiced down that hideous, humorous face, "I don't blame you. You are a little more presentable stern-foremost; but then you're a damsite more likable this way." Kenneth was scared stiff, but he wouldn't show it, not even to an old graven image.

"That's much better," said the idol, blinking the mud out of its eyes. Kenneth sat down weakly on the nozzle of the hose. This was the payoff.

"Don't sit there looking so stupid!" said the idol irritably. "Besides, you'll catch cold, holding down that hose."

Kenneth's breath came out in a rush. "This is too much," he gasped. He was more than a little hysterical. "I . . . I . . . in just a minute I'll wake up and smell coffee and bacon. I don't believe there *is* a crusty old idol, or that it talked, or that—"

"Get off that hose," said the idol, and added meaningly. "And dry up."

Kenneth rose and absently began wringing his clothes. "What sort of a critter are you?"

"I'm a god," said the idol. "Name's Rakna. What's yours?"

"K-Kenneth Courtney."

"Stop stammering, man! I'm not going to hurt you. What's the matter; didn't you ever see a god before?"

"No," said Kenneth, a little relieved. "You don't seem like . . . I mean—" Suddenly something about the god, something in his incredibly deep eyes, made it very easy to talk. "I thought gods lived up in the clouds, sort of. And anything I ever read about it said that gods come to earth in fire, or lightning, or in the shape of some kind of animal, or—"

"Nuts," said the god.

Kenneth was startled. "Well, gods don't talk like that . . . uh . . . do they?"

"You heard me, didn't you?" asked Rakna. "Think I'm a liar?" The piercing gaze made Kenneth wince. "Like you? No, you dope; I was created by common people, who thought common thoughts and spoke in a common way. Not in this language, of course, or in this time. But people are pretty much the same, by and large. Think the same way, y'know."

"Well, what people were you the god of?"

"Oh, you wouldn't know if I told you. They disappeared quite a while back. Used to be one of them buried near me. Had his thigh bone poking into my . . . well, never mind. Anyhow, he faded out. There's not a trace of those people left anywhere. This earth has been here quite a while, you know. They come and they go."

"How come you can speak English, then?"

"Because I know everything you know, which isn't much, by the way, and considerable besides. Every time a thought passes in that gab factory of yours I know what it is. You drive a truck. You're wife's named Marjorie. She's very capable; knows all about budgets and calories and such. She thinks you're a liar."

"If you're a god," Kenneth said quickly, to change the subject, "why couldn't you dig yourself out?"

"Listen, lamebrain, who said I wanted to dig myself out? Can't a god grab forty winks once in a while?"

"Forty winks? How long were you asleep?"

"*I* don't know. Couple of hundred million years, maybe. I'll tell you when I get a chance to look at the stars."

But there wasn't any earth that long ago!"

Rakna leered at him. "Vas you dere?"

Kenneth sat down again, this time on dry ground. Standing was too much of a strain.

"Hm-m-m . . . I see steam's back again. Electricity? Yes. You're getting along, you people. Atomic power? Oh, well, it won't be long now. Levitation? Trans—"

Kenneth had the uncomfortable feeling that he was being read like a newspaper—a back number at that. He was a little annoyed, and besides, those waves of beneficence still flowed from Rakna's eyes. Kenneth's fear departed completely, and he rose to his feet and said:

"Listen. All this is a little too strong for me. As far as I'm concerned, your somebody's half-ton Charlie McCarthy. Or maybe you're wired for sound."

Rakna chuckled deep in his jowls. "Aha!" he rumbled. "A skeptic, no less! Know what happens to little mortals who get cocky? They suffer for it. In lots of ways. For instance, I can increase the density of your bones so that your own skeleton will crush you to death. Like *this!*"

The deep eyes turned on Kenneth, and he fell to the ground, crushed there by an insupportable and increasing weight.

"Or I can put your eyes on your fingertips so that you have to see with your hands."

Kenneth found himself on his feet again. He was staring at the ground, although his head was up. He saw the world reel about him as he clapped his seeing hands to his face. He cried out in an ecstasy of terror.

"Or," continued the god conversationally, "I can finish your lily pool for you and drown you in it."

Kenneth was hurled forward into shallow water, where no water had been before. He bumped his head stunningly on a solid concrete surface and lay there, immersed and strangling. Suddenly he found himself before the idol again. His clothes were dry; his eyes were in place; everything was quite, quite normal. Except that damned idol, and the brand-new lily pool. It had all taken possibly eight seconds.

"Or—" said the idol.

"O.K., O.K.," said Kenneth weakly. "You win."

"That's better," smirked Rakna. "Now listen to me. I don't want you to think I intend any harm! I don't. But unfortunately for my character I was created in more or less a man's image. The only faults I have are human ones, and even though I have improved considerably, I still possess those faults. One of them is vanity. I don't like to be called a weakling any more than you do. You'll take a poke at someone who calls you a pansy; all right, so will I. Savvy?"

Kenneth nodded.

"Right. All I want from you is a little consideration. Keep your mouth shut about me; I don't mind being admired, but I don't want to be a museum piece." Amused pity suddenly manifested itself on those craggy features. "Look, Kenneth, I've been a little hard on you. After all, you did give me a comfortable place to sit. Anything I could do for you?" Again those fear-erasing waves of friendliness. Kenneth stopped trembling.

"Why . . . I don't know. I've got a good job, and about everything I want."

"How about your wife? Are you altogether happy?"

"Why, sure I am. Well . . . that is—"

"Never mind the details. I know all about it. She calls you a liar and she's right, and you wish something could be done about it. Want me to make you incapable of telling a lie? I can do it."

"You mean—"

"I mean that every time anyone asks you a question you'll be able to tell them only the truth. How much money you have, what you did that night in Denver"—Kenneth quailed at that—"what you honestly think of your boss—"

"Oh, no!" said Kenneth. "That doesn't sound so hot."

Rakna grinned. "All right. Let's do it this way. Everything you say will be the truth. If you say black is white, it will be white. If you tell your wife you were working late instead of playing poker, then it will be true. See what I mean?"

Kenneth couldn't see anything wrong in that. "By golly, Rakna, you've got something there. Can you do it?"

"I've done it," said Rakna. "Look. See that chain hoist you hauled me up with?"

Kenneth glanced at it. "Yeah."

"Now tell me it's not lying here, but it's in the shed."

"It's in the shed," said Kenneth obediently.

The hoist vanished. A clinking of chain drifted down the garden path. Rakna grinned.

"Hot cha!" exclaimed Kenneth. "Nothing but the truth. Thanks a million, Rakna. You're an ace!"

"Skip it," said the god. "Now beat it. I want to think."

Kenneth started up the path, his surliness quite gone and a new spring in his step. Rakna gazed after him and chuckled deeply.

"Cocky little devil," he said. "This ought to be good." He relaxed and let his mind dwell casually on profound matters.

As he came to the turn in the path and out of the range of old Rakna's quizzical gaze, Kenneth's steps suddenly slowed and he began to wonder a little at all this. Surely a thing like this couldn't be true! He found himself in a very precarious mental state. He could go back again and see if there really was a god in his garden, or he could blindly believe everything that had happened, or he could go on as usual and try to forget the whole thing. The worst part of it all was that if it all was a dream, he was probably nuts. If it wasn't a dream, who was nuts? He shrugged. Once you got used to the idea of having a god in your back yard you could get a kick out of it. But how did the old sourpuss think he could prove his power by making Kenneth speak the absolute truth? Not, of course, that there was anything in it.

Marjorie heard him coming into the house.

"Hurry and wash up, darling," she called briskly. "Supper's on!"

"Be right with you, kid!" He scrubbed up, put on a clean shirt and came down to the dining room. In one of the steaming dishes on the table was turnips. He frowned. His wife noticed, and said forlornly:

"Oh, dear, I forgot. You don't like turnips!"

"Don't be silly," he lied gallantly. "I love 'em."

No sooner had he said the words than the lowly turnips seemed to take on a glamour, a gustatory perfection. His mouth watered for them, his being cried out for them—turnips were the most delicious, the most nourishing and delightful food ever to be set on a man's table. He loved 'em.

A little startled, he sat down and began to eat—turnips more than anything else. "Most delicious meal I ever had," he told a gratified Marjorie. No sooner said than done. It *was*. And as a matter of fact, it was strictly a budget meal—one of those meals that good little managers like Marjorie Courtney throw together to make up for yesterday's spring chicken. She was vastly flattered.

"You must have worked terribly hard to fix up a

meal like this," Kenneth said with his mouth full. "You must be tired."

She was, suddenly, a little. Kenneth laid down his fork. "You *look* tired, dear." Lines appeared on her fresh little face. "Darling!" he said anxiously. "You're terribly tired!"

"I don't know what's the matter," she said haggardly.

"Marjorie, sweet, you're sick! What is it?"

"I don't know," she said faintly. "All of a sudden I feel—" Her head dropped on the table. He caught her in his arms.

"Buck up, kid. I'll carry you upstairs. Hang on, now. I'll get you settled and call a doctor." He crossed the room and started up the stairs.

"I'm too heavy—" she murmured.

"Nonsense!" he scoffed. "You're as light as a feather!"

Her body seemed to lift out of his arms. He was halfway up the stairs by this time, poised on one leg, about to take another step. The sudden lightening of her body had the effect, on him, of a kick on the chin. Down he went, head over heels, to the bottom of the stairs.

It was a nasty jolt, and for the moment he couldn't see anything but stars. "'Marge!" he muttered. "You all right?" Say you're all right!"

A whimpering cry cleared his head. Marjorie was settling gently down toward him, bumping each step lightly—lightly, like a floating feather.

He reached out dazedly and took her hand. She came drifting down toward him as he sprawled there, until their bodies rested together.

"Oh, God," moaned Kenneth. "What am I going to do?"

He rose and tried to help her up. His gentle pull on her arm sent her flying up over his head. She was crying weakly, hysterically. He walked into the living room, his wife literally streaming out behind him, and held her poised over the day bed until she rested on it. Then he ran for the telephone.

But as the singsong "Operator!" came over the wire he laid down the receiver, struck with a thought. Bit by insane bit he pieced the thing together; Rakna's promise; the power that he now had over the truth—the whole crazy affair. In the last few hectic minutes he had all but forgotten. Well, if he could do it, he could undo it.

He went back to his wife, drew a deep breath, and said:

"You're not sick. You weigh one hundred and fourteen."

Marjorie bounced up out of the day bed, shook her head dizzily, and advanced toward him. Kenneth sensed thunder in the air.

"What sort of a joke was that?" she demanded, her voice trembling. Kenneth thought a little faster this time. "Why, darling! Nothing has happened to you!"

Marjorie's face cleared. She stopped, then went on into the dining room, saying: "What on earth made us wander out here when we should be eating?"

"Nothing," said Kenneth; and that seemed to tie up all the threads. He felt a little weak; this power of his was a little too big to be comfortable. He noticed another thing, too: he could make his wife forget anything that happened, but he still knew about it. Lord! He'd have to be careful. He had a splitting headache, as always when he was excited, and that didn't help any. Marjorie noticed it.

"Is something the matter, Kenny?" she asked. "Have you a headache?"

"No," he said automatically; and as he said it, it was true! For the first time he grinned at the idea of his power. Not bad! No more toothache, stomachache, business worries—business— Holy smoke! He was rich! Watch.

"Marge," he said as she put two lumps in his coffee, "we have twenty thousand dollars in the bank."

"Yes. I know. Isn't it nice? Cream?"

"You know? How did you know?"

"Silly! I've always known. You told me, didn't you? Anyway, I've known about it quite a while, it seems to me. Why?"

"Why?" Kenneth was floored. Then he shrugged. The truth was like that, he guessed. If a thing was true, it required no explanation; it just *was*. He finished his coffee and pushed back his chair. "Let's go to a show, kiddo."

"That would be nice," she said. "Just as soon as I get the dishes done."

"Oh," he said airily. "They're done."

She turned astonished eyes to him. It occurred to him then that if he persisted in this sort of thing he might make her doubt her sanity. A bank account was one thing; but the dishes—

"I mean," he explained. "We did them."

"Oh . . . of course. I . . . well, let's go."

He made up his mind to go a little easy thereafter.

That was the beginning of a hectic three weeks for Kenneth Courtney. Hectic, but fun, by golly. Everything came his way; everything he said was true, and if everything he did wasn't quite right, it could be fixed. Like the time he was driving his big twelve-speed Diesel tractor-trailer job through the mountains one night, and a light sedan whipped around a hairpin turn and steered straight between his headlights.

"Look out!" he called to Johnny Green, his helper, who was in the bunk over the seat. "We're going to smash!"

And as the car approached, as their bumpers practically kissed, Kenneth remembered his powers. "We missed him!" he bellowed.

Miss him they did. The car vanished, and a second

later its careening tail light appeared in the rear-view mirror. It just wasn't possible—but it was true.

He did learn to be careful, though. There was the time when he casually remarked that it was raining cats and dogs. That mistake cost him half an hour of running madly around telling people that it really wasn't raining cats and dogs, you know, just raining hard. The thing would have made quite a sensation if he had not thought of declaring that it had not rained at all that day.

His influence was far-reaching. one night he happened to tune into a radio soprano who was mutilating Italian opera to such an extent that Kenneth inadvertently remarked: "She's lousy!" Thirty seconds later the loud-speaker gave vent to a series of squeaks and squalls which had no conceivable connection with Italian opera.

He had to watch his language. No author or orator was ever so careful about avoiding clichés and catch phrases as was Kenneth Courtney in the weeks in which he enjoyed his powers. A friend once remarked that he had been working all day; "I'm dead!" he said. Kenneth turned pale and solemnly swore that he would never use *that* expression again. He began to notice things about the way we speak: "I'm starved." "You're crazy." "You look like a ghost." "I hate you." "You're a half-wit," or "idiot" or "imbecile. "You never grew up."

At first Kenneth was a good man to have around the house. From his easychair he did the housework, made the beds, cooked a delicious series of meals, redecorated the living room, and renewed every article of clothing and linen in the house. Pretty soft. But he found that the wear and tear of the thing was too much for his wife.

Though Marjorie had every evidence that the work was done, still she had no memory of doing it—unless, of course, she remarked on it to Kenneth. In that case she would be told, and truthfully, that she had done the work herself. But she began to worry a little about her memory; at times she thought she was losing it altogether. You don't cook a six-course dinner without remembering anything about it except the fact that you cooked it; and Marjorie even had to be told about that. So Kenneth, after a while, left the house to its appointed boss, and amused himself elsewhere.

And Kenneth never told her—or anyone—about Rakna and what he had done. Why? Because the conviction that matter-of-fact, efficient little Marjorie Courtney wouldn't believe such a far-fetched tale was so deep-rooted that it never occurred to him to use his power on her. She had, in the past, called him a liar so many times with justice that he felt subconsciously that she would do it again. That, incidentally, *might* have been Rakna's doing.

Well, for three weeks this went on. Kenneth had money to burn, all the leisure time he wanted—he worked now for the fun of it—and life was a song—in swingtime, of course, but still a song. He had been so busy experimenting and amusing himself that he hadn't thought of really celebrating. And on one memorable Saturday night he went downtown and threw a wingding that made history.

Only an old sailor or an ex-soldier or a man with Kenneth's powers can throw that sort of a binge. He was not a heavy drinker; but every time that sickly, cloying feeling came over him he'd say, like every other swiller: "*I'm* not drunk. I may be tight, but I'm not drunk." And then he could start over. Never mind the details; but let this suffice: the next morning, stocks on liquor jumped two points, and on the various hangover remedies, six to ten points. Not a sober man went out of a barroom anywhere in town that night. Kenneth painted the town bright, bright red; and he and all the tipplers he could possibly find—and everything was possible to Kenneth! —literally drank the town dry.

He reeled home about six in the morning. He had poured some two hundred gallons of the best down his throat, and his breath would fell a strong man at thirty yards. Yet he was only delightfully high; he even remembered to eradicate the breath as he came in the door, by remarking that it was sweet as a baby's.

Marjorie was up when he entered rockily, flinging his hat to the right, his coat to the left, and himself on the carpet. She said nothing, which was bad; just walked daintily around him and upstairs. He called her, but she kept on going.

"Oh, oh!" he said, He started after her, found the stairs a little too much for him, and so declared himself on the second floor. Once there, he stumbled in on Marjorie. She was packing.

"What goes on?" he wanted to know.

"I'm going to stay with mother for a while," she said tiredly. "Till you sober up."

"Sober up?" he repeated. "Why, I'm perfectly sober!" It was true, of course; but that made no difference. Just because a thing is basically, unalterably true doesn't mean that a woman and a wife is going to believe it. She kept packing.

"Now wait a minute, darling. Haven't I been good to you? What do you want me to do? Marjorie!" This was the first time she had pulled anything like this. He was flabbergasted.

She turned toward him. "Kenneth, I'm sorry, but I've got to go away from you for a while. Maybe forever," she added forlornly. "You see, something's happened to me . . . to us . . . in the last few weeks. I don't know what it is, but I think sometimes that I'm losing my mind. I forget things . . . and you, Kenneth! I can't understand what you're up to, with all your running around at all hours of the night, and the strange things that are happening. The other day I was in the living room and just happened to be looking at Aunt Myrtle's vase when it disappeared . . . vanished, just like that." She snapped her fingers.

Kenneth swore under his breath. That was a slip. He had hated that eyesore, and happened to think of it one day when he was on the road. He had stated that it no longer existed, forgetting that his wife might be in the room at the time.

"So you see I need a rest, Kenneth." She began to cry, but turned to her packing all the same. Kenneth tried to put his arms around her, but she pushed him away.

Now Kenneth had learned during his year or so of marriage that the only way to stop one of these bickerings was to tell the truth, take his medicine like a man, and then be forgiven. Well, he reasoned, the truth wouldn't be so hard to tell this time. Again, it never occurred to him to tell her that nothing was the matter, that she wasn't angry and frightened. No, the only thing he could think of that would fill the bill was to share his secret about the god in the garden. That was the cause of it all, so it might be the cure.

"Marjorie . . . I can explain everything."

"Oh, yes," she said bitterly. "You always can."

He swallowed that and tried again. "Listen, darling, please. I was digging our lily pool, and—"

As the story unfolded she stopped her packing and sank down on the edge of the bed. His words carried a peculiar conviction, and he thrilled to the dawning belief in her face.

"—and so last night I thought of celebrating it. It would do no harm that couldn't be set right. See? So don't go, sweetheart. There's no need—"

The remark brought her engrossed mind back to the fact that she had been in the midst of leaving his bed and board when he had interrupted with this story, this—yes—preposterous story. She remembered that she was angry at him, and that fact was quite sufficient. He was so horribly smug, so terribly in the right about everything. Marjorie Courtney was by no means the first woman who, incensed, refused to believe the absolute truth simply because that truth put her in the wrong.

"I don't believe any of it!" she said firmly. Suddenly she drew back a little. "Kenneth . . . I do believe that it's *you* who are losing your mind, not I . . . Ohhh—"

Kenneth realized then that if she kept that up any longer she'd have herself convinced. That wouldn't do. He took her by the arm, hurried her out and down the stairs. "Come on," he said grimly. "You're about to be introduced to a god. That'll show you who's crazy."

She struggled a little, but allowed herself to be forced out into the yard and down the garden path. She wouldn't believe it! She wouldn't!

As they reached the pool she looked up at Kenneth's face. It was grimly determined; she was frightened. She did not see old Rakna grin and raise his carven eyebrows.

"Rakna!" called Kenneth. "My wife won't believe in you. What can I do to convince her?"

Majorie said brokenly: "It's just an old statue . . . I know . . . I saw the hideous thing last week . . . it can't talk . . . It's stone—"

Rakna said: "I *am* stone, to her. I told you I didn't want anybody but you knowing anything about me."

"But . . . she's my wife!" cried Kenneth.

Marjorie said: "What?"

"You see," said Rakna, "she can't hear me. She thinks you're talking to a piece of stone." The god laughed richly. "I don't blame her for thinking you're nuts!"

"Skip that," Kenneth said angrily. "She's going to leave me if I can't convince her I'm sane. She just won't believe me. I thought you said I would always speak the absolute truth? Why won't she believe me?"

"Kenneth!" gasped Marjorie hysterically. "Stop it! Stop talking to that awful statue! Please, Kenneth!"

Rakna laughed again. "Look, dope, don't you know that truth, as such, does not exist to an angry woman, unless she happens to agree with it? As for my doing anything about this, that's up to you. You got yourself into this. I found it most amusing, too. now get yourself out. That ought to be funnier."

"Why you old . . . Listen, Rakna, give me a break, will you?" said Kenneth desperately.

Rakna just chuckled.

Suddenly Marjorie fell on her knees beside Kenneth. She looked up at him with tear-filled, imploring eyes. She was incredibly lovely, lovely and pitiful as she knelt there.

"Kenneth," she moaned. "Oh, darling, I love you . . . I always will, no matter what happens to you, no matter—" She drew a great shuddering sigh, and Kenneth's heart and soul went out to her. "Tell me you're all right, Kenneth. Tell me this is all a dream. Oh, God . . . Kenneth! I'm your wife, and I'm crying for you! You're out of your mind! This idol . . . its power over you—"

Kenneth dropped beside her and held her close. Rakna chuckled again—his last chuckle.

Kenneth whispered in Majorie's ear: "Darling, it's all right! I'm quite sane, truly I am. Just forget everything. There is no Rakna . . . you're right. Just a brownstone idol. Rakna has no power over me. I have no powers that he gave me—" Anything to comfort her. He murmured on and on.

They crouched there, those two young people, at the foot of an incredibly old brownstone idol, who was once Rakna, a god with the power of a god. The stone idol had no power over Kenneth Courtney, for Kenneth had spoken the truth when he said those words.

They lived, of course, happily ever after. And if you visit them, Kenneth may take you into the rock garden and show you his ugly old idol. It has a craggy, aristocratic face, with an expression on it of rueful humor. He was a good sport, that Rakna. Kenneth, by the way, still lies to his wife.

EVEN THE ANGELS

Malcolm Jameson

Mr. Herbert P. McQuigley died, was buried, and duly mourned. He was a good man, as men are judged in Pearlburg. He did not smoke, drink, dance, or play at cards. He married early, and he was the kind of man that did not take his marriage vows lightly. His private life, in short, was impeccable. His reputation for utter rectitude had never been clouded by the slightest breath of scandal except for one brief rumor that turned out later to be a base canard. At a time when Mr. McQuigley was attending a bankers' convention in Cincinnati, the police happened to raid a gambling dive. Part of their haul chanced to be a man, quite drunk, who was clicking a stack of chips with one hand while his disengaged arm held a chorine he was dandling on his knee. The culprit gave his name as H. P. McQuigley of Pearlburg, and the thing got in the papers. But all that was straightened out and explained, and the appropriate apologies made public by the papers. The fellow happened to be a ne'er-do-well cousin, of the reprobate Orangetown branch.

So much for Mr. McQuigley's private life. He was a lawyer by profession, but eventually got into business where he was acclaimed to be a success. He became president of the local bank and acquired the town's leading mercantile establishment in addition to much good farmland. Disgruntled persons who had had business dealings with him often complained he was a hard bargainer and a merciless collector, but to those Mr. McQuigley always said—and the logic of it is indisputable—that since he never demanded more than was due, he should not be expected to concede less. To those who complained that the laws were unfair, he suggested they change the law. In politics he was a conservative.

But as previously stated, he died and was buried. His widow and the brethren of the First Orthodist Church, of which he was a deacon, gave him an imposing funeral. He was buried in a private burial ground and a modest stone placed to mark the spot. A few centuries rolled by, and in the course of them the headstone sagged and fell into the patch of weeds that had taken the plot. The world passed on, busy with its own affairs, not knowing or caring that once the McQuigley name was one to conjure with in Pearlburg. *Sic transit gloria mundi!*

Not so, however, in Heaven. Or rather, in that sector of it given over to the Orthodists. Two hundred years, four months and five days after the demise of Mr. McQuigley, a routine report from the Heavenly Auditor to the Rectifier of Wrongs started a chain of activities whose reverberations continued to echo in the Hereafter for a long time to come. Perhaps as good a way as any to plot the course and expose the anatomy of that Celestial headache is to offer the Heavenly file, enriched by the interpolation of certain unofficial memoranda exchanged among the harassed angels and demons concerned.

The very first entry is the Auditor's report alluded to above. It is dated the 204th day of the year 88,011, absolute—which is meaningless to us. The report itself is self-explanatory, except that Mesram's use of the word "recently" will bear a little interpretation. He is no doubt alluding to the two-hundred-and-odd years that had intervened between the passing of Mr. McQuigley and his own entry into the case. It must be borne in mind that to an immortal such a period of time is not impressive. Here is the report:

From: The Heavenly Auditor
To: The Rectifier of Wrongs.
In Re: Satanic Complaint about Allotment.

Your Reverence:

Pursuant to your gracious instructions I have looked into His Malevolency's demand for a larger allotment for fuel and his request for additional appropriation for salaries and upkeep of one demon and three imps. I regret to state that for once His Devilship appears to have a well-grounded complaint. A comparison of the rosters of the Blest and the Damned with an actual head count on the job shows that there is one soul too many in the Pits of Gehenna, while the Celestial Chorus is shy one tenor.

A superficial investigation indicates that this unfortunate soul is one Herbert P. McQuigley, a devout Orthodist, recently admitted, known on the records as Inmate 1,218. He was received on the night of August 14, 1941; Gate Tender, Saleph, angel, second class; Deputy Recording Angel of the Watch, Mosoch; Sorter of the Sheep from the Goats, Riphath. The latter, acting on a transcript of the record furnished by Mosoch, sentenced McQuigley to an eternity in the Pits. Curiously, the transcript upon which he acted has since disappeared. Sorter Riphath, when interviewed, said that to the best of his recollection the alleged sins were gambling, drunkenness and lascivious conduct. These sins do not appear in the official record.

A miscarriage of justice may have occurred. I recommend a searching inquiry into the whole matter of McQuigley's entry and commitment. But may I suggest to Your Reverence that it is high time someone put a bug in Satan's ear? He is no doubt a good angel for his job, but it seems to me he lies awake nights thinking up ways to worry and embarrass us here in Heaven. After all, *we* aren't damned.

Yours faithfully,
Mesram

From: *Rectifier of Wrongs,*
To: *The Heavenly Auditor.*
In Re: *Your Report.*

Submissive Sir:

Your report received and will be acted upon.

The last four lines of your report are rejected and you are hereby rebuked for having written them. When your opinion is desired on such matters, it will be asked for.

Abimael.

Unofficial scribble to First Deputy Recording Angel, attributed to Judith, private secretary to Abimael.

"Stand by, sanctikins, to go through the wringer. It's about that McQuigley mixup. Somebody's going to sizzle for it. Satan squawked and old nosy Mesram has been poking around. So far he's pinned it on Riphath, but you can bet your last bowl of ambrosia that that holy old coot isn't going to accept the buck. You'd better tip Thiras off so he can be thinking up the answers—I just finished engrossing the official scroll. It'll hit you in a day or so. For ever and ever,
Judy.

From: Special Investigator Nahum,
To: The Rectifier of Wrongs.
In Re: Scandalous Laxity in Bureau of Records of the
Living.

Your Reverence:

I have the honor to report that the Angel Riphath, though guilty as charged of having wrongfully committed Inmate 1,218 while sitting as Sorter of the Day, is completely exonerated. He had no choice but to proceed from the Divine Record, a presumably authentic copy of which was before him at the time.

The fault lies in the Recording Bureau, whence the false document emanated. After a very painful investigation the following facts have come to light:

On New Year's Eve of the first day of 88,000, absolute, they threw a party in the Recorder's office—much nectar and nec— Well, you know—the usual thing. Present were: First Deputy Sarug and Judith, of the your own office, and a brace of Soothers of the Blest, and several minor deputies. Thiras, who was on watch at the time, joined them and lost contact with his watchees for the space of several hours. To cover up, he later used the current Earthly AP dispatches as a source of recordable sins, on the theory that only stuff that gets into the papers is serious enough to be worth writing down anyhow. In the interim a report had come through to the effect that H. P. McQuigley—Inmate 1,218—had been arrested in Cincinnati on various charges and that his guilt was apparent, which Phiras inscribed on the blotter.

Somewhat later a correction came through and was duly made, but it was delayed somehow and in the meantime the said McQuigley had died, been received and committed, leading to the unhappy dilemma we have now to face. It scared Sarug and Thiras. They rectified the records, but there was no way to undo the commitment without exposing themselves, so they entered into a conspiracy to forget the whole thing, trusting no one would pay attention to McQuigley's wails that it was all a mistake.

These are the facts. I have no recommendations to make.

Nahum.

From: The Rectifier of Wrongs,
To: Sarug, Thiras, Judith.
In Re: Your Misconduct.

Children:
Report to me at once for assignment of penance.

From: The Rectifier of Wrongs,
To: The Archangel Asarmoth, Chief of Legal Department.
In Re: Erroneous Commitment.

Your Holiness:
Please advise me how to rectify the foregoing error.
Abimael.

Unofficial note, Asarmoth to Abimael.

You can't. Best thing to do is forget it. What is one damned, more or less, among the Orthodists? I've never been able to figure out how any of 'em get by, their views are so strict. Anyway, what makes their Heaven any more desirable than their Hell? We only work here, you know, but we can't help having our personal opinions.

But seriously, old boy, you're up against something. The fellow has a legitimate kick, I suppose, but we can't back down on the doctrine of the infallibility of our courts. And you are perfectly aware of what we will be letting ourselves in for if we admit a single instance of error in the records. Every damned soul in Hell will be clamoring for a review. No, old-timer, it won't do. Why not send one of your slick-tongued persuaders down there and have a talk with him?

As for Satan, there is no pleasing him. I've never liked him, but then I am not omniscient. What's more to the point, I'm not omnipotent. You might hush him up by giving him what he asks for, but mind you, not an obulus more. He'll get the idea he has something on you, and then there *will* be Hell to pay! Excuse the pun, old fellow, but Heaven is a dull place at times.

Cordially,

Asarmoth.

From: The Rectifier of Wrongs,
To: Special Investigator Nahum.
In Re: McQuigley.

Dear Servitor:

Go to Hell. In Pit 47 in Subdivision 3 of West Gehenna you will find Inmate 1,218. Have him fished out and cooled off and have a talk with him. You know all the facts. Tell him as little as you have to—maybe the best thing to say is that we have arranged a pardon for him. In any case, give him a thorough brushing off and tell him we are transferring him to Heaven. That ought to do it. Let me know as early as possible how you make out.

Abimael.

Copy of requisition on Celestial Stores and Supplies, submitted by Rachel, secretary to Nahum.

Please furnish at once:

Item 1. Two brand-new wings, size 38, style XIV-B. To replace former ones, badly singed and unfeathered by trip to Hell.

Item 2. Fresh head of hair, as per sample—only a couple of shades redder, and slightly more curly, if you don't mind. Same reason as above, except there was no defeathering.

Item 3. Complete new outfit of robes, as above.

P. S. If I've got to do this again, for Heaven's sake, furnish asbestos weave—especially the skirt. You should have seen those poor sinners writhe! It was too, too cruel.

From: Special Investigator Nahum,
To: The Rectifier of Wrongs,
In Re: McQuigley.

Your Reverence:

This McQuigley is a tough egg. He has the legal mind. To make a long story short, he won't play ball except on his own terms.

First off, he was stubborn and wouldn't get out of the pool. Said he'd stood it for two centuries and would stand it as many more. All he wanted was justice. That is, justice *and* retribution. He kept saying that over and over, and all the while he was splashing that damned vitriol all over us. Rachel was taking down the chatter, and it made her pretty sore. She was all burned up, and I'm not being funny about it, either.

But to get to the point. He claimed he had been framed and could prove it. Said he had been through the same thing on Earth and came out on top, and what's more, got big damages. Says he expects as much or more here. I promised him Heaven, but he said that was not enough. He rated Heaven. In addition, he wants to know, what does he get for two hundred years of torment in blazing brimstone and boiling vitriol? He was entitled to damages. What are we offering to keep him from blabbing to the Big Boss?

That smacks of blackmail, I know, but he is shrewd, and knows where he has got us. I pointed out that it was impossible to add anything to Heaven, since Heaven itself is the gratification of every proper human desire. He snorted at that; said he'd settle for an archangelship. I made the counteroffer of a demonship, but he said no. Archangelship or nothing. Well, that's out, I know. An archangel is allowed a few faults, but one thing he must have, and that is some understanding and sympathy for human beings. An Orthodist of his type has neither. What's more, he would start out with a grievance against all the Blest, because they had been there from the first, while he had just come from the Pit.

It looks bad. I borrowed a few yards of unused vitriol strainer and wrapped Rachel up in it and brought her home. Fortunately the parchment she used was acidproof, so the transcript of the interview has been preserved. It is enclosed herewith.

Nahum.

Unofficial, Asarmoth to Abimael.

Herewith the sequel. Read it and weep. Now what?

Unofficial: Asarmoth to Abimael.

Nahum did quite right. But send him back to talk some more. Keep on fishing for counterproposals. Sooner or later the bird will come across with one we can handle. It's likely to be a slick proposition, for McQuigley was a lawyer and a clever one. But then, I'm a lawyer, too. Let me worry about our angle.

From: Special Investigator Nahum,
To: The Rectifier of Wrongs.
In Re: The McQuigley case.

Your Reverence:
Things came out better this time. He refuses absolutely to accept a pardon for a sin he did not commit, but says he has no scruples against accepting one for

a sin he *did* commit. It seems that the basic cause of his bellyache is that he has had to suffer for some alleged concentrated sinning that he didn't get any fun out of. I gather that he spent most of his life yearning to go on a big bust, get pie-eyed, watch the little ball fall, and the rest of it, but being a pillar of society in a hick town and getting rich at it, he didn't dare. Anyhow, what he wants now is to be permitted to go back to Earth for a week end with an understanding in advance that he can shoot the works and get away with it. Then he will come back to Heaven with no hard feelings.

Nahum.

Unofficial, Abimael to Asarmoth.

I am afraid of this. It is revolutionary. But it may be an out. What do you think?

Same: Asarmoth to Abimael.

It's worth a shot, but not via the pardon route. To get such a pardon we would have to go to the Big Boss. He must know, of course, since He knows everything, but since He chooses to pretend not to notice, it's a hint to us not to emphasize it. Suppose we do it by contract—I will draw up the contract—and sign it with him? We'll have lots of witnesses so he can't squirm out of it later.

By the way, it wouldn't do him any good to go back to Earth now. Things have changed. Better cut him back to his own time—say, swap his personality with that of the erring cousin who got him into this mess. That'll take a miracle, but I guess you can wangle that out of the Miracle Bureau without going higher. We don't want this small time chiseler's wails to make too much noise.

From: The Rectifier of Wrongs,
To: Chief of Bureau, Miracles and Apparitions.
In Re: Case of H. P. McQuigley—brief of transcript attached.

From the inclosure you will readily see the dilemma we are facing. Knowing nothing is impossible to you. I want to ask a favor. Will you—without making too much fuss about it—arrange to have this soul transferred back to 9:15 the night of Saturday, the 15th of June, 1940, and kept there until 3:22 the following Monday morning? House it in the body of his black sheep cousin Hank. I presume you can do the necessary juggling of the consciousnesses of the parties concerned so that the substitution will go unnoticed.

Abimael.

Unofficial (very). From Miraclist's Helper Joel, to Nahum.

Your chief sure wished an assignment on us this time! Boy! You should have seen that sainted hellion of yours perform. He did everything, and how! He lapped it up. He went at his sinning like an old-timer and added a few touches of his own. First he socked the roulette layout for a couple of grand, and then he shifted to stud. He played his cards like a fish, but he had 'em, so he mopped up. And drink—wow! I've heard of the unquenchable thirst of the Pit, but I never saw it in action before. He settled down to straight rum finally, and polished off two full bottles by dawn.

He slept awhile after that—who wouldn't—and then got up and tapered off on champagne. By mid-afternoon, when the chorines came, in, he was in form again. He didn't miss any bets with them, either. That night they danced awhile and shot craps in the intermissions. He never let down a minute until the cops came in and the show was over.

Anyhow, your miracle is done, and I hope it helps. But for Pete's sake, what's it all about? How is a guy like that going to stand it in the Orthodist Heaven?

Canceled pass, lifted from hook in the gatekeeper's lodge, Southern Portal of the Pearly Gates:

Good for one exit from Hell and one re-entry to Heaven. Signed, Abimael; countersigned, Asarmoth. Taken up by Gatekeeper Ebal, 240th day, the year 88,011.

From: Satan,
To: The Rectifier of Wrongs.
In Re: Your pet, McQuigley.

Think you've pulled a fast one, don't you? Wait. That guy belongs in my joint, if I know anything about sinners. Anyhow, I'm keeping the fires going in his pit and his demon Meroz on the job, and if you know what's good for you, you'll pay the bills. Here's something else to put in your pipe—when you start raiding my place to populate yours, you're simply raising Hell! He! He!

                                    Beelzebub.

From: Supervisor of Distribution of Blessings.
To: Rectifier of Wrongs.

Your Reverence:

My flock is turning sour and something's got to be done about it. A new saint hit here the other day, but there is something fishy about him. He has a low number, for one thing. Moreover, he grouses all the time, which no true saint ever does. He threw his first goblet of nectar in the cherub's face and howled because it didn't have kick enough to make a gnat grunt. And his manner with the lady saints is . . . well, uh . . . unsaintly. That's not all, he openly boasts of having sinned on Earth and says he is going to get away with it. The rest of my charges are deeply offended. Do you suppose a hatch was left open and the fellow crawled up from Downside?

Shadrach.

Unofficial, Abimael to Asarmoth.

Now look what you got me into. I'm sunk. What do we do next—build him a special private heaven? I'm afraid there will be riots both here and down there. One thing the Big Boss'll never stand for and that is discrimination. You said you'd do the worrying. Well, hop to it. I'm worried out.

Asarmoth to Abimael.

Ah, ye of little faith! Leave it to Uncle Dudley. How long since he came back—five months, Earth time, isn't it? Send for a couple of Michael's strongarm angels and have them give him the bum's rush. His old pit is warm and ready.

Abimael to Asarmoth.

He'll holler. Then we'll have an investigation.

Asarmoth to Abimael.

Let him holler. Tell him to file an appeal in your court. Then send for me.

Transcript of significant portions of hearing before Special Court of Rectification held in Gehenna, Justice Abimael sitting. Satan is present as an interested party. The demon Meroz is acting as sergeant at arms. Attorney General Asarmoth is acting for the authorities, the shade of Herbert P. McQuigley as his own counsel—at his own insistence. The Miraclist Joel has testified as to the sins committed. Satan, and various shades, both from the Pits and from among the Blest, have appeared as character witnesses. Their testimony is unanimous on one point. McQuigley is a typical nonrepentant sinner of the most arrogant variety. At last McQuigley takes the stand, Asarmoth questioning.

Q. You complain that you were tormented for the space of two hundred years and five months? And without justifiable reason?

A. I do. And fearfully. There was no justice in it. I should have spent that term in Heaven.

Q. Quite so. The court concedes it. Since then you have spent five months in Heaven?

A. Yes, after much——

Q. Never mind that. You admit it. Now, as a member in good standing of the Orthodist sect, what do you think is a fitting punishment for a man who gets beastly drunk and fritters away his substance in gaming?

A. Eternal damnation!

Q. Good. Yet you did that very thing?

A. Yes, all but the frittering part. (Witness smirks.) But I had in my pocket——

Q. We know what you had in your pocket. It was this. I show you a contract. Do you recognize it? Do you admit it to be your own free act, done without coercion or any promise given outside the terms set down and agreed upon in its text?

A. Sure. Why not? (Defiantly.)

Q. One more question and then we will examine the contract. Was it not a lifelong tenet of yours that one should be satisfied with the letter of a contract, neither demanding more nor accepting less?

A. Absolutely. It still is.

Asarmoth opens contract and reads.

Q. The essence of this agreement is in Stipulation III. I read:

"Having been unlawfully deprived of two hundred

years and five months of Paradise and in lieu of it having been compelled to suffer a like period of the most bitter torment, the party of the second part—that is, McQuigley—contends that he is thereby entitled to whatever benefits that may have flowed from the alleged sins for which he was punished; and that in order to possess himself of those intangible benefits, it is necessary that he be released from Hell long enough to commit the sins from which they flow—" Correct, Mr. McQuigley?

A. (Witness nods emphatically.) To the dot!

Q. (Continuing reading): "—and to achieve that end he voluntarily consents to accept that punishment appropriate to the deeds which he has already suffered, and further waives all right, title and interest in the two hundred years of bliss of which he has been defrauded, provided the party of the first part concurs. The party of the first part—The Heavenly Authorities— agree." Still correct, Mr. McQuigley?

A. (Smugly): What could be righter? The text is plain.

Q. Quite so. You came here an innocent man. Through a clerical error you wrongfully suffered a period of punishment—an extremely short period, I may say, in view of the extent of Eternity. As soon as the error was discovered you were offered any atonement within our power, but you rejected everything but this—your own idea. We have carried out the contract. You accepted the period of punishment and waived the two hundred years of bliss. The five-odd months of Paradise to which your original entry entitled you has been given you. The accounts are balanced, all terms fulfilled. There is nothing left to do but file this document among the archives.

Asarmoth, turning toward the bench: Your Reverence, the case is complete. The sinner's plea is frivolous. Let Meroz take him back to his pit.

McQuigley: Hey! You can't do that to me. What

about the rest of it—what you promised? From now on—

Justice Abimael: You came here in the beginning as a flawless soul, so far as the record showed, meriting eternal bliss. There was an unfortunate error made, but it has since been compensated for on terms of your own dictation. Justice is satisfied. But in your second coming, you appear as a confessed and unregenerate sinner and thus merit a perpetuity of damnation. It is by your own act that—

McQuigley: B-but I understood . . . it was implied . . . that is, I . . . uh . . . thought that—

Justice Abimael, shaking his head wearily: Not in the contract! Meroz, take him away!

Most unofficial, from the Archangel Asab, Keeper of the Great Seal of All the Heavens and personal attendant on the All Highest.

To Asarmoth:

God's in his Heaven and all's right with the world. I heard the Big Boss chuckle last night—the first time in eons. You got away with it, kid, but for a while you were on awfully thin ice. Don't stick your neck out again!

SMOKE GHOST

Fritz Leiber

Miss Millick wondered just what had happened to Mr. Wran. He kept making the strangest remarks when she took dictation. Just this morning he had quickly turned around and asked, "Have you ever seen a ghost, Miss Millick?" And she had tittered nervously and replied, "When I was a girl there was a thing in white that used to come out of the closet in the attic bedroom when I slept there, and moan. Of course it was just my imagination. I was frightened of lots of things." And he had said, "I don't mean that kind of ghost. I mean a ghost from the world today, with the soot of the factories on its face and the pounding of machinery in its soul. The kind that would haunt coal yards and slip around at night through deserted office buildings like this one. A real ghost. Not something out of books." And she hadn't known what to say.

He'd never been like this before. Of course he might be joking, but it didn't sound that way. Vaguely

129

Miss Millick wondered whether he mightn't be seeking some sort of sympathy from her. Of course, Mr. Wran was married and had a little child, but that didn't prevent her from having daydreams. The daydreams were not very exciting, still they helped fill up her mind. But now he was asking her another of those unprecedented questions.

"Have you ever thought what a ghost of our times would look like, Miss Millick? Just picture it. A smoky composite face with the hungry anxiety of the unemployed, the neurotic restlessness of the person without purpose, the jerky tension of the high-pressure metropolitan worker, the uneasy resentment of the striker, the callous opportunism of the scab, the aggressive whine of the panhandler, the inhibited terror of the bombed civilian, and a thousand other twisted emotional patterns. Each one overlying and yet blending with the other, like a pile of semitransparent masks?"

Miss Millick gave a little self-conscious shiver and said, "That would be terrible. What an awful thing to think of."

She peered furtively across the desk. She remembered having heard that there had been something impressively abnormal about Mr. Wran's childhood, but she couldn't recall what it was. If only she could do something—laugh at his mood or ask him what was really wrong. She shifted the extra pencils in her left hand and mechanically traced over some of the shorthand curlicues in her notebook.

"Yet, that's just what such a ghost or vitalized projection would look like, Miss Millick," he continued, smiling in a tight way. "It would grow out of the real world. It would reflect the tangled, sordid, vicious things. All the loose ends. And it would be very grimy. I don't think it would seem white or wispy, or favor graveyards. It wouldn't moan. But it would mutter unintelligibly, and twitch at your sleeve.

Like a sick, surly ape. What would such a thing want from a person, Miss Millick? Sacrifice? Worship? Or just fear? What could you do to stop it from troubling you?"

Miss Millick giggled nervously. There was an expression beyond her powers of definition in Mr. Wran's ordinary, flat-cheeked, thirtyish face, silhouetted against the dusty window. He turned away and stared out into the gray downtown atmosphere that rolled in from the railroad yards and the mills. When he spoke again his voice sounded far away.

"Of course, being immaterial, it couldn't hurt you physically—at first. You'd have to be peculiarly sensitive to see it, or be aware of it at all. But it would begin to influence your actions. Make you do this. Stop you from doing that. Although only a projection, it would gradually get its hooks into the world of things as they are. Might even get control of suitably vacuous minds. Then it could hurt whomever it wanted."

Miss Millick squirmed and read back her shorthand, like the books said you should do when there was a pause. She became aware of the failing light and wished Mr. Wran would ask her to turn on the overhead. She felt scratchy, as if soot were sitting down onto her skin.

"It's a rotten world, Miss Millick," said Mr. Wran, talking at the window. "Fit for another morbid growth of superstition. It's time the ghosts, or whatever you call them, took over and began a rule of fear. They'd be no worse than men."

"But"—Miss Millick's diaphragm jerked, making her titter inanely—"of course, there aren't any such things as ghosts."

Mr. Wran turned around.

"Of course there aren't, Miss Millick," he said in a loud, patronizing voice, as if she had been doing the talking rather than he. "Science and common sense and psychiatry all go to prove it."

She hung her head and might even have blushed if she hadn't felt so all at sea. Her leg muscles twitched, making her stand up, although she hadn't intended to. She aimlessly rubbed her hand along the edge of the desk.

"Why, Mr. Wran, look what I got off your desk," she said, showing him a heavy smudge. There was a note of clumsily playful reproof in her voice. "No wonder the copy I bring you always gets so black. Somebody ought to talk to those scrubwomen. They're skimping on your room."

She wished he would make some normal joking reply. But instead he drew back and his face hardened.

'Well, to get back," he rapped out harshly, and began to dictate.

When she was gone, he jumped up, dabbed his finger experimentally at the smudged part of the desk, frowned worriedly at the almost inky smears. He jerked open a drawer, snatched out a rag, hastily swabbed off the desk, crumpled the rag into a ball and tossed it back. There were three or four other rags in the drawer, each impregnated with soot.

Then he went over to the window and peered out anxiously through the dusk, his eyes searching the panorama of roofs, fixing on each chimney and water tank.

"It's a neurosis. Must be. Compulsions. Hallucinations," he muttered to himself in a tired, distraught voice that would have made Miss Millick gasp. "It's that damned mental abnormality cropping up in a new form. Can't be any other explanation. But it's so damned real. Even the soot. Good thing I'm seeing the psychiatrist. I don't think I could force myself to get on the elevated tonight." His voice trailed off, he rubbed his eyes, and his memory automatically started to grind.

It had all begun on the elevated. There was a particular little sea of roofs he had grown into the habit of glancing at just as the packed car carrying him homeward lurched around a turn. A dingy, melancholy little world of tar-paper, tarred gravel and smoky brick. Rusty tin chimneys with odd conical hats suggested abandoned listening posts. There was a washed-out advertisement of some ancient patent medicine on the nearest wall. Superficially it was like ten thousand other drab city roofs. But he always saw it around dusk, either in the smoky half-light, or tinged with red by the flat rays of a dirty sunset, or covered by ghostly windblown white sheets of rain-splash, or patched with blackish snow; and it seemed unusually bleak and suggestive; almost beautifully ugly though in no sense picturesque; dreary, but meaningful. Unconsciously it came to symbolize for Catesby Wran certain disagreeable aspects of the frustrated, frightened century in which he lived, the jangled century of hate and heavy industry and total wars. The quick daily glance into the half darkness became an integral part of his life. Oddly, he never saw it in the morning, for it was then his habit to sit on the other side of the car, his head buried in the paper.

One evening toward winter he noticed what seemed to be a shapeless black sack lying on the third roof from the tracks. He did not think about it. It merely registered as an addition to the well-known scene and his memory stored away the impression for further reference. Next evening, however, he decided he had been mistaken in one detail. The object was a roof nearer than he had thought. Its color and texture, and the grimy stains around it, suggested that it was filled with coal dust, which was hardly reasonable. Then, too, the following evening it seemed to have been blown against a rusty ventilator by the wind—which could hardly have happened if it were at all heavy. Perhaps it was filled with leaves. Catesby was surprised to find himself anticipating his next daily glance with a minor note of apprehension. There was something unwholesome in the posture of the thing that stuck in his mind—a bulge in the sacking that suggested a misshaped head peering around the ventilator. And his apprehension was justified, for that evening the thing was on the nearest roof, though on the farther side, looking as if it had just flopped down over the low brick parapet.

Next evening the sack was gone. Catesby was annoyed at the momentary feeling of relief that went through him, because the whole matter seemed too unimportant to warrant feelings of any sort. What difference did it make if his imagination had played tricks on him, and he'd fancied that the object was slowly crawling and hitching itself closer across the roofs? That was the way any normal imagination worked. He deliberately chose to disregard the fact that there were reasons for thinking his imagination was by no means a normal one. As he walked home from the elevated, however, he found himself wondering whether the sack was really gone. He seemed to recall a vague, smudgy trail leading across the gravel to the nearer side of the roof, which was masked by a parapet. For an instant an unpleasant picture formed in his mind—that of an inky, humped creature crouched behind the parapet, waiting.

The next time he felt the familiar grating lurch of the car, he caught himself trying not to look out. That angered him. He turned his head quickly. When he turned it back, his compact face was definitely pale. There had been only time for a fleeting rearward glance at the escaping roof. Had he actually seen in silhouette the upper part of a head of some sort peering over the parapet? Nonsense, he told himself. And even if he had seen something, there were a thousand explanations which did not involve the supernatural or even true hallucination. Tomorrow he would take a good look and clear up the whole matter. If necessary, he would visit the roof personally, though he hardly knew where to find it and disliked in any case the idea of pampering a silly fear.

He did not relish the walk home from the elevated that evening, and visions of the thing disturbed his dreams, and were in and out of his mind all next day at the office. It was then that he first began to relieve his nerves by making jokingly serious remarks about the supernatural to Miss Millick, who seemed properly mystified. It was on the same day, too, that he became aware of a growing antipathy to grime and soot. Everything he touched seemed gritty, and he found himself mopping and wiping at his desk like an old lady with a morbid fear of germs. He reasoned that there was no change really in his office, and that he'd just now become sensitive to the dirt that had always been there, but there was no denying an increasing nervousness. Long before the car reached the curve, he was straining his eyes through the murky twilight, determined to take in every detail.

Afterward he realized he must have given a muffled cry of some sort, for the man beside him looked at him curiously, and the woman ahead gave him an unfavorable stare. Conscious of his own pallor and uncontrollable trembling, he stared back at them hungrily, trying to regain the feeling of security he had completely lost. They were the usual reassuringly wooden-faced people everyone rides home with on the elevated. But suppose he had pointed out to one of them what he had seen—that sodden, distorted face of sacking and coal dust, that boneless paw which waved back and forth, unmistakably in his direction, as if reminding him of a future appointment—he involuntarily shut his eyes tight. His thoughts were racing ahead to tomorrow evening.

He pictured this same windowed oblong of light and packed humanity surging around the curve—then an opaque monstrous form leaping out from the roof in a parabolic swoop—an unmentionable face pressed close against the window, smearing it with wet coal dust—huge paws fumbling sloppily at the glass—

Somehow he managed to turn off his wife's anxious inquiries. Next morning he reached a decision and made an appointment for that evening with a psychiatrist a friend had told him about. It cost him a considerable effort, for Catesby had a well-grounded distaste for anything dealing with psychological abnormality. Visiting a psychiatrist meant raking up an episode in his past which he had never fully described even to his wife. Once he had made the decision, however, he felt considerably relieved. The psychiatrist, he told himself, would clear everything up. He could almost fancy him saying, "Merely a bad case of nerves. However, you must consult the oculist whose name I'm writing down for you, and you must take two of these pills in water every four hours," and so on. It was almost comforting, and made the coming revelation he would have to make seem less painful.

But as the smoky dusk rolled in, his nervousness had returned and he had let his joking mystification of Miss Millick run away with him until he had realized he wasn't frightening anyone but himself.

He would have to keep his imagination under better control, he told himself, as he continued to peer out restlessly at the massive, murky shapes of the downtown office buildings. Why, he had spent the whole afternoon building up a kind of neo-medieval cosmology of superstition. It wouldn't do. He realized then that he had been standing at the window much longer than he'd thought, for the glass panel in the door was dark and there was no noise coming

from the outer office. Miss Millick and the rest must
have gone home.

It was then he made the discovery that there
would have been no special reason for dreading the
swing around the curve that night. It was, as it
happened, a horrible discovery. For, on the shad-
owed roof across the street and four stories below, he
saw the thing huddle and roll across the gravel and,
after one upward look of recognition, merge into the
blackness beneath the water tank.

As he hurriedly collected his things and made for
the elevator, fighting the panicky impulse to run, he
began to think of hallucination and mild psychosis as
very desirable conditions. For better or for worse, he
pinned all his hopes on the psychiatrist.

"So you find yourself growing nervous and . . . er
. . . jumpy, as you put it," said Dr. Trevethick,
smiling with dignified geniality. "Do you notice any
more definite physical symptoms? Pain? Headache?
Indigestion?"

Catesby shook his head and wet his lips. "I'm
especially nervous while riding in the elevated," he
murmured swiftly.

"I see. We'll discuss that more fully. But I'd like
you first to tell me about something you mentioned
earlier. You said there was something about your
childhood that might predispose you to nervous ail-
ments. As you know, the early years are critical ones
in the development of an individual's behavior
pattern."

Catesby studied the yellow reflections of frosted
globes in the dark surface of the desk. The palm of
his left hand aimlessly rubbed the thick nap of the
armchair. After a while he raised his head and looked
straight into the doctor's small brown eyes.

"From perhaps my third to my ninth year," he

began, choosing the words with care, "I was what you might call a sensory prodigy."

The doctor's expression did not change. "Yes?" he inquired politely.

"What I mean is that I was supposed to be able to see through walls, read letters through envelopes and books through their covers, fence and play ping-pong blindfolded, find things that were buried, read thoughts." The words tumbled out.

"And could you?" The doctor's voice was toneless.

"I don't know. I don't suppose so," answered Catesby, long-lost emotions flooding back into his voice. "It's all confused now. I thought I could, but then they were always encouraging me. My mother . . . was . . . well . . . interested in psychic phenomena. I was . . . exhibited. I seem to remember seeing things other people couldn't. As if most opague objects were transparent. But I was very young. I didn't have any scientific criteria for judgment."

He was reliving it now. The darkened rooms. The earnest assemblages of gawking, prying adults. Himself alone on a little platform, lost in a straight-backed wooden chair. The black silk handkerchief over his eyes. His mother's coaxing, insistent questions. The whispers. The gasps. His own hate of the whole business, mixed with hunger for the adulation of adults. Then the scientists from the university, the experiments, the big test. The reality of those memories engulfed him and momentarily made him forget the reason why he was disclosing them to a stranger.

"Do I understand that your mother tried to make use of you as a medium for communicating with the . . . er . . . other world?"

Catesby nodded eagerly.

"She tried to, but she couldn't. When it came to getting in touch with the dead, I was a complete failure. All I could do—or thought I could do—was see real, existing, three-dimensional objects beyond the vision of normal people. Objects anyone could have seen except for distance, obstruction, or darkness. It was always a disappointment to mother."

He could hear her sweetish, patient voice saying, "Try again, dear, just this once. Katie was your aunt. She loved you. Try to hear what she's saying." And he had answered, "I can see a woman in a blue dress standing on the other side of Dick's house." And she had replied, "Yes, I know, dear. But that's not Katie. Katie's a spirit. Try again. Just this once, dear." The doctor's voice gently jarred him back into the softly gleaming office.

"You mentioned scientific criteria for judgment, Mr. Wran. As far as you know, did anyone ever try to apply them to you?"

Catesby's nod was emphatic.

"They did. When I was eight, two young psychologists from the university got interested in me. I guess they did it for a joke at first, and I remember being very determined to show them I amounted to something. Even now I seem to recall how the note of polite superiority and amused sarcasm drained out of their voices. I suppose they decided at first that it was very clever trickery, but somehow they persuaded mother to let them try me out under controlled conditions. There were lots of tests that seemed very businesslike after mother's slipshod little exhibitions. They found I was clairvoyant—or so they thought. I got worked up and on edge. They were going to demonstrate my supernormal sensory powers to the university psychology faculty. For the first time I began to worry about whether I'd come through. Perhaps they kept me going at too hard a pace, I don't know. At any rate, when the test came, I couldn't do a thing. Everything became opaque. I got desperate and made things up out of my imagination. I lied. In the end I failed utterly, and I believe the two young psychologists got into a lot of hot water as a result."

He could hear the brusque, bearded man saying, "You've been taken in by a child, Flaxman, a mere child. I'm greatly disturbed. You've put yourself on the same plane as common charlatans. Gentlemen, I ask you to banish from your minds this whole sorry episode. It must never be referred to." He winced at the recollection of his feeling of guilt. But at the same time he was beginning to feel exhilarated and almost light-hearted. Unburdening his long-repressed memories had altered his whole viewpoint. The episodes on the elevated began to take on what seemed their proper proportions as merely the bizarre workings of overwrought nerves and an overly suggestible mind. The doctor, he anticipated confidently, would disentangle the obscure subconscious causes, whatever they might be. And the whole business would be finished off quickly, just as his childhood experience— which was beginning to seem a little ridiculous now— had been finished off.

"From that day on," he continued, "I never exhibited a trace of my supposed powers. My mother was frantic and tried to sue the university. I had something like a nervous breakdown. Then the divorce was granted, and my father got custody of me. He did his best to make me forget it. We went on long outdoor vacations and did a lot of athletics, associated with normal matter-of-fact people. I went to business college eventually. I'm in advertising now. But," Catesby paused, "now that I'm having nervous symptoms, I've wondered if there mightn't be a connection. It's not a question of whether I was really clairvoyant or not. Very likely my mother taught me a lot of unconscious deceptions, good enough to fool even young psychology instructors. But don't you think it may have some important bearing on my present condition?"

For several moments the doctor regarded him with a professional frown. Then he said quietly, "And is there some . . . er . . . more specific connection between your experiences then and now? Do you by any chance find that you are once again beginning to . . . er . . . see things?"

Catesby swallowed. He had felt in increasing eagerness to unburden himself of his fears, but it was not easy to make a beginning, and the doctor's shrewd question rattled him. He forced himself to concentrate. The thing he thought he had seen on the roof loomed up before his inner eye with unexpected vividness. Yet it did not frighten him. He groped for words.

Then he saw that the doctor was not looking at him but over his shoulder. Color was draining out of the doctor's face and his eyes did not seem so small. Then the doctor sprang to his feet, walked past Catesby, threw up the window and peered into the darkness.

As Catesby rose, the doctor slammed down the window and said in a voice whose smoothness was marred by a slight, persistent gasping, "I hope I haven't alarmed you. I saw the face of . . . er . . . a Negro prowler on the fire escape. I must have frightened him, for he seems to have gotten out of sight in a hurry. Don't give it another thought. Doctors are frequently bothered by *voyeurs* . . . er . . . Peeping Toms."

"A Negro?" asked Catesby, moistening his lips.

The doctor laughed nervously. "I imagine so, though my first odd impression was that it was a white man in blackface. You see, the color didn't seem to have any brown in it. It was dead-black."

Catesby moved toward the window. There were smudges on the glass. "It's quite all right, Mr. Wran."

The doctor's voice had acquired a sharp note of impatience, as if he were trying hard to reassume his professional authority. "Let's continue our conversation. I was asking you if you were"—he made a face— "seeing things."

Catesby's whirling thoughts slowed down and locked into place. "No, I'm not seeing anything that other people don't see, too. And I think I'd better go now. I've been keeping you too long." He disregarded the doctor's half-hearted gesture of denial. "I'll phone you about the physical examination. In a way you've already taken a big load off my mind." He smiled woodenly. "Goodnight, Dr. Trevethick."

Catesby Wran's mental state was a peculiar one. His eyes searched every angular shadow, he glanced sideways down each chasm-like alley and barren basement passageway, and kept stealing looks at the irregular line of the roofs, yet he was hardly conscious of where he was going. He pushed away the thoughts that came into his mind, and kept moving. He became aware of a slight sense of security as he turned into a lighted street where there were people and high buildings and blinking signs. After a while he found himself in the dim lobby of the structure that housed his office. Then he realized why he couldn't go home, why he daren't go home—after what had happened at the office of Dr. Trevethick.

"Hello, Mr. Wran," said the night elevator man, a burly figure in overalls, sliding open the grille-work door to the old-fashioned cage. "I didn't know you were working nights now, too."

Catesby stepped in automatically. "Sudden rush of orders," he murmured inanely. "Some stuff that has to be gotten out."

The cage creaked to a stop at the top floor. "Be working very late, Mr. Wran?"

He nodded vaguely, watched the car slide out of

sight, found his keys, swiftly crossed the outer office, and entered his own. His hand went out to the light switch, but then the thought occurred to him that the two lighted windows, standing out against the dark bulk of the building, would indicate his whereabouts and serve as a goal toward which something could crawl and climb. He moved his chair so that the back was against the wall and sat down in the semidarkness. He did not remove his overcoat.

For a long time he sat there motionless, listening to his own breathing and the faraway sounds from the streets below: the thin metallic surge of the crosstown streetcar, the farther one of the elevated, faint lonely cries and honkings, indistinct rumblings. Words he had spoken to Miss Millick in nervous jest came back to him with the bitter taste of truth. He found himself unable to reason critically or connectedly, but by their own volition thoughts rose up into his mind and gyrated slowly and rearranged themselves with the inevitable movement of planets.

Gradually his mental picture of the world was transformed. No longer a world of material atoms and empty space, but a world in which the bodiless existed and moved according to its own obscure laws or unpredictable impulses. The new picture illuminated with dreadful clarity certain general facts which had always bewildered and troubled him and from which he had tried to hide: the inevitability of hate and war, the diabolically timed mischances which wreck the best of human intentions, the walls of willful misunderstanding that divide one man from another, the eternal vitality of cruelty and ignorance and greed. They seemed appropriate now, necessary parts of the picture. And superstition only a kind of wisdom.

Then his thoughts returned to himself and the question he had asked Miss Millick, "What would such a thing want from a person? Sacrifices? Worship, Or just fear? What could you do to stop it from troubling you?" It had become a practical question.

With an explosive jangle, the phone began to ring, "Cate, I've been trying everywhere to get you," said his wife. "I never thought you'd be at the office. What are you doing? I've been worried."

He said something about work.

"You'll be home right away?" came the faint anxious question. "I'm a little frightened. Ronny just had a scare. It woke him up. He kept pointing to the window saying, 'Black man, black man.' Of course it's something he dreamed. But I'm frightened. You will be home? What's that, dear? Can't you hear me?"

"I will. Right away," he said. Then he was out of the office, buzzing the night bell and peering down the shaft.

He saw it peering up the shaft at him from the deep shadows three floors below, the sacking face pressed against the iron grilled-work. it started up the stair at a shockingly swift, shambling gait, vanishing temporarily from sight as it swung into the second corridor below.

Catesby clawed at the door to the office, realized he had not locked it, pushed it in, slammed and locked it behind him, retreated to the other side of the room, cowered between the filing cases and the wall. His teeth were clicking. He heard the groan of the rising cage. A silhouette darkened the frosted glass of the door, blotting out part of the grotesque reverse of the company name. After a little the door opened.

The big-globed overhead light flared on and, standing inside the door, her hand on the switch, was Miss Millick.

"Why, Mr. Wran," she stammered vacuously, "I didn't know you were here. I'd just come in to do some extra typing after the movie. I didn't . . . but the lights weren't on. What were you— "

He stared at her. He wanted to shout in relief, grab hold of her, talk rapidly. He realized he was grinning hysterically.

"Why, Mr. Wran, what's happened to you?" she asked embarrassedly, ending with a stupid titter. "Are you feeling sick? Isn't there something I can do for you?"

He shook his head jerkily and managed to say, "No, I'm just leaving. I was doing some extra work myself."

"But you *look* sick," she insisted, and walked over toward him. He inconsequentially realized she must have stepped in mud, for her high-heeled shoes left neat black prints.

"Yes, I'm sure you must be sick. You're so terribly pale." She wounded like an enthusiastic, incompetent nurse. Her face brightened with a sudden inspiration. "I've got something in my bag, that'll fix you up right away," she said. "It's for indigestion."

She fumbled at her stuffed oblong purse. He noticed that she was absent-mindedly holding it shut with one hand while she tried to open it with the other. Then, under his very eyes, he saw her bend back the thick prongs of metal locking the purse as if they were tinfoil, or as if her fingers had become a pair of steel pliers.

Instantly his memory recited the words he had spoken to Miss Millick that afternoon. "It couldn't hurt you physically—at first . . . gradually get its hooks into the world . . . might even get control of suitably vacuous minds. Then it could hurt whomever it wanted." A sickish, cold feeling grew inside him. He began to edge toward the door.

But Miss Millick hurried ahead of him.

"You don't have to wait, Fred," she called. "Mr. Wran's decided to stay a while longer."

The door to the cage shut with a mechanical rattle. The cage creaked. Then she turned around in the door.

"Why, Mr. Wran," she gurgled reproachfully, "I just couldn't think of letting you go home now. I'm sure you're terribly unwell. Why, you might collapse in the street. You've just got to stay here until you feel different."

The creaking died away. He stood in the center of the office, motionless. His eyes traced the coal-black course of Miss Millick's footprints to where she stood blocking the door. Then a sound that was almost a scream was wrenched out of him, for it seemed to him that the blackness was creeping up her legs under the thin stockings.

"Why, Mr. Wran," she said. "You're acting as if you were crazy. You must lie down for a while. Here, I'll help you off with your coat."

The nauseously idiotic and rasping note was the same; only it had been intensified. As she came toward him he turned and ran through the storeroom, clattered a key desperately at the lock of the second door to the corridor.

"Why, Mr. Wran," he heard her call, "are you having some kind of a fit? You must let me help you."

The door came open and he plunged out into the corridor and up the stairs immediately ahead. It was only when he reached the top that he realized the heavy steel door in front of him led to the roof. He jerked up the catch.

"Why, Mrs. Wran, you mustn't run away. I'm coming after you."

Then he was out on the gritty gravel of the roof. The night sky was clouded and murky, with a faint pinkish glow from the neon signs. From the distant mills rose a ghostly spurt of flame. He ran to the edge. The street lights glared dizzily upward. Two men were tiny round blobs of hat and shoulders. He swung around.

The thing was in the doorway. The voice was no longer solicitous but moronically playful, each sentence ending in a titter.

"Why, Mr. Wran, why have you come up here? We're all alone. Just think, I might push you off."

The thing came slowly toward him. He moved backward until his heels touched the low parapet. Without knowing why, or what he was going to do, he dropped to his knees. He dared not look at the face as it came nearer, a focus for the worst in the world, a gathering point for poisons from everywhere. Then the lucidity of terror took possession of his mind, and words formed on his lips.

"I will obey you. You are my god," he said. "You have supreme power over man and his animals and his machines. You rule this city and all others. I recognize that."

Again the titter, closer. "Why, Mr. Wran, you never talked like this before. Do you mean it?"

"The world is yours to do with as you will, save or tear to pieces," he answered fawningly, the words automatically fitting themselves together in vaguely liturgical patterns. "I recognize that. I will praise, I will sacrifice. In smoke and soot I will worship you forever."

The voice did not answer. He looked up. There was only Miss Millick, deathly pale and swaying drunkenly. Her eyes were closed. He caught her as she wobbled toward him. His knees gave way under the added weight and they sank down together on the edge of the roof.

After a while she began to twitch. Small noises came from her throat and her eyelids edged open.

"Come on, we'll go downstairs," he murmured jerkily, trying to draw her up. "You're feeling bad."

"I'm terribly dizzy," she whispered. "I must have

fainted. I didn't eat enough. And then I'm so nervous lately, about the war and everything, I guess. Why, we're on the roof! Did you bring me up here to get some air? Or did I come up without knowing it? I'm awfully foolish. I used to walk in my sleep, my mother said."

As he helped her down the stairs, she turned and looked at him. "Why, Mr. Wran," she said, faintly, "you've got a big black smudge on your forehead. Here, let me get it off for you." Weakly she rubbed at it with her handkerchief. She started to sway again and he steadied her.

"No, I'll be all right," she said. "Only I feel cold. What happened, Mr. Wran? Did I have some sort of fainting spell?"

He told her it was something like that.

Later, riding home in the empty elevated car, he wondered how long he would be safe from the thing. It was a purely practical problem. He had no way of knowing, but instinct told him he had satisfied the brute for some time. Would it want more when it came again? Time enough to answer that question when it arose. It might be hard, he realized, to keep out of an insane asylum. With Helen and Ronny to protect, as well as himself, he would have to be careful and tightlipped. He began to speculate as to how many other men and women had seen the thing or things like it.

The elevated slowed and lurched in a familiar fashion. He looked at the roofs near the curve. They seemed very ordinary, as if what made them impressive had gone away for a while.

NOTHING IN THE RULES

L. Sprague De Camp

Not many spectators turn out for a meet between two minor women's swimming clubs, and this one was no exception. Louis Connaught, looking up at the balcony, thought casually that the single row of seats around it was about half full, mostly with the usual bored-looking assortment of husbands and boy friends, and some of the Hotel Creston's guests who had wandered in for want of anything better to do. One of the bellboys was asking an evening-gowned female not to smoke, and she was showing irritation. Mr. Santalucia and the little Santalucias were there as usual to see mamma perform. They waved down at Connaught.

Connaught—a dark devilish-looking little man— glanced over to the other side of the pool. The girls were coming out of the shower rooms, and their shrill conversation was blurred by the acoustics of the pool room into a continuous buzz. The air was faintly steamy. The stout party in white duck pants was

149

Laird, coach of the Knickerbockers and Connaught's arch rival. He saw Connaught and boomed: "Hi, Louie!" The words rattled from wall to wall with a sound like a stick being drawn swiftly along a picket fence. Wambach of the A.A.U. Committee, who was refereeing, came in with his overcoat still on and greeted Laird, but the booming reverberations drowned his words before they got over to Connaught.

Then somebody else came through the door; or rather, a knot of people crowded through it all at once, facing inward, some in bathing suits and some in street clothes. It was a few seconds before Coach Connaught saw what they were looking at. He blinked and looked more closely, standing with his mouth half open.

But not for long. *"Hey!"* he yelled in a voice that made the pool room sound like the inside of a snare drum in use. "Protest! PROTEST! *You can't do that!*"

It had been the preceding evening when Herbert Laird opened his front door and shouted, "H'lo, Mark, come on in." The chill March wind was making a good deal of racket but not as much as all that. Laird was given to shouting on general principles. He was stocky and bald.

Mark Vining came in and deposited his briefcase. He was younger than Laird—just thirty, in fact— with octagonal glasses and rather thin severe features that made him look more serious than he was, which was fairly serious.

"Glad you could come, Mark," said Laird. "Listen, can you make our meet with the Crestons tomorrow night?"

Vining pursed his lips thoughtfully. "I guess so. Loomis decided not to appeal, so I don't have to work nights for a few days anyhow. Is something special up?"

Laird looked sly. "Maybe. Listen, you know that

Mrs. Santalucia that Louie Connaught has been cleaning up with for the past couple of years? I think I've got that fixed. But I want you along to think up legal reasons why my scheme's O.K."

"Why," said Vining cautiously. "What's your scheme?"

"Can't tell you now. I promised not to. But if Louie can win by entering a freak—a woman with webbed fingers—"

"Oh, look here, Herb, you know those webs don't really help her—"

"Yes, yes, I know all the arguments. You've already got more water-resistance to your arms than you've got muscle to overcome it with, and so forth. But I know Mrs. Santalucia has webbed fingers, and I know she's the best woman swimmer in New York. And I don't like it. It's bad for my prestige as a coach." He turned and shouted into the gloom: "Iantha!"

"Yes?"

"Come here, will you please? I want you to meet my friend Mr. Vining. Here, we need some light."

The light showed the living room as usual buried under disorderly piles of boxes of bathing suits and other swimming equipment, the sale of which furnished Herbert Laird with most of his income. It also showed a young woman coming in in a wheel chair.

One look gave Vining a feeling that, he knew, boded no good for him. He was unfortunate in being a pushover for any reasonably attractive girl, and at the same time being cursed with an almost pathological shyness where women were concerned. The facts that both he and Laird were bachelors and took their swimming seriously were the main ties between them.

This girl was more than reasonably attractive. She was, thought the dazzled Vining, a wow, a ten-strike, a direct sixteen-inch hit. Her smooth, rather flat features and high cheekbones had a hint of Asian or American Indian, and went oddly with her light-gold hair, which, Vining could have sworn, had a faint greenish tinge. A blanket was wrapped around her legs.

He came out of his trance as Laird introduced the exquisite creature as "Miss Delfoiros."

Miss Delfoiros didn't seem exactly overcome. As she extended her hand, she said with a noticeable accent: "You are not from the newspapers, Mr. Vining?"

"No," said Vining. "Just a lawyer. I specialize in wills and probate and things. Not thinking of drawing up yours, are you?"

She relaxed visibly and laughed. "No. I 'ope I shall not need one for a long, long time."

"Still," said Vining seriously, "you never know—"

Laird bellowed: "Wonder what's keeping that sister of mine. Dinner ought to be ready. *Martha!*" He marched out, and Vining heard Miss Laird's voice, something about "—but Herb, I had to let those things cool down—"

Vining wondered with a great wonder what he should say to Miss Delfoiros. Finally he said, "Smoke?"

"Oh, no, thank you very much. I do not do it."

"Mind if I do?"

"No, not at all."

"Whereabouts do you hail from?" Vining thought the question sounded both brusque and silly. He never did get the hang of talking easily under these circumstances.

"Oh, I am from Kip—Cyprus, I mean. You know, the island."

"Really? That makes you a British subject, doesn't it?"

"Well . . . no, not exactly. Most Cypriots are, but I am not."

"Will you be at this swimming meet?"

"Yes, I think so."

"You don't"—he lowered his voice—"know what scheme Herb's got up his sleeve to beat La Santalucia?"

"Yes . . . no . . . I do not . . . what I mean is, I must not tell."

More mystery, thought Vining. What he really wanted to know was why she was confined to a wheel chair; whether the cause was temporary or permanent. But you couldn't ask a person right out, and he was still trying to concoct a leading question when Laird's bellow wafted in: "All right, folks, soup's on!" Vining would have pushed the wheel chair in, but before he had a chance, the girl had spun the chair around and was halfway to the dining room.

Vining said: "Hello, Martha, how's the schoolteaching business?" But he wasn't really paying much attention to Laird's capable spinster sister. He was gaping at Miss Delfoiros, who was quite calmly emptying a teaspoonful of salt into her water glass and stirring.

"What . . . what?" he gulped.

"I 'ave to," she said. "Fresh water makes me—like what you call drunk."

"Listen, Mark!" roared his friend. "Are you sure you can be there on time tomorrow night? There are some questions of eligibility to be cleared up, and I'm likely to need you badly."

"Will Miss Delfoiros be there?" Vining grinned, feeling very foolish inside.

"Oh, sure. Iantha's out . . . say, listen, you know that little eighteen-year-old Clara Havranek? She did the hundred in one-o-five yesterday. She's championship material. We'll clean the Creston Club yet—" He went on, loud and fast, about what he was going to do to Louie Connaught's girls. The while, Mark Vining tried to concentrate on his own food, which was good, and on Iantha Delfoiros, who was charming but evasive.

There seemed to be something special about Miss Delfoiros's food, to judge by the way Martha Laird had served it. Vining looked closely and saw that it had the peculiarly dead and clammy look that a dinner once hot but now cold has. He asked about it.

"Yes," she said. "I like it cold."

"You mean you don't eat *anything* hot?"

She made a face. " 'ot food? No, I do not like it. To us it is—"

"Listen, Mark! I hear the W.S.A. is going to throw a post-season meet in April for novices only—"

Vining's dessert lay before him a full minute before he noticed it. He was too busy thinking how delightful Miss Delfoiros's accent was.

When dinner was over, Laird said, "Listen, Mark, you know something about these laws against owning gold? Well, look here—" He led the way to a candy box on a table in the living room. The box contained, not candy, but gold and silver coins. Laird handed the lawyer several of them. The first one he examined was a silver crown, bearing the inscription "Carolus II Dei Gra" encircling the head of England's Merry Monarch with a wreath in his hair—or, more probably, in his wig. The second was an eighteenth-century Spanish collar. The third was a Louis d'Or.

"I didn't know you went in for coin collecting, Herb," said Vining. "I suppose these are all genuine?"

"They're genuine all right. But I'm not collecting 'em. You might say I'm taking 'em in trade. I have a chance to sell ten thousand bathing caps, if I can take payment in those things."

"I shouldn't think the U.S. Rubber Company would like the idea much."

"That's just the point. What'll I do with 'em after I

get 'em? Will the government put me in jail for having 'em?"

"You needn't worry about that. I don't think the law covers old coins, though I'll look it up to make sure. Better call up the American Numismatic Society —they're in the 'phone book—and they can tell you how to dispose of them. But look here, what the devil is this? Ten thousand bathing caps to be paid for in pieces-of-eight? I never heard of such a thing."

"That's it exactly. Just as the little lady here." Laird turned to Iantha, who was nervously trying to signal him to keep quiet. "The deal's her doing."

"I did . . . did—" She looked as if she were going to cry. " 'Erbert, you should not have said that. You see," she said to Vining, "we do not like to 'ave a lot to do with people. Always it causes us troubles."

"Who," asked Vining, "do you mean by 'we'?"

She shut her mouth obstinately. Vining almost melted. But his legal instincts came to the surface. If you don't get a grip on yourself, he thought, you'll be in love with her in another five minutes. And that might be a disaster. He said firmly: "Herb, the more I see of this business the crazier it looks. Whatever's going on, you seem to be trying to get me into it. But I won't let you before I know what it's all about."

"Might as well tell him, Iantha," said Laird. "He'll know when he sees you swim tomorrow, anyhow."

She said: "You will not tell the newspaper men Mr. Vining?"

"No. I won't say anything to anybody."

"You promise?"

"Of course. You can depend on a lawyer to keep things under his hat."

"Under his—I suppose you mean not to tell. So, look." She reached down and pulled up the lower end of the blanket.

Vining looked. Where he expected to see feet, there was a pair of horizontal flukes, like those of a porpoise.

Louis Connaught's having kittens, when he saw what his rival coach had sprung on him, can thus be easily explained. First he doubted his own senses. Then he doubted whether there was any justice in the world.

Meanwhile Mark Vining proudly pushed Iantha's wheel chair in among the cluster of judges and time-keepers at the starting end of the pool. Iantha herself, in a bright green bathing cap, held her blanket around her shoulders, but the slate-gray tail with its flukes was smooth and the flukes were horizontal; artists who show mermaids with scales and a vertical tail fin, like a fish's, simply don't know their zoölogy.

"All right, all right," bellowed Laird. "Don't crowd around. Everybody get back to where they belong. Everybody, please."

One of the spectators, leaning over the rail of the balcony to see, dropped a fountain pen into the pool. One of Connaught's girls, a Miss Black, dove in after it. Ogden Wambach, the referee, poked a finger at the skin of the tail. He was a well-groomed, gray-haired man.

"Laird," he said, "is this a joke?"

"Not at all. She's entered in the back stroke and all the free styles, just like any other club member. She's even registered with the A.A.U."

"But . . . but . . . I mean, is it alive? Is it real?"

Iantha spoke up. "Why do you not ask me those questions, Mr. . . . Mr. . . . I do not know you—"

"Good grief," said Wambach. "It talks! I'm the referee, Miss—"

"Delfoiros. Iantha Delfoiros."

"My word. Upon my word. That means—let's see—Violet Porpoise-tail, doesn't it? *Delphis* plus *oura*—"

"You know Greek? Oh, 'ow nice!" She broke into a string of Romaic.

Wambach gulped a little. "Too fast for me, I'm afraid. And that's *modern* Greek, isn't it?"

"Why, yes. I am modern, am I not?"

"Dear me. I suppose so. But is that tail really real? I mean, it's not just a piece of costumery?"

"Oh, but yes." Iantha threw off the blanket and waved her flukes.

"Dear me," said Ogden Wambach. "Where are my glasses? You understand, I just want to make sure there's nothing spurious about this."

Mrs. Santalucia, a muscular-looking lady with a visible mustache and fingers webbed down to the first joint, said, "You mean I gotta swim against *her?*"

Louis Connaught had been sizzling like a dynamite fuse. "You can't do it!" he shrilled. "This is a woman's meet! I protest!"

"So what?" said Laird.

"But you can't enter a fish in a woman's swimming meet! Can you, Mr. Wambach?"

Mark Vining spoke up. He had just taken a bunch of papers clipped together out of his pocket, and was running through them.

"Miss Delfoiros," he asserted, "is not a fish. She's a mammal."

"How do you figure that?" yelled Connaught.

"*Look* at her."

"Um-m-m," said Ogden Wambach. "I see what you mean."

"But," howled Connaught, "she still ain't human!"

"There is a question about that, Mr. Vining," said Wambach.

"No question at all. There's nothing in the rules against entering a mermaid, and there's nothing that says the competitors have to be human."

*   *   *

Connaught was hopping about like an overwrought cricket. He was now waving a copy of the current A.A.U. swimming, diving and water polo rules. "I still protest! Look here! All through here it only talks about two kinds of meets, men's and women's. She ain't a woman, and she certainly ain't a man. If the Union had wanted to have meets for mermaids they'd have said so."

"Not a woman?" asked Vining in a manner that juries learned meant a rapier thrust at an opponent. "I beg your pardon, Mr. Connaught. I looked the question up." He frowned at his sheaf of papers. "Webster's International Dictionary, Second Edition, defines a woman as 'any female person.' And it further defines 'person' as 'a being characterized by conscious apprehension, rationality, and a moral sense.' " He turned to Wambach. "Sir, I think you'll agree that Miss Delfoiros has exhibited conscious apprehension and rationality during her conversation with you, won't you?"

"My word . . . I really don't know what to say, Mr. Vining . . . I suppose she has, but I couldn't say—"

Horwitz, the scorekeeper, spoke up. "You might ask her to give the multiplication table." Nobody paid him any attention.

Connaught exhibited symptoms alarmingly suggestive of apoplexy. "But you can't— What are you talking about . . . conscious ap-ap—"

"Please, Mr. Connaught!" said Wambach. "When you shout that way I can't understand you because of the echoes."

Connaught mastered himself with a visible effort. Then he looked crafty. "How do I know she's got a moral sense?"

Vining turned to Iantha. "Have you ever been in jail, Iantha?"

Iantha laughed. "What a funny question, Mark! But of course, I have not."

"That's what *she* says," sneered Connaught. "How you gonna prove it?"

"We don't have to," said Vining loftily. "The burden of proof is on the accuser, and the accused is legally innocent until proved guilty. That principle was well established by the time of King Edward the First."

"That wasn't the kind of moral sense I meant," cried Connaught. "How about what they call moral turp-turp— You know what I mean."

"Hey," growled Laird, "what's the idea? Are you trying to cast— What's the word, Mark?"

"Aspersions?"

"—cast aspersions on one of my swimmers? You watch out, Louie. If I hear you be— What's the word, Mark?"

"Besmirching her fair name?"

"—besmirching her fair name I'll drown you in your own tank."

"And after that," said Vining, "we'll slap a suit on you for slander."

"Gentlemen! Gentlemen!" said Wambach. "Let's not have any more personalities, please. This is a swimming meet, not a lawsuit. Let's get to the point."

"We've made ours," said Vining with dignity. "We've shown that Iantha Delfoiros is a woman, and Mr. Connaught has stated, himself, that this is a woman's meet. Therefore, Miss Delfoiros is eligible. Q.E.D."

"Ahem," said Wambach. "I don't quite know—I never had a case like this to decide before."

Louis Connaught almost had tears in his eyes; at least he sounded as if he did. "Mr. Wambach, you can't let Herb Laird do this to me. I'll be a laughing-stock."

Laird snorted. "How about your beating me with your Mrs. Santalucia? I didn't get any sympathy from you when people laughed at me on account of that. And how much good did it do me to protest against her fingers?"

"But," wailed Connaught, "if he can enter this Miss Delfurrus, what's to stop somebody from entering a trained sea lion or something? Do you want to make competitive swimming into a circus?"

Laird grinned. "Go ahead, Louie. Nobody's stopping you from entering anything you like. How about it, Ogden? Is she a woman?"

"Well . . . really . . . oh, dear—"

"Please!" Iantha Delfoiros rolled her violet-blue eyes at the bewildered referee. "I should so like to swim in this nice pool with all these nice people!"

Wambach sighed. "All right, my dear, you shall!"

"Whoopee!" cried Laird, the cry being taken up by Vining, the members of the Knickerbocker Swimming Club, the other officials, and lastly the spectators. The noise in the enclosed space made sensitive eardrums wince.

"Wait a minute," yelped Connaught when the echoed had died. "Look here, page 19 of the rules. 'Regulation Costume, Women: Suits must be of dark color, with skirt attached. Leg is to reach—' and so forth. Right here it says it. She can't swim the way she is, not in a sanctioned meet."

"That's true," said Wambach. "Let's see—"

Horwitz looked up from his little score-sheet littered table. "Maybe one of the girls has a halter she could borrow," he suggested. "That would be *something.*"

"Halter, phooey!" snapped Connaught. "This means a regular suit with legs and skirt, and everybody knows it."

"But she hasn't got any legs!" cried Laird. "How could she get into—"

"That's just the pernt! If she can't wear a suit with legs, and the rules say you gotta have legs, she can't wear the regulation suit, and she can't compete! I gotcha that time! Ha-ha, I'm sneering!"

"I'm afraid not, Louie," said Vining, thumbing his own copy of the rule book. He held it up to the light and read: " 'Note.—These rules are approximate, the idea being to bar costumes which are immodest, or will attract undue attention and comment. The referee shall have the power'—et cetera, et cetera. If we cut the legs out of a regular suit, and she pulled the rest of it on over her head, that would be modest enough for all practical purposes. Wouldn't it, Mr. Wambach?"

"Dear me—I don't know—I suppose it would."

Laird hissed to one of his pupils, "Hey, listen, Miss Havranek! You know where my suitcase is? Well, you get one of the extra suits out of it, and there's a pair of scissors in with the first-aid things. You fix that suit up so Iantha can wear it."

Connaught subsided. "I see now," he said bitterly, "why you guys wanted to finish with a 300-yard free style instead of a relay. If I'd'a' known what you were planning—and, you, Mark Vining, if I ever get in a jam, I'll go to jail before I hire you for a lawyer, so help me."

Mrs. Santalucia had been glowering at Iantha Delfoiros. Suddenly she turned to Connaught. "Thissa no fair. I swim against people. I no gotta swim against moimaids."

"Please, Maria, don't *you* desert me," wailed Connaught.

"I no swim tonight."

Connaught looked up appealingly to the balcony. Mr. Santalucia and the little Santalucias, guessing what was happening, burst into a chorus of: "Go on, mamma! You show them, mamma!"

"Aw right. I swim one, maybe two races. If I see I no got a chance, I no swim no more."

"That's better, Maria. It wouldn't really count if she beat you anyway." Connaught headed for the door, saying something about "telephone" on the way.

Despite the delays in starting the meet, nobody left the pool room through boredom; in fact the empty seats in the balcony were full by this time and people were standing up behind them. Word had got around the Hotel Creston that something was up.

By the time Louis Connaught returned, Laird and Vining were pulling the altered bathing suit on over Iantha's head. It didn't reach quite as far as they expected, having been designed for a slightly slimmer swimmer. Not that Iantha was fat. But her human part, if not exactly plump, was at least comfortably upholstered, so that no bones showed. Iantha squirmed around in the suit a good deal, and threw a laughing remark in Greek to Wambach, whose expression showed that he hoped it didn't mean what he suspected it did.

Laird said, "Now listen, Iantha, remember not to move till the gun goes off. And remember that you swim directly over the black line on the bottom, not between two lines."

"Are they going to shoot a gun? Oh, I am afraid of shooting!"

"It's nothing to be afraid of; just blank cartridges. They don't hurt anybody. And it won't be so loud inside that cap."

"Herb," said Vining, "won't she lose time getting off, not being able to make a flat dive like the others?"

"She will. But it won't matter. She can swim a mile in *four* minutes, without really trying."

Ritchey, the starter, announced the 50-yard free style. He called: "All right, everybody, line up."

Iantha slithered off her chair and crawled over to the starting platform. The other girls were all standing with feet together, bodies bent forward at the hips, and arms pointing backward. Iantha got into a curious position of her own, with her tail under her and her weight resting on her hands and flukes.

"Hey! Protest!" shouted Connaught. "The rules say that all races, except back strokes, are started with dives. What kind of a dive do you call that?"

"Oh, dear," said Wambach. "What—"

"That," said Vining urbanely, "is a mermaid dive. You couldn't expect her to stand upright on her tail."

"But that's just it!" cried Connaught. "First you enter a non-regulation swimmer. Then you put a non-regulation suit on her. Then you start her off with a non-regulation dive. Ain't there anything you guys do like other people?"

"But," said Vining, looking through the rule book, "It doesn't say—here it is. 'The start in all races shall be made with a dive.' But there's nothing in the rules about what kind of dive shall be used. And the dictionary defines a dive simply as a 'plunge into water.' So if you jump in feet first holding your nose, that's a dive for the purpose of the discussion. And in my years of watching swimming meets I've seen some funnier starting-dives than Miss Delfoiros's."

"I suppose he's right," said Wambach.

"O.K., O.K.," snarled Connaught. "But the next time I have a meet with you and Herb, I bring a lawyer along too, see?"

Ritchey's gun went off. Vining noticed that Iantha flinched a little at the report, and perhaps was slowed down a trifle in getting off by it. The other girls' bodies shot out horizontally to smack the water loudly, but Iantha slipped in with the smooth, unhurried motion of a diving seal. Lacking the advantage of feet to push off with, she was several yards behind the other swimmers before she really got started. Mrs. Santalucia had taken her usual lead, foaming along with the slow strokes of her webbed hands.

Iantha didn't bother to come to the surface except at the turn, where she had been specifically ordered to come up so the judge of the turns wouldn't raise arguments as to whether she had touched the end, and at the finish. She hardly used her arms at all, except for an occasional flip of her trailing hands to steer her. The swift up-and-down flutter of the powerful tail-flukes sent her through the water like a torpedo, her wake appearing on the surface six or eight feet behind her. As she shot through the as yet unruffled waters at the far end of the pool on the first leg, Vining, who had gone around to the side to watch, noticed that she had the power of closing her nostrils under water, like a seal or hippopotamus.

Mrs. Santalucia finished the race in the very creditable time of 29.8 seconds. But Iantha Delfoiros arrived, not merely first, but in the time of 8.0 seconds. At the finish she didn't reach up to touch the starting-platform, and then hoist herself out by her arms the way human swimmers do. She simply angled up sharply, left the water like a leaping trout, and came down with a moist smack on the concrete, almost bowling over a timekeeper. By the time the other contestants had completed the turn she was sitting on the platform with her tail curled under her. As the girls foamed laboriously down the final leg, she smiled dazzlingly at Vining, who had had to run to be in the finish.

"That," she said, "was much fun, Mark. I am so glad you and 'Erbert put me in these races."

Mrs. Santalucia climbed out and walked over to Horwitz's table. That young man was staring in disbelief at the figures he had just written.

"Yes," he said, "that's what it says. Miss Iantha Delfoiros, 8.0; Mrs. Maria Santalucia, 29.8. Please don't drip on my score sheets, lady. Say, Wambach, isn't this a world's record or something?"

"My word!" said Wambach. "It's less than a half the existing short-course record. Less than a third, maybe; I'd have to check it. Dear me, I'll have to take it up with the Committee. I don't know whether they'd allow it; I don't think they will, even though there isn't any specific rule against mermaids."

Vining spoke up. "I think we've complied with all the requirements to have records recognized, Mr. Wambach. Miss Delfoiros was entered in advance like all the others."

"Yes, yes, Mr. Vining, but don't you see, a record's a serious matter. No ordinary human being could ever come near a time like that."

"Unless he used an outboard motor," said Connaught. "If you allow contestants to use tail fins like Miss Delfurrus, you ought to let 'em use propellers. I don't see why these guys should be the only ones to be let bust rules all over the place, and then think up lawyer arguments why it's O.K. I'm gonna get me a lawyer, too."

"That's all right, Ogden," said Laird. "You take it up with the Committee, but we don't really care much about the records anyway, so long as we can lick Louie here." He smiled indulgently at Connaught, who sputtered with fury.

"I no swim," announced Mrs. Santalucia. "This is all crazy business. I no get a chance."

"Now, Maria," said Connaught, taking her aside, "just once more, won't you please? My reputation—" The rest of his words were drowned in the general reverberation of the pool room. But at the end of them the redoubtable female appeared to have given into his entreaties.

The 100-yard free style started in much the same manner as the 50-yard. Iantha didn't flinch at the gun this time, and got off to a good start. She skimmed along just below the surface, raising a wake like a tuna-clipper. These waves confused the swimmer in the adjacent lane, who happened to be Miss Breitenfeld of the Creston Club. As a result, on her first return leg, Iantha met Miss Breitenfeld swimming athwart her—Iantha's—lane, and rammed the unfortunate girl amidships, Miss Breitenfeld went down without even a gurgle, spewing bubbles.

Connaught shrieked: "Foul! Foul!" though in the general uproar it sounded like "Wow, wow!" Several swimmers who weren't racing dove in to the rescue, and the race came to a stop in general confusion and pandemonium. When Miss Breitenfeld was hauled out it was found that she had merely had the wind knocked out of her and had swallowed considerable water.

Mark Vining, looking around for Iantha, found her holding onto the edge of the pool and shaking her head. Presently she crawled out, crying: "Is she 'urt? Is she 'urt? Oh, I am so sorree! I did not think there would be anybody in my lane, so I did not look ahead."

"See?" yelled Connaught. "See, Wambach? See what happens? They ain't satisfied to walk away with the races with their fish-woman. No, they gotta try to cripple my swimmers by butting their slats in. Herb," he went on nastily, "why dontcha get a pet swordfish? Then when you rammed one of my poor girls she'd be out of competition for good."

"Oh," said Iantha. "I did not mean . . . it was an accident!"

"Accident my foot!"

"But it was. Mr. Referee, I do not want to bump people. My 'ead 'urts, and my neck also. You think I try to break my neck on purpose?" Iantha's altered suit had crawled up under her armpits, but nobody noticed particularly.

"Sure it was an accident," bellowed Laird. "Anybody could see that. And, listen, if anybody was fouled it was Miss Delfoiros."

"Certainly," chimed in Vining. "She was in her own lane, and the other girl wasn't."

"Oh, dear me," said Wambach. "I suppose they're right again. This'll have to be re-swum anyway. Does Miss Breitenfeld want to compete?"

Miss Breitenfeld didn't but the others lined up again. This time the race went off without untoward incident. Iantha again made a spectacular leaping finish, just as the other three swimmers were half-way down the second of their four legs.

When Mrs. Santalucia emerged this time, she said to Connaught: "I swim no more. That is final."

"Oh, but Maria—" It got him nowhere. Finally he said, "Will you swim in the races that she don't enter?"

"Is there any?"

"I think so. Hey, Horowitz, Miss Delfurrus ain't entered in the breast stroke, is she?"

Horowitz looked. "No, she isn't," he said.

"That's something. Say, Herb, how come you didn't put your fish-woman in the breast stroke?"

Vining answered for Laird. "Look at your rules, Louie. 'The feet shall be drawn up simultaneously, the knees bent and open,' etcetera. The rules for back stroke and free style don't say anything about how the legs shall be used, but those for breast stroke do. So no legs, no breast stroke. We aren't giving you a chance to make any legitimate protests."

"Legitimate protests!" Connaught turned away, sputtering.

While the dives were being run off, Vining, watching, became aware of an ethereal melody. First he thought it was in his head. Then he was sure it was coming from one of the spectators. He finally located the source; it was Iantha Delfoiros, sitting in her wheel chair and singing softly. By leaning nearer he could make out the words:

> *"Die schonstte Jungfrau sitzet*
> *Dort ober wunderbar;*
> *Ihr goldnes Geschmeide blitzet;*
> *Sie kaemmt ihr goldenes Haar."*

Vining went over quietly. "Iantha," he said. "Pull your bathing suit down, and don't sing."

She complied, looking up at him with a giggle. "But that is a nice song! I learn it from a wrecked German sailor. It is about one of my people."

"I know, but it'll distract the judges. They have to watch the dives closely, and the place is too noisy as it is."

"Such a nice man you are, Mark, but so serious!" She giggled again.

Vining wondered at the subtle change in the mermaid's manner. Then a horrible thought struck him.

"Herb!" he whispered. "Didn't she say something last night about getting drunk on fresh water?"

Laird looked up. "Yes. She— The water in the pools' fresh! I never thought of that. Is she showing signs?"

"I think she is."

"Listen, Mark, what'll we do?"

"I don't know. She's entered in two more events, isn't she. Back stroke and 300-yard free style?"

"Yes."

"Well, why not withdraw her from the back stroke, and give her a chance to sober up before the final event?"

"Can't. Even with all her firsts we aren't going to win by any big margin. Louie has the edge on us in the dives, and Mrs. Santalucia'll win the breast stroke. In the events Iantha's in, if she takes first and Louie's girls take second and third, that means five points for us but four for him, so we have an advantage of only one point. And her world's record times don't give us any more points."

"Guess we'll have to keep her in and take a chance," said Vining glumly.

Iantha's demeanor was sober enough in lining up for the back stroke. Again she lost a fraction of a second in getting started by not having feet to push off with. But once she got started, the contest was even more one-sided than the free style races had been. The human part of her body was practically out of water, skimming the surface like the front half of a speedboat. She made paddling motions with her arms, but that was merely for technical reasons; the power was all furnished by the flukes. She didn't jump out onto the starting platform this time; for a flash Vining's heart almost stopped as the emerald-green bathing cap seemed about to crash into the tiles at the end of the pool. But Iantha had judged the distance to a fraction of an inch, and braked to a stop with her flukes just before striking.

The breast stroke was won easily by Mrs. Santalucia, though her slow plodding stroke was less spectacular than the butterfly of her competitors. The shrill cheers of the little Santalucias could be heard over the general hubbub. When the winner climbed out, she glowered at Iantha and said to Connaught: "Louie, if you ever put me in a meet wit' moimaids again, I no swim for you again, never. Now I go home." With which she marched off to the shower room.

Ritchey was just about to announce the final event, the 300-yard free style, when Connaught plucked his sleeve. "Jack," he said, "wait a second. One of my swimmers is gonna be delayed a coupla minutes." He went out a door.

Laird said to Vining: "Wonder what Louie's grinning about. He's got something nasty, I bet. He was 'phoning earlier, you remember."

"We'll soon see— What's that?" A hoarse bark wafted in from somewhere and rebounded from the walls.

Connaught reappeared carrying two buckets. Behind him was a little round man in three sweaters. Behind the little round man gallumped a glossy California sea lion. At the sight of the gently rippling, jade-green pool the animal barked joyously and skidded into the water, swam swiftly about, and popped out onto the landing-platform, barking. The bark had a peculiarly nerve-racking effect in the echoing pool room.

Ogden Wambach seized two handfuls of his sleek gray hair and tugged. "Connaught!" he shouted. "What is that?"

"Oh, that's just one of my swimmers, Mr. Wambach."

"Hey, listen!" rumbled Laird. "We're going to protest this time. Miss Delfoiros is at least a woman, even if she's a kind of peculiar one. But you can't call *that* a woman."

Connaught grinned like Satan looking over a new shipment of sinners. "Didn't you just say to go ahead and enter a sea lion if I wanted to?"

"I don't remember saying—"

"Yes, Herbert," said Wambach, looking haggard. "You did say it. There didn't used to be any trouble in deciding whether a swimmer was a woman or not. But now that you've brought in Miss Delfoiros, there doesn't seem to be any place we can draw a line."

"But look here, Ogden, there is such a thing as going too far—"

"That's just what I said about you!" shrilled Connaught.

Wambach took a deep breath. "Let's not shout, please. Herbert, technically you may have an argument. But after we allowed Miss Delfoiros to enter, I think it would be only sporting to let Louis have his sea lion. Especially after you told him to get one if he could."

Vining spoke up. "Oh, we're always glad to do the sporting thing. But I'm afraid the sea lion wasn't entered at the beginning of the meet as is required by the rules. We don't want to catch hell from the Committee—"

"Oh, yes, she was," said Connaught. "See!" He pointed to one of Horowitz's sheets. "Her name's Alice Black, and there it is."

"But," protested Vining, "I thought *that* was Alice Black." He pointed to a slim dark girl in a bathing suit who was sitting on a window ledge.

"It is," grinned Connaught. "It's just a coincidence that they both got the same name."

"You don't expect us to believe *that*?"

"I don't care whether you believe or not. It's so. Ain't the sea lion's name Alice Black?" He turned to the little fat man, who nodded.

"Let it pass," moaned Wambach. "We can't take time off to get this animal's birth certificate."

"Well, then," said Vining, "how about the regulation suit? Maybe you'd like to try to put a suit on your sea lion?"

"Don't have to. She's got one already. It grows on her. Yah, yah, yah, gotcha that time."

"I suppose," said Wambach, "that you *could* consider a natural sealskin pelt as equivalent to a bathing-suit."

"Sure you could. That's the pernt. Anyway the idea of suits is to be modest, and nobody gives a care about a sea lion's modesty."

Vining made a final point. "You refer to the animal as 'her,' but how do we know it's a female? Even Mr. Wambach wouldn't let you enter a male sea lion in a women's meet."

Wambach spoke: "How do you tell on a sea lion?"

Connaught looked at the little fat man. "Well, maybe we had better not go into that here. How would it be if I put up a ten-dollar bond that Alice is a female, and you checked on her sex later?"

"That seems fair," said Wambach.

Vining and Laird looked at each other. "Shall we let 'em get away with that, Mark?" asked the latter.

Vining rocked on his heels for a few seconds. Then he said, "I think we might as well. Can I see you outside a minute, Herb? You people don't mind holding up the race a couple of minutes more, do you? We'll be right back."

Connaught started to protest about further delay, but thought better of it. Laird presently reappeared looking unwontedly cheerful.

" 'Erbert!" said Iantha.

"Yes?" he put his head down.

"I'm afraid—"

"You're afraid Alice might bite you in the water? Well, I wouldn't want that—"

"Oh, no, not afraid that way. Alice, poof! If she gets nasty I give her one with the tail. But I am afraid she can swim faster than me."

"Listen, Iantha, you just go ahead and swim the best you can. Twelve legs, remember. And don't be surprised, no matter what happens."

"What you two saying?" asked Connaught suspiciously.

"None of your business, Louie. Whatcha got in that pail? *Fish?* I see how you're going to work this. Wanta give up and concede the meet now?"

Connaught merely snorted.

The only competitors in the 300-yard free style race were Iantha Delfoiros and the sea lion, allegedly named Alice. The normal members of both clubs declared that nothing would induce them to get into the pool with the animal. Not even the importance of collecting a third-place point would move them.

Iantha got into her usual starting position. Beside her the little round man maneuvered Alice, holding her by an improvised leash made of a length of rope. At the far end, Connaught had placed himself and one of the buckets.

Ritchey fired his gun; the little man slipped the leash and said: "Go get 'em, Alice!" Connaught took a fish out of his bucket and waved it. But Alice, frightened by the shot, set up a furious barking and stayed where she was. Not till Iantha had almost reached the far end of the pool did Alice sight the fish at the other end. Then she slid off and shot down the water like a streak. Those who have seen sea lions merely loafing about a pool in a zoo or aquarium have no conception of how fast they can go when they try. Fast as the mermaid was, the sea lion was faster. She made two bucking jumps out of water before she arrived and oozed out onto the concrete. One gulp and the fish had vanished.

Alice spotted the bucket and tried to get her head into it. Connaught fended her off as best he could with his feet. At the starting end, the little round man had taken a fish out of the other bucket and was waving it, calling: "Here, Alice!" Alice didn't get the idea until Iantha had finished her second leg. Then she went like the proverbial bat from hell.

The same trouble occurred at the starting end of the pool; Alice didn't see why she should swim twenty-five yards for a fish when there were plenty of them a few feet away. The result was that at the half-way-mark Iantha was two legs ahead. But then Alice, who was no dope as sea lions go, caught on. She caught up with and passed Iantha in the middle of her eighth leg, droozling out of the water at each end long enough to gulp a fish and then speeding down

to the other end. In the middle of the tenth leg she
was ten yards ahead of the mermaid.

At that point Mark Vining appeared through the
door, running. In each hand he held a bowl of goldfish by the edge. Behind him came Miss Havranek
and Miss Tufts, also of the Knickerbockers, both
similarly burdened. The guests of the Hotel Creston
had been mildly curious when a dark, severe-looking
young man and two girls in bathing suits had dashed
into the lobby and made off with the six bowls. But
they had been too well-bred to inquire directly about
the rape of the goldfish.

Vining ran down the side of the pool to a point
near the far end. There he extended his arms and
inverted the bowls. Water and fish cascaded into the
pool. Miss Havranek and Miss Tufts did likewise at
other points along the edge of the pool.

Results were immediate. The bowls had been large,
and each had contained about six or eight fair-sized
goldfish. The forty-odd bright-colored fish, terrified
by their rough handling, darted hither and thither
about the pool, or at least went as fast as their
inefficient build would permit them. Alice, in the
middle of her ninth leg, angled off sharply. Nobody
saw her snatch the fish; one second it was there, and
the next it wasn't. Alice doubled with a swirl of
flippers and shot diagonally across the pool. Another
fish vanished. Forgotten were her master and Louis
Connaught and their buckets. This was much more
fun. Meanwhile, Iantha finished her race, narrowly
avoiding a collision with the seat lion on her last leg.

Connaught hurled the fish he was holding as far as
he could. Alice snapped it up and went on hunting.
Connaught ran toward the starting-platform, yelling:
"Foul! Foul! Protest! Protest! Foul! Foul!"

He arrived to find the timekeepers comparing
watches on Iantha's swim, Laird and Vining doing a

kind of war dance, and Ogden Wambach looking like
the March Hare on the twenty-eighth of February.
"Stop!" cried the referee. "Stop, Louie! If you shout
like that you'll drive me mad! I'm almost mad now! I
know what you're going to say."

"Well . . . well . . . why don't you do something,
then? Why don't you tell these crooks where to head
in? Why don't you have 'em expelled from the Union?
Why don't you—"

"Relax, Louie," said Vining. "We haven't done
anything illegal."

"*What?* Why, you dirty—"

"Easy, easy." Vining looked speculatively at his
fist. The little man followed his glance and quieted
somewhat. "There's nothing in the rules about putting fish into a pool. Intelligent swimmers, like Miss
Delfoiros, know enough to ignore them when they're
swimming a race."

"But . . . what . . . why you—"

Vining walked off, leaving the two coaches and the
referee to fight it out. He looked for Iantha. She was
sitting on the edge of the pool, paddling in the water
with her flukes. Beside her were four feebly flopping
goldfish laid out in a row on the tiles. As he approached, she picked one up and put the front end of
it in her mouth. There was a flash of pearly teeth
and a spasmodic flutter of the fish's tail, and the front
half of the fish was gone. The other half followed
immediately.

At that instant Alice spotted the three remaining
fish. The sea lion had cleaned out the pool, and was
now slithering around on the concrete, barking and
looking for more prey. She galumphed past Vining
toward the mermaid.

Iantha saw her coming. The mermaid hoisted her
tail out of the water, pivoted where she sat, swung
the tail up in a curve, and brought the flukes down
on the sea lion's head with a loud *spat*. Vining, who

was twenty feet off, could have sworn he felt the wind of the blow.

Alice gave a squawk of pain and astonishment and slithered away, shaking her head. She darted past Vining again, and for reasons best known to herself hobbled over to the center of the argument and bit Ogden Wambach in the leg. The referee screeched and climbed up on Horowitz's table.

"Hey," said the scorekeeper. "You're scattering my papers!"

"I still say they're publicity-hunting crooks!" yelled Connaught, waving his copy of the rule book at Wambach.

"Bunk!" bellowed Laird. "He's just sore because we can think up more stunts than he can. He started it, with his web-fingered woman."

"I'm going mad!" screamed Wambach. "You hear? Mad, mad, mad! One more word out of either of you and I'll have you suspended from the Union!"

"*Ow, ow, ow!*" barked Alice.

Iantha had finished her fish. She started to pull the bathing suit down again; changed her mind, pulled it off over her head, rolled it up, and threw it across the pool. Halfway across it unfolded and floated down onto the water. The mermaid then cleared her throat, took a deep breath, and in a clear singing soprano, launched into the heart-wrenching strains of:

> "Rheingold!
> Reines Gold,
> Wie lauter und hell
> Leuchtest hold du uns!
> Um dich, du klares—"

"Iantha!"

"What is it, Markee?" she giggled.

"I said, it's getting time to go home!"

"Oh, but I do not want to go home. I am having much fun.

> *"Nun wir klagen!*
> *Gebt uns das Gold—"*

"No, really, Iantha, we've got to go." He laid a hand on her shoulder. The touch made his blood tingle. At the same time it was plain that the remains of Iantha's carefully husbanded sobriety had gone where the woodbine twineth. The last race in fresh water had been like three oversized Manhattans. Through Vining's head ran an absurd but apt paraphrase of an old song:

> *"What shall we do with a drunken mermaid*
> *At three o'clock in the morning?"*

"Oh, Markee, always you are so serious when people are 'aving fun. But if you say 'please' I will come."

"Very well, please come. Here, put your arm around my neck, and I'll carry you to your chair."

Such, indeed was Mark Vining's intention. He got one hand around her waist and another under her tail. Then he tried to straighten up. He had forgotten that Iantha's tail was a good deal heavier than it looked. In fact, that long and powerful structure of bone, muscle, and cartilage ran the mermaid's total weight up to the surprising figure of over two hundred and fifty pounds. The result of his attempt was to send himself and his burden headlong into the pool. To the spectators it looked as though he had picked Iantha up and then deliberately dived in with her.

He came up and shook the water off of his head. Iantha popped up in front of him.

"So!" she gurgled. "You are 'aving fun with Iantha!

I think you are serious, but you want to play games! All right, I show you!" She brought her palm down smartly, filling Vining's mouth and nose with water. He struck out blindly for the edge of the pool. He was a powerful swimmer, but his street clothes hampered him. Another splash cascaded over his luckless head. He got his eyes clear in time to see Iantha's head go down and her flukes up.

"Markeeee!" The voice was behind him. He turned, and saw Iantha holding a large black block of soft rubber. This object was a plaything for users of the Hotel Creston's pool, and it had been left lying on the bottom during the meet.

"Catch!" cried Iantha gayly, and let drive. The block took Vining neatly between the eyes.

The next thing he knew he was lying on the wet concrete. He sat up and sneezed. His head seemed to be full of ammonia. Louis Connaught put away the smelling-salts bottle, and Laird shoved a glass containing a snort of whiskey at him. Beside him was Iantha, sitting on her curled-up tail. She was actually crying.

"Oh, Markee, you are not dead? You are all right? Oh, I am so sorry! I did not mean to 'it you."

"I'm all right, I guess," he said thickly. "Just an accident. Don't worry."

"Oh, I am so glad!" She grabbed his neck and gave it a hug that made its vertebrae creak alarmingly.

"Now," he said, "if I could dry out my clothes. Louie, could you . . . uh—"

"Sure," said Connaught, helping him up. "We'll put your clothes on the radiator in the men's shower room, and I can lend you a pair of pants and a sweatshirt while they're drying."

When Vining came out in his borrowed garments, he had to push his way through the throng that crowded the starting end of the pool room. He was relieved to note that Alice had disappeared. In the crowd Iantha in her wheel chair was holding court. In front of her stood a large man in a dinner jacket and a black coat, with his back to the pool.

"Permit me," he was saying. "I am Joseph Clement. Under my management nothing you wished in the way of a dramatic or musical career would be beyond you. I heard you sing, and I know that with but little training even the doors of the Metropolitan would fly open at your approach."

"No, Mr. Clement. It would be nice, but tomorrow I 'ave to leave for 'ome." She giggled.

"But my dear Miss Delfoiros—where is your home, if I may presume to ask?"

"Cyprus."

"Cyprus? Hm-m-m—let's see, where's that?"

"You do not know where Cyprus is? You are not a nice man. I do not like you. Go away."

"Oh, but my dear, dear Miss Del—"

"Go away I said. Scram."

"But—"

Iantha's tail came up and lashed out, catching the cloaked man in the solar plexus.

Little Miss Havranek looked at her teammate, Miss Tufts, as she prepared to make her third rescue of the evening. "Poisonally," she said, "I am getting sick of pulling dopes out of this pool."

The sky was just turning gray the next morning when Laird drove his huge old town car out into the driveway of his house in the Bronx. Although he always drove himself, he couldn't resist the dirt-cheap prices at which second-hand town cars can be obtained. Now the car had the detachable top over the driver's seat in place, with good reason; the wind was driving a heavy rain almost horizontally.

He got out and helped Vining carry Iantha into the car. Vining got in the back with the mermaid. He spoke into the voice tube: "Jones Beach, Chauncey."

"Aye, aye, sir," came the reply. "Listen, Mark, you sure we remembered everything?"

"I made a list and checked it." He yawned. "I could have done with some more sleep last night. Are you sure you won't fall asleep at the wheel?"

"Listen, Mark, with all the coffee I got sloshing around in me, I won't get to sleep for a week."

"We certainly picked a nice time to leave."

"I know we did. In a coupla hours the place'll be covered six deep with reporters. If it weren't for the weather, they might be arriving now. When they do, they'll find the horse has stolen the stable door—that isn't what I mean, but you get the idea. Listen, you better pull down some of those curtains until we get out on Long Island."

"Righto, Herb."

Iantha spoke up in a small voice. "Was I very bad last night when I was drunk, Mark?"

"Not very. At least, not worse than I'd be if I went swimming in a tank of sherry."

"I am so sorry—always I try to be nice, but the fresh water gets me out of my head. And that poor Mr. Clement, that I pushed into the water—"

"Oh, he's used to temperamental people. That's his business. But I don't know that it was such a good idea on the way home to stick your tail out of the car and biff that cop under the chin with it."

She giggled. "But he looked so surprised!"

"I'll say he did! But a surprised cop is sometimes a tough customer."

"Will that make trouble for you?"

"I don't think so. If he's a wise cop, he won't report it at all. You know how the report would read: 'Attacked by mermaid at corner Broadway and Ninety-eighth Street, 11:45 p.m.' And *where* did you learn the unexpurgated version of 'Barnacle Bill the Sailor'?"

"A Greek sponge diver I met in Florida told me.

'E is a friend of us mer-folk, and he taught me my first English. 'E used to joke about my Cypriot accent when we talked Greek. It is a pretty song, is it not?"

"I don't think 'pretty' is exactly the word I'd use."

" 'Oo won the meet? I never did 'ear."

"Oh, Louie and Herb talked it over, and decided they'd both get so much publicity out of it that it didn't much matter. They're leaving it up to the A.A.U., who will get a first-class headache. For instance, we'll claim we didn't foul Alice, because Louie had already disqualified her by his calling and fish-waving. You see that's coaching, and coaching a competitor during an event is illegal. But, look here, Iantha, why do you have to leave so abruptly?"

She shrugged. "My business with 'Erbert is over, and I promised to get back to Cyprus before my sister's baby was born."

"You don't lay eggs? But of course you don't. Didn't I just prove last night you were mammals?"

"Markee, what an idea! Anyway, I do not want to stay around. I like you and I like 'Erbert, but I do not like living on land. You just imagine living in water for yourself, and you get an idea. And if I stay, the newspapers come, and soon all New York knows about me. We mer-folk do not believe in letting the land men know about us."

"Why?"

"We used to be friends with them sometimes, and always it made trouble. And now they 'ave guns and go around shooting things a mile away, to collect them, my great-uncle was shot in the tail last year by some aviator man who thought he was a porpoise or something. We don't like being collected. So when we see a boat or an airplane coming, we duck down and swim away quick."

"I suppose," said Vining slowly, "that that's why there were plenty of reports of mer-folks up a few centuries ago, and then they stopped, so that now people don't believe they exist."

"Yes. We are smart, and we can see as far as the land men can. So you do not catch us very often. That is why this business with 'Erbert, to buy ten thousand caps for the mer-folk, 'as to be secret. Not even his company will know about it. But they will not care if they get their money. And we shall not 'ave to sit on rocks drying our 'air so much. Maybe later we can arrange to buy some good knives and spears the same way. They would be better than the shell things we use now."

"I suppose you get all these old coins out of wrecks?"

"Yes. I know of one just off . . . no, I must not tell you. If the land men know about a wreck, they come with divers. Of course, the very deep ones we do not care about, because we cannot dive down that far. We 'ave to come up for air, like a whale."

"How did Herb happen to suck you in on that swimming meet?"

"Oh, I promised him when he asked—when I did not know 'ow much what-you-call-it fuss there would be. When I found out, he would not let me go back on my promise. I think he 'as a conscience about that, and that is why he gave me that nice fish spear."

"Do you ever expect to get back this way?"

"No, I do not think so. We 'ad a committee to see about the caps, and they chose me to represent them. But now that is arranged, and there is no more reason for me going out on land again."

He was silent for a while. Then he burst out: "Iantha, I just can't believe that you're starting off this morning to swim the Atlantic, and I'll never see you again."

She patted his hand. "Maybe you cannot, but that is so. Remember, friendships between my folks and yours always make people un'appy. I shall remember you a long time, but that is all there will ever be to it."

He growled something in his throat, looking straight in front of him.

She said: "Mark, you know I like you, and I think you like me. 'Erbert 'as a moving-picture machine in his house, and he showed me some pictures of 'ow the land folk live.

"These pictures showed a custom of the people in this country, when they like each other. It is called—kissing, I think. I should like to learn that custom."

"Huh? You mean *me*?" To a man of Vining's temperament, the shock was almost physically painful. But her arms were already sliding around his neck. Presently twenty firecrackers, six Roman candles, and a skyrocket seemed to go off inside him.

"Here we are, folks," called Laird. Getting no response, he repeated the statement more loudly. A faint and unenthusiastic "Yeah" came through the voice tube.

Jones Beach was bleak under the lowering March clouds. The wind drove the rain against the car windows.

They drove down the beach road a way, till the tall tower was lost in the rain. Nobody was in sight.

The men carried Iantha down onto the beach and brought the things she was taking. These consisted of a boxful of cans of sardines, with a trap to go over the shoulders; a similar but smaller container with her personal belongings, and the fish spear, with which she might be able to pick up lunch on the way.

Iantha peeled off her land-woman's clothes and pulled on the emerald bathing cap. Vining, watching her with the skirt of his overcoat whipping about his

legs, felt as if his heart was running out of his damp
shoes onto the sand.

They shook hands, and Iantha kissed them both.
She squirmed down the sand and into the water.
Then she was gone. Vining thought he saw her wave
back from the crest of a wave, but in that visibility he
couldn't be sure.

They walked back to the car, squinting against the
drops. Laird said: "Listen, Mark, you look as if you'd
just taken a right to the button."

Vining merely grunted. He had got in front with
Laird, and was drying his glasses with his handkerchief, as if that were an important and delicate
operation.

"Don't tell me you're hooked?"

"So what?"

"Well, I suppose you know there's absolutely nothing you can do about it."

"Herb?" Vining snapped angrily. "Do you have to
point out the obvious?"

Laird, sympathizing with his friend's feelings, did
not take offense. After they had driven a while,
Vining spoke on his own initiative. "That," he said,
"is the only woman I've ever known that made me
feel at ease. I could talk to her."

Later, he said, "I never felt so mixed up in
my life. I doubt whether anybody else ever did,
either. Maybe I ought to feel relieved it's over. But
I don't."

Pause. Then: "You'll drop me in Manhattan on
your way back, won't you?"

"Sure, anywhere you say. Your apartment?"

"Anywhere near Times Square will do. There's a
bar there I like."

So, thought Laird, at least the normal male's instincts were functioning correctly in the crisis.

When he let Vining out on Forth-sixth Street,

the young lawyer walked off into the rain whistling.
The whistle surprised Laird. Then he recognized the
tune as one that was written for one of Kipling's
poems. But he couldn't, at the moment, think which
one.

A GOOD KNIGHT'S WORK

Robert Bloch

I am stepping on the gas, air is pouring into the truck and curses are pouring out, because I feel like I get up on the wrong side of the gutter this morning.

Back in the old days I am always informing the mob how I am going to get away from it all and buy a little farm in the country and raise chickens. So now I raise chickens and wish I am back in the old days raising hell.

It is one of those things, and today it is maybe two or three of them, in spades. Perhaps you are lucky and do not live in the Corn Belt, so I will mention a few items to show that the guy naming it knows what he's talking about.

This morning I wake up at four a.m. because fifty thousand sparrows are holding a Communist rally under the window. I knock my shins over a wheel-barrow in the back yard because the plumbing is remote. When I get dressed I have to play tag with fifty chickens I am taking to market, and by the time

187

that's over I am covered with more feathers than a senator who gets adopted by Indians in a newsreel. After which all I do is load the cacklers on the truck, drive fifty miles to town, sell biddies at a loss, and drive back—strictly without breakfast.

Breakfast I must catch down the road at the tavern, where I got to pay ten bucks to Thin Tommy Malloon for protection.

That is my set-up and explains why I am not exactly bubbling over with good spirits. There is nothing to do about it but keep a stiff upper lip— mostly around the bottle I carry with me on the trip back.

Well, I am almost feeling better after a few quick ones, and am just about ready to stop my moans and groans when I spot this sign on the road.

I don't know how it is with you. But this is how it is with me. I do not like signs on the road a bit, and of all the signs I do not like, the SIAMESE SHAVE signs I hate in spades.

They stand along the highway in series, and each of them has a line of poetry on it so when you pass them all you read a little poem about SIAMESE SHAVE. They are like the Old Lady Goose rhymes they feed the juveniles, and I do not have any love for Ma Goose and her poetry.

Anyhow, when I see this first sign I let out some steam and take another nip. But I cannot resist reading the sign because I always do. It says:

"DON'T WEAR A LONG BEARD."

And a little further on the second one reads:

"LIKE A GOAT."

Pretty soon I come to the third one, saying:

"JUST TAKE A RAZOR."

And all at once I'm happy, hoping maybe somebody made a mistake and the fourth sign will say:

"AND CUT YOUR THROAT!"

So I can hardly wait to see the last one, and I'm

looking ahead on the road, squinting hard. Then I slam on the brakes.

No, I don't see a sign. There is a *thing* blocking the road, instead. *Two* things.

One of these things is a horse. At least, it looks more like a horse than anything else I could see on four drinks. It is a horse covered with a kind of awning, or tent that hangs down over its legs and out on its neck. In fact, I noticed that this horse is wearing a mask over its head with eyeholes, like it belonged to the Ku Klux Klan.

The other *thing* is riding the horse. It is all silver, from head to foot, and I notice that there is a long plume growing out of its head. It looks like a man, and it has a long, sharp pole in one hand and the top off a garbage can in the other.

Now when I look at this party I am certain of only one thing. This is not the Lone Ranger.

When I drive a little closer my baby-blue eyes tell me that what I am staring at is a man dressed up in a suit of armor, and that the long sharp pole is nothing but a little thing like a twelve-foot spear with a razor on the end.

Who he is and why he is dressed up this way may be very interesting to certain parties like the State police, but I am very far away from being one. Also I am very far away from Thin Tommy Malloon who is waiting for my ten bucks protection money. Thin Tommy is not the kind of a man who likes waiting, especially for money.

So when I see Old Ironsides blocking the road, I place my head outside the window and request, "Get the hell out of the way, buddy!" in a loud but polite voice.

Which turns out to be a mistake, in spades and no trump.

*   *   *

The party in the tin tuxedo just looks at the truck coming his way, and cocks his iron head when he sees steam coming from the carburetor. The exhaust is beginning to make trombone noises, because I am stepping hard on the gas, and this seems to make up the heavy dresser's mind for him.

"Yoicks!" howls his voice behind his helmet. "A dragon!"

And all at once he levels that lance of his, knocks his tootsies against the horse's ribs, and starts coming head-on for the truck.

"For Pendragon and England!" he bawls, over the clanking. And charges straight ahead like a baby tank.

That twelve-foot razor of his is pointed straight for my radiator, and I do not wish him to cut my motor, so naturally I swing the old truck out of the way.

This merely blows the carburetor cap higher than the national debt, and out shoots enough steam and hot air to supply a dozen congressmen.

The horse rears up, and the tintype lets out a yap, letting his lance loose. Instead of hitting the radiator, it smashes my windshield.

Also my temper. I stop the truck and get out, fast. "Now, listen, buddy," I reason with him.

"Aha!" comes the voice from under the helmet. "A wizard!" He uses a brand of double-talk I do not soon forget. "Halt ye, for it is Pallagyn who speaks."

I am in no mood for orations, so I walk up to him, waving a pipe wrench.

"Bust my windows, eh, buddy? Monkey business on a public highway, is it? I'm going to—Yow!"

I am a personality that seldom hollers "Yow!" even at a burlesque show, but when this armor-plated jockey slides off his horse and comes for me, he is juggling a sharp six feet of sword. And six feet of sword sailing for your neck is worth a "Yow!" any day, I figure.

I also figure I had better duck unless I want a shave and a haircut, and it is lucky for me that Iron-lung has to move slow when he whams his sword down at me.

I come up under his guard and give him a rap on the old orange with my pipe wrench.

There is no result.

The steel king drops his sword and lets out another roar, and I caress his helmet again with the wrench. Still no result. I get my result on the third try. The wrench breaks.

And then his iron arms grab me, and I am in for it.

The first thing I know, everything is turning black as solitary, and my sparring partner is reaching for a shiver at his belt. I get my foot there, fast.

All I can do is push forward, but it works. About a hundred and fifty pounds of armor loses balance, and there is nothing for the guy inside to do except go down with it. Which he does, on his back. Then I am on his chest, and I roll up the Venetian blind on the front of his helmet.

"Hold, enough!" comes the double-talk from inside. "Prithee, hold!"

"O.K., buddy. But open up the mail box of yours. I want to see the face of the damned fool that tries to get me into a traffic accident with a load of tin."

He pulls up the shutters, and I get a peek at a purple face decorated with red whiskers. There are blue eyes, too, and they look down, ashamed.

"Ye are the first, O Wizard, to gaze upon the vanquished face of Sir Pallagyn of the Black Keep," he mumbles.

I get off his chest like it was the hot seat. Because, although I am very fond of nuts, I like them only in fruit cakes.

"I've got to be going," I mention. "I don't know who you are or why you are running around like this, and I maybe ought to have you run in, but I got business up the road, see? So long."

I start walking away and turn around. "Besides, my name is not O. Wizard."

"Verily," says the guy who calls himself Sir Pallagyn, getting up slow, with a lot of rattling. "Ye are a wizard, for ye ride a dragon breathing fire and steam—"

I am thinking of the fire and steam Thin Tommy Malloon is breathing right now, so I pay little or no attention, but get in the truck. Then this Pallagyn comes running up and yells, "Wait!"

"What for?"

"My steed and arms are yours by right of joust."

Something clicks inside my head, and even if it is an eight ball, I get interested. "Wait a minute," I suggest. "Just who are you and where do you hang out?"

"Why," says he, "as I bespoke, O Wizard—I am Sir Pallagyn of the Black Keep, sent here ensorcelled by Merlin, from Arthur's court at Camelot. And I hang out at the greaves in my armor," he adds, tucking in some cloth sticking out of the chinks and joints in his heavy suit.

"Huh?" is about the best I can do.

"And having bested me in fair combat, ye gain my steed and weapons, by custom of the joust." He shakes his head, making a noise like a Tommy-gun. "Merlin will be very angry when he hears of this, I wot."

"Merlin?"

"Merlin, the Gray Wizard, who sent me upon the quest," he explains. "He it was who sped me forward in Time, to quest for the Cappadocian Tabouret."

Now I am not altogether a lug—as you can tell by the way I look up some of the spelling on these items—and when something clicks inside my noggin it means I am thinking, but difficult.

I know I am dealing with the worst kind of screwball—the kind that bounces—but still there is some sense in what he is saying. I see this King Arthur and this Merlin in a picture once, and I see also some personalities in armor that are called knights, which means they are King Arthur's trigger men. They hang out around a big table in a stone hide-out and are always spoiling for trouble and going off on quests—which means, putting the goniff on stuff which doesn't belong on them, or copping dames from other knights.

But I figure all this happens maybe a hundred years ago, or so, over in Europe, before they throw away their armor and change into colored shirts to put the rackets on an organized paying basis.

And this line about going forward in Time to find something is practically impossible, unless you go for Einstein's theory, which I don't, preferring Ann Sheridan.

Still, it is you might say unusual, so I answer this squirrel. "What you're trying to tell me is that you come here from King Arthur's court and some magician sends you to find something?"

"Verily, O Wizard. Merlin counseled me that I might not be believed," says Pallagyn, sadlike. He chews on his mustache, without butter. He almost looks like he is promoting a weeper.

"I believe you, buddy," I say, wanting to cheer him up and also get out of here.

"Then take my mount and weapons—it is required by law of the joust," he insists.

Right then I figure I would rather take a drink. I do. It makes me feel better. I get out and walk over to the oat-burner. "I don't know what to do with this four-legged blue barrel," I tell him, "or your manicure set, either. But if it makes you happy, I will take them with me."

So I grab the nag and take him around back of the truck, let down the ramp and put him in. When I get back, Sir Pallagyn is piling his steel polo set into the front seat.

"I place these on the dragon for thee," he says.

"This isn't a dragon," I explain. "It's a Ford."

"Ford? Merlin did not speak of that creature." He climbs into the seat after his cutlery, looking afraid the steering wheel will bite him.

"Hey, where you going?"

"With thee, O Wizard. The steed and weapons are thine, but I must follow them, even into captivity. It is the law of the quest."

"You got laws on the brain, that's your trouble. Now listen, I don't like hitchhikers—"

Then I gander at my ticker and see it is almost ten and remember I am to meet Thin Tommy at eight. So I figure, why not? I will give this number a short lift down the pike and dump him where it is quiet and forget him. Maybe I can also find out whether or not there is somebody missing from Baycrest, which is the local laughing academy, and turn him in. Anyway, I have my date to keep, so I start the truck rolling.

This Pallagyn lets out a sort of whistle through his whiskers when I hit it up, so I say, "What's the matter, buddy, are you thirsty?"

"No," he gasps. "But we are flying!"

"Only doing forty," I tells him. "Look at the speedometer."

"Forty what? Speedometer?"

My noggin is clicking like a slot machine in a church bazaar. This baby isn't faking! I get another look at his armor and see it is solid stuff—not like fancy-dress costumes, but real heavy, with little designs in gold and silver running through it. And he doesn't know what a car is, or a speedometer!

"You need a drink," I says, taking it for him, and then passing him the bottle.

"Mead?" he says.

"No, Haig & Haig. Try a slug."

He tilts the bottle and takes a terrific triple-tongue. He lets out a roar and turns redder than his whiskers.

"I am bewitched!" he yells. "Ye black wizard!"

"Hold it. You'll cool off in a minute. Besides, I'm not a wizard. I'm a truck farmer, believe it or not, and don't let them kid you down at the Bastille. I'm through with the rackets."

He gets quieter in a minute and begins to ask me questions. Before I know it, I am explaining who I am and what I am doing, and after another drink it doesn't seem so screwy to me any more.

Even when he tells me about this Merlin baby putting a spell on him and sending him through Time to go on a quest, I swallow it like my last shot. I break down and tell him to call me Butch. In a few minutes we're practically cell mates.

"Ye may call me Pallagyn," he says.

"O.K., Pal. How about another slug?"

This time he is more cautious, and it must go down fairly well, because he smacks his lips and doesn't hardly even turn pink.

"Might I inquire as to your destination, O Butch?" he lets out, after a minute or so.

"You might," I says. "There it is, straight ahead."

I point out the building we are just coming to. It is a roadhouse and tavern called "The Blunder Inn," and it is in this rat hole that Thin Tommy Malloon hangs his hat and holster. This I explain to Pal.

"It doth not resemble a rat hole," he comments.

"Any place where Thin Tommy gets in must be a rat hole," I tell him, "because Thin Tommy is a rat. He is a wrongo but strongo. Nevertheless, I must now go in and pay him his ten dollars for protection or he will sprinkle lye on my alfalfa."

"What do you mean?" asks Pallagyn.

So I explain to him very simple in words of three letters how Thin Tommy use to be a high number in the rackets back in town but decides to retire. How he buys this roadhouse and clips customers at night, but being naturally a very energetic type of guy, he gets bored unless he can clip customers by day, also. So he figures out that he can sell protection to farmers in the country just like he sells it to grocery stores and gas stations in the city.

"Protection?" interrupts Pallagyn.

"Yes, Pal. I have a little farm, and I must pay Thin Tommy ten a week or else I will have trouble, such as finding ground glass in my hen mash, or a pineapple in my silo."

"Ye pay to keep vandals from despoiling the crops?" asks the knight. "Would it not be expedient to discover the miscreants and punish them?"

"I *know* who would wreck the farm if I didn't pay," I reply. "Thin Tommy."

"Ah, now methinks I comprehend thy plight. Thou art a serf, and this Thin Thomas is thy overlord."

Somehow this remark, and the way Pallagyn says it, seems to show me up for a sucker. And I have just enough drink in me to resent it.

"I am no serf," I shout. "As a matter of fact, I am waiting a long time to fix the clock of this Thin Tommy. So today I pay him no ten dollars, and I am going in to tell him so to what he calls his face."

Pallagyn listens to me kind of close, because he seems pretty ignorant on English and grammar, but he catches on and smiles.

"Spoken like a right true knight," he says. "I shall accompany ye on this mission, for I find in my heart a liking for thy steadfast purpose, and a hatred of Thin Thomas."

"Sit where you are," I says, fast. "I will handle this myself. Because Thin Tommy does not like strangers coming into his joint in the daytime without an invitation, and you are dressed kind of loud and conspicuous. So you stay here," I tell him, "and have a drink."

And I pull up and climb out of the car and march into the tavern fast.

My heart is going fast also, because what I am about to do is enough to make any heart go fast in case Thin Tommy gets an idea to stop it from beating altogether. Which he sometimes does when he is irked, particularly over money.

Even so I walk up to the bar and sure enough, there is Thin Tommy standing there polishing the glasses with boxing gloves on. Only when I look again I realize these are not boxing gloves at all, but merely Thin Tommy's hands.

Thin Tommy is not really thin, you understand, but is called that because he weighs about three hundred fifty pounds, stripped—such as once a month, when he takes a bath.

"So, it's you!" he says, in a voice like a warden.

"Hello, Thin Tommy," I greet him. "How are tricks?"

"I will show you how tricks are if you do not cough up those ten berries fast and furious," grunts Thin Tommy. "All of the others have been here two or three hours ago, and I am waiting to go to the bank."

"Go right ahead," I tell him. "I wouldn't stop you."

Thin Tommy drops the glass he is polishing and leans over the bar. "Hand it over," he says through his teeth. They are big yellow teeth, all smashed together in not such a pleasant grin.

I grin right back at him because how can he see my knees shaking?

"I have nothing for you, Tommy," I get out. "In fact, that is why I stopped in, to tell you that from now on I do not require protection any longer."

"Ha!" yells Thin Tommy, pounding on the bar and then jumping around it with great speed for a man of his weight. "Bertram!" he calls. "Roscoe!"

Bertram and Roscoe are Tommy's two waiters, but I know Tommy is not calling them in to serve me.

They come running out of the back, and I see they have experience in such matters before, because Bertram is carrying a blackjack and Roscoe has a little knife in his hand. This knife worries me most, because I am practically certain that Roscoe is never a boy scout.

By the time I see all this, Thin Tommy is almost on top of me, and he lets go with one arm for my jaw. I bend my head down just in time, but Thin Tommy's other hand catches me from the side and slaps me across the room. I fall over a chair, and by this time Bertram and Roscoe are ready to wait on me. In fact, one of them pulls out the chair I fell over, and tries to hit me on the head with it.

I let out a yell and grab up a salt cellar from the table. This I push down Bertram's mouth, and I am just ready to throw a little pepper in Roscoe's eyes when Thin Tommy crashes over, grabs the knife from Roscoe's hand, and backs me into the corner.

All at once I hear a crash outside the door, and somebody hollers, "Yoicks! Pendragon and Pallagyn!"

Into the room gallops Sir Pallagyn. He has got his sword in one hand, and the empty bottle in the other, and he is full to the eyeballs with courage.

He lets the bottle go first and it catches Bertram in the side of the head, just when he is getting the salt cellar out of his mouth. Bertram slides down with a sort of moan, and Roscoe and Tommy turn around.

"It's one of them there rowboats, like I seen at the Fair!" remarks Thin Tommy.

"Yeah," says Roscoe, who is all at once very busy when Pallagyn comes for him with his sword. In fact Roscoe is so busy he falls over the chair and lands on his face, which gets caught in a cuspidor. Pallagyn is ready to whack him one when Thin Tommy drops hold of me and lets out a grunt.

He grabs up the blackjack and the dagger both in the same hand and lets fly. They bounce off Pallagyn's helmet, of course, so Thin Tommy tries a chair. This doesn't work, either, so he picks up the table.

Pallagyn just turns kind of surprised and starts coming for him. And Thin Tommy backs away.

"No . . . no—" he says. All at once he reaches into his hip pocket and pulls out the old lead poisoner.

"Watch out!" I yell, trying to get to Tommy before he can shoot. "Duck, Pal—duck!"

Pallagyn ducks, but he is still running forward and his armor is so heavy he can't stop if he wants to keep from falling over.

The gun goes off over his head, but then Sir Pallagyn is going on, and he runs right into Thin Tommy, butting his head into his stomach. Thin Tommy just gives one "Oooof!" and sits down backward, holding his belly where the helmet hit it, and he turns very green indeed.

Pallagyn sticks out his sword, but I say, "Never mind. This ought to teach him a lesson."

Going out, Thin Tommy just manages to whisper to me, "Who is that guy?"

"That," I tell him, "is my new hired man. So if I was you, I wouldn't plant any pineapples on my farm, because he is allergic to fruit."

So we leave and climb back into the truck.

"Thanks, Pal," I say. "You not only threw a scare into that monkey but you also saved my life. I am in debt to you, whoever you are, and if Thin Tommy didn't serve such rotgut, I would take you back in and buy you a drink."

"Verily, 'tis a trifle," says Pallagyn.

"I'll do you the same some day, Pal," I tell him. "You are my buddy."

"Ye could help me now, methinks."

"How?"

"Why, in pursuit of my quest. I was sent here by Merlin to seek the Cappadocian Tabouret."

"I do not know anything about the new night clubs," I tell him. "I am not an uptown boy any longer."

"The Cappadocian Tabouret," says Pallagyn, ignoring me, "is the table on which the Holy Grail will rest, once we find it."

"Holy Grail?"

So Pallagyn began to tell me a long yarn about how he is living in a castle with this King Arthur and a hundred other triggers who are all knights like he is. As near as I get it, all they do is sit around and drink and fight each other, which makes it look like this King Arthur is not so good in controlling his mob.

The brain in this outfit is this guy Merlin, who is a very prominent old fuddy in the Magician's Union. He is always sending the lads out to rescue dames that have been snatched, or to knock off the hoods of other mobs, but what he is really interested in is this Holy Grail.

I cannot catch exactly what the Holy Grail is, except it's kind of a loving cup or trophy that has disappeared from some hock shop back there in the Middle Ages. But everybody is hot to find it, including the big boys in the mob like Sir Galahad and Sir Lancelot.

When Pallagyn mentions these two I know I have heard of them some place, so naturally I ask questions and find out quite a bit about ancient times and knights and how they live and about the tournaments—which are pretty much the same as the Rose Bowl games, without a take—and many other items which are of great interest to an amateur scholar like myself.

But to slice a long story thin, Merlin cannot put the finger on this Holy Grail yet, although he is sending out parties every day to go on these quests for it. But he is a smart cookie in many another way, and one of his little tricks is to get himself coked up and then look into the future. For example, he tells King Arthur that he is going to have trouble some time ahead, and Pallagyn says he may be right, because he personally notices this Sir Lancelot making pigeon noises at Arthur's skirt. But gossip aside, one of the things Merlin sees in the future is this Cappadocian Tabouret, which is a sacred relic on which the Holy Grail is supposed to sit.

So the old hophead calls in Sir Pallagyn and says he is sending him on a quest for the glory of Britain, to get this table for the Holy Grail and bring it back.

All Merlin can do to help him is to put a spell on him and send him into the future to the time where he sees the Tabouret.

And he tells him a little about these times and this country, sprinkles a little powder on him, and all at once Pallagyn is sitting on his horse in the middle of County Trunk AA, where I find him.

"That is not exactly the easiest story in the world to believe," I remark, when Pallagyn finishes.

"Here I am," says the knight, which is about as good an answer as any.

For a minute I think I can understand how he must feel, being shipped off through Time into a new territory, without even a road map to help him. And since he is a good guy and saved my life, I figure the least I can do is try.

"Didn't this old snowbird give you a hint where it might be?" I ask.

"Merlin? Forsooth, he spoke of seeing it in a House of the Past."

"What kind of house?"

"House of the Past, methinks he named it."

"Never heard of it," I says, "unless he means a funeral parlor. And you don't catch me going into any stiff hotel."

I say this as we are driving into my yard, and I stop the truck.

"Let's grab a plate of lunch," I suggest. "Maybe we can think of something."

"Lunch?"

"Grub—hay—food."

"Here?"

"Yeah. This is my dump—house."

I salvage Pallagyn out of the car and take him inside. Then, while I fix the food, he sits there in the kitchen and asks me a thousand screwy questions. He is very ignorant about everything.

It turns out that back in his times, there is not enough civilization to put in your ear. He doesn't know what a stove is, or gas, and I can see why they call them the Dark Ages when he tells me he hasn't ever seen an electric light.

So I tell him everything, about cars and trains and airplanes and tractors and steamships, and then I break down and give him a few inside tips on how citizens live.

I hand it to him about the mobs and the rackets and the bluecoats, and politics and elections. Then I give him a few tips about science—machine guns and armored cars and tear gas and pineapples and fingerprints, all the latest stuff.

It is very hard to explain these matters to such an

ignorant guy as this Pallagyn, but he is so interested and grateful that I want to give him the right steer.

I even show him how to eat with a knife and fork, as it turns out at lunch that King Arthur's court doesn't go in for fancy table manners.

But I am not a schoolteacher, and after all, we are not getting any closer to Sir Pallagyn's problem, which is snatching this Tabouret in his quest.

So I begin asking him all over again about what it is and what it looks like and where this fink Merlin said he could find it.

And all he manages to come clean with is that it's in the House of the Past, and that Merlin sees it in a jag.

"Big place," he says. "And the Tabouret is guarded by men in blue."

"Police station?" I wonder.

"It is in a transparent coffin," he says.

I never see any of these, though I hear Stinky Raffelano is buried in one when he catches his slugs last year.

"Ye can see but cannot touch it," he remembers.

All at once I get it.

"It's under glass," I tell him. "In a museum."

"Glass?"

"Never mind what that is," I say. "Sure—guards. House of the Past. It's a museum in town."

I tell him what a museum is, and then start thinking.

"First thing to do is get a line on where it is. Then we can figure out how to pull the snatch."

"Snatch?"

"Steal it, Pal. Say—do you know what it looks like?"

"Verily. Merlin described it in utmost detail, lest I err and procure a spurious Tabouret."

"Good. Give me a line on it, will you?"

"Why, it is but a wooden tray of rough boards, with four short legs set at the corners. Brown is its hue, and it spans scarce-four hands in height. Plain it is, without decoration or adornment, for it was but crudely fashioned by the good Cappadocian Fathers."

"So," I say. "I think maybe I have a notion. Wait here," I tell him, "and improve your education."

And I hand him a copy of a movie magazine. I go down to the cellar, and when I come up after a while, Sir Pallagyn comes clanking up to me, all excited.

"Pray, and who is this fair damsel?" he asks, pointing out a shot of Ann Sothern in a bathing suit. "She has verily the appearance of the Lady of the Lake," he remarks. "Albeit with more . . . more—"

"You said it, Pal," I agree. "Much more, in spades. But here—does this look like the table you're after?"

"Od's blood, it is the very thing! From whence didst thou procure it?"

"Why it's nothing but a piece of old furniture I find laying down in the basement. A footstool, but I knock the stuffing out of it and scrape off some varnish. Now, all you got to do is get this Merlin to wave his wand and call you back, and you hand him over the goods. He will never catch wise," I say, "and it will save us a lot of trouble."

Pallagyn's puss falls in a little and he starts chewing his red mustache again.

"I fear, Sir Butch, thy ethics are not of the highest. I am aquest, nor could I present a spurious Tabouret in sight of mine own conscience."

So I see I am in for it. Of course it will be easy for me to tell this tin can to go chase his quest, but somehow I feel I owe him a good turn.

"I will work things out in a jiffy, Pal. You just go out and put your nag in the stable, and when you come back, I will have things fixed up."

"On thy honor?" he says, smiling all of a sudden.

"Sure. Shake."

He shakes until his armor rattles.

"Never mind," I say. "Take care of the nag and leave it to me."

He clunks out and I get busy on the phone.

When he comes back I am set.

"Come on out and hop in the truck," I invite. "We are on our way to pick up that furniture for you."

"Indeed? Then we really quest together, Sir Butch?"

"Don't ask any questions," I remark. "On your way."

I notice he fumbles with that movie magazine a minute, and when he sees me looking he blushes.

"I wouldst carry the image of this fair lady, as is the custom of the quest," he admits, tucking the picture of Ann Sothern in his helmet, so only her legs stick out over his forehead.

"O. K. by me, Pal. But come on, we got a drive ahead of us."

I grab up a pint, the fake Tabouret, and a glass cutter; head for the truck, and we're off.

It is a long drive, and I have plenty of time to explain the lay of the land to Sir Pallagyn. I tell him how I call the museum and find out if they have this table in hock. Then I hang up and call back in a different voice, telling them that I am an express man with a suit of armor on hand for them which I will send over.

"Pretty neat, eh, Pal?" I ask.

"But I do not comprehend. How did you talk to the museum if it is in the city and—"

I do not understand the telephone so good myself, because I never see the movie. "Young Tom Edison" or whatever, so I just pass it over.

"I am a wizard myself," I let it go.

"Still, I fail to perceive the plan. What place has armor in a House of the Past?"

"Why, it's a relic. Don't you know nobody wears armor no more? It's all bulletproof vests."

"Still, how doth that contrive for us to—snatch—the Tabouret?"

"Don't you get it? I'll carry you into the museum like an empty suit of armor. Then we will spot this Tabouret, I will set you down in a corner, and when the joint closes up you can snatch it very quick indeed. You can use this glass cutter to get it out, substitute this fake furniture in the case, and nobody will be hep to it the next morning. Simple."

"By're Lady, 'tis a marvel of cunning!"

I admit it sounds pat myself. But I notice we are now coming into some traffic, so I stop the truck and say, 'From now on you are nothing but a suit of armor with nothing inside. You climb into the back of the truck so citizens will not give you the queer eye, and lie quiet. When we get to the museum I will drag you out, and you just hold still. Remember?"

"Verily."

So Pallagyn hops into the back of the truck and lies down and I head into the city. Before I get too far I take myself a couple of quick ones because I am a little nervous, being so long since I pulled a job.

I am not exactly floating but my feet do not touch bottom when we get downtown. Which is why I accidentally touch a fender of the car ahead of me when we stop in traffic. In fact I touch it so that it drops off.

It is a big black job, and an old Whitey with a mean-looking puss opens the door and leans out and says:

"Here now, you ruffian!"

"Who are you calling a ruffian, you bottle-nosed old baboon?" I answer, hoping to pass it off quiet.

"Aaaaargh!" says Whitey, climbing out of his buggy. "Come along, Jefferson, and help me deal with this hoodlum."

It is funny he should call me such when I feel sure he never sets peepers on me before in his life, but then it is a small world. And the chauffeur that hauls out after him is much too big to be running around in a small world. He is not only big but mean-looking, and he comes marching right at me along with old Whitey.

"Why don't you go away and soak your feet!" I suggest, still wanting to be diplomatic and avoid trouble. But Whitey does not go for my good advice.

"Let me have the number of your license," he growls. "I am going to do something about reckless drivers that smash into cars."

"Yeah," says the big chauffeur, sticking his red face into the window. "Maybe this fellow would slow down a little if he was driving with a couple of black eyes."

"Now wait a minute," I suggest. "I am very sorry if I bump into you and lose my temper, but I am on my way to the museum in a hurry with a rush order. If you look in the back of the truck, you will see a suit of armor I am delivering there."

As it turns out this is not such a hot suggestion at that. Because when I see Whitey and the chauffeur marching at me I have presence of mind to toss the whiskey bottle in the back of the truck. And now Sir Pallagyn has got a gander at it, so when Whitey hangs his nose over the side, there is Pal taking a snifter.

When he sees the old guy coming he stops still with his arm in the air, snapping his visor down with the bottle in his mouth.

"Here, what's this?" snaps Whitey.

"Huh?"

"What's that bottle doing stuck in the visor of this helmet? And what's making the arm hold on to it?"

"I don't know, mister. That's how I find it when I unpack it this morning."

"Something wrong," insists old Whitey. "They didn't drink whiskey way back then."

"It's pretty old whiskey," I tell him.

"I'll vouch for that," he says, real nasty, "if your breath is any indication. I think you ought to be run in for drunken driving."

"Say," pipes up Jefferson, the big chauffeur. "Maybe this mug doesn't even own the truck like he says. He might have stole this armor."

Whitey smiles like a desk sergeant. "I never thought of that. Now, sir"—and he wheels on me fast—"if you know so much about this particular bit of armor, perhaps you can tell me the name of its original wearer."

"Why . . . why . . . Sir Pallagyn of the Round Table," I stammer.

"Pallagyn? Pallagyn? Never heard of him," snaps Whitey. "He never sat at the Round Table."

"He was always under it," I say. "He was a lush."

"Preposterous! This is all a fraud of some sort."

"Look!" Jefferson yells. "The whiskey!"

We all look around, and sure enough the whiskey is disappearing from the bottle because Pallagyn is gargling it down very quiet.

"Fraud!" says Whitey, again, and taps the helmet with his cane.

"Come on, where you steal this from?" growls Jefferson, grabbing me by the collar. And Whitey keeps hitting the helmet.

"Desist, by blessed St. George!" roars Pallagyn, sitting up. "Desist, ere I let air through thy weasand, thou aged conskiter!"

Whitey stands there with the cane in the air and his mouth is open wide enough to hang a canary in. Pal sees the cane and grabs for his sword.

"A joust, is it?" he yells.

And all around us the citizens are honking their horns and staring out startled like, but when they

see Pallagyn standing up and waving his pocketknife
they drive away very fast in high.

"Robot!" mumbles Whitey.

"Rodent, am I?" and Pallagyn begins to slice away
at Whitey's breadbasket.

"Hey!" yells the chauffeur, dropping me. "Cut
that!" He makes a dive for the knight, but he sees
him climbing up into the truck and bops him with
the whiskey bottle. The big guy falls down and sits
still. Whitey dances around for a minute and then
runs for his car.

"I am a trustee of the museum," he bawls. "And
whatever that thing is, it isn't going on display. Witch-
craft, that's what it is!"

Now this is a fine time for a bluecoat to show up,
but when he does I quick-motion to Pal to hold still
and grab the duckfoot by the collar.

"This guy and his chauffeur back into me," I say.
"And if you smell the chauffeur you see he is drunk;
as a matter of fact he is passed out. That old bird is
also a lush, but me," and I step on the gas, "I am in a
hurry to deliver this armor to a museum, and I do
not wish to press charges."

"Hey—" says the beat daddy, but I pull away fast.
I am around the corner before he has time to cry
"Wolf!" and I take it up several alleys.

Meanwhile I bawl out Pallagyn in all suits.

"From now on," I tell him, "you don't make a
move, no matter what happens. Understand?"

"*Hic*," says Pallagyn.

"The only way I can get you into the museum is
for you to be quiet and lay limp," I say.

"Hic."

"And stop those hiccups or it's good-by quest!"

"*Hic*."

"Here we are," I tell him, pulling up in back of
the big gray building, into the loading zone.

"*Hic*."

"Shut your trap," I snarl.

Pallagyn pulls down his visor.

"No, wait." He is still hiccuping, so I yank his plume off and stuff it into his mouth.

"Now be quiet and leave it to me," I say. I get the table under one arm and slip the glass cutter into one pocket. Then I open the back of the truck and slide Pallagyn down the ramp to the ground.

"Ugh! Oooof!" he groans, under his helmet.

"*Sh!* Here we go!"

It is not so easy to drag Pallagyn along by the arms, but I manage to hoist him up the platform and get him past the door. There is a guard standing there.

"New armor," I tell him. "Where is your hardware department?"

"Funny. Nobody told me to expect a delivery. Oh, well, I'll let you set it up. Dr. Peabody will probably arrange to place it tomorrow."

He looks at me, all red in the puss, trying to drag Pallagyn along.

"Funny it should be so weighty. I thought armor was light."

"This baby must be wearing heavy underwear," I tell him. "How about giving me a hand?"

He helps lift Pallagyn and we carry him through a lot of halls into a big room.

There are a lot of suits of armor standing around the walls, and several are hanging on wires from the ceiling, but I see something else and let out a snort.

Sure enough, in the center of the room is a glass case, and inside it is standing a little table just like the one I have under my arm.

I set the thing down and the guard notices it for the first time.

"What you got here?" he asks.

"The armor is supposed to stand on it," I explain. "It comes with the set."

"Oh. Well, just stand it up against the wall. I got to get back to the door."

And he goes away. I take a quick gander up and down and see the place is deserted. It is getting dark and I figure it is closing time already.

"Here we are," I whisper.

"*Hic*," says Pallagyn.

He opens his visor and takes a look at the Tabouret.

"Verily, it is that for which I seek," he whispers. "My thanks, a thousandfold."

"Forget it. Now all you got to do is wait till it gets a little darker, then make the snatch."

I go up to the case and tap it.

"Why," I say, "this is real luck. It opens from the back and you don't even have to use the glass cutter."

But Pallagyn is not paying any attention. He is looking around at the armor on the walls.

"Gawain!" he snorts.

"What?"

" 'Tis the veritable armor of Sir Gawain!" he yaps. "One of the Brotherhood of the Round Table."

"You don't say!"

"Aye—and yonder stands the coat of mail of Sir Sagramore! Indeed! I recognize the main of Eldeford, he that is cousin to Sir Kay. And Maligaint—"

He is rattling off the names of old friends, clanking around and tapping the tin, but it all looks like a bunch of spare parts in a hot car hide-out to me.

"I am among friends," he chuckles.

"Yeah? Don't be too sure. If these museum babies ever find out what you're up to, it's good-by quest. Now get to work, quick. I got to be going back." I push him over to the case. "I'll watch the door for you in case anyone is coming," I whisper. "You switch the Tabourets. Snap into it."

So I stand there, and Pallagyn makes for the case, trying not to clank too loud. It is dark and quiet, and creepy.

Pallagyn gets the case open in no time, but he has trouble in hauling out the Tabouret, because it is nailed down.

He is grunting and yanking on it and I am shaking because he is maybe going to rouse a guard.

"I cannot say much for this guy Merlin," I comment. "He is supposed to help you knights over the hard spots, but I do not notice he has done you a good turn yet."

"Nay, I have thee to thank for my success," says Pallagyn. "For, lo, my quest is ended!"

And he rips the Tabouret loose and slides the other one in. Then he closes the glass again and marches over across the room.

Only right in the middle of it he lets out a squawk and falls down on the stone floor when his foot slips.

There is a loud crash like all hell was breaking loose.

It does.

Guys are yelling down the hall and I hear feet running this way. I get over to Pallagyn and help him up, but just as I am easing him onto his feet a squad of guards charges into the room and the heat is very much on.

"Stop, thief!" yells the guy in the lead, and the whole gang charges down on us. Pallagyn is trying to stand still again and I am yanking open a window, but when he sees them coming, Pal lets out a whoop and drops the Tabouret, waving his sword around.

"Stand back ere I skewer thy livers!" he howls. Then he turns to me. "Make haste, Sir Butch, and effect thy escape whilst I told off yon varlets."

"Give me that," I say, grabbing at the sword. "I'll

hold them off and you get out of here and gallop back to your Merlin with the Bank Nite prize."

"There he is, men!" yells a new voice. Coming through the door is none other than old Whitey in person, and behind him are about eight cops. Then the cops are ahead of him, because they are coming for us, fast. A fat sergeant has his gun extremely out.

"Pendragon and England!" yells Pallagyn, patting the first cop on his bald spot with the flat side of his sword.

"Hell and damnation!" bawls the sergeant. He lets go a slug, which bounces off the helmet.

"Superman!" hollers another cop.

"Get him, boys!" screams Whitey.

It is a picnic without ants. I plant one on the sergeant's neck, and Pal wades in with his sword. But the other six push us back into a corner, and the guards come up behind them. As fast as we knock them down, the others close in. They swarm over us like a gang of Airdales on a garbage heap.

"Here we go," I gasp out, punching away.

"Be of good . . . uh . . . heart!" roars Pallagyn. He slices away. All at once he slips and the sword falls. And two coppers jump him before he can get up. The sergeant gets his gun out again and points it at me.

"Now then—" he says. The boys grab us and push us forward.

All at once Pallagyn closes his eyes. "Merlin!" he whispers. "Aid!"

Something very unusual happens here. The first thing I notice is a lot of clanking, and scraping coming from the dark corners of the room.

And then there is more noise, like Pallagyn's armor makes, only louder.

"For Arthur and England!" Pallagyn yells. "Gawain, Sagramore, Eldeford, Maligaint!—"

"Aye, we come!"

Out of the dark crashes a half dozen suits of armor; but there are men in them now. It is the armor from the walls, and I see Pallagyn's gang is here.

"Merlin sent help!" he grunts. And then he grabs his sword and wades in.

The others are whacking up the cops already, and there is a smashing of tinware. Some of the duckfeet are running and the guards make for the door. As fast as they get there, the suits of armor hanging on the walls drop down on their necks and throw them.

In a minute it is all over.

Pallagyn stands in the center of the room holding the Tabouret and all the guys in armor huddle around him.

"The quest is over," he says. "Thanks to Merlin, and Sir Butch, here—"

But I am not here any more. I am sneaking out of the window, fast, because I have had enough trouble and do not like to get mixed up in hocus-pocus or magician's unions. So I do not stay, but drop over the ledge.

Before I do so I think I see a flash of lightning or something, but cannot be sure. Anyway, I look around once more and see the museum room is empty. There are a lot of cops lying on the floor and a lot of empty suits of armor are standing around, but there is nothing in them. I look for Pallagyn's suit and it is gone. So I blink my eyes and head for the truck, which I drive the hell away from there.

That is how it is, and I do a lot of thinking on my way home. Also the air helps to sober me up and I remember that I have been practically drunk all the time since morning.

In fact, I am drunk since before I meet this Pallagyn if I ever do meet him and it is not my imagination.

Because when I look back in the museum I do not see him any more and I wonder if it is all something

I dream up out of air and alcohol. It bothers me, and I know that whatever happens at the museum will not leak out in print, because cops are touchy about such matters and as far as they know nothing is stolen.

Then I figure maybe Thin Tommy Malloon can tell me if I drop in, so on the way home I park the car at his tavern and step inside.

Nobody is behind the bar but Bertram, and when he sees me he is very polite.

"I would like to speak with Thin Tommy," I say.

Bertram gulps. "He is upstairs lying down," he says. "In fact he does not feel so chipper since you bop him in the belly this morning."

"What do you mean *I* bop him?" I ask. "My buddy does that."

"You come in alone," Bertram tells me. He gives me a long look, but there are customers in the joint so I just shrug and walk out.

So the rest of the way home I am no better off, because I figure either Bertram is lying to me or I am nuts. And right now I would just as soon be a little nuts as admit anything so screwy could happen.

Which is how it stands with me. I am sober, and I am done with chasing around for the day. If I lay off drinking shellac, I will not see any more knights in armor with dopey stories about magicians and quests. I will let bygones be bygones and be a good boy.

That suits me, so I back the car into the garage.

And then I get out and start cursing all over again.

All at once I know for sure whether or not it all happens.

Because standing there in the garage is that dizzy nag with the mask over the head that I have Sir Pallagyn put into the stable.

Do you know anybody who wants to buy a horse, cheap?

THE DEVIL WE KNOW

Henry Kuttner

For days the thin, imperative summons had been whispering deep in Carnevan's brain. It was voiceless and urgent, and he likened his mind to a compass needle that would swing, inevitably, toward the nearest magnetic point. It was fairly easy to focus his attention on the business of the moment, but it was, as he had found, somewhat dangerous to relax. The needle wavered and swung imperceptibly, while the soundless cry grew stronger, beating at the citadel of his consciousness. Yet the meaning of the message remained unknown to him.

There was not the slightest question of insanity. Gerald Carnevan was as neurotic as most, and knew it. He held several degrees, and was junior partner in a flourishing New York advertising concern, contributing most of the ideas. He golfed, swam and played a fair hand of bridge. He was thirty-seven years old, with the thin, hard face of a Puritan—which he was not—and was being blackmailed, in a

mild degree, by his mistress. This he did not especially resent, for his logical mind had summoned up
the possibilities, arrived at a definite conclusion, and
then had forgotten.

And yet he had not forgotten. In the depths of his
subconscious the thought remained, and it came to
Carnevan now. That, of course, might be the explanation of the—the "voice." A suppressed desire to
solve the problem completely. It seemed to fit fairly
well, considering Carnevan's recent engagement to
Phyllis Mardrake. Phyllis, of Boston stock, would not
overlook her fiancé's amours—if they were dragged
out into the open. Diana, who was shameless as well
as lovely, would not hesitate to do that if matters
came to a head.

The compass needle quivered again, swung, and
came to a straining halt. Carnevan, who was working
late in his office that night, grunted angrily. On an
impulse, he leaned back in his chair, tossed his cigarette out of the open window, and waited.

Suppressed desires, according to the teachings of
psychology, should be brought out into the open,
where they could be rendered harmless. With this in
mind, Carnevan smoothed all expression from his
thin, harsh face and waited. He closed his eyes.

Through the window came the roaring murmur of
a New York street. It faded and dimmed almost
imperceptibly. Carnevan tried to analyze his sensa-
tions. His consciousness seemed inclosed in a sealed
box, straining all in one direction. Light patterns
faded on his closed lids as the retina adjusted itself.

Voiceless a message came into his brain. He could
not understand. It was too alien—incomprehensible.

But at last words formed. A name. A name that
hovered on the edge of the darkness, nebulous, inchoate. *Nefert. Nefert.*

He recognized it now. He remembered the seance
last week, which he had attended with Phyllis at her

request. It had been cheap, ordinary claptrap—trumpets and lights, and voices whispering. The medium held seances thrice a week, in an old brownstone near Columbus Circle. Her name was Madame Nefert—or so she claimed, though she looked Irish rather than Egyptian.

Now Carnevan knew what the voiceless command was. *Go to Madame Nefert,* it told him.

Carnevan opened his eyes. The room was quite unchanged. This was as he had expected. Already some vague theory had formed within his mind, germinating an annoyed anger that someone had been tampering with his most exclusive possession—his *self*. It was he, he thought, hypnotism. Somehow, during the seance, Madame Nefert had managed to hypnotize him, and his curious reactions of the past week were due to post-hypnotic suggestion. It was somewhat farfetched, but certainly not impossible.

Carnevan, as an advertising man, inevitably followed certain lines of thought. Madame Nefert would hypnotize a client. That client would return to her, worried and not understanding what had happened, and the medium would probably announce that spirits were taking a hand. When the client had been properly convinced—the first step in advertising campaigns—Madame Nefert would show her hand, whatever she had to sell.

It was the first tenet of the game. Make the customer believe he needs something. Then sell it to him.

Fair enough. Carnevan rose, lit a cigarette and pulled on his coat. Adjusting his tie before the mirror, he examined his face closely. He seemed in perfect health, his reactions normal, and his eyes well under control.

The telephone rang sharply. Carnevan picked up the receiver.

"Hello . . . Diana? How are you, dear?" Despite Diana's blackmailing activities, Carnevan preferred to keep matters running along smoothly, lest they grow more complicated. So he substituted "dear" for another epithet that came to his mind.

"I can't," he said at last. "I've an important call to make tonight. Now wait—I'm not turning you down! I'll put a check in the mail tonight."

This seemed satisfactory, and Carnevan hung up. Diana did not yet know of his forthcoming marriage to Phyllis. He was a little worried about how she would take the news. Phyllis, for all her glorious body, was quite stupid. At first Carnevan had found this attribute relaxing, giving him an illusory feeling of power in the moments when they were together. Now, however, Phyllis's stupidity might prove a handicap.

He'd cross that bridge later. First of all, there was Nefert. *Madame* Nefert. A wry smile touched his lips. By all means, the title. Always look for the trade-mark. It impresses the consumer.

He got his car from the garage of the office building and drove uptown on the parkway, turning off into Columbus Circle. Madame Nefert had a front parlor and a few tawdry rooms which no one ever saw, since they probably contained her equipment. A placard on the window proclaimed the woman's profession.

Carnevan mounted the steps and rang. He entered at the sound of a buzzer, turned right, and pushed through a half-open door which he closed behind him. Drapes had been drawn over the windows. The room was illuminated by a dim, reddish glow from lamps in the corners.

It was bare. The carpet had been pushed aside. Signs had been made on the floor with luminous chalk. A blackened pot stood in the center of a pentagram. That was all, and Carnevan shook his head disgustedly. Such a stage setting would impress only the most credulous. Yet he decided to play along till he got to the bottom of this most peculiar advertising stunt.

A curtain was twitched aside, revealing an alcove in which Madame Nefert sat on a hard, plain chair. The woman had not even troubled to don her customary masquerade, Carnevan saw. With her beefy, red face and her stringy hair, she resembled a charwoman out of some Shavian comedy. She wore a flowered wrapper, hanging open to reveal a dirty white slip at her capacious bosom.

The red light flickered on her face.

She looked at Carnevan with glassy, expressionless eyes. "The spirits are—" she began, and fell suddenly silent, a choking rattle deep in her throat. Her whole body twitched convulsively.

Suppressing a smile, Carnevan said, "Madame Nefert, I'd like to ask you a few questions."

She didn't answer. There was a long, heavy silence. After a time Carnevan made a tentative movement toward the door, but still the woman did not rouse.

She was playing the game to the hilt. He glanced around, saw something white in the blackened pot, and stepped closer to peer down into the interior. Then he retched violently, clawed out a handkerchief and, holding it over his mouth, whirled to confront Madame Nefert.

But he could not find words. Sanity came back. He breathed deeply, realized that a clever papier-maché image had almost destroyed his emotional balance.

Madame Nefert had not moved. She was leaning forward, breathing in stertorous, rasping gasps. A faint, insidious odor crept into Carnevan's nostrils.

Someone said sharply, "Now!"

The woman's hand moved in a fumbling, uncertain gesture. Simultaneously, Carnevan was conscious of a newcomer in the room. He whirled, to see, seated in the middle of the pentagram, a small huddled figure that was regarding him steadily.

The red light was dim. All Carnevan could see was a head, and a shapeless body concealed by a dark cloak as the man—or boy—squatted. Yet the sight of that head was enough to make his heart jump excitedly.

For it was not entirely human. At first Carnevan had thought it was a skull. The face was thin, with pale, translucent skin of finest ivory laid lightly over the bone, and it was completely hairless. It was triangular, delicately wedge-shaped, without the ugly protruding knobs of the cheekbones which make human skulls so often hideous. The eyes were certainly human. They slanted up almost to where the hairline would have been had the being possessed hair, and they were like cloudy, gray-green stone, flecked with opalescent dancing lights, red-tinted now by the light.

It was a singularly beautiful face, with the clear, passionless perfection of polished bone. The body Carnevan could not see, hidden as it was by the cloak.

Was that strange face a mask? Carnevan knew it was not. By the subtle, unmistakable revolt of his whole physical being, he knew that he looked upon a horror.

With an automatic reflex, he took out a cigarette and lighted it. The being had made no move meanwhile, and Carnevan abruptly realized that the compass needle in his brain had vanished.

Smoke coiled up from his cigarette. He, Gerald Carnevan, was standing in this dim, red-lit room, with a fake medium in, presumably, a fake trance behind him, and—something—crouching only a few feet away. Outside, a block distant, was Columbus Circle, with electric signs and traffic.

Electric lights meant advertising. A key clicked in Carnevan's brain. *Get the customer wondering.* In this case he seemed to be the customer. The direct approach was hell on salesmen and their foreplanned tactics. Carnevan began to walk directly toward the being.

The soft, pink, childish lips parted. "Wait," a singularly gentle voice commanded. "Don't cross the pentagram, Carnevan. You can't anyway, but you might start a fire."

"That tears it," the man remarked, almost laughing. "Spirits don't speak colloquial English. What's the idea?"

"Well," said the other, not moving, "to begin with, you may call me Azazel. I'm not a spirit. I'm rather more of a demon. As for colloquial English, when I enter your world I naturally adjust myself to it—or am adjusted. My own tongue cannot be heard here. I'm speaking it, but you hear the Earthly equivalent. It's automatically adjusted to your capabilities."

"All right," Carnevan said. "Now what?" He blew smoke through his nostrils.

"You're skeptical," Azazel said, still motionless. "I could convince you in a moment by leaving the pentagram, but I can't do that without your help. At present, the space I'm occupying exists in both our worlds, coincidentally. I *am* a demon, Carnevan, and I want to strike a bargain with you."

"I expect flashlight bulbs to go off in a moment. But you can fake all the photos you want, if that's the game. I won't pay blackmail," Carnevan said, thinking of Diana and making a mental reservation.

"You do," Azazel remarked, and gave a brief, pithy history of the man's relations with Diana Bellamy.

Carnevan felt himself flushing. "That's enough," he said curtly. "It *is* blackmail, eh?"

"Please let me explain—from the beginning. I got in touch with you first at the seance last week. It's incredibly difficult for inhabitants of my . . . my dimension to establish contact with human beings. But in this case I managed it. I implanted certain thoughts in your subconscious mind and held you by those."

"What sort of thoughts?"

"Gratifications," Azazel said. "The death of your senior partner. The removal of Diana Bellamy. Wealth. Power. Triumph. Secretly you treasured those thoughts, and so a link was established between us. Not enough, however, for I couldn't really communicate with you till I'd worked on Madame Nefert."

"Go on," Carnevan said quietly. "She's a charlatan, of course."

"So she is." Azazel smiled. "But she is a Celt. A violin is useless without a violinist. I managed to control her somewhat, and induced her to make the necessary preparations so I could materialize. Then I drew you here."

"Do you expect me to believe you?"

The other's shoulders stirred restlessly. "That is the difficulty. If you accept me, I can serve you well—very well indeed. But you will not do that until you believe."

"I'm not Faust," Carnevan said. "Even if I did believe you, why do you think I'd want to—" He stopped.

"You are human," Azazel said.

For a second there was silence. Carnevan angrily dropped his cigarette and crushed it out. "All the legends of history," he muttered. "Folklore—all full of it. Bargains with demons. And always at a price. But I'm an atheist, or an agnostic. Not sure which. A soul—I can't believe I have one. When I die, it's a blackout."

Azazel studied him thoughtfully. "There must be a fee, of course." A curious expression crossed the being's face. There was mockery in it, and fear, too. When he spoke again his voice was hurried.

"I can serve you, Carnevan. I can give you anything you desire—everything, I believe."

"Why did you choose me?"

"The seance drew me. You were the only one present I could touch."

Scarcely flattered, Carnevan frowned. It was impossible for him to believe. He said, at last, "I wouldn't mind—if I thought this wasn't merely some trick. Tell me more about it. Just what you could do for me."

Azazel spoke further. When he had finished, Carnevan's eyes were glistening.

"Even a little of that—"

"It is easy enough," Azazel urged. "All is ready. The ceremony does not take long, and I'll guide you step by step."

Carnevan clicked his tongue, smiling. "There it is. I can't believe. I tell myself that you're real—but deep inside my brain I'm trying to find a logical explanation. And that's all too easy. If I were convinced you are what you say and can—"

Azazel interrupted. "Do you know anything about teratology?"

"Eh? Why—just the layman's knowledge."

The being stood up slowly. He was wearing, Carnevan saw, a voluminous cloak of some dark, opaque, shimmering material.

He said, "If there is no other way of convincing you—and since I cannot leave the pentagram—I must take this means."

A sickening premonition shot through Carnevan as

he saw delicate, slim hands fumbling at the fastenings of the cloak. Azazel cast it aside.

Almost instantly he wrapped the garment around him. Carnevan had not moved. But there was blood trickling down his chin.

Then silence till the man tried to speak, a hoarse, croaking noise that rasped through the room. Carnevan found his voice.

Unexpectedly his words came out in a half shriek. Abruptly he whirled and went to a corner, where he stood with his forehead pressed hard against the wall. When he returned, his face was more composed, though sweat gleamed on it.

"Yes," he said. "Yes?"

"This is the way—" Azazel began.

The next morning Carnevan sat at his desk and talked quietly to the demon, who lounged in a chair, invisible to all but one man, and his voice equally masked. Sunlight slanted in through the windows, and a cool breeze brought in the muffled clamor of traffic. Azazel seemed incredibly real sitting there, his body muffled by the cloak, his skull-like, beautiful head whitened by the sunlight.

"Speak softly," the demon cautioned. "No one can hear me, but they can hear you. Whisper—or just think. It will be clear to me."

"Fair enough." Carnevan rubbed his freshly shaven cheek. "We'd better lay out a plan of campaign. You'll have to earn my soul, you know."

"Eh?" For a second the demon looked puzzled; then he laughed softly. "I'm at your service."

"First—we must arouse no suspicion. Nobody would believe the truth, but I don't want them thinking I'm insane—as I may be," Carnevan continued logically. "But we'll not consider that point just now. What about Madame Nefert? How much does she know?"

"Nothing at all," Azazel said. "She was in a trance

while under my control. She remembered nothing when she woke. Still if you prefer, I can kill her."

Carnevan held up his hand. "Steady now! That's just where people like Faust made their mistakes. They went hogwild, got drunk on power, and wrapped themselves up till they couldn't even move. Any murders we may commit must be necessary. Here! Just how much control have I over you?"

"A good deal," Azazel admitted.

"Suppose I asked you to kill yourself—told you to do so?"

For answer, the demon picked up a paper knife from the desk and thrust it deeply into his cloak. Remembering what lay under that garment, Carnevan glanced away hurriedly.

Smiling, Azazel replaced the knife. "Suicide is impossible to a demon, by any means."

"Can't you be killed at all?"

There was a little silence. Then— "Not by you," Azazel said.

Carnevan shrugged. "I'm checking up all the angles. I want to know just where I stand. You must obey me, though. Is that right?"

Azazel nodded.

"So. Now I don't want a million dollars in gold dumped into my lap. Gold's illegal, anyway, and people would ask questions. Any advantages I get must come naturally, without arousing the slightest suspicion. If Eli Dale died, the firm would be without a senior partner. I'd get the job. It carries enough money for my purposes."

"I can get you the largest fortune in the world," the demon suggested.

Carnevan laughed a little. "And then? Everything would be far too easy for me. I want to feel the thrill of achieving things myself—with some help from you. If you cheat once at solitaire, it's different from cheating all through the game. I have a good deal of faith in myself, and want to justify that—build up my ego. People like Faust grew jaded. King Solomon must have been bored to death. Then, too, he never used his brain, and I'll bet it atrophied. Look at Merlin!" Carnevan smiled. "He got so used to calling up devils to do what he wanted that a young snip got the best of him without any trouble. No, Azazel—I want Eli Dale to die, but naturally."

The demon looked at his slim, pale hands.

Carnevan shrugged. "Can you change your form?"

"Of course."

"Into anything?"

For answer, Azazel became, in rapid succession, a large black dog, a lizard, a rattlesnake, and Carnevan himself. Finally he resumed his own form and relaxed again in the chair.

"None of those disguises would help you kill Dale," Carnevan grunted. "We want something that won't be suspected. Do you know what disease germs are, Azazel?"

"I know, from your mind," the other nodded.

"Could you transform yourself into toxins?"

"Why not? If I knew which one you wished, I'd locate a specimen, duplicate its atomic structure, and enter it with my own life force."

"Spinal meningitis," Carnevan said thoughtfully. "That's fatal enough. It'd knock over a man in Dale's senile condition. But I forgot whether it's a germ or virus."

"That doesn't matter," Azazel said. "I'll locate a slide or specimen of the stuff—some hospital should do—and then materialize inside Dale's body as the disease."

"Will it be the same thing?"

"Yes."

"Good enough. The toxin will propagate, I suppose, and that'll be the end of Dale. If it isn't, we'll try something else."

He turned back to his work, and Azazel vanished. The morning dragged past slowly. Carnevan ate at a nearby restaurant, wondering what his familiar demon was doing, and was rather surprised to find that he had a hearty appetite. During the afternoon, Diana phoned. She had, apparently, found out about Carnevan's engagement to Phyllis. She had already telephoned Phyllis.

Carnevan hung up, rigidly repressing his violent rage. After a brief moment he dialed Phyllis' number. She was not at home, he was told.

"Tell her I'll be out to see her tonight," he growled, and slammed the receiver down in its cradle. It was rather a relief to look up and see the shrouded form of Azazel in the chair.

"It's done," the demon said. "Dale has spinal meningitis. He doesn't know it yet, but the toxin propagated very rapidly. A curious experiment. But it worked."

Carnevan tried to focus his mind. It was Phyllis he was thinking of now. He was in love with her, of course—but she was so rigid, so incredibly Puritanical. He had made one slip in the past. In her eyes, that might be enough. Would she break the engagement? Surely not! In this day and age, amorous peccadilloes were more or less taken for granted, even by a girl who had been reared in Boston. Carnevan considered his fingernails.

After a time he made an excuse to see Eli Dale, asking his advice on some unimportant business problem, and scrutinized carefully the old man's face. Dale was flushed and bright-eyed, but otherwise seemed normal. Yet the mark of death was on him, Carnevan knew. He would die, the senior partnership would devolve on someone else—and the first step in Carnevan's plan was taken.

As for Phyllis and Diana—why, after all, he owned a familiar demon! With the powers at his control, he could solve this problem, too. Just how he would do that, Carnevan did not know as yet; ordinary methods, he thought, should be used first in every case. He must not grow too dependent on magic.

He dismissed Azazel for the time and drove that night to Phyllis' home. But before that, he made a stop at Diana's apartment. The scene was brief and stormy while it lasted.

Dark, slim, furious and lovely, Diana said she wouldn't let him marry.

"Why not?" Carnevan wanted to know. "After all, my dear, if you want money, I can arrange that."

Diana said unpleasant things about Phyllis. She hurled an ash tray down and stamped on it. "So I'm not good enough to marry! But she is!"

"Sit down and be quiet," Carnevan suggested. "Try and analyze your feelings—"

"You cold-blooded fish!"

"—and see just where you stand. You're not in love with me. Dangling me on a string gives you a feeling of power and possession. You don't want any other woman to have me."

"I pity any woman who does," Diana remarked, selecting another ash tray. She looked remarkably pretty, but Carnevan was in no mood to appreciate beauty.

"All right," he said. "Listen to me. If you string along, you won't lack for money—or anything. But if you try to cause trouble again, you'll certainly regret it."

"I don't scare easily," Diana snapped. "Where are you going? Off to see that yellow-haired wench, I suppose?"

Carnevan favored her with an imperturbable smile, donned his topcoat, and vanished. He drove to the home of the yellow-haired wench, where he encountered not-unforeseen difficulties. But finally he outargued the maid and was ushered in to face an icicle sitting silently on a couch. It was Mrs. Mardrake.

"Phyllis does not wish to see you, Gerald," she said, her prim mouth biting off the words.

Carnevan girded his loins and began to talk. He talked well. So convincing was his story that he almost persuaded himself that Diana was a myth—that the whole affair had been cooked up by some personal enemy. Mrs. Mardrake finally capitulated, after an internal struggle of some length.

"There must be no scandal," she said at last. "If I thought there was a word of truth in what that woman said to Phyllis—"

"A man in my position has enemies," Carnevan said, thus reminding his hostess that, maritally speaking, he was a fish worth hooking. She sighed.

"Very well, Gerald. I'll ask Phyllis to see you. Wait here."

She swept out of the room, and, Carnevan suppressed a smile. Yet he knew it would not be this easy to convince Phyllis.

She did not appear immediately. Carnevan guessed that Mrs. Mardrake was having difficulty in persuading her daughter of his bona fides. He wandered about the room, taking out his cigarette case and then, with a glance at the surroundings, putting it back. What a Victorian house!

A heavy family Bible on its stand caught his eye. For want of anything else to do, he went toward it, opening the book at random. A passage leaped up at him.

"If any man worship the beast and his image, and receive his mark on his forehead, or in his hand, the same shall drink of the wine of the wrath of God."

It was, perhaps, an instinctive reaction that made

Carnevan reach up to touch his forehead. He smiled at the conceit. Superstition! Yes—but so were demons.

At that moment Phyllis came in, looking like Evangeline in Acadia, with much the same martyred expression Longfellow's heroine might have worn. Suppressing an ungallant impulse to kick her, Carnevan reached for her hands, failed to capture them, and followed her to a couch.

Puritanism and a pious upbringing has its drawbacks, he thought. This became more evident when, after ten minutes, Phyllis still remained unconvinced of Carnevan's innocence.

"I didn't tell mother everything," she said quietly. "That woman said some things— Well, I could see she was telling the truth."

"I love you," Carnevan said inconsequentially.

"You don't. Or you'd never have taken up with this woman."

"Even if it happened before I knew you?"

"I could forgive many things, Gerald," she said, "but not that."

"You," Carnevan remarked, "don't want a husband. You want a graven image."

It was impossible to break through her calm self-righteousness. Carnevan lost his self-possession. He argued and pleaded, despising himself as he did so. Of all the women in the world, he had to fall in love with the most hide-bound and Puritanical of them all. Her silence had the quality of enraging him almost to hysteria. He had an impulse to shout obscenities into the room's quiet, religious atmosphere. Phyllis, he knew, was humiliating him horribly, and deep within him something cowered rawly under the lashing he could not stop himself from giving it.

"I love you, Gerald," was all she would say. "But you don't love me. I can't forgive you this. Please go before you make it worse."

He flung out of the house, seething with fury, hot and sick with the realization that he had failed to maintain his poise. Phyllis, Phyllis, Phyllis! An imperturbable iceberg. She knew nothing of humanity. Emotions had never existed in her breast unless they were well-schooled, dainty as an antimacassar of lace. A china doll, expecting the rest of the world to be of china. Carnevan stood by his car, shaking with rage, wishing more than anything else on earth to hurt Phyllis as he himself had been hurt.

Something stirred inside the car. It was Azazel, the cloak shrouding his dark body, the bone-white face expressionless.

Carnevan flung out an arm behind him, pointing. "The girl!" he said hoarsely. "She . . . she—"

"You need not speak," Azazel murmured. "I read your thoughts. I shall—do as you wish."

He was gone. Carnevan sprang into the car, inserted the key, savagely started the motor. As the vehicle began to move he heard a thin, knife-edged scream lancing out from the house he had left.

He stopped the car and raced back, chewing his lip.

As the hastily summoned physician said, Phyllis Mardrake had suffered a severe nervous shock. The reason was unknown, but, presumably, it might have been the ordeal of her interview with Carnevan, who said nothing to dispel the illusion. Phyllis simply lay and twitched, her eyes staring glassily. Sometimes her lips formed words.

"The cloak— Under the cloak—"

And then she would alternately laugh and scream until exhaustion claimed her.

She would recover, but it would take some time. In the meanwhile, Phyllis was sent to a private sanitarium, where she fell into hysterics whenever she saw Dr. Joss, who happened to be bald-headed. Her jabbering about cloaks grew less frequent, and occasionally Carnevan was permitted to visit her. She asked for him. The quarrel had been patched up, and Phyllis almost half admitted that she had been wrong in her stand.

When she had completely recovered she would marry Carnevan. But there must be no more slips.

The horror she had seen was buried deep in her mind, emerging only during delirium, and in her frequent nightmares. Carnevan was thankful that she did not remember Azazel. Yet he saw much of the demon these days—for he was fulfilling a malicious, cruel little scheme of his own.

It was started soon after Phyllis's breakdown, when Diana kept telephoning him at the office. At first Carnevan spoke shortly to her. Then he realized that she, actually, was responsible for Phyllis's near-madness.

It was, of course, right that she should suffer. Not death. Anyone might die. Eli Dale, for example, was already fatally ill with spinal meningitis. But a more subtle form of punishment—a torture such as Phyllis had undergone.

Carnevan's face wore an expression that was not pleasant to see as he summoned the demon and issued instructions.

"Slowly, gradually, she will be driven insane," he said. "She will be given time to realize what is happening. Give her—glimpses, so to speak. A cumulative series of inexplicable happenings. I'll give you the detailed directions when I work them out. She told me that she isn't easily frightened," Carnevan finished, and rose to pour himself a drink. He offered one to the demon, but it was refused.

Azazel sat motionless in a dark corner of the apartment, occasionally glancing out of the window to where Central Park lay far below.

Carnevan was struck by a sudden thought. "How

do you react to this? Demons are supposed to be evil. Does it give you pleasure to . . . hurt people?"

The beautiful skull face was turned toward him. "Do you know what evil is, Carnevan?"

The man splashed soda into his rye. "I see. A matter of semantics. Of course, it's an arbitrary term. Humanity has set up its own standards—"

Azazel's slanted, opalescent eyes glittered. "That is moral anthropomorphism. And egotism. You haven't considered environment. The physical properties of this world of yours caused good and evil, as you know it."

It was Carnevan's sixth drink, and he felt argumentative. "That I don't quite understand. Morality comes from the mind and the emotions."

"A river has its source," Azazel countered. "But there's a difference between the Mississippi and the Colorado. If human beings had evolved in—well, my world, for example—the whole pattern of good and evil would have been entirely different. Ants have a social structure. But it isn't like yours. The environment is different."

"There's a difference between insects and men, too."

The demon shrugged. "We are not alike. Less alike than you and an ant. For both of you have, basically, two common instincts. Self-preservation and propagation of the species. Demons can't propagate."

"Most authorities agree on that," Carnevan granted. "Possibly it explains the reason for changelings, too. How is it there are so many kinds of demons?"

Azazel questioned him with his eyes.

"Oh—you know. Gnomes and kobolds and trolls and jinn and werewolves and vampires and—"

"There are more kinds of demons than humanity knows," Azazel explained. "The reason is pretty obvious. Your world tends toward a fixed pattern—a state of stasis. You know what entropy is. The ultimate aim of your universe is a unity, changeless and eternal. Your branches of evolution will finally meet and remain at one fixed type. Such offshoots as the moa and the auk will die out, as dinosaurs and mammoths have died. In the end there will be stasis. My universe tends toward physical anarchy. In the beginning there was only one type. In the end it will be ultimate chaos."

"Your universe is like a negative of mine," Carnevan pondered. "But—wait! You said demons can't die. And they can't propagate. How can there be any progress at all?"

"I said demons can't commit suicide," Azazel pointed out. "Death may come to them, but from an outside source. That applies to procreation, too."

It was too confused for Carnevan. "You must have emotions. Self-preservation implies fear of death."

"Our emotions are not yours. Clinically, I can analyze and understand Phyllis's reactions. She was reared very rigidly, and subconsciously she has resented that oppression. She never admitted, even to herself, her desire to break free. But you were a symbol to her. Secretly she admired and envied you, because you were a man and, as she thought, able to do whatever you wanted. Love is a false synonym for propagation, as the soul is a wish fulfillment creation growing out of self-preservation. Neither exists. Phyllis's mind is a maze of inhibitions, fears and hopes. Puritanism, to her, represents security. That was why she couldn't forgive you for your affair with Diana. It was an excuse for retreating to the security of her former life pattern."

Carnevan listened interestedly. "Go on."

"When I appeared to her, the psychic shock was violent. Her subconscious ruled for a time. That was why she became reconciled to you. She is an escapist; her previous security seemed to have failed, so she fulfills both her escape wish and her desire for protection by agreeing to marry you."

Carnevan mixed himself another drink. He remembered something.

"You just said the soul is nonexistent—eh?"

Azazel's body stirred under the shrouding cloak. "You misunderstood me."

"I don't think so," Carnevan said, feeling a cold, deadly horror under the warm numbness of liquor. "Our bargain was that you serve me in exchange for my soul. Now you imply that I have no soul. What was your real motive?"

"You're trying to frighten yourself," the demon murmured, his strange eyes alert. "All through history, religion has been founded on the hypothesis that souls exist."

"Do they?"

"Why not?"

"What is a soul like?" Carnevan asked.

"You couldn't imagine," Azazel said. "There'd be no standard of comparison. By the way, Eli Dale died two minutes ago. You're now the senior partner of the firm. May I congratulate you?"

"Thank you," Carnevan nodded. "We'll change the subject, if you like. But I intend to find out the truth sooner or later. If I have no soul, you're up to something else. However—let's get back to Diana."

"You wish to drive her mad."

"I wish *you* to drive her mad. She is the schizophrenic type—slim and long boned. She has a stupid sort of self-confidence. She has built her life on a foundation of things she knows to be real. Those things must be removed."

"Well?"

"She is afraid of the dark," Carnevan said, and his smile was quite unpleasant. "Be subtle, Azazel. She will hear voices. She will see people following her.

Delusions of persecution. One by one her senses will begin to fail her. Or, rather, deceive her. She'll smell things no one else does. She'll hear voices. She'll taste poison in her food. She'll begin to feel things—unpleasant things. If necessary, she may, at the last—see things."

"This is evil, I suppose," Azazel observed, rising from his chair. "My interest is purely clinical. I can reason that such matters are important to you, but that's as far as it goes."

The telephone rang. Carnevan learned that Eli Dale was dead—spinal meningitis.

To celebrate the occasion, he poured another drink and toasted Azazel, who had vanished to visit Diana. Carnevan's thin, hard face was only slightly flushed by the liquor he had consumed. He stood in the center of the apartment and revolved slowly, eyeing the furnishings, the books, the bric-a-brac. It would be well to find another place—something a bit more swanky. A place suitable for a married couple. He wondered how long it would be before Phyllis was completely recovered.

Azazel— Just what was the demon after?—he wondered. Certainly not his soul. What, then?

One night two weeks later, he rang the bell of Diana's apartment. The girl's voice asked who was there, and she opened the door a slight crack before admitting Carnevan. He was shocked at the change in her.

There was little tangible alteration. Diana was holding herself under iron control, but her makeup was too heavy. That in itself was revealing. It was a symbol of the mental shield she was trying to erect against the psychical invasion. Carnevan said solicitously, "Diana, what's wrong? You sounded hysterical over the phone. I told you last night you should see a doctor."

She fumbled for a cigarette, which trembled slightly in her hands as Carnevan lit it. "I have. He . . . he wasn't much help, Jerry. I'm so glad you're not angry at me any more."

"Angry? Here, sit down. That's it. I'll mix a drink. No, I got over being angry; we get along together, and Phyllis—well, we couldn't very well have a *ménage a trois*. She's in a sanitarium, you know, and it'll be a long while before she gets out. Even then she may be a lunatic—" Carnevan sucked in his breath. "Sorry."

Diana pushed back her dark hair and turned to face him on the couch. "Jerry, do you think I'm going crazy?"

"No, I don't," he said. "I think you need a rest, or a change."

She didn't hear. Her head was tilted to one side, as though she listened to a soundless voice. Glancing up, Carnevan saw Azazel standing across the room— invisible to the girl, but apparently not inaudible.

"Diana!" he said sharply.

Her lips parted. Her voice was unsteady as she looked at him. "Sorry. You were saying?"

"What did the doctor tell you?"

"Nothing much." She did not wish to follow up the line of discussion. Instead, she took the drink Carnevan had mixed, eyed it and sipped the highball. Then she put down the glass.

"Anything wrong?" the man asked.

"No. How does it taste to you?"

"All right."

Carnevan wondered just what Diana had tasted in her drink. Bitter almonds, perhaps. Another of Azazel's deft illusions. He ran his fingers through the girl's hair, feeling a thrill of power as he did so. A nasty sort of revenge, he thought. Odd that Diana's distress did not touch him in the slightest degree. Yet he was not basically evil, Carnevan knew. The old, old problem of arbitrary standards—right and wrong.

Azazel said—and his words were heard by Carnevan alone: "Her control cannot last much longer. I think she'll break tomorrow. A manic-depressive may commit suicide, so I'll guard against that. Every dangerous weapon she touches will seem red-hot to her."

Abruptly, without warning, the demon vanished. Carnevan grunted and finished his drink. From the corner of his eye he saw something move.

Slowly he turned his head, but it was gone. What had it been? Like a black shadow. Formless, inchoate. Without reason, Carnevan's hands were shaking. Utterly amazed, he put down his drink and surveyed the apartment.

Azazel's presence had never affected him thus before. It was probably a reaction—no doubt he had been keeping a tight control over his nerves, without noticing it. After all, demons *are* supernatural.

From the corner of his eye he again saw the cloudy blackness. This time he did not move as he tried to analyze it. The thing hovered just on the edge of his range of vision. Imperceptibly, his eyes moved slightly, and it was gone.

A formless black cloud. Formless? No, it was, he thought, spindle-shaped, motionless and upright on its axis. His hands were shaking more than ever.

Diana was eyeing him. "What's the matter, Jerry? Am I making you nervous?"

"Too much work at the office," he said. "I'm the new senior partner, you know. I'll push off now. You'd better see that doctor again tomorrow."

She did not reply, only watched him as he let himself out of the apartment. Driving home, Carnevan again caught a brief glimpse of the black, foggy spindle. Not once could he get a clear view of it. It hovered just on the border of his vision. He sensed, though he could not see, certain features cloudily discerned in it. What they were he could not guess. But his hands trembled.

Coldly, furiously, his intellect fought against the unreasonable terror of his physical structure. He faced the alien. Or— No—he did not face it. It slid away and vanished. Azazel?

He called the demon's name, but there was no response. Hurtling toward his apartment, Carnevan sucked at his lower lip and thought hard. How— Why—

What was so unreasonably, subtly horrifying about this—this apparition?

He did not know, unless it was, perhaps, that vague hint of features in the blackness which he could never face directly. He sensed that those features were unspeakable, and yet he had a perverse curiosity to behold them directly. Once safe in his apartment, he again glimpsed the black spindle, at the edge of his vision, near the window. He swung swiftly to face it; it vanished. But at that moment a shock of unreasoning horror gripped Carnevan, a deadly, sickening feeling that he might see that against which his whole physical being revolted.

"Azazel," he called softly.

Nothing.

"Azazel!"

Carnevan poured a drink, lit a cigarette and found a magazine. He was untroubled until bedtime and during the night, but in the morning, when first he opened his eyes, something black and spindle-shaped skittered away as he looked toward it.

He telephoned Diana. She seemed much better, she said. Apparently Azazel wasn't on the job. Unless the black thing *was* Azazel. Carnevan hurriedly drove to his office, had black coffee sent up, and then drank milk instead. His nerves needed soothing rather than stimulating.

* * *

Twice that morning the black spindle appeared in the office. Each time there was that horrifying knowledge that if Carnevan looked at it directly, the features would be clear to him. And in spite of himself, he tried to look. Vainly, of course.

His work suffered. Presently he knocked off and drove to the sanitarium to see Phyllis. She was much better, and spoke of the forthcoming marriage. Carnevan's palms were clammy as a black spindle retreated hurriedly across the sunny, pleasant room.

Worst of all, perhaps, was the realization that if he *did* succeed in looking squarely at the phantasm, he would not go mad. But he would want to. That he realized quite well. His instinctive physical reaction told him as much. Nothing belonging to his universe or any remotely kindred one could bring about the empty hollowness within his body, the shocking feeling that his cellular structure was trying to shrink away from the—the spindle.

He drove to Manhattan, narrowly avoiding an accident on the George Washington Bridge as he closed his eyes to avoid seeing what wasn't there when he opened them again. It was past sundown. The jeweled towers of New York rose against a purple sky. Their geometrical neatness looked devoid of warmth, inhospitable and unhelpful. Carnevan stopped at a bar, drank two whiskeys, and left when a black spindle ran across the mirror.

Back in his apartment, he sat with his head in his hands for perhaps five minutes. When he stood up, his face was hard and vicious. His eyes flickered slightly; then he caught himself.

"Azazel," he said—and, more loudly: "Azazel! I am your master! Appear to me!"

His thought probed out, forceful, hard as iron. Behind it lay unformed terror. Was Azazel the black spindle? Would he appear—completely?

"Azazel! I am your master! Obey me! I summon you!"

The demon stood before Carnevan, materializing from empty air. The beautiful face of pale bone was expressionless; the slanted, opalescent, pupilless eyes were impassive. Under the dark cloak, Azazel's body shivered once and was still.

With a sigh, Carnevan sank down in his chair. "All right," he said. "Now what's up? What's the idea?"

Azazel said quietly, "I went back to my own world. I would have remained there had you not summoned me."

"What is this—spindle thing?"

"It is not of your world," the demon said. "It is not of mine. It pursues me."

"Why?"

"You have your stories of men who have been haunted. Sometimes by demons. In my world—I have been haunted."

Carnevan licked his lips. "By this thing?"

"Yes."

"What is it?"

Azazel's shoulders seemed to hunch together. "I do not know. Except that it is very horrible, and it pursues me."

Carnevan lifted his hands and pushed hard at his eyes. "No. No. It's too crazy. *Something* haunting a demon. Where did it come from?"

"I know of my universe and yours. That is all. This thing came from outside both our time sectors, I think."

With a sudden flash of insight, Carnevan said, "That was why you offered to serve me."

Azazel's face did not change. "Yes. The thing was getting closer, and closer to me. I thought if I entered your universe, I might escape it. But it followed."

"And you couldn't enter this world without my help. All that talk about my soul was so much guff."

"Yes. The thing followed me. I fled back to my universe, and it did not pursue. Perhaps it could not. It may be able to move in only one direction—from its world to mine, and then to yours, but not the other way. It remained here, I know."

"It remained," Carnevan said, very white, "to haunt me."

"You feel the same horror toward it? I wondered. We are so unlike physically—"

"I never see it directly. It has—features?"

Azazel did not answer. Silence hung in the room.

At last Carnevan bent forward in his chair. "The thing haunts you—unless you go back to your own world. Then it haunts me. Why?"

"I don't know. It's alien to me, Carnevan."

"But you're a demon! You have supernatural powers—"

"Supernatural to you. There are powers supernatural to demons."

Carnevan poured himself a drink. His eyes were narrowed.

"Very well. I have enough power over you to keep you in this world, or you wouldn't have returned when I summoned you. So it's a deadlock. As long as you stay here, that thing will haunt you. I won't let you go to *your* world, for then it would haunt me—as it has been doing. Though it seems to be gone now."

"It has not gone," Azazel said tonelessly.

Carnevan's body shook uncontrollably. "Mentally I can tell myself not to be frightened. Physically the thing is . . . is—"

"It is horrible even to me," Azazel said. "Remember, I have seen it directly. Eventually it will destroy me, if you keep me in this world of yours."

"Humans have exorcised demons," Carnevan pointed out. Isn't there any way you can exorcise that thing?"

"No."

"A blood sacrifice?" Carnevan suggested nervously. "Holy water? Bell, book and candle?" He sensed the foolishness of the proposals as he made them.

But Azazel looked thoughtful. "None of those. But perhaps—life force." The dark cloak quivered.

Carnevan said, "Elementals have been exorcised, according to folklore. But first it's necessary to make them visible and tangible. Giving them octoplasm—blood—I don't know."

The demon nodded slowly. "In other words, translating the equation to its lowest common denominator. Humans cannot fight a disembodied spirit. But if that spirit is drawn into a vessel of flesh, it is subject to earthly physical laws. I think that is the way, Carnevan."

"You mean—"

"The thing that pursues me is entirely alien. But if I can reduce it to its lowest common denominator, I can destroy it. As I could destroy you, had I not promised to serve you. And, of course, if your destruction would help me. Suppose I give that thing a sacrifice. It must, for a time, partake of the nature of the thing it assimilates. Human life force should do."

Carnevan listened eagerly. "Will it work?"

"I think it will. I will give the thing a human sacrifice. It will become, briefly, and partially, human, and a demon can easily destroy a human being."

"A sacrifice—"

"Diana. It will be easiest, since I already have weakened the fortress of her consciousness. I must break down all the barriers of her brain—a psychical substitute for the sacrificial knife of pagan religions."

Carnevan gulped the last of his drink. "Then you can destroy the thing?"

Azazel nodded. "That is my belief. But what will

be left of Diana will be in no way human. You will be asked questions by the authorities. However, I shall try to protect you."

And with that he vanished before Carnevan could raise an objection. The apartment was deadly still. Carnevan looked around, half expecting to see the black spindle flashing away as he glanced toward it. But there was no trace of anything supernatural.

He was still sitting in the chair, half an hour later, when the telephone rang. Carnevan answered it.

"Yes . . . Who? . . . *What?* Murdered? . . . No, I . . . I'll be right over."

He replaced the receiver and straightened, eyes aglow. Diana was—was dead. Murdered, quite horribly, and there were certain factors that puzzled the police. Well, he was safe. Suspicion might point to him, but nothing could ever be proved. He had not gone near Diana all that day.

"Congratulations, Azazel," Carnevan said softly. He crushed out his cigarette and turned to get his topcoat from the closet.

The black spindle had been waiting behind him. This time it did not flash away as he looked at it.

It did not flash away, Carnevan saw it. He saw it distinctly. He saw every feature of what he had mistakenly imagined to be a spindle of black fog.

The worst part of it was that Carnevan didn't go mad.

THE ANGELIC ANGLEWORM

Fredric Brown

Charlie Wills shut off the alarm clock and kept right on moving, swinging his feet out of bed and sticking them into his slippers as he reached for a cigarette. Once the cigarette was lighted, he let himself relax a moment, sitting on the side of the bed.

He still had time, he figured, to sit there and smoke himself awake. He had fifteen minutes before Pete Johnson would call to take him fishing. And twelve minutes was enough time to wash his face and throw on his old clothes.

It seemed funny to get up at five o'clock, but he felt swell. Golly, even with the sun not up yet and the sky a dull pastel through the window, he felt great. Because there was only a week and a half to wait now.

Less than a week and a half, really, because it was ten days. Or—come to think of it—a bit more than ten days from this hour in the morning. But call it ten days, anyway. If he could go back to sleep again now, damn it, when he woke up it would be that much closer to the time of the wedding. Yes, it was swell to sleep when you were looking forward to something. Time flies by and you don't even hear the rustle of its wings.

But no—he couldn't go back to sleep. He'd promised Pete he'd be ready at five-fifteen, and if he wasn't, Pete would sit out front in his car and honk the horn and wake the neighbors.

And the three minutes grace was up, so he tamped out the cigarette and reached for the clothes on the chair.

He began to whistle softly: "I'm Going to Marry Yum Yum, Yum Yum" from *The Mikado*. And tried—in the interests of being ready in time—to keep his eyes off the silver-framed picture of Jane on the bureau.

He must be just about the luckiest guy on earth. Or anywhere else, for that matter, if there was anywhere else.

Jane Pemberton, with soft brown hair that had little wavelets in it and felt like silk—no, nicer than silk—and with the cute go-to-hell tilt to her nose, with long graceful sun-tanned legs, with—damn it, with everything that it was possible for a girl to have, and more. And the miracle that she loved him was so fresh that he still felt a bit dazed.

Ten days in a daze, and then—

His eye fell on the dial of the clock, and he jumped. It was ten minutes after five, and he still sat there holding the first sock. Hurriedly, he finished dressing. Just in time! It was almost five-fifteen on the head as he slid into his corduroy jacket, grabbed his fishing tackle, and tiptoed down the stairs and outside into the cool dawn.

Pete's car wasn't there yet.

Well, that was all right. It'd give him a few minutes to rustle up some worms, and that would save time later on. Of course he couldn't really dig in Mrs. Grady's lawn, but there was a bare area of border around the flower bed along the front porch, and it wouldn't matter if he turned over a bit of the dirt there.

He took his jackknife out and knelt down beside the flower bed. Ran the blade a couple of inches in the ground and turned over a clod of it. Yes, there were worms all right. There was a nice big juicy one that ought to be tempting to any fish.

Charlie reached out to pick it up.

And that was when it happened.

His fingertips came together, but there wasn't a worm between them, because something had happened to the worm. When he'd reached out for it, it had been a quite ordinary-looking angleworm. A three-inch juicy, slippery, wriggling angleworm. It most definitely had *not* had a pair of wings. Nor a—

It was quite impossible, of course, and he was dreaming or seeing things, but there it was.

Fluttering upward in a graceful slow spiral that seemed utterly effortless. Flying past Charlie's face with wings that were shimmery-white, and not at all like butterfly wings or bird wings, but like—

Up and up it circled, now above Charlie's head, now level with the roof of the house, then a mere white—somehow a *shining* white—speck against the gray sky. And after it was out of sight, Charlie's eyes still looked upward.

He didn't hear Pete Johnson's car pull in at the curb, but Pete's cheerful hail of "Hey," caught his attention, and he saw that Pete was getting out of the car and coming up the walk.

Grinning. "Can we get some worms here, before we start?" Pete asked. Then: " 'Smatter? Think you see a flying saucer? And don't you know never to look up with your mouth open like you were doing when I pulled up? Remember that pigeons—Say, *is* something the matter? You look white as a sheet."

Charlie discovered that his mouth was still open, and he closed it. Then he opened it to say something, but couldn't think of anything to say—or rather, of any way of saying it—so he closed his mouth again.

He looked back upward, but there wasn't anything in sight any more, and he looked down at the earth of the flower bed, and it looked like ordinary earth.

"Charlie!" Pete's voice sounded seriously concerned now. "Snap out of it! Are you all right?"

Again Charlie opened his mouth, and closed it. Then he said weakly, "Hello, Pete."

"For God's sake, Charlie. Did you go to sleep out here and have a nightmare or what? Get up off your knees and—Listen, are you *sick*? Shall I take you to Doc Palmer instead of us going fishing?"

Charlie got to his feet slowly, and shook himself. He said, "I—I guess I'm all right. Something funny happened. But—All right, come on. Let's go fishing."

"But what? Oh, all right, tell me about it later. But before we start, shall we dig some—Hey, don't look like that! Come on, get in the car; get some fresh air and maybe that'll make you feel better."

Pete took his arm, and Pete picked up the tackle box and led Charlie out to the waiting car. He opened the dashboard compartment and took out a bottle. "Here, take a snifter of this."

Charlie did, and as the amber fluid gurgled out of the bottle's neck and down Charlie's he felt his brain begin to rid itself of the numbness of shock. He would think again.

The whisky burned on the way down, but it put a pleasant spot of warmth where it landed, and he felt better. Until it changed to warmth, he hadn't realized that there had been a cold spot in the pit of his stomach.

He wiped his lips with the back of his hand and said, "Gosh."

"Take another," Pete said, his eyes on the road. "Maybe too it'll do you good to tell me what happened and get it out of your system. That is, if you want to."

"I—I guess so," said Charlie. "It—it doesn't sound like much to tell it, Pete. I just reached for a worm, and it flew away. On white, shining wings."

Pete looked puzzled. "You reached for a worm, and it flew away. Well, why not? I mean, I'm no entomologist, but maybe there are worms with wings. Come to think of it, there probably are. There are winged ants, and caterpillars turn into butterflies. What scared you about it?"

"Well, this worm didn't have wings until I reached for it. It looked like an ordinary angleworm. Damn it, it *was* an ordinary angleworm until I went to pick it up. And then it had a—a—oh, skip it. I was probably seeing things."

"Come on, get it out of your system. Give."

"Damn it, Pete, *it had a halo!*"

The car swerved a bit, and Pete eased it back to the middle of the road before he said, "A what?"

"Well," said Charlie defensively, "it looked like a halo. It was a little round golden circle just above its head. It didn't seem to be attached; it just floated there."

"How'd you know it was its head? Doesn't a worm look alike on both ends?"

"Well," said Charlie, and he stopped to consider the matter. How *had* he known? "Well," he said, "since it was a halo, wouldn't it be kind of silly for it to have a halo around the wrong end? I mean, even sillier than to have—Hell, you know what I mean."

Pete said, "Hmph." Then, after the car was around a curve: "All right, let's be strictly logical. Let's assume you saw, or thought you saw, what you—uh—

thought you saw. Now, you're not a heavy drinker so it wasn't D.T.s. Far as I can see, that leaves three possibilities."

Charlie said, "I see two of them. It could have been a pure hallucination. People do have 'em, I guess, but I never had one before. Or I suppose it could have been a dream, maybe. I'm sure I didn't, but I suppose that I could have gone to sleep there and dreamed I saw it. But *that* isn't it. I'll concede the possibility of an hallucination, but not a dream. What's the third?"

"Ordinary fact. That you really saw a winged worm. I mean, that there is such a thing, for all I know. And you were just mistaken about it not having wings when you first saw it, because they were folded. And what you thought looked like a halo was some sort of a crest or antenna or something. There are some damn funny-looking bugs."

"Yeah," said Charlie. But he didn't believe it. There may be funny-looking bugs, but none that suddenly sprout wings and halos and ascend unto—

He took another drink.

II

Sunday afternoon and evening he spent with Jane, and the episode of the ascending angleworm slipped into the back of Charlie's mind. Anything, except Jane, tended to slip there when he was with her.

At bedtime when he was alone again, it came back. The thought, not the worm. So strongly that he couldn't sleep and he got up and sat in the armchair by the window and decided the only way to get it out of his mind was to think it through.

If he could pin things down and decide what had really happened out there at the edge of the flower bed, then maybe he could forget it completely.

Okay, he told himself, let's be strictly logical.

Pete had been right about the three possibilities. Hallucination, dream, reality. Now to begin with, it *hadn't* been a dream. He'd been wide awake; he was as sure of that as he was sure of anything. Eliminate that.

Reality? That was impossible, too. It was all right for Pete to talk about the funniness of insects and the possibility of antennae, and such—but Pete hadn't *seen* the damn thing. Why, it had flown past only inches from his eyes. And that halo had really *been* there.

Antennae? Nuts.

And that left hallucination. That's what it must have been, hallucination. After all, people *do* have hallucinations. Unless it happened often it didn't necessarily mean you were a candidate for the booby hatch. All right, then accept it was an hallucination, and so what? So forget it.

With that decided, he went to bed and—by thinking about Jane again—happily to sleep.

The next morning was Monday and he went back to work.

And the morning after that was Tuesday.

And on Tuesday—

III

It wasn't an ascending angleworm this time. It wasn't anything you could put your finger on, unless you can put your finger on sunburn, and that's painful sometimes.

But sunburn—in a rainstorm—

It was raining when Charlie Wills left home that morning, but it wasn't raining hard at that time, which was a few minutes after eight. A mere drizzle. Charlie pulled down the brim of his hat and but-

toned up his raincoat and decided to walk to work
anyway. He rather liked walking in the rain. And he
had time: he didn't have to be there until eight-thirty.

Three blocks away from work, he encountered the
Pest, bound in the same direction. The Pest was
Jane Pemberton's kid sister, and her right name was
Paula, and most people had forgotten the fact. She
worked at the Hapworth Printing Company, just as
Charlie did; but she was a copyholder for one of the
proofreaders and he was assistant production manager.

But he'd met Jane through her, at a party given for
employees.

He said, "Hi there, Pest. Aren't you afraid you'll
melt?" For it was raining harder now, definitely
harder.

"Hello, Charlie-warlie. I like to walk in the rain."

She *would*, thought Charlie bitterly. At the hated
nickname Charlie-warlie, he winced. Jane had called
him that once, but—after he'd talked reason to her—
never again. Jane was reasonable. But the Pest had
heard it—And Charlie was mortally afraid, ever after, that she'd sometime call him that at work, with
other employees in hearing. And if *that* ever happened—

"Listen," he protested, "can't you forget that damn
fool nickname? I'll quit calling you Pest if you quit
calling me—uh—*that*."

"But I like to be called the Pest. Why don't you
like to be called Charlie-warlie?"

She grinned at him, and Charlie writhed inwardly.
Because she was *who* she was, he didn't dare—

There was pent-up anger in him as he walked into
the blowing rain, head bent low to keep it out of his
face. Damn the brat—

With vision limited to a few yards of sidewalk
directly ahead of him, Charlie probably wouldn't
have seen the teamster and the horse if he hadn't
heard the cracks that sounded like pistol shots.

He looked up, and saw. In the middle of the street, maybe fifty feet ahead of Charlie and the Pest and moving toward them came an overloaded wagon. It was drawn by an aged, despondent horse, a horse so old and bony that the slow walk by which it progressed seemed to be its speediest possible rate of movement.

But the teamster obviously didn't think so. He was a big ugly man with an unshaven, swarthy face. He was standing up, swinging his heavy whip for another blow. It came down, and the old horse quivered under it and seemed to sway between the shafts.

The whip lifted again.

And Charlie yelled, "Hey, there!" and started toward the wagon.

He wasn't certain yet just what he was going to do about it if the brute beating the other brute refused to stop. But it was gong to be something. Seeing an animal mistreated was one thing Charlie Wills just couldn't stand. And wouldn't stand.

He yelled, "Hey!" again, because the teamster didn't seem to have heard him the first time, and he started forward at a trot, along the curb.

The teamster heard that second yell, and he might have heard the first. Because he turned and looked squarely at Charlie. Then he raised the whip again, even higher, and brought it down on the horse's welt-streaked back with all his might.

Things went red in front of Charlie's eyes. He didn't yell again. He knew darned well now what he was going to do. It began with pulling that teamster down off the wagon where he could get at him. And then he was going to beat him to a pulp.

He heard Paula's high heels clicking as she started after him and called out, "Charlie, be caref—"

But that was all of it that he heard. Because, just at that moment, it happened.

A suddenly blinding wave of intolerable heat, a sensation as though he had just stepped into the heart of a fiery furnace. He gasped once for breath, as the very air in his lungs and in his throat seemed to be scorching hot. And his skin—

Blinding pain, just for an instant. Then it was gone, but too late. The shock had been too sudden and intense, and as he felt again the cool rain in his face, he went dizzy and rubbery all over, and lost consciousness. He didn't even feel the impact of his fall.

Darkness.

And then he opened his eyes into a blur of white that resolved itself into white walls and white sheets over him and a nurse in a white uniform, who said, "Doctor! He's regained consciousness."

Footsteps and the closing of a door, and there was Doc Palmer frowning down on him.

"Well, Charles, what have you been up to now?"

Charlie grinned a bit weakly. He said, "Hi, Doc. I'll bite. What *have* I been up to?"

Doc Palmer pulled up a chair beside the bed and sat down in it. He reached out for Charlie's wrist and held it while he looked at the second hand of his watch. Then he read the chart at the end of the bed and said, "Hmph."

"Is that the diagnosis," Charlie wanted to know, "or the treatment? Listen, first what about that teamster? That is, if you know—"

"Paula told me what happened. Teamster's under arrest, and fired. You're all right, Charles. Nothing serious."

"Nothing serious? What's it a non-serious case of? In other words, what happened to me?"

"You keeled over. Prostration. And you'll be peeling for a few days, but that's all. Why didn't you use a lotion of some kind yesterday?"

Charlie closed his eyes and opened them again slowly. And said, "Why didn't I use a—For *what?*"

"The sunburn, of course. Don't you know you can't go swimming on a sunny day and not get—"

"But I wasn't swimming yesterday, Doc. Nor the day before. Gosh, not for a couple weeks, in fact. What do you mean, sunburn?"

Doc Palmer rubbed his chin. He said. "You better rest a while, Charles. If you feel all right by this evening, you can go home. But you better not work tomorrow."

He got up and went out.

The nurse was still there, and Charlie looked at her blankly. He said, "Is Doc Palmer going—Listen, what's this all about?"

The nurse was looking at him queerly. She said, "Why you were—I'm sorry, Mr. Wills, but a nurse isn't allowed to discuss a diagnosis with a patient. But you haven't anything to worry about; you heard Dr. Palmer say you could go home this afternoon or evening."

"Nuts," said Charlie. "Listen, what time is it? Or aren't nurses allowed to tell that?"

"It's ten-thirty."

"Golly, and I've been here about two hours." He figured back; remembering now that he'd passed a clock that said twenty-four minutes after eight just as they'd turned the corner for that last block. And, if he'd been awake again for five minutes, then he'd been unconscious for two full hours.

"Anything else you want, sir?"

Charlie shook his head slowly. And then because he wanted her to leave so he could sneak a look at that chart, he said, "Well, yes. Could I have a glass of orange juice?"

As soon as she was gone, he sat up in bed. It hurt a little to do that, and he found his skin was a bit tender to the touch. He looked at his arms, pulling up the sleeves of the hospital nightshirt they'd put on him, and the skin was pinkish. Just the shade of pink that meant the first stage of a mild sunburn.

He looked down inside the nightshirt, and then at his legs, and said, "What the hell—" Because the sunburn, if it *was* sunburn, was uniform all over.

And that didn't make sense, because he hadn't been in the sun enough to get burned at any time recently, and he hadn't been in the sun at all without his clothes. And—yes, the sunburn extended even over the area which would have been covered by trunks if he *had* gone swimming.

But maybe the chart would explain. He reached over the foot of the bed and took the clipboard with the chart off the hook.

Reported that patient fainted suddenly on street without apparent cause. Pulse 135, respiration labored, temperature 104, upon admission. All returned to normal within first hour. Symptoms seem to approximate those of heat prostration, but . . .

Then there were a few qualifying comments which were highly technical-sounding. Charlie didn't understand them, and somehow he had a hunch that Doc Palmer didn't understand them either. They had a whistling-in-the-dark sound to them.

Click of heels in the hall outside and he put the chart back quickly and ducked under the covers. Surprisingly, there was a knock. Nurses wouldn't knock, would they?

He said, "Come in."

It was Jane. Looking more beautiful than ever, with her big brown eyes a bit bigger with fright.

"Darling! I came as soon as the Pest called home and told me. But she was awfully vague. What on earth happened?"

By that time she was within reach, and Charlie put his arms around her and didn't give a damn, just then, what had happened to him. But he tried to explain. Mostly to himself.

IV

People always try to explain.

Face a man, or a woman, with something he doesn't understand, and he'll be miserable until he classifies it. Lights in the sky. And a scientist tells him it's the aurora borealis—or the aurora australis—and he can accept the lights, and forget them.

Something knocks pictures off a wall in an empty room, and throws a chair downstairs. Consternation, until it's named. Then it's only a poltergeist.

Name it, and forget it. Anything with a name can be assimilated.

Without one, it's—well unthinkable. Take away the name of anything, and you've got blank horror.

Even something as familiar as a commonplace ghoul. Graves in a cemetery dug up, corpses eaten. Horrible thing, it may be; but it's merely a ghoul; as long as it's named—But suppose, if you can stand it, there was no such word as *ghoul* and no concept of one. *Then* dug-up half-eaten corpses are found. Nameless horror.

Not that the next thing that happened to Charlie Wills had anything to do with a ghoul. Not even a werewolf. But I think that, in a way, he'd have found a werewolf more comforting than the duck, under the circumstances. One expects strange behavior of a werewolf, but a duck—

Like the duck in the museum.

Now there is nothing intrinsically terrible about a duck. Nothing to make one lie awake at night, with cold sweat coming out on top of peeling sunburn. On the whole, a duck is a pleasant object, particularly if it is roasted. This one wasn't.

It happened on Thursday. Charlie's stay in the hospital had been for eight hours; they'd released him late in the afternoon, and he'd eaten dinner downtown and then gone home. The boss had insisted on his taking the next day off from work. Charlie hadn't protested much.

Home, and, after stripping to take a bath, he'd studied his skin with blank amazement. Definitely a first-degree burn. Definitely, all over him. Almost ready to peel.

It did peel, the next day.

He took advantage of the holiday by taking Jane out to the ball game, where they sat in a grandstand so he could be out of the sun. It was a good game, and Jane understood and liked baseball.

Thursday, back to work.

At eleven twenty-five, Old Man Hapworth, the big boss, came into Charlie's office.

"Wills," he said, "we got a rush order to print ten thousand handbills, and the copy will be here in about an hour. I'd like you to follow the thing right through the Linotype room and the composing room and get it on the press the minute it's made up. It's a close squeak whether we make deadline on it, and there's a penalty if we don't."

"Sure, Mr. Hapworth. I'll stick right with it."

"Fine. I'll count on you. But listen—it's a bit early to eat, but just the same you better go out for your lunch hour now. The copy will be here about the time you get back, and you can stick right with the job. That is, if you don't mind eating early."

"Not at all," Charlie lied. He got his hat and went out.

Damn it, it was too early to eat. But he had an hour off and he could eat in half that time, so maybe if he walked half an hour first, he could work up an appetite.

The museum was two blocks away, and the best place to kill half an hour. He went there, strolled down the central corridor without stopping, except to stare for a moment at a statue of Aphrodite that reminded him of Jane Pemberton and made him remember—even more strongly than he already remembered—that it was only six days now until his wedding.

Then he turned off into the room that housed the numismatic collection. He'd used to collect coins when he was a kid, and although the collection had been broken up since then, he still had a mild interest in looking at the big museum collection.

He stopped in front of a showcase of bronze Romans.

But he wasn't thinking about them. He was still thinking about Aphrodite, or Jane, which was quite understandable under the circumstances. Most certainly, he was not thinking about flying worms or sudden waves of burning heat.

Then he chanced to look across toward an adjacent showcase. And within it, he saw the duck.

It was a perfectly ordinary-looking duck. It had a speckled breast and greenish-brown markings on its wings and a darkish head with a darker stripe starting just above the eye and running down along the short neck. It looked like a wild rather than a domestic duck.

And it looked bewildered at being there.

For just a moment, the complete strangeness of the duck's presence in a showcase of coins didn't register with Charlie. His mind was *still* on Aphrodite. Even while he stared at a wild duck under glass inside a showcase marked "Coins of China."

Then the duck quacked, and waddled on its awkward webbed feet down the length of the showcase and butted against the glass of the end, and fluttered its wings and tried to fly upward, but hit against the glass of the top. And it quacked again and loudly.

Only then did it occur to Charlie to wonder what a live duck was doing in a numismatic collection. Apparently, to judge from its actions, the duck was wondering the same thing.

And only then did Charlie remember the angelic worm and the sunless sunburn.

And somebody in the doorway said, "*Psst.* Hey."

Charlie turned, and the look on his face must have been something out of the ordinary because the uniformed attendant quit frowning and said, "Something wrong, mister?"

For a brief instant, Charlie just stared at him. Then it occurred to Charlie that this was the opportunity he'd lacked when the angleworm had ascended. Two people couldn't see the same hallucination. If it was an—

He opened his mouth to say, "Look," but he didn't have to say anything. The duck beat him to it by quacking loudly and again trying to flutter through the glass of the case.

The attendant's eyes went past Charlie to the case of Chinese coins and he said, "Gaw!"

The duck was still there.

The attendant looked at Charlie again and said, "Did *you*—" and then stopped without finishing the question and went up to the showcase to look at close range. The duck was still struggling to get out, but more weakly. It seemed to be gasping for breath.

The attendant said, "Gaw!" again, and then over his shoulder to Charlie: "Mister, *how* did you—That there case is her-hermetchicallay sealed. It's airproof. Lookit that bird. It's—"

It already had; the duck fell over, either dead or unconscious.

The attendant grasped Charlie's arm. He said firmly. "Mister, you come with me to the boss." And less firmly, "Uh—*how* did you get that thing in there? And don't try to tell me you didn't, mister. I was through here five minutes ago, and you're the only guy's been in here since."

Charlie opened his mouth, and closed it again. He had a sudden vision of himself being questioned at the headquarters of the museum and then at the police station. And if the police started asking questions about him, they'd find out about the worm and about his having been in the hospital for—And they'd get an alienist maybe, and—

With the courage of sheer desperation, Charlie smiled. He tried to make it an ominous smile; it may not have been ominous, but it was definitely unusual. "How would you like," he asked the attendant, "to find *yourself* in there?" And he pointed with his free arm through the entrance and out into the main hallway at the stone sarcophagus of King Mene-Ptah. "I can do it, the same way I put that duck—"

The museum attendant was breathing hard. His eyes looked slightly glazed, and he let go of Charlie's arm. He said, "Mister, did you really—"

"Want me to show you how?"

"Uh—Gaw!" said the attendant. He ran.

Charlie forced himself to hold his own pace down to a rapid walk, and went in the opposite direction to the side entrance that led out into Becker Street.

And Becker Street was still a very ordinary-looking street, with lots of midday traffic, and no pink elephants climbing trees and nothing going on but the hurried confusion of a city street. Its very noise was soothing, in a way; although there was one bad moment when he was crossing at the corner and heard a sudden noise behind him. He turned around, startled, afraid of what strange thing he might see there.

But it was only a truck.

He managed to get out of its way in time to avoid being run over.

V

Lunch. And Charlie was definitely getting into a state of jitters. His hand shook so that he could scarcely pick up his coffee without slopping it over the edge of the cup.

Because a horrible thought was dawning in his mind. *If* something was wrong with him, was it fair to Jane Pemberton for him to go ahead and marry her? Is it fair to saddle the girl one loves with a husband who might go to the icebox to get a bottle of milk and find—God knows what?

And he was deeply, madly in love with Jane.

So he sat there, an unbitten sandwich on the plate before him, and alternated between hope and despair as he tried to make sense out of the three things that had happened to him within the past week.

Hallucination?

But the attendant too had seen the duck!

How comforting it had been—it seemed to him now—that, after seeing the angelic angleworm, he had been able to tell himself it had been an hallucination. *Only* an hallucination.

But wait. Maybe—

Could not the museum attendant have been part of the same hallucination as the duck? Granted that he, Charlie, could have seen a duck that wasn't there, couldn't he also have included in the same category a museum attendant who professed to see the duck? Why not? A duck and an attendant who sees it—the combination could be as illusory as the duck alone.

And Charlie felt so encouraged that he took a bite out of his sandwich.

But the *burn?* Whose hallucination was that? Or *was* there some sort of a natural physical ailment that could produce a sudden skin condition approximating mild sunburn? But, if there were such a thing, then evidently Doc Palmer didn't know about it.

Suddenly Charlie caught a glimpse of the clock on the wall, and it was one o'clock, and he almost strangled on the bite of sandwich when he realized that he was over half an hour late, and must have been sitting in the restaurant almost an hour.

He got up and ran back to the office.

But all was well; Old Man Hapworth wasn't there. And the copy for the rush circular was late and got there just as Charlie arrived.

He said, *"Whew!"* at the narrowness of his escape, and concentrated hard on getting that circular through the plant. He rushed it to the Linotypes and read proof on it himself, then watched make-up over the compositor's shoulder. He knew he was making a nuisance of himself, but it killed the afternoon.

And he thought, "Only one more day to work after today, and then my vacation, and on *Wednesday*—"

Wedding on Wednesday.

But—

If—

The Pest came out of the proofroom in a green smock and looked at him. "Charlie," she said, "you look like something no self-respecting cat would drag in. Say, what's wrong with you? Really?"

"Uh—nothing. Say, Paula, will you tell Jane when you get home that I may be a bit late this evening? I got to stick here till these handbills are off the press."

"Sure, Charlie. But tell me—"

"Nix. Run along, will you? I'm busy."

She shrugged her shoulders, and went back into the proofroom.

The machinist tapped Charlie's shoulder. "Say, we got that new Linotype set up. Want to take a look?"

Charlie nodded and followed. He looked over the installation, and then slid into the operator's chair in front of the machine. "How does she run?"

"Sweet. Those Blue Streak models are honeys. Try it."

Charlie let his fingers play over the keys, setting words without paying any attention to what they were. He sent in three lines to cast, then picked the slugs out of the stick. And found that he had set: "For men have died and worms have eaten them and ascendeth unto Heaven where it sitteth upon the right hand—"

"Gaw!" said Charlie. And *that* reminded him of—

VI

Jane noticed that there was something wrong. She couldn't have helped noticing. But instead of asking questions, she was unusually nice to him that evening.

And Charlie, who had gone to see her with the resolution to tell her the whole story, found himself weakening. As men always weaken when they are with the women they love and the parlor lamp is turned low.

But she did ask: "Charles—you *do* want to marry me, don't you? I mean, if there's any doubt in your mind and that's what has been worrying you, we can postpone the wedding till you're sure whether you love me enough—"

"*Love* you?" Charlie was aghast. "Why—"

And he proved it pretty satisfactorily.

So satisfactorily, in fact, that he completely forgot his original intention to suggest that very postponement. But *never* for the reason she suggested. With his arms around Jane—well, the poor chap was only human.

A man in love is a drunken man, and you can't exactly blame a drunkard for what he does under the influence of alcohol. You can blame him, of course, for getting drunk in the first place; but you can't put even that much blame on a man in love. In all probability, he fell through no fault of his own. In all probability his original intentions were strictly dishonorable; then, when those intentions met resistance, the subtle chemistry of sublimation converted them into the stuff that stars are made of.

Probably that was why he didn't go to see an alienist the next day. He was a bit afraid of what an alienist might tell him. He weakened and decided to wait and see if anything else happened.

Maybe nothing else would happen.

There was a comforting popular superstition that things went in groups of three, and three things had happened already.

Sure, that was it. From now on, he'd be all right. After all, there wasn't anything basically wrong; there couldn't be. He was in good health. Aside from Tuesday, he hadn't missed a day's work at the print shop in two years.

And—well, by now it was Friday noon and nothing had happened for a full twenty-four hours, and nothing was going to happen again.

Nothing did, Friday, but he read something that jolted him out of his precarious complacency.

A newspaper account.

He sat down in the restaurant at a table at which a previous diner had left a morning paper. Charlie read it while he was waiting for his order to be taken. He finished scanning the front page before the waitress came, and the comic section while he was eating his soup, and then turned idly to the local page.

GUARD AT MUSEUM SUSPENDED

Curator Orders Investigation

And the cold spot in his stomach got larger and colder as he read, for there it was in black and white.

The wild duck had really been in the showcase. No one could figure out how it had been put there. They'd had to take the showcase apart to get it out, and the showcase showed no indication of having been tampered with. It had been puttied up airtight to keep out dust, and the putty had not been damaged.

A guard, for reasons not clearly given in the article, had been given a three-day suspension. One gathered from the wording of the story that the curator of the museum had felt the necessity of doing *something* about the matter.

Nothing of value was missing from the case. One Chinese coin with a hole in the middle, a haikwan tael, made of silver, had not been found after the affair; but it wasn't worth much. There was some doubt as to whether it had been stolen by one of the workmen who had disassembled the showcase or whether it had been accidentally thrown out with the debris of old putty.

The reporter, telling the thing humorously, suggested that probably the duck had mistaken the coin for a doughnut because of the hole, and had eaten it. And that the curator's best revenge would be to eat the duck.

The police had been called in, but had taken the attitude that the whole affair must have been a practical joke. By whom or how accomplished, they didn't know.

Charlie put down the paper and stared moodily across the room.

Then it definitely *hadn't* been a double hallucination, a case of his imagining both duck and attendant. And until now that the bottom had fallen out of that idea, Charlie hadn't realized how strongly he'd counted on the possibility.

Now he was back where he'd started.

Unless—

But that was absurd. Of course, theoretically, the newspaper item he had just read *could* be an hallucination too, but—no, that was too much to swallow. According to that line of reasoning, if he went around to the museum and talked to the curator, the curator himself would be an hallucin—

"*Your duck,* sir."

Charlie jumped halfway out of his chair.

Then he saw it was the waitress standing at the side of the table with his entree, and that she had spoken because he had the newspaper spread out and there wasn't room for her to put it down.

"Didn't you order roast duck, sir? I—"

Charlie stood up hastily, averting his eyes from the dish.

He said, "Sorry-gotta-make-a-phone-call," and hastily handed the astonished waitress a dollar bill and strode out. Had he really ordered—Not exactly; he'd told her to bring him the special.

But eat duck? He'd rather eat—no, not fried angleworms either. He shuddered.

He hurried back to the office, despite the fact that he was half an hour early, and felt better once he was within the safe four walls of the Hapworth Printing Company. Nothing out of the way had happened to him there.

As yet.

VII

Basically, Charlie Wills was quite a healthy young man. By two o'clock in the afternoon, he was so hungry that he sent one of the office boys downstairs to buy him a couple of sandwiches.

And he ate them. True, he lifted up the top slice of bread on each and looked inside. He didn't know what he expected to find there, aside from boiled ham and butter and a piece of lettuce, but if he had found—in lieu of one of those ingredients—say, a Chinese silver coin with a hole in the middle, he would not have been more than ordinarily surprised.

It was a dull afternoon at the plant, and Charlie had time to do quite a bit of thinking. Even a bit of research. He remembered that the plant had printed, several years before, a textbook on entomology. He found the file copy and industriously paged through it looking for a winged worm. He found a few winged things that might be called worms, but none that even remotely resembled the angleworm with the halo. Not even, for that matter, if he disregarded the golden circle, and tried to make identification solely on the basis of body and wings.

No flying angleworms.

There weren't any medical books in which he could look up—or try to look up—how one could get sunburned without a sun.

But he looked up "tael" in the dictionary, and found that it was equivalent to a liang, which was one-sixteenth of a catty. And that one official liang is equivalent to a hectogram.

None of which seemed particularly helpful.

Shortly before five o'clock he went around saying good-by to everyone, because this was the last day at the office before his two weeks' vacation, and the good-bys were naturally complicated by good wishes on his impending wedding—which would take place in the first week of his vacation.

He had to shake hands with everybody but the Pest, whom, of course, he'd be seeing frequently during the first few days of his vacation. In fact, he went home with her from work to have dinner with the Pembertons.

And it was a quiet, restful, pleasant dinner that left him feeling better than he'd felt since last Sunday morning. Here in the calm harbor of the Pemberton household, the absurd things that had happened to him seemed so far away and so utterly fantastic that he almost doubted if they had happened at all.

And he felt utterly, completely certain that it was all over. Things happened in threes, didn't they? *If* anything else happened—But it wouldn't.

It didn't, that night.

Jane solicitously sent him home at nine o'clock to get to bed early. But she kissed him good night so tenderly, and withal so effectively, that he walked down the street with his head in rosy clouds.

Then suddenly—out of nothing, as it were—Charlie remembered that the museum attendant had been suspended, and was losing three days' pay, because of the episode of the duck in the showcase. And if that duck business was Charlie's fault—even indirectly —didn't he owe it to the guy to step forward and explain to the museum directors that the attendant had been in no way to blame, and that he should not be penalized?

After all, he, Charlie, had probably scared the poor attendant half out of his wits by suggesting that he could repeat the performance with a sarcophagus instead of a showcase, and the attendant had told such a disconnected story that he hadn't been believed.

But—*had* the thing been his fault? *Did* he owe—

And there he was butting his head against that brick wall of impossibility again. Trying to solve the unsolvable.

And he knew, suddenly, that he had been weak in not breaking his engagement to Jane. That what had happened three times within the short space of a week might all too easily happen again.

Good God! Even at the ceremony. Suppose he reached for the wedding ring and pulled out a—

From the rosy clouds of bliss to the black mire of despair had proved to be a walk of less than a block.

Almost he turned back toward the Pemberton home to tell them tonight, then decided not to. Instead, he'd stop by and talk with Pete Johnson.

Maybe Pete—

What he really hoped was that Pete would talk him out of his decision.

VIII

Pete Johnson had a gallon jug, almost full, of wine. Mellow sherry. And Pete had sampled it, and was mellow too.

He refused even to listen to Charlie, until his guest had drunk one glass and had a second on the table in front of him. Then he said, "You got something on your mind. O. K., shoot."

"Lookit, Pete. I told you about that angleworm business. In fact, you were practically there when it happened. And you know about what happened Tuesday morning on my way to work. But yesterday— well, what happened was worse, I guess. Because another guy saw it. It was a duck."

"What was a duck?"

"In a showcase at—Wait, I'll start at the beginning." And he did, and Pete listened.

"Well," he said thoughtfully, "the fact that it was in the newspaper quashes one line of thought. Fortunately. Listen, I don't see what you got to worry about. Aren't you making a mountain out of a few molehills?"

Charlie took another sip of the sherry and lighted a cigarette and said, "How?" quite hopefully.

"Well, three screwy things have happened. But

you take any one by itself and it doesn't amount to a hill of beans, does it? Any one of them can be explained. Where you bog down is in sitting there insisting on a blanket explanation for all of them.

"How do you know there is any connection at all? Now take them separately—"

"You take them," suggested Charlie. "How would you explain them so easy as all that?"

"First one's a cinch. Your stomach was upset or something and you had a pure hallucination. Happens to the best people once in a while. Or—you got a second choice just as simple—maybe you saw a new kind of bug. Hell, there are probably thousands of insects that haven't been classified yet. New ones get on the list every year."

"Um," said Charlie. "And the heat business?"

"Well, doctors don't know everything. You got too mad seeing that teamster beating the horse, and anger has a physical effect, hasn't it? You slipped a cog somewhere. Maybe it affected your thermodermal gland?"

"What's a thermodermal gland?"

Pete grinned. "I just invented it. But why not? The medicos are constantly finding new ones or new purposes of old ones. And there's *something* in your body that acts as a thermostat and keeps your skin temperature constant. Maybe it went wrong for a minute. Look what a pituitary gland can do for you or against you. Not to mention the parathyroids and the pineal and the adrenals and so on.

"Nothing to it, Charlie. Have some more wine. Now, let's take the duck business. If you don't think about it with the other two things in mind, there's nothing exciting about it. Undoubtedly just a practical joke on the museum or by somebody working there. It was just coincidence that *you* walked in on it."

"But the showcase—"

"Bother the showcase! It could have been done somehow; you didn't check that showcase yourself, and you know what newspapers are. And, for that matter, look what Thurston and Houdini could do with things like that, and let you examine the receptacles before and after. Maybe, too, it wasn't just a joke. Maybe somebody had a purpose putting it there, but why think that purpose had any connection with you? You're an egotist, that's what you are."

Charlie sighed. "Yes, but—But you take the three things together, and—"

"Why take them together? Look, this morning I saw a man slip on a banana peel and fall; this afternoon I had a slight toothache; this evening I got a telephone call from a girl I haven't seen in years. Now why should I take those three events and try to figure one common cause for all of them? One underlying motif for all three? I'd go nuts, if I tried."

"Um," said Charlie. "Maybe you got something there. But—"

Despite the "but—" he went home feeling cheerful, hopeful, and mellow. And he was going through with the wedding just as though nothing had happened. Apparently nothing of importance *had* happened. Pete was sensible.

Charlie slept soundly that Saturday morning, and didn't awaken until almost noon.

And Saturday nothing happened.

IX

Nothing, that is, unless one considered the matter of the missing golf ball as worthy of record. Charlie decided it wasn't; golf balls disappear all too often. In fact, for a dub golfer, it is only normal to lose at least one ball on eighteen holes.

And it was in the rough, at that.

He'd sliced his drive off the tee on the long four-teenth, and he'd seen it curve off the fairway, hit, bounce, and come to rest behind a big tree; with the tree directly between the ball and the green.

And Charlie's "Damn!" had been loud and fervent, because up to that hole he had an excellent chance to break a hundred. Now he'd have to lose a stroke chipping the ball back onto the fairway.

He waited until Pete had hooked into the woods on the other side, and then shouldered his bag and walked toward the ball.

It wasn't there.

Behind the tree and at about the spot where he thought the ball had landed, there was a wreath of wilted flowers strung along a purple cord that showed through at intervals. Charlie picked it up to look under it, but the ball wasn't there.

So, it must have rolled farther, and he looked but couldn't find it. Pete, meanwhile, had found his own ball and hit his recovery shot. He came across to help Charlie look and they waved the following four-some to play on through.

"I thought it stopped right here," Charlie said, "but it must have rolled on. Well, if we don't find it by the time that foursome's played through us, I'll drop another. Say, how'd this thing get here?"

He discovered he still had the wreath in his hand. Pete looked at it and shuddered. "Golly, what a color combination. Violet and red and green on a purple ribbon. It stinks." The thing did smell a bit, although Pete wasn't close enough to notice that and it wasn't what he meant.

"Yeah, but what *is* it? How'd it get—"

Pete grinned. "Looks like one of those things Hawaiians wear around their necks. Leis, don't they call them? Hey!"

He caught the suddenly stricken look on Charlie's face and firmly took the thing out of Charlie's hand

and threw it into the woods. "Now, son," he said, "don't go adding *that* damned thing to your string of coincidences. What's the difference who dropped it here or why? Come on, find your ball and let's get ready. The foursome's on the green already."

They didn't find the ball.

So Charlie dropped another. He got it out into the middle of the fairway with a niblick and then a screaming brassie shot straight down the middle put him on, ten feet from the pin. And he one-putted for a par five on the hole, even with the stroke penalty for a lost ball.

And broke a hundred after all. True, back in the clubhouse while they were getting dressed, he said, "Listen, Pete, about that ball I lost on the fourteenth. Isn't it kind of funny that it—"

"Nuts," Pete grunted. "Didn't you ever lose a ball before? Sometimes you think you see where they land, and it's twenty or even forty feet off from where it really is. The perspective fools you."

"Yeah, but—"

There was that "but" again. It seemed to be the last word on everything that happened recently. Screwy things happen one after another and you can explain each one if you consider it alone, *but*—

"Have a drink," Pete suggested, and handed over a bottle.

Charlie did, and felt better. He had several. It didn't matter, because tonight Jane was going to a shower given by some girl friends and she wouldn't smell it on his breath.

He said, "Pete, got any plans for tonight? Jane's busy, and it's one of my last bachelor evenings—"

Pete grinned. "You mean, what are we going to do or get drunk? O.K., count me in. Maybe we can get a couple more of the gang together. It's Saturday, and none us has to work tomorrow."

X

And it was undoubtedly a good thing that none of them did have to work Sunday for few of them would have been able to. It was a highly successful stag evening. Drinks at Tony's, and then a spot of bowling until the manager of the alleys began to get huffy about people bowling balls that started down one alley, jumped the groove, and knocked down pins in the allay adjacent.

And then they'd gone—

Next morning Charlie tried to remember all the places they'd been and all the things they'd done, and decided he was glad he couldn't. For one thing, he had a confused recollection of having tried to start a fight with a Hawaiian guitar player who was wearing a lei, and that he had drunkenly accused the guitarist of stealing his golf ball. But the others had dragged him out of the place before the police got there.

And somewhere around one o'clock they'd eaten, and Charlie had been so stubborn that he'd insisted on trying four eateries before they found one which served duck. He was going to avenge his golf ball by eating duck.

All in all, a very silly and successful spree. Undoubtedly worth a mild hangover.

After all, a guy gets married only once. At least, a man who has a girl like Jane Pemberton in love with him gets married only once.

Nothing out of the ordinary happened Sunday. He saw Jane and again had dinner with the Pembertons. And every time he looked at Jane, or touched her, Charlie had somewhat the sensation of a green pilot making his first outside loop in a fast plane, but that was nothing out of the ordinary. The poor guy was in love.

XI

But on Monday—

Monday was the day that really upset the apple cart. After five fifty-five o'clock Monday afternoon, Charlie knew it was hopeless.

In the morning, he made arrangements with the minister who was to perform the ceremony, and in the afternoon he did a lot of last minute shopping in the wardrobe line. He found it took him longer than he'd thought.

At five-thirty he began to doubt if he was going to have time to call for the wedding ring. It had been bought and paid for previously, but was still at the jewelers' being suitably engraved with initials.

He was still on the other side of town at five-thirty, awaiting alterations on a suit, and he phoned Pete Johnson from the tailor's:

"Say, Pete, can you do an errand for me?"

"Sure, Charlie. What's up?"

"I want to get the wedding ring before the store closes at six, so I won't have to come downtown at all tomorrow. It's right in the block with you, Scorwald & Benning's store. It's paid for; will you pick it up for me? I'll phone 'em to give it to you."

"Glad to. Say, where are you? I'm eating downtown tonight; how's about putting the feed bag on with me?"

"Sure, Pete. Listen, maybe I can get to the jewelers' in time: I'm just calling you to play safe. Tell you what; I'll meet you there. You be there at five minutes to six to be sure of getting the ring, and I'll get there at the same time if I can. If I can't, wait for me outside. I won't be later than six-fifteen at latest."

And Charlie hung up the receiver and found the tailor had the suit ready for him. He paid for it, then went outside and began to look around for a taxi.

It took him ten minutes to find one, and still he

saw he was going to get to the jewelry store in time. In fact, it wouldn't have been necessary for him to have phoned Pete. He'd get there easily by five fifty-five.

And it was just a few seconds before that time when he stepped out of the cab, paid off the driver, and strode up to the entrance.

It was just as his first foot crossed the threshold of the Scorwald & Benning store that he noticed the peculiar odor. He had taken one step farther before he recognized what it was, and then it was too late to do anything about it.

It had him. Unconsciously, he'd taken a deep sniff of identification, and the stuff was so strong, so pure, that he didn't need a second. His lungs were filled with it.

And the floor seemed to his distorted vision to be a mile away, but coming up slowly to meet him. Slowly, but getting there. He seemed to hang suspended in the air for a measurable time. Then, before he landed, everything was mercifully black and blank.

XII

"Ether."

Charlie gawked at the white-uniformed doctor. "But how the d-devil could I have got a dose of ether?"

Peter was there, too, looking down at him over the doctor's shoulder. Pete's face was white and tense. Even before the doctor shrugged, Pete was saying: "Listen, Charlie, Doc Palmer is on his way over here. I told 'em—"

Charlie was sick at his stomach, very sick. The doctor who had said, "Ether," wasn't there, and neither was Doc Palmer, but Pete now seemed to be arguing with a tall distinguished-looking gentleman who had a spade beard and eyes like a chicken hawk.

Pete was saying, "Let the poor guy alone. Damn it, I've known him all his life. He doesn't need an alienist. Sure he said screwy things while he was under, but doesn't anybody talk silly under ether?"

"But, my young friend"—the tall man's voice was unctuous—"you quite misinterpret the hospital's motives in asking that I examine him. I wish to prove him sane. If possible. He may have had a legitimate reason for taking the ether. And also the affair of last week when he was here for the first time. Surely a normal man—"

"But damn it, he *didn't take* that ether himself. I saw him coming in the doorway after he got out of the cab. He walked naturally, and he had his hands down at his sides. Then, all of a sudden, he just keeled over."

"You suggest someone near him did it?"

"There *wasn't* anybody near him."

Charlie's eyes were closed but by the psychiatrist's tone of voice, he could tell that the man was smiling. "Then how, my young friend, *do* you suggest that he was anesthetized?"

"Damn it, I don't know. I'm just saying he didn't—"

"Pete!" Charlie recognized his own voice and found that his eyes were open again. "Tell him to go to hell. Tell him to certify me if he wants. Sure I'm crazy. Tell him about the worm and the duck. Take me to the booby hatch. Tell him—"

"Ha." Again the voice with the spade beard. "You have had previous—ah—delusions?"

"Charlie, shut up! Doc, he's still under the influence of the ether; don't listen to him. It isn't *fair* to psych a guy when he doesn't know what he's talking about. For two cents, I'd—"

"Fair? My friend, psychiatry is not a game. I assure you that I have this young man's interests at heart. Perhaps his—ah—aberration is curable, and I wish to—"

Charlie sat up in bed. He yelled, *"Get out of here before I—"*

Things went black again

The tortuous darkness, thick and smoky and sickening. And he seemed to be creeping through a narrow tunnel toward a light. Then suddenly he knew that he was conscious again. But maybe there was somebody around who would talk to him and ask him questions if he opened his eyes, so he kept them tightly shut.

He kept his eyes tightly shut, and thought.

There must be an answer.

There wasn't any answer.

An angelic angleworm.

Heat wave.

Duck in a showcase of coins.

Wilted wreath of ugly flowers.

Ether in a doorway.

Connect them; there *must* be a connection. It *had* to make sense. It had to *make sense!*

Least common denominator. Something that connects them, that welds them into a coherent series, something that you can understand, something that you can maybe do something about. Something you can fight.

Worm.

Heat.

Duck.

Wreath.

Ether.

Worm.

Heat.

Duck.

Wreath.

Ether.

Worm, heat, duck, wreath, ether, worm, heat, duck wreath—

They pounded through his head like beating on a tom-tom; they screamed at him out of the darkness and gibbered.

XIII

He must have slept, if you could call it sleep.

It was broad daylight again, and there was only a nurse in the room. He asked, "What—day is it?"

"Wednesday afternoon, Mr. Wills. Is there anything I can do for you?"

Wednesday afternoon. Wedding day.

He wouldn't have to call it off now. Jane knew. Everybody knew. It had been called off for him. He'd been weak not to have done it himself, before—

"There are people waiting to see you, Mr. Wills. Do you feel well enough to entertain visitors?"

"I—Who?"

"A Miss Pemberton and her father. And a Mr. Johnson. Do you want to see them?"

Well, did he?

"Look," he said, "what exactly's wrong with me? I mean—"

"You've suffered a severe shock. But you've slept quietly for the last twelve hours. Physically, you are quite all right. Even able to get up, if you feel you want to. But, of course, you mustn't leave."

Of *course* he mustn't leave. They had him down as a candidate for the booby hatch. An excellent candidate. Young man most likely to succeed.

Wednesday. Wedding day.

Jane.

He couldn't bear to see—

"Listen," he said, "will you send in Mr. Pemberton, alone? I'd rather—"

"Certainly. Anything else I can do for you?"

Charlie shook his head sadly. He was feeling most horribly sorry for himself. Was there anything *anybody* could do for him?

Mr. Pemberton held out his hand quietly. "Charles, I can't begin to tell you how sorry I am—"

Charlie nodded. "Thanks. I—I guess you understand why I don't want to see Jane. I realize that—that of course we can't—"

Mr. Pemberton nodded. "Jane—un—understands, Charles. She wants to see you, but realizes that it might make both of you feel worse, at least right now. And Charles, if there's anything any of us can do—"

What was there anybody could do?

Pull the wings off an angleworm?

Take a duck out of a showcase?

Find a missing golf ball?

Pete came in after the Pembertons had gone away. A quieter and more subdued Pete than Charlie had ever seen.

He said, "Charlie, do you feel up to talking this over?"

Charlie sighed. "If it'd do any good, yes. I feel all right physically. But—"

"Listen, you've got to keep your chin up. There's an answer somewhere. Listen, I was wrong. There is a connection, a tie-up between these screwy things that happened to you. There's got to be."

"Sure," said Charlie, wearily. "What?"

"That's what we've got to find out. First place, we'll have to outsmart the psychiatrists they'll sick on you. As soon as they think you're well enough to stand it. Now, let's look at it from their point of view so we'll know what to tell 'em. First—"

"How much do they know?"

"Well, you raved while you were unconscious, about the worm business and about a duck and a golf ball, but you can pass that off as ordinary raving. Talking in your sleep. Dreaming. Just deny knowing anything about them, or anything connected with any of them. Sure, the duck business was in the newspapers, but it wasn't a big story and your name wasn't in it. So they'll never tie that up. If they do, deny it. Now that leaves the two times you keeled over and were brought here unconscious."

Charlie nodded. "And what do they make of them?"

"They're puzzled. The first one they can't make anything much of. They're inclined to leave it lay. The second one—Well, they insist that you must, somehow, have given yourself that ether."

"But why? Why would anybody give himself ether?"

"No sane man would. That's just it; they doubt your sanity because they think you did. If you can convince them you're sane, then—Look, you *got* to buck up. They are classifying your attitude as acute melancholia, and that sort of borders on manic depressive. See? You got to act cheerful."

"Cheerful? When I was to be married at two o'clock today? By the way, what time is it now?"

Pete glanced at his wrist watch and said, "Uh— never mind that. Sure, if they ask why you feel lousy mentally, tell them—"

"Damn it, Pete, I wish I *was* crazy. At least, being crazy makes sense. And if this stuff keeps up, I *will* go—"

"*Don't talk like that.* You got to fight."

"Yeah," said Charlie, listlessly. "Fight what?"

There was a low rap on the door and the nurse looked into the room. "Your time is up, Mr. Johnson. You'll have to leave."

XIV

Inaction, and the futility of circling thought-patterns that get nowhere. Finally, he had to do something or go mad.

Get dressed? He called for his clothes and got them, except that he was given slippers instead of his shoes. Anyway, getting dressed took up time.

And sitting in a chair was a change from lying in bed. And then walking up and down was a change from sitting in a chair.

"What time is it?"

"Seven o'clock, Mr. Wills."

Seven o'clock; he should have been married five hours by now.

Married to Jane; beautiful, gorgeous, sweet, loving, understanding, kissable, soft, lovable Jane Pemberton. Five hours ago this moment she should have become Jane Wills.

Nevermore.

Unless—

The problem.

Solve it.

Or go mad.

Why would a worm wear a halo?

"Dr. Palmer is here to see you, Mr. Wills. Shall I—"

"Hello, Charles. Came as soon as I could after I learned you were out of your—uh—coma. Had an o.b. case that kept me. How do you feel?"

He felt terrible.

Ready to scream and tear the paper off the wall only the wall was painted white and didn't have any paper. And scream, scream—

"I feel swell, Doc," said Charlie.

"Anything—uh—strange happen to you since you've been here?"

"Not a thing. But, Doc, how would you explain—"

Doc Palmer explained. Doctors always explain. The air crackled with words like psychoneurotic and autohypnosis and traumata.

Finally, Charlie was alone again. He'd managed to say good-bye to Doc Palmer, too, without yelling and tearing him to bits.

"What time is it?"

"Eight o'clock."

Six hours married.

Why a *duck?*

Solve it.

Or go mad.

What would happen next? "Surely this thing shall follow me all the days of my life and I shall dwell in the bughouse forever."

Eight o'clock.

Six hours married.

Why a lei? Ether? Heat?

What have they in common? And why a duck?

And what would it be *next time?* When would next time be? Well, maybe he could guess that. How many things happened to him thus far? Five—if the missing golf ball counted. How far apart? Let's see— the angleworm was Sunday morning when he went fishing; the heat prostration was Tuesday; the duck in the museum was Thursday noon, the second-last day he worked; the golf game and the lei was Saturday; the either Monday—

Two days apart.

Periodicity?

He'd been pacing up and down the room, now suddenly he felt in his pocket and found pencil and a notebook, and sat down in the chair.

Could it be—*exact* periodicity?

He wrote down "Angleworm" and stopped to think. Pete was to call for him to go fishing at five-fifteen and he'd gone downstairs at just that time, and right to the flower bed to dig—Yes, five-fifteen A.M. He wrote it down.

"Heat." Hm-m-m, he'd been a block from work and was due there at eight-thirty, and when he'd passed the corner clock he'd looked and seen that he had five minutes to get there, and then had seen the teamster and—He wrote it down. "Eight twenty-five." And calculated.

Two days, three hours, ten minutes.

Let's see, which was next? The duck in the museum. He could time that fairly well, too. Old Man Hapworth had told him to go to lunch early, and he'd left at—uh—eleven twenty-five and it took him, say, ten minutes to walk the block to the museum and down the main corridor and into the numismatic room—say, eleven thirty-five.

He subtracted that from the previous one.

And whistled.

Two days, three hours, ten minutes.

The lei? Um, they'd left the clubhouse about one-thirty. Allow an hour and a quarter, say, for the first thirteen holes, and—Well, say between two-thirty and three. Strike an average at two forty-five. That would be pretty close. Subtract it.

Two days, three hours, ten minutes.

Periodicity.

He subtracted the next one first—the fourth episode should have happened at five fifty-five on Monday. If—

Yes, it had been *exactly* five minutes of six when he'd walked through the door of the jewelry shop and been anesthetized.

Exactly.

Two days, three hours, ten minutes.

Periodicity.

PERIODICITY.

A connection, at last. Proof that the screwy events

were all of a piece. Every—uh—fifty-one hours and ten minutes *something screwy happened*.

But why?

He stuck his head out in the hallway.

"Nurse. NURSE. What time is it?"

"Half past eight, Mr. Wills. Anything I can bring you?"

Yes. No. Champagne. Or a strait jacket. Which?

He'd solved the problem. But the answer didn't make any more sense than the problem itself. Less, maybe. And today—

He figured quickly.

In thirty-five minutes.

Something would happen to him in thirty-five minutes!

Something like a flying angleworm or like a quacking duck suffocating in an air-tight showcase, or—

Or maybe something *dangerous* again? Burning heat, sudden anesthesia—

Maybe something worse?

A cobra, unicorn, devil, werewolf, vampire, unnamable monster?

At nine-five. In half an hour.

In a sudden draft from the open window, his forehead felt cold. Because it was wet with sweat.

In half an hour.

XV

Pace up and down, four steps one way, four steps back. Think, think, THINK.

You've solved part of it; what's the rest? Get it, or it will get you.

Periodicity; that's part of it. Every two days, three hours, ten minutes—

Something happens.

Why?

What?

How?

They're connected, those things, they are part of a pattern and they make sense somehow or they wouldn't be spaced an exact interval of time apart.

Connect: angleworm, heat, duck, lei, ether—

Or go mad.

Mad. *Mad.* MAD.

Connect: Ducks eat angleworms, or do they? Heat is necessary to grow flowers to make leis. Angleworms might eat flowers for all he knew, but what have they to do with leis, and what is ether to a duck? Duck is animal, lei is vegetable, heat is vibration, ether is gas, worm is—what the hell is a worm? And why a worm that flies? Why was the duck in the showcase? What about the missing Chinese coin with the hole? Do you add or subtract the golf ball, and if you let x equal a halo and y equal one wing, then x plus 2y plus 1 angleworm equals—

Outside, somewhere, a clock strikes in the gathering darkness.

One, two, three, four, five, six, seven, eight, nine—

Nine o'clock.

Five minutes to go.

In five minutes something was going to happen again.

Cobra, unicorn, devil, werewolf, vampire. Or something cold and slimy and without a name.

Anything.

Pace up and down, four steps one way, four steps back.

Think, THINK.

Jane forever lost. Dearest Jane, in whose arms was all of happiness. Jane, darling, I'm not mad, I'm worse than mad. I'm—

WHAT TIME IS IT?

It must be two minutes after nine. Three.

What's coming? Cobra, devil, werewolf—

What will it be this time?

At five minutes after nine—WHAT?

Must be four after now; yes, it had been at least four minutes, maybe four and a half—

He yelled, suddenly. He couldn't stand the waiting.

It couldn't be solved. But he had to solve it.

Or go mad.

MAD.

He must be mad already. Mad to tolerate living, trying to fight something you couldn't fight, trying to beat the unbeatable. Beating his head against—

He was running now, out the door, down the corridor.

Maybe if he hurried, he could kill himself before five minutes after nine. He'd never have to know. DIE, DIE AND GET IT OVER WITH. THAT'S THE ONLY WAY TO BUCK THIS GAME.

Knife.

There'd be a knife somewhere. A scalpel is a knife.

Down the corridor. Voice of a nurse behind him, shouting. Footsteps.

Run. Where? Anywhere.

Less than a minute left. Maybe seconds.

Maybe it's nine-five now. Hurry!

Door marked "Utility"—he jerked it open.

Shelves of linen. Mops and brooms. You can't kill yourself with a mop or broom. You can smother yourself with linen, but not in less than a minute and with doctors and interns coming.

Uniforms. Bucket. Kick the bucket, but *how?* Ah. There on the upper shelf—

A cardboard carton, already opened, marked "Lye."

Painful? Sure, but it wouldn't last long. Get it over with. The box in his hand, the opened corner and tilted the contents into his mouth.

But it was not a white, searing powder. All that had come out of the cardboard carton was a small copper coin. He took it out of his mouth and held it, and looked at it with dazed eyes.

It was five minutes after nine, then; out of the box of lye had come a small foreign copper coin. No, it wasn't the Chinese haikwan tael that had disappeared from the showcase in the museum, because that was silver and had a hole in it. And the lettering on this wasn't Chinese. If he remembered his coins, it looked Rumanian.

And then strong hands took hold of Charlie's arms and led him back to his room and somebody talked to him quietly for a long time.

And he slept.

XVI

He awoke Thursday morning from a dreamless sleep, and felt strangely refreshed and, oddly, quite cheerful.

Probably because, in that awful thirty-five minutes of waiting he'd experienced the evening before, he'd hit rock bottom. And bounced.

A psychiatrist might have explained it by saying that he had, under stress of great emotion, suffered a temporary lesion and gone into a quasi-state of manic-depressive insanity. Psychiatrists like to make simple things complicated.

The fact was that the poor guy had gone off his rocker for a few minutes.

And the absurd anticlimax of that small copper coin had been the turning point. Look for something horrible, unnamable—and get a small copper coin. Practically a prophylactic treatment, if you've got enough stuff in you to laugh.

And Charlie had laughed last night. Probably that was why his room this morning seemed to be a different room. The window was in a different wall, and it had bars across it. Psychiatrists often misinterpret a sense of humor.

But this morning he felt cheerful enough to overlook the implications of the barred windows. Here it was a bright new day with the sun streaming through the bars, and it was *another* day and he was still alive and had another chance.

Best of all, he knew he wasn't insane.

Unless—

He looked and there were his clothes hanging over the back of a chair and he sat up and put his legs out of bed, and reached for his coat pocket to see if the coin was still where he'd put it when they'd grabbed him.

It was.

Then—

He dressed slowly, thoughtfully.

Now in the light of morning, it came to him that the thing could be solved. Six—now there were six—screwy things, but they were definitely connected. Periodicity proved it.

Two days, three hours, ten minutes.

And whatever the answer was, it as not malevolent. It was impersonal. If it had wanted to kill, it had a chance last night; it need merely have affected something else other than the lye in that package. There'd *been* lye in the package when he'd picked it up; he could tell that by the weight. And then it had been five minutes after nine instead of lye there'd been the small copper coin.

It wasn't friendly, either; or it wouldn't have subjected him to heat and anesthesia. It must be something impersonal.

A coin instead of lye.

Were they all substitutions of one thing for another?

Hm-m-m. Lei for a golf ball. A coin for lye. A duck for a coin. But the heat? The ether? The angleworm?

He went to the window and looked out for a while

into the warm sunlight falling on the green lawn, and he realized that life was very sweet. And that if he took this thing calmly and didn't let it get him down again, he might yet lick it.

The first clue was already his.

Periodicity.

Take it calmly; think about other things. Keep your mind off the merry-go-round and maybe the answer will come.

He sat down on the edge of the bed and felt in his pocket for the pencil and notebook and they were still there, and the paper on which he'd made his calculations of timing. He studied those calculations carefully.

Calmly.

And at the end of the list he put down "9:05" and added the word "lye" and a dash. Lye had turned to—what? He drew a bracket and began to fill in words that could be used to describe the coin: coin—copper—disk—But those were general. There must be a specific name for the thing.

Maybe—

He pressed the button that would light a bulb outside his door and a moment later heard a key turn in the lock and the door opened. It was a male attendant this time.

Charlie smiled at him. "Morning," he said. "Serve breakfast here, or do I eat the mattress?"

The attendant grinned, and looked a bit relieved. "Sure. Breakfast's ready; I'll bring you some."

"And—uh—"

"Yes?"

"There's something I want to look up," Charlie said. "Would there be an unabridged dictionary any-where handy? And if there is, would it be asking too much for you to let me see it a few minutes?"

"Why—I guess it will be all right. There's one down in the office and they don't use it very often."

"That's swell. Thanks."

But the key turned in the lock when he left.

Breakfast came half an hour later, but the dictionary didn't arrive until the middle of the morning. Charlie wondered if there had been a staff meeting to discuss its lethal possibilities. But anyway, it came.

He waited until the attendant had left and then put the big volume on the bed and opened it to the color plate that showed coins of the world. He took the copper coin out of his pocket and put it alongside the plate and began to compare it with the illustrations, particularly those of coins of the Balkan countries. No, nothing just like it among the copper coins. Try the silver—yes, there was a silver coin with the same mug on it. Rumanian. The lettering— yes, it was identically the same lettering except for the denomination.

Charlie turned to the coinage table. Under Rumania—

He gasped.

It couldn't be.

But it was.

It was impossible that the six things that had happened to him could have been—

He was breathing hard with excitement as he turned to the illustrations at the back of the dictionary, found the pages of birds, and began to look among the ducks. Speckled breast and short neck and darker stripe starting just above the eye—

And he knew he'd found the answer.

He'd found the factor, besides periodicity, that connected the things that had happened. If it fitted the others, he could be sure. The angleworm? Why— *sure*—and he grinned at that one. The heat wave? Obvious. And the affair on the golf course? That was harder, but a bit of thought gave it to him.

The matter of the ether stumped him for a while.

It took a lot of pacing up and down to solve that one, but finally he managed to do it.

And then? Well, what could he *do* about it?

Periodicity? Yes, that fitted in. If—

Next time would be—hm-m-m—12:15 Saturday morning.

He sat down to think it over. The whole thing was completely incredible. The answer was harder to swallow than the problem.

But—they *all* fitted. Six coincidences, spaced an exact length of time apart?

All right then, forget how incredible it is, and what are you going to do about it? How are you going to get there to let them know?

Well—maybe take advantage of the phenomenon itself?

The dictionary was still there and Charlie went back to it and began to look in the gazetteer. Under "H—"

"*Whew!*" There was one that gave him a *double* chance. And within a hundred miles.

If he could get out of here—

He rang the bell, and the attendant came. "Through with the dictionary," Charlie told him. "And listen, could I talk to the doctor in charge of my case?"

It proved that the doctor in charge was still Doc Palmer, and that he was coming up anyway.

He shook hands with Charlie and smiled at him. That was a good sign, or was it?

Well, now if he could lie convincingly enough—

"Doc, I feel swell this morning," said Charlie. "And listen—I remembered something I want to tell you about. Something that happened to me Sunday, couple of days before that first time I was taken to the hospital."

"What was it, Charles?"

"I *did* go swimming, and that accounts for the sunburn that was showing up on Tuesday morning, and maybe for some other things. I'd borrowed Pete Johnson's car—" Would they check up on that? Maybe not. "—and I got lost off the road and found a swell pool and stripped and went in. And I remember now that I dived off the bank and I think I must have grazed my head on a rock because the next thing I remember I was back in town."

"H-m-m," said Doc Palmer. "So *that* accounts for the sunburn, and maybe it can account for—"

"Funny that it just came back to me this morning when I woke up," said Charlie. "I guess—"

"I told those fools," said Doc Palmer, "that there couldn't be any connection between the third-degree burns and your fainting. Of course there was, in a way. I mean your hitting your head while you were swimming would account—Charles, I'm sure glad this came back to you. At least we now know the cause of the way you've acted, and we can treat it. In fact, maybe you're cured already."

"I think so, Doc. I sure feel swell now. Like I was just waking up from a nightmare. I guess I made a fool of myself a couple of times. I have a vague recollection of buying some ether once, and something about some lye—but those are like things that happened in a dream, and now my mind's as clear as a bell. Something seemed to pop this morning, and I was all right again."

Doc Palmer sighed. "I'm relieved, Charles. Frankly, you had us quite worried. Of course, I'll have to talk this over with the staff and we'll have to examine you pretty thoroughly, but I think—"

There were other doctors and they asked questions and they examined his skull—but whatever lesion had been made by the rock seemed to have healed. Anyway, they couldn't find it.

If it hadn't been for his suicide attempt of the evening before, he could have walked out of the hospital then and there. But because of that, they

insisted on his remaining under observation for twenty-
four hours. And Charlie agreed; that would let him
out some time Friday afternoon, and it wasn't
until twelve-fifteen Saturday morning that *it* would
happen.

Plenty of time to go a hundred miles.

If he just watched everything he did and said in
the meantime and made no move or remark which a
psychiatrist could interpret—

He loafed and rested.

And at five o'clock Friday afternoon it was all
right, and he shook hands all the way around, and
was a free man again. He'd promised to report to
Doc Palmer regularly for a few weeks.

But he was free.

XVII

Rain and darkness.

A cold, unpleasant drizzle that started to find its
way through his clothes and down the back of his
neck and into his shoes even as he stepped off the
train onto the small wooden platform.

But the station was there, and on the side of it was
the sign that told him the name of the town. Charlie
looked at it and grinned, and went into the station.
There was a cheerful little coal stove in the middle of
the room. He had time to get warmed up before he
started. He held out his hands to the stove.

Over at one side of the room, a grizzled head
regarded him curiously through the ticket window.
Charlie nodded at the head and the head nodded
back.

"Stayin' here a while, stranger?" the head asked.

"Not exactly," said Charlie. "Anyway, I hope not.
I mean—" Hell, after those whoppers he'd told the
psychiatrists back at the hospital, he shouldn't have

any trouble lying to a ticket agent in a little country town. "I mean, I don't think so."

"Ain't no more trains out tonight, mister. Got a place to stay? If not, my wife sometimes takes in boarders for short spells."

"Thanks," said Charlie. "I've made arrangements." He started to add, "I hope," and then realized that it would lead him further into discussion.

He glanced at the clock and at his wrist watch and saw that both agreed that it was a quarter to twelve.

"How big is this town?" he asked. "I don't mean population. I mean, how far out the turnpike is it to the township line? The border of town."

" 'Tain't big. Half a mile maybe, or a little better. You goin' out to the Tolivers, maybe? They live just past and I heard tell he was sendin' to th' city for a—nope, you don't look like a hired man."

"Nope," said Charlie. "I'm not." He glanced at the clock again and started for the door. He said, "Well, be seeing you."

"You goin' to—"

But Charlie had already gone out the door and was starting down the street behind the railroad station. Into the darkness and the unknown and—Well, he could hardly tell the agent about his real destination, could he?

There was the turnpike. After a block, the sidewalk ended and he had to walk along the edge of the road, sometimes ankle deep in mud. He was soaked through by now, but that didn't matter.

It proved to be more than half a mile to the township line. A big sign there—an oddly big sign considering the size of the town—read:

YOU ARE NOW ENTERING HAVEEN

Charlie crossed the line and faced back. And waited, an eye on his wrist watch.

At twelve-fifteen he'd have to step across. It was ten minutes after already. Two days, three hours, ten minutes after the box of lye had held a copper coin, which was two days, three hours, ten minutes after he'd walked into the anesthesia in the door of a jewelry store, which was two days, three hours, ten minutes after—

He watched the hands of his accurately set wrist watch, first the minute hand until twelve-fourteen. Then the second hand.

And when it lacked a second of twelve-fifteen he put forth his foot and at *the* fatal moment he was stepping slowly across the line.

Entering Haveen.

XVIII

And as with each of the others, there was no warning. But suddenly:

It wasn't raining any more. There was bright light, although it didn't seem to come from a visible source. And the road beneath his feet wasn't muddy; it was smooth as glass and alabaster-white. The white-robed entity at the gate ahead stared at Charlie in astonishment.

He said: "How did *you* get here? You aren't even—"

"No," said Charlie. "I'm not even dead. But listen, I've got to see the-uh—who's in charge of the printing?"

"The Head Compositor, of course. But you can't—"

"I've got to see him, then," said Charlie.

"But the rules forbid—"

"Look, it's important. Some *typographical errors* are going through. It's to your interests up here as well as to mine, that they be corrected, isn't it? Otherwise things can get into an awful mess."

"Errors? Impossible. You're joking."

"Then how," asked Charlie, reasonably, "did I get to Heaven without dying?"

"But—"

"You see I was supposed to be entering Haveen. There is an e-matrix that—"

"Come."

XIX

It was quite pleasant and familiar, that office. Not a lot different from Charlie's own office at the Hapworth Printing Company. There was a rickety wooden desk, littered with papers, and behind it sat a small bald-headed Chief Compositor with printer's ink on his hands and a smear of it on his forehead. Past the closed door was a monster roar and clatter of typesetting machines and presses.

"Sure," said Charlie. "They're supposed to be perfect, so perfect that you don't even need proofreaders. But maybe once out of infinity something can happen to perfection, can't it? Mathematically, once out of infinity *anything* can happen. Now look; there is a separate typesetting machine and operator for the records covering each person, isn't there?"

The Head Compositor nodded. "Correct, although in a manner of speaking the operator and the machine are one, in that the operator is a function of the machine and the machine a manifestation of the operator and both are extensions of the ego of the— but I guess that is a little too complicated for you to understand."

"Yes, I—well, anyway, the channels that the matrices run in must be tremendous. On our linotypes at the Hapworth Printing Company, an e-mat would make the circuit every sixty seconds or so, and if one was defective it would cause one mistake a minute, but up here—Well, is my calculation of fifty hours and ten minutes correct?"

"It is," agreed the Head Compositor. "And since there is no way you could have found out that fact except—"

"Exactly. And once every that often the defective e-matrix comes round and falls when the operator hits the e-key. Probably the ears of the mat are worn; anyway it falls through a long distributor front and falls too fast and lands ahead of its right place in the word, and a typographical error goes through. Like a week ago Sunday, I was supposed to pick up an *angleworm*, and—"

"Wait."

The Head Compositor pressed a buzzer and issued an order. A moment later, a heavy book was brought in and placed on his desk. Before the Head Compositor opened it, Charlie caught a glimpse of his own name on the cover.

"You said at five-fifteen A.M.?"

Charlie nodded. Pages turned.

"I'll be—blessed!" said the Head Compositor. "*Angleworm!* It must have been something to see. Don't know I've ever heard of an angelworm before. And what was next?"

"The e fell wrong in the word 'hate'—I was going after a man who was beating a horse, and—Well, it came out 'heat' instead of 'hate.' The e dropped two characters early that time. And I got heat prostration and sunburn on a rainy day. That was eight twenty-five Tuesday, and then at eleven thirty-five Thursday at the museum—"

"Yes?" prompted the Head Compositor.

"A tael. A Chinese silver coin I was supposed to see. It came out 'teal' and because a teal is a duck, there was a wild duck fluttering around in an airtight showcase. One of the attendants got in trouble; I hope you'll fix that."

The Head Compositor chuckled. "I shall," he said. "I'd like to have seen that duck. And the next time would have been two forty-five Saturday afternoon. What happened then?"

"Lei instead of lie, sir. My golf ball was stymied behind a tree and it was supposed to be a poor lie—but it was a poor lei instead. Some wilted, mismatched flowers on a purple cord. And the next was the hardest for me to figure out, even when I had the key. I had an appointment at the jewelry store at five fifty-five. But that was the fatal time. I got there at five fifty-five, but the e-matrix fell four characters out of place that time, clear back to the start of the word. Instead of getting *there* at five fifty-five, I got *ether*."

"*Tch, tch.* That one was unfortunate. And next?"

"The next was just the reverse, sir. In fact, it happened to save my life. I want temporarily insane and tried to kill myself by taking lye. But the bad e fell in lye and it came our *ley*, which is a small Rumanian copper coin. I've still got it, for a souvenir. In fact when I found out the name of the coin, I guessed the answer. It gave me the key to the others."

The Head Compositor chuckled again. "You've shown great resource," he said. "And your method of getting here to tell us about it—"

"That was easy, sir. If I timed it so I'd be entering Haveen at the right instant, I had a double chance. If either of the two e's in that word turned out to be the bad one and fell—as it did—too early in the word, I'd be entering Heaven."

"Decidedly ingenious. You may, incidentally, consider the errors corrected. We've taken care of all of them, while you talked; except the last one, of course. Otherwise, you wouldn't still be here. And the defective mat is removed from the channel."

"You mean that as far as people down there know, none of those things ever—"

"Exactly. A revised edition is now on the press, and nobody on Earth will have any recollection of any of those events. In a way of speaking, they no longer ever happened. I mean, they did, but now they didn't for all practical purposes. When we return you to Earth, you'll find the status there just what it would have been if the typographical errors had not occurred."

"You mean, for instance, that Pete Johnson won't remember my having told him about the angleworm, and there won't be any record at the hospital about my having been there? And—"

"Exactly. The errors are *corrected*."

"*Whew!*" said Charlie. "I'll be—I mean, well, I was supposed to have been married Wednesday afternoon, two days ago. Uh—will I be? I mean, *was* I? I mean—"

The Head Compositor consulted another volume, and nodded. "Yes, at two o'clock Wednesday afternoon. To one Jane Pemberton. Now if we return you to Earth as of the time you left there—twelve-fifteen Saturday morning, you'll find yourself—let's see—spending your honeymoon in Miami. At that exact moment, you'll be in a taxicab en route—"

"Yes, but—" Charlie gulped.

"But what?" The Head Compositor looked surprised. "I certainly thought that was what you wanted, Wills. We owe you a big favor for having used such ingenuity in calling those typographical errors to our attention, but I thought that being married to Jane was what you wanted, and if you go back and find yourself—"

"Yes, but—" said Charlie again. "But—I mean— Look, I'll have been married two days. I'll miss—I mean, couldn't I—"

Suddenly the Head Compositor smiled.

"How stupid of me," he said, "of course. Well, the time doesn't matter at all. We can drop you anywhere in the continuum. I can just as easily return you as of two o'clock Wednesday afternoon, at the moment of the ceremony. Or Wednesday morning, just before. Any time at all."

"Well," said Charlie, hesitantly. "It isn't exactly that I'd miss the wedding ceremony. I mean, I don't like receptions and things like that, and I'd have to sit through a long wedding dinner and listen to toasts and speeches and, well, I mean. I—"

The Head Compositor laughed. He said, "Are you ready?"

"Am I—Sure!"

Click of train wheels over the rails, and the stars and moon bright above the observation platform of the speeding train.

Jane in his arms. His wife, and it was Wednesday evening. Beautiful, gorgeous, sweet, loving, soft, kissable, lovable Jane—

She snuggled closer to him, and he was whispering, "It's—it's eleven o'clock, darling. Shall we—"

Their lips met, clung.

Then, hand in hand, they walked through the swaying train. His hand turned the knob of the stateroom door and, as it swung slowly open, he picked her up to carry her across the threshold.

DAHUT, Book III
Dahut is the daughter of the King, Gratillonius, and her story is one of mythic power . . . and ancient evil. The senile gods of Ys have decreed that Dahut must become a Queen of the Christ-cursed city of Ys while her father still lives. 65371-7 $3.95

THE DOG AND THE WOLF, Book IV
Gratillonius, the once and future King, strives first to save the surviving remnant of the Ysans from utter destruction, and then to save civilization itself as barbarian night extinguishes the last flickers of the light that once was Rome! 65391-1 $4.50

ANDERSON, POUL
THE BROKEN SWORD
Come with us now to 11th-century Scandinavia, when Christianity is beginning to replace the old religon, but the Old Gods still have power, and men are still oppressed by the folk of the Faerie.

65382-2 $2.95

ASIRE, NANCY
TWILIGHT'S KINGDOMS
For centuries, two nearly-immortal races—the Krotahnya, followers of Light, and the Leishoranya, servants of Darkness—have been at war, struggling for final control of a world that belongs to neither. "The novel-length debut of an important new talent . . . I enthusiastically recommend it."—C.J. Cherryh

65362-8 $3.50

BROWN, MARY
THE UNLIKELY ONES
Thing is a young girl who hides behind a mask; her companions include a crow, a toad, a goldfish, and a

kitten. Only the Dragon of the Black Mountain can restore them to health and happiness—but the questers must total seven to have a chance of success. "An imaginative and charming book."—*USA Today*. "You've got a winner here . . ."—Anne McCaffrey.

65361-X $3.95

DAVIDSON, AVRAM and DAVIS, GRANIA
MARCO POLO AND THE SLEEPING BEAUTY
Held by bonds of gracious but involuntary servitude in the court of Kublai Khan for ten years, the Polos—Marco, his father Niccolo, and his uncle Maffeo—want to go home. But first they must complete one simple task: bring the Khan the secret of immortality!

65372-5 $3.50

EMERY, CLAYTON
TALES OF ROBIN HOOD
Deep within Sherwood Forest, Robin Hood and his band have founded an entire community, but they must be always alert against those who would destroy them: Sir Guy de Gisborne, Maid Marion's ex-fiance and Robin's sworn enemy; the sorceress Taragal, who summons a demon boar to attack them; and even King Richard the Lion-Hearted, who orders Robin and his men to come and serve his will in London. And who is the false Hood whose men rape, pillage and burn in Robin's name?

65397-0 $3.50

AB HUGH, DAFYDD
HEROING
A down-on-her-luck female adventurer, a would-be boy hero, and a world-weary priest looking for new faith are comrades on a quest for the World's Dream.

65344-X $3.50

HEROES IN HELL

created by Janet Morris

The greatest heroes of history meet the greatest names of science fiction—and each other!—in the greatest meganovel of them all! (Consult "The Whole Baen Catalog" for the complete listing of HEROES IN HELL.)

MORRIS, JANET & GREGORY BENFORD,
C.J. CHERRYH, ROBERT SILVERBERG, more!
ANGELS IN HELL (Vol. VII)
Gilgamesh returns for blood; Marilyn Monroe kisses the Devil; Stalin rewrites the Bible; and Altos, the unfallen Angel, drops in on Napoleon and Marie with good news: Marie will be elevated to heaven, no strings attached! Such a deal! (So why is Napoleon crying?) 65360-1 $3.50

MORRIS, JANET, & LYNN ABBEY, NANCY ASIRE,
C. J. CHERRYH, DAVID DRAKE, BILL KERBY,
CHRIS MORRIS, more.
MASTERS IN HELL (Vol. VIII)
Feel the heat as the newest installment of the infernally popular HEROES IN HELL® series roars its way into your heart! This is Hell—where you'll find Sir Francis Burton, Copernicus, Lee Harvey Oswald, J. Edgar Hoover, Napoleon, Andropov, and other masters and would-be masters of their fate.
65379-2 $3.50

REAVES, MICHAEL
THE BURNING REALM
A gripping chronicle of the struggle between human magicians and the very *in*human Chthons with their

demon masters. All want total control over the whirling fragments of what once was Earth, before the Necromancer unleashed the cataclysm that tore the world apart. "A fast-paced blend of fantasy, martial arts, and unforgettable landscapes."—Barbara Hambly   65386-5 $3.50

EMPIRE OF THE EAST
by Fred Saberhagen

THE BROKEN LANDS, **Book I**
A masterful blend of high technology and high sorcery; a unique adventure in a world on the brink of ultimate change; a world where magic rules—and science struggles to live again! "The work of a master." —*The Magazine of Fantasy & Science Fiction*
65380-6 $2.95

THE BLACK MOUNTAINS, **Book II**
East meets West in bloody conflict on a world where magic rules, but technology is revolting! "A fine mix of fantasy and science fiction, action and speculation." —Roger Zelazny   65390-3 $2.75

ARDNEH'S WORLD, **Book III**
The gripping climax of the "Empire of the East" series. "Ranks favorably with Tolkien. Exceptional in sheer unbridled zest and imaginative sweep." —*School Library Journal*   65404-7 $2.95

SPRINGER, NANCY
CHANCE—AND OTHER GESTURES OF THE HAND OF FATE
Chance is a low-born forester who falls in love with

the lovely Princess Halimeda—but the story begins when Halimeda's brother discovers Chance's feelings toward the Princess. It's a story of power and jealousy, taking place in the mysterious Wirral forest, whose inhabitants are not at all human . . .

65337-7 $3.50

THE HEX WITCH OF SELDOM (hardcover)
The King, the Sorceress, the Trickster, the Virgin, the Priest . . . together they form the Circle of Twelve, the primal human archetypes whose powers are manifest in us all. Young Bobbi Yandro, can speak with them at will—and when she becomes the mistress of a horse who is more than a horse, events sweep her into the very hands of the Twelve . . .

65389-X $15.95

To order any Baen Book listed above, send the code number, title, and author, plus 75 cents postage and handling per book (no cash, please) to Baen Books, Dept. CT, 260 Fifth Avenue, New York, NY 10001.

To order by phone (VISA and MasterCard accepted), call our distributor, Simon & Schuster, at (212) 698-7408.

ENTER A NEW WORLD
OF FANTASY . . .

Sometimes an author grows in stature so steadily that it seems as if he has always been a master. Such a one is David Drake, whose rise to fame has been driven equally by his archetypal creation, Colonel Alois Hammer's armored brigade of future mercenaries, and his non-series science fiction novels such as **Ranks of Bronze**, and **Fortress**.

Now Drake commences a new literary Quest, this time in the universe of fantasy. Just as he has become the acknowledged peer of such authors as Jerry Pournelle and Gordon R. Dickson in military and historically oriented science fiction, he will now take his place as a leading proponent of fantasy adventure. So enter now . . .

AUGUST 1988 65424-1 352 PP. $3.95

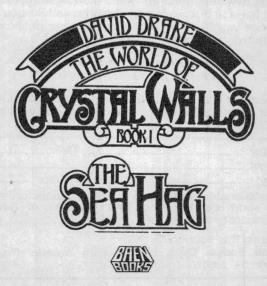

DAVID DRAKE
THE WORLD OF
CRYSTAL WALLS
BOOK I

THE SEA HAG

BAEN BOOKS